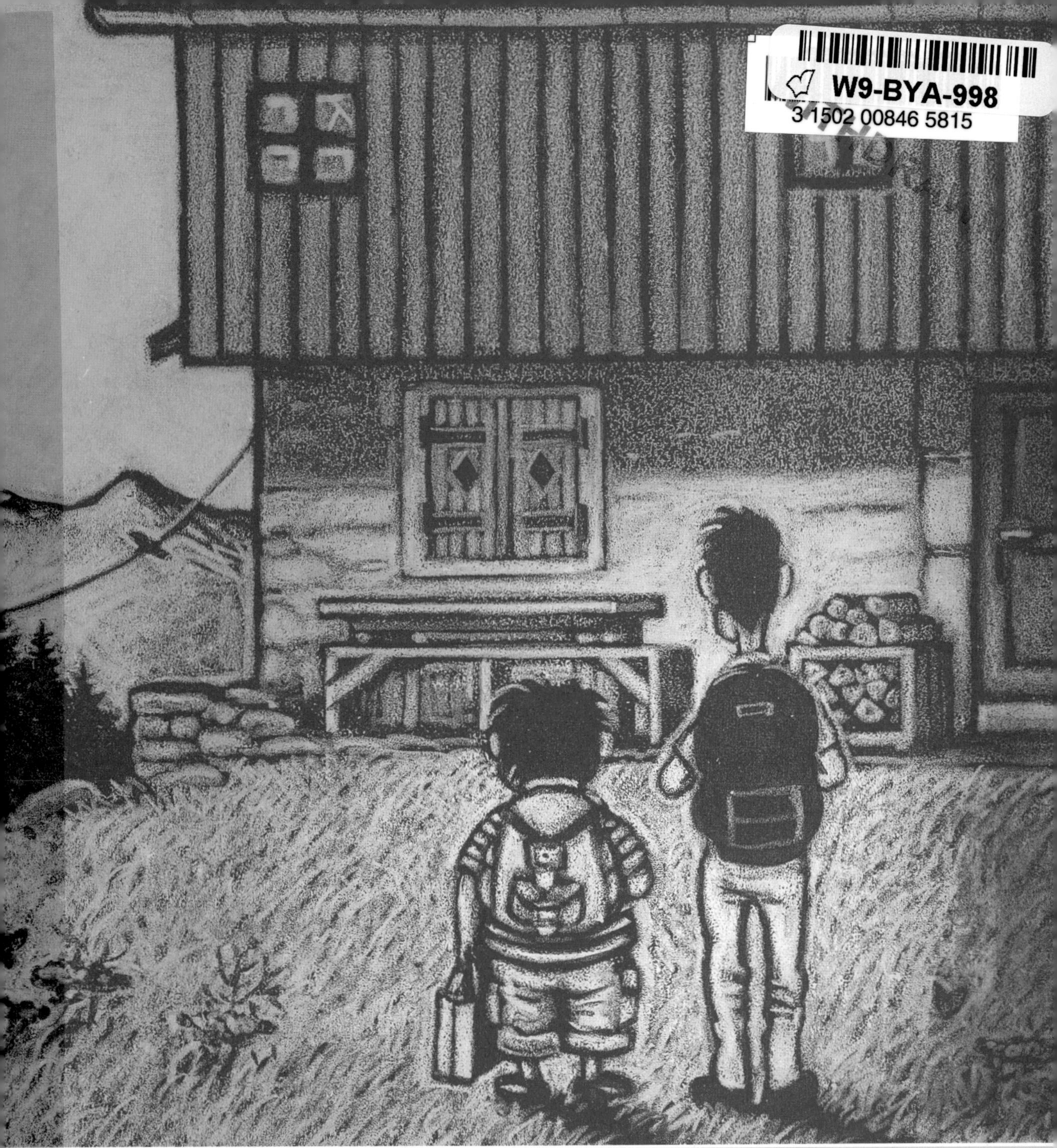

PIERRE WAZEM & TOM TIRABOSCO

THE RETREAT

HUMANOIDS

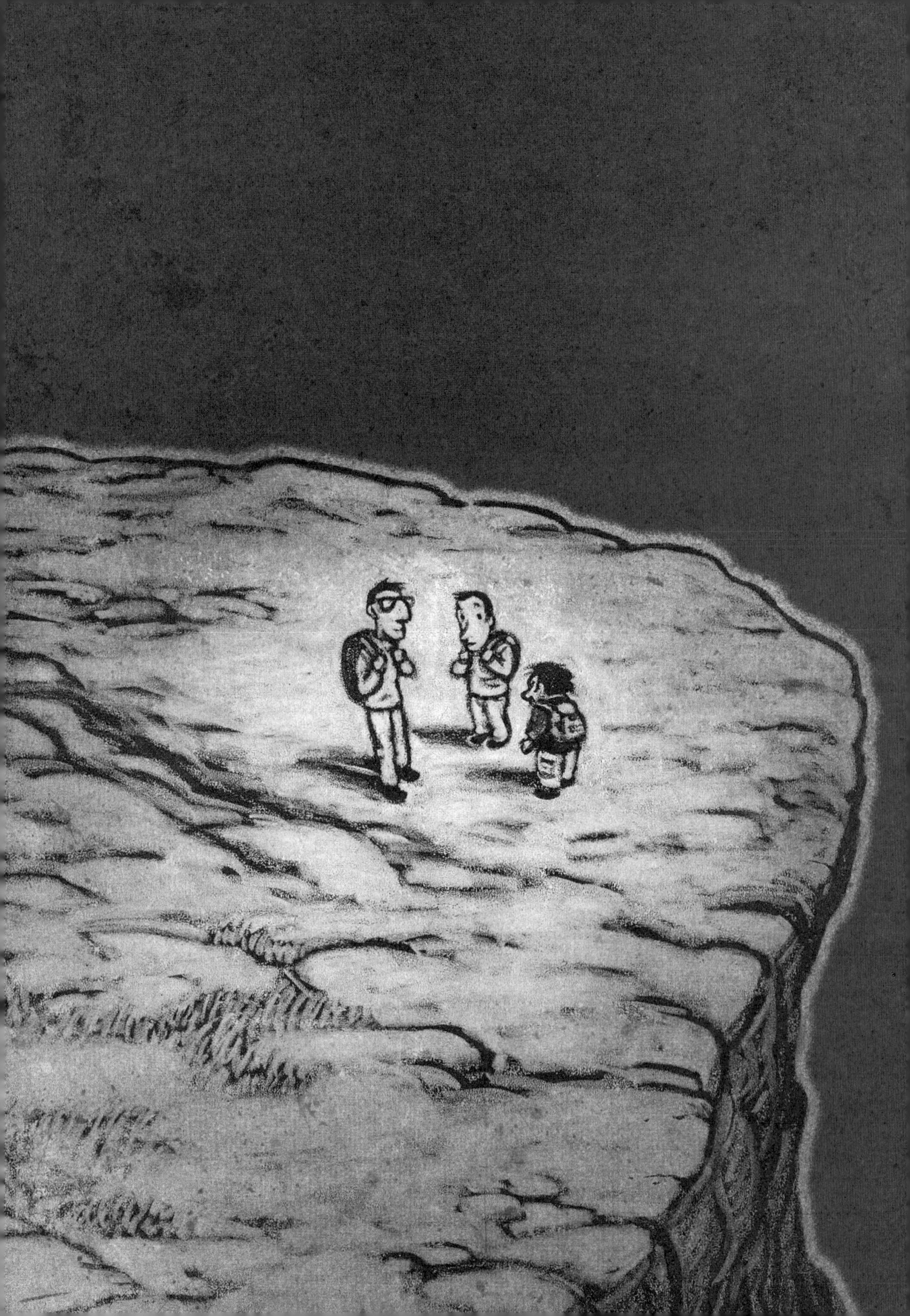

PIERRE WAZEM
Writer

TOM TIRABOSCO
Artist

MARK BENCE
Translator

JERRY FRISSEN
Senior Art Director

**ALEX DONOGHUE
& TIM PILCHER**
U.S. Edition Editors

FABRICE GIGER
Publisher

•

Rights & Licensing - licensing@humanoids.com
Press and Social Media - pr@humanoids.com

THE RETREAT
This title is a publication of Humanoids, Inc. 8033 Sunset Blvd. #628, Los Angeles, CA 90046.
Copyright © 2017 Humanoids, Inc., Los Angeles (USA). All rights reserved.
Humanoids and its logos are ® and © 2017 Humanoids, Inc.

Originally published in French by Les Humanoïdes Associés (Paris, France).

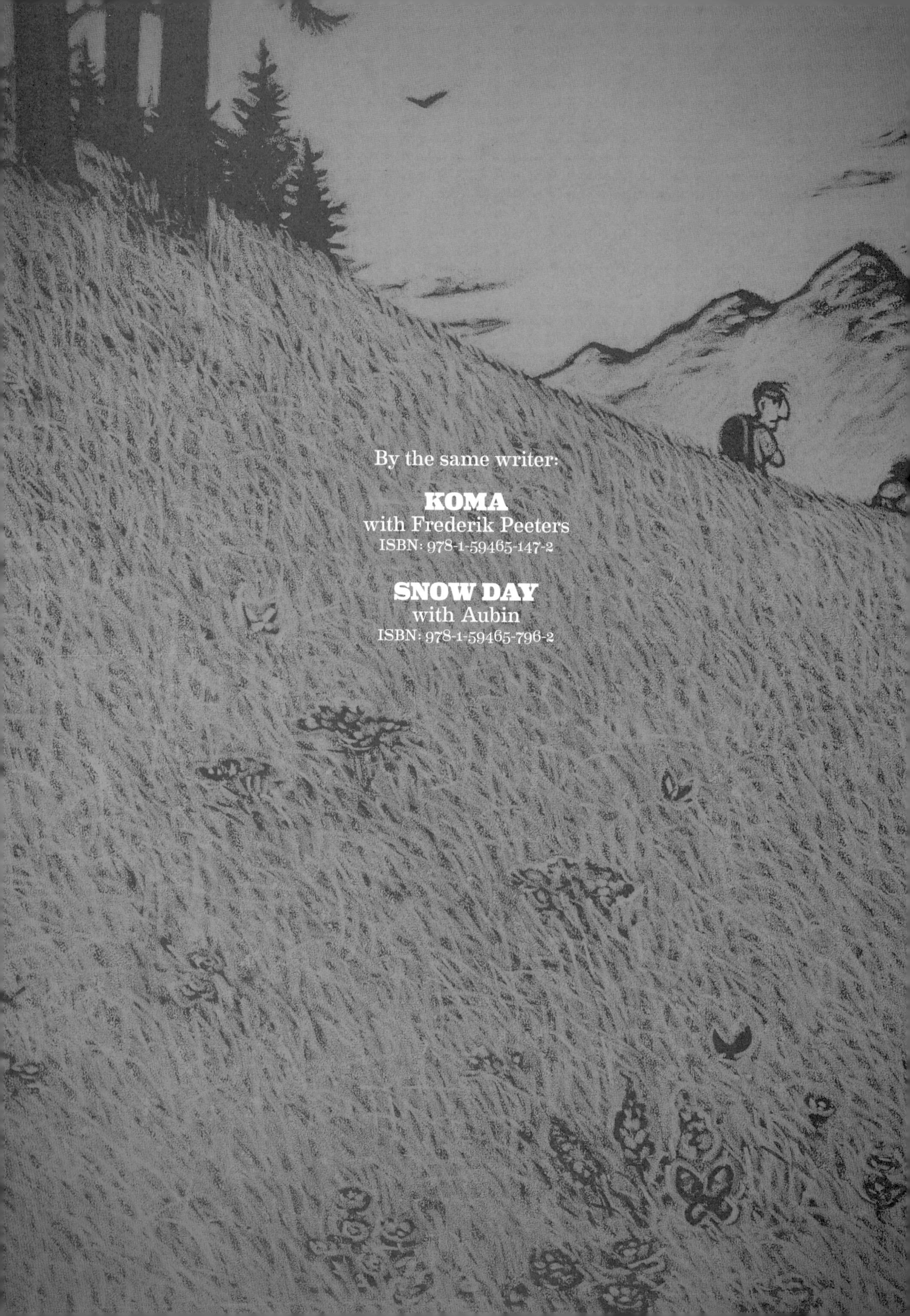

By the same writer:

KOMA
with Frederik Peeters
ISBN: 978-1-59465-147-2

SNOW DAY
with Aubin
ISBN: 978-1-59465-796-2

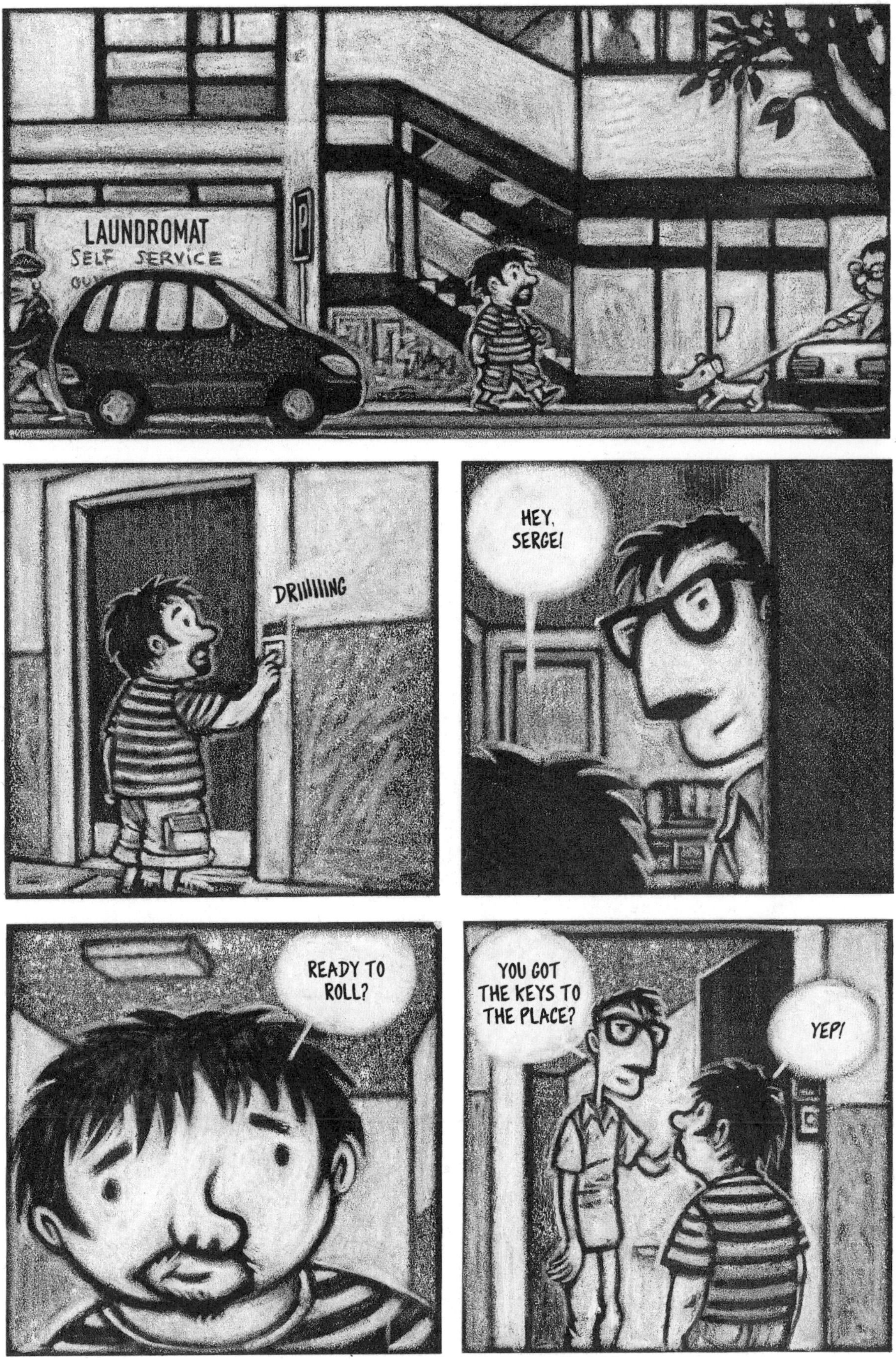
LAUNDROMAT
SELF SERVICE
DRIIIIIIING
HEY, SERGE!
READY TO ROLL?
YOU GOT THE KEYS TO THE PLACE?
YEP!

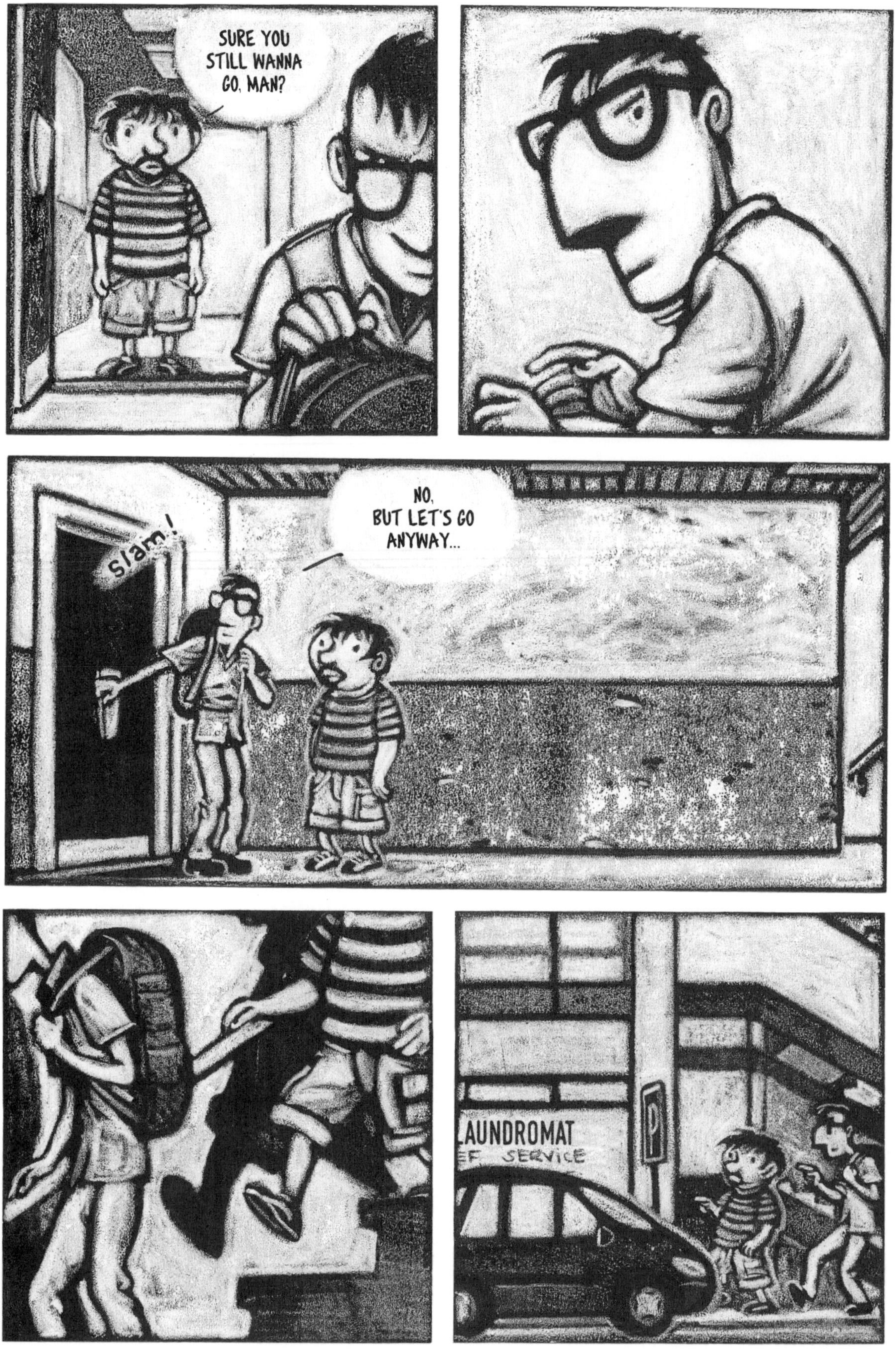
SURE YOU STILL WANNA GO, MAN?
NO, BUT LET'S GO ANYWAY...
slam!
LAUNDROMAT
SERVICE

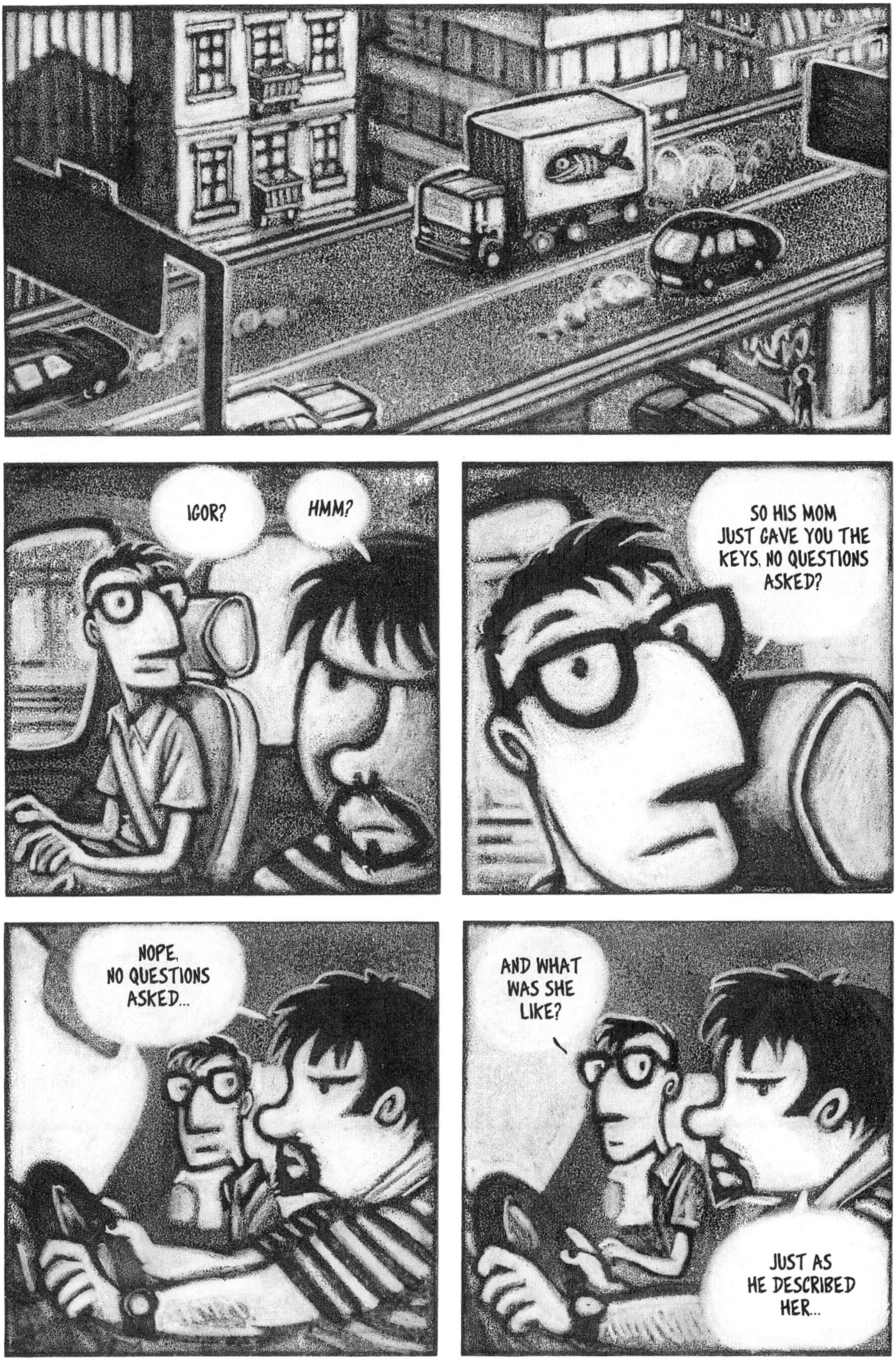
IGOR?
HMM?
SO HIS MOM JUST GAVE YOU THE KEYS, NO QUESTIONS ASKED?
NOPE, NO QUESTIONS ASKED...
AND WHAT WAS SHE LIKE?
JUST AS HE DESCRIBED HER...

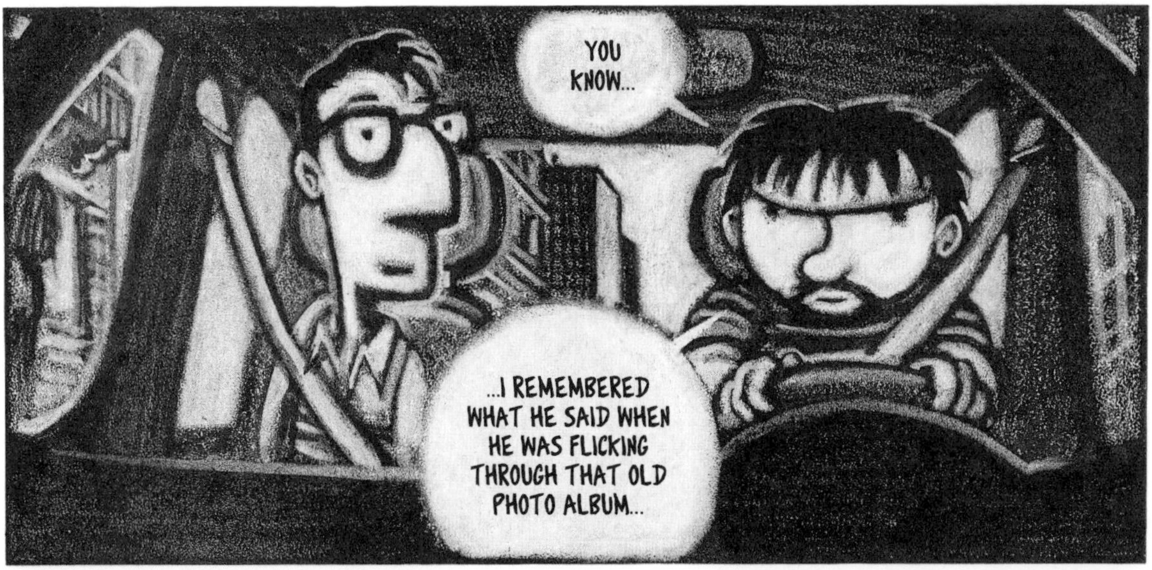
YOU KNOW...
...I REMEMBERED WHAT HE SAID WHEN HE WAS FLICKING THROUGH THAT OLD PHOTO ALBUM...

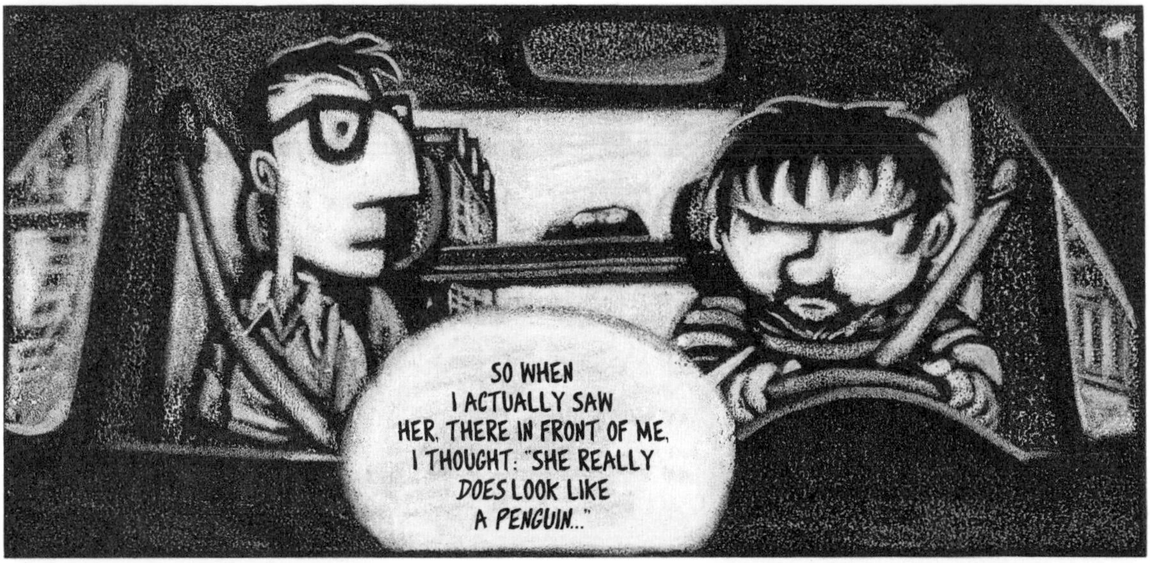
SO WHEN I ACTUALLY SAW HER, THERE IN FRONT OF ME, I THOUGHT: "SHE REALLY *DOES* LOOK LIKE A *PENGUIN*..."

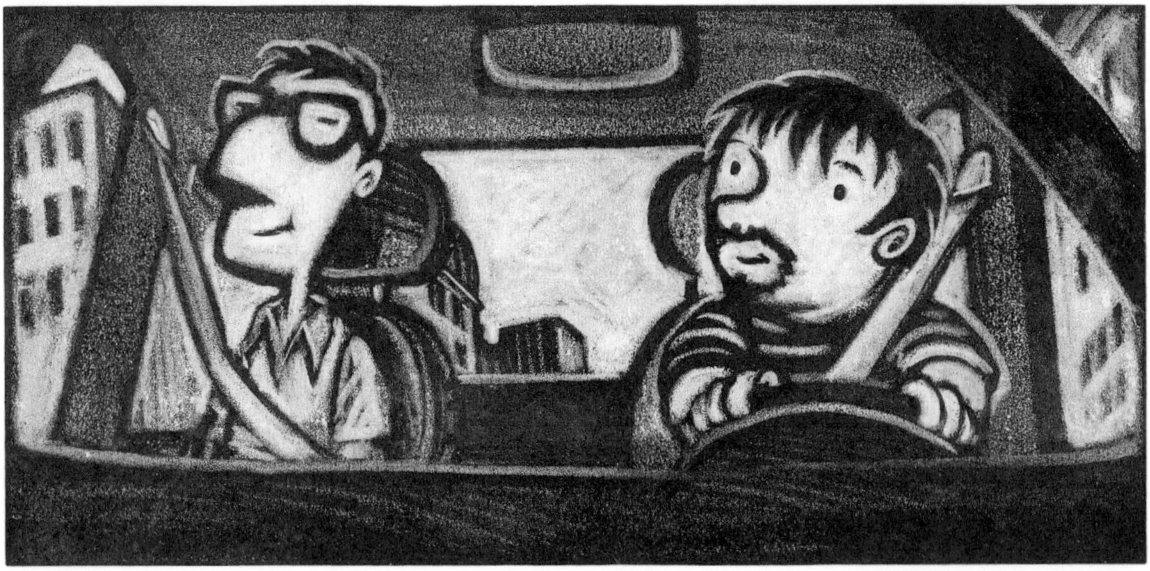

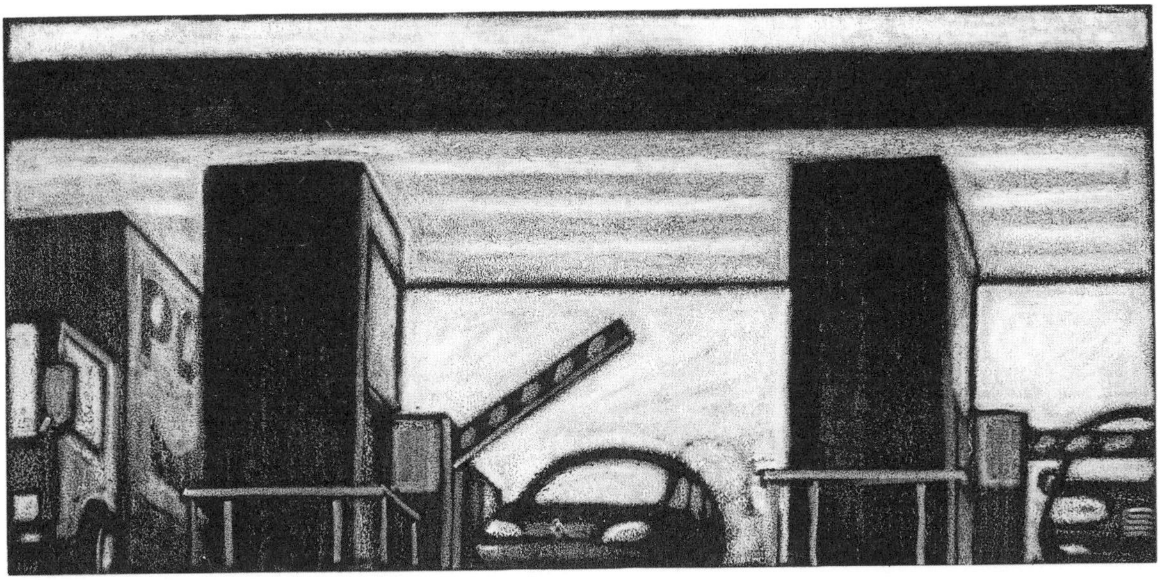

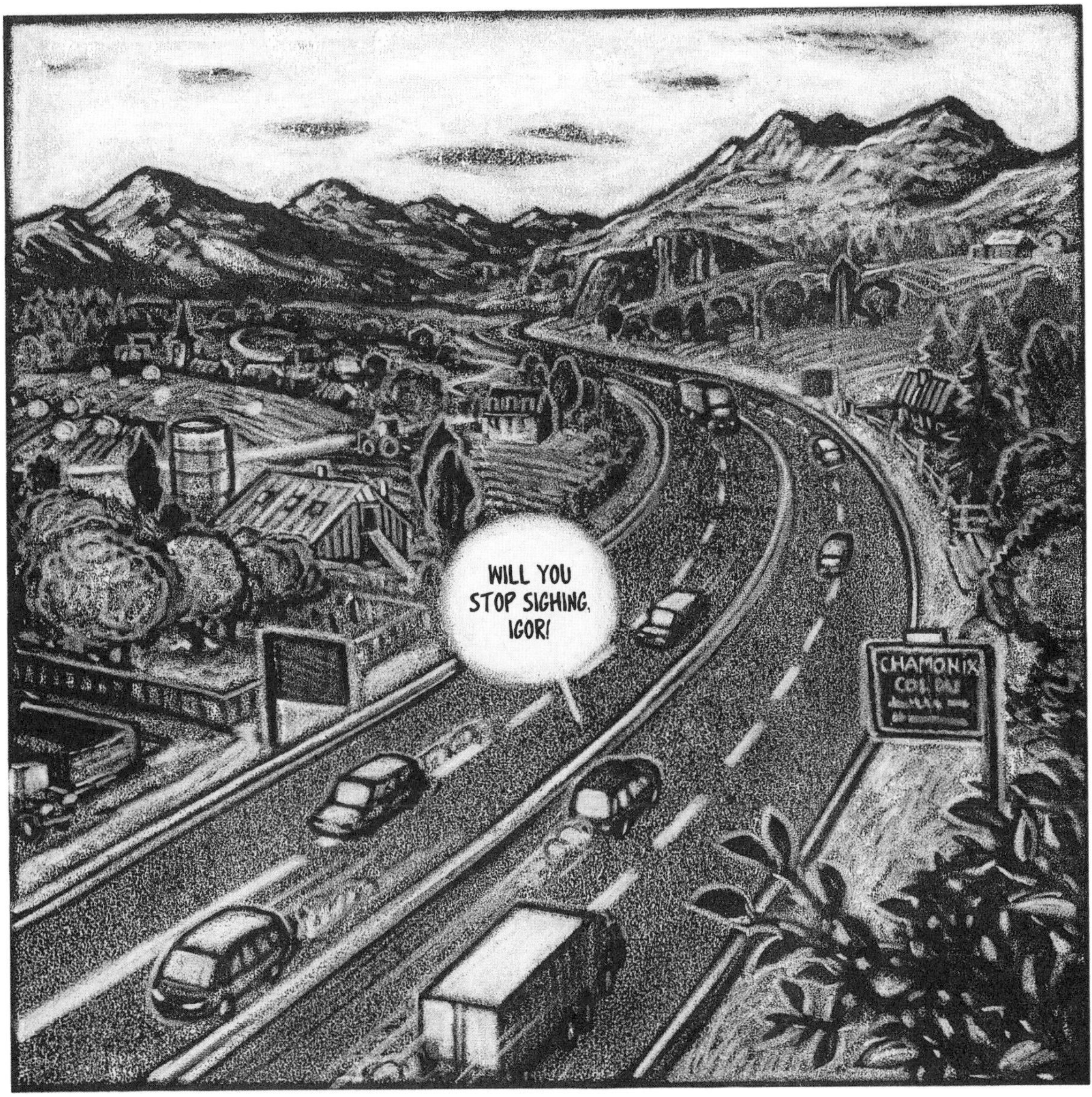
WILL YOU STOP SIGHING, IGOR!
CHAMONIX

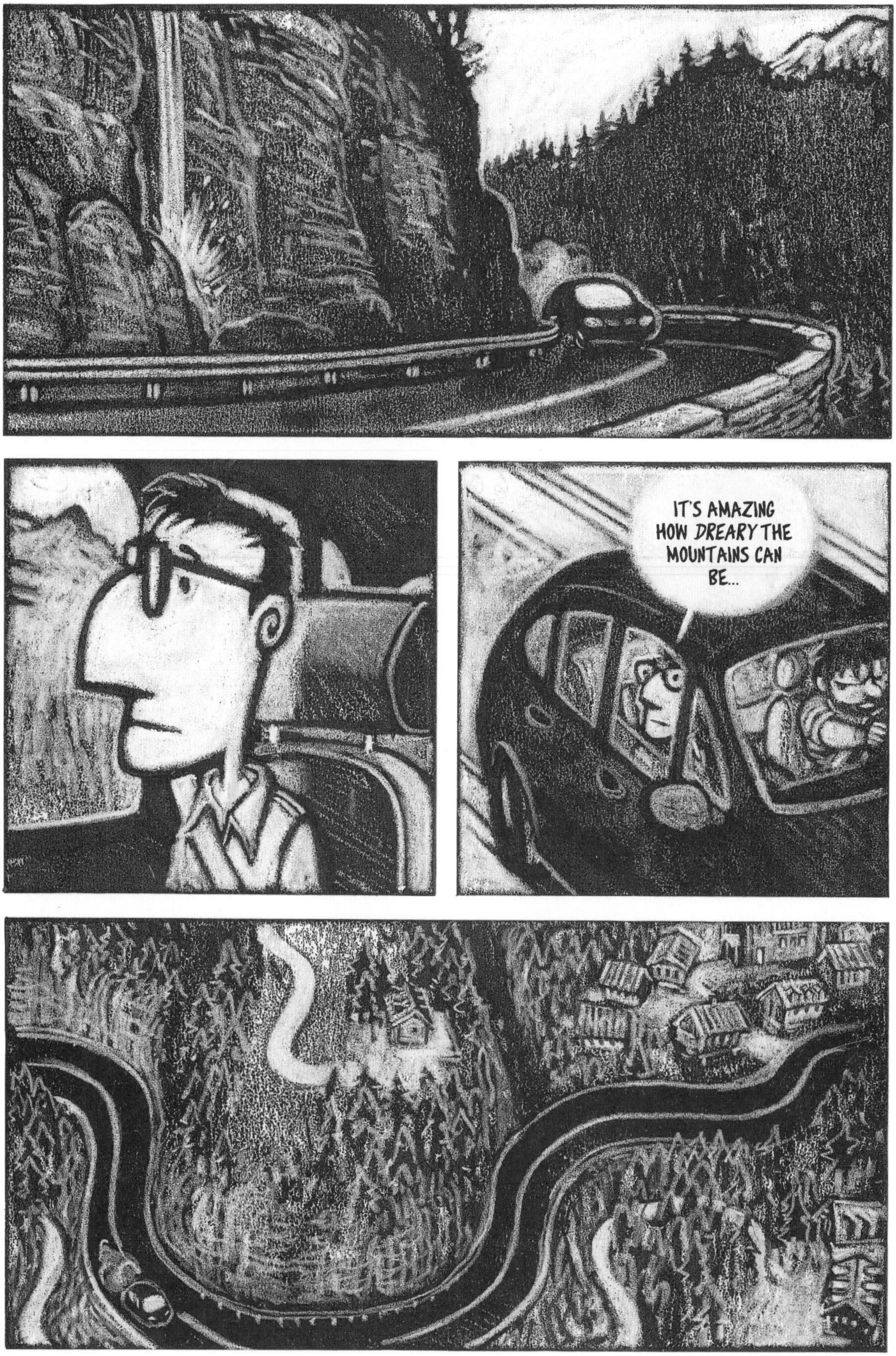
IT'S AMAZING HOW DREARY THE MOUNTAINS CAN BE...

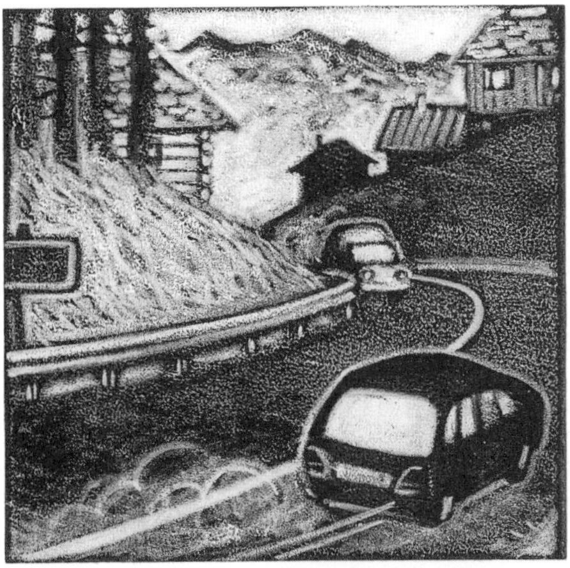

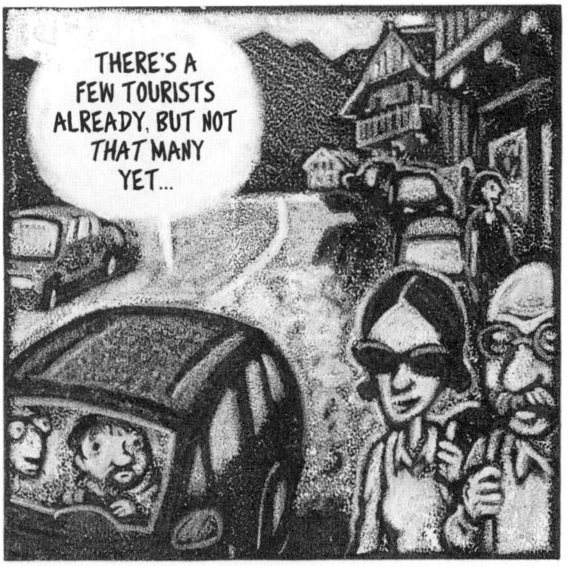
THERE'S A FEW TOURISTS ALREADY, BUT NOT THAT MANY YET...

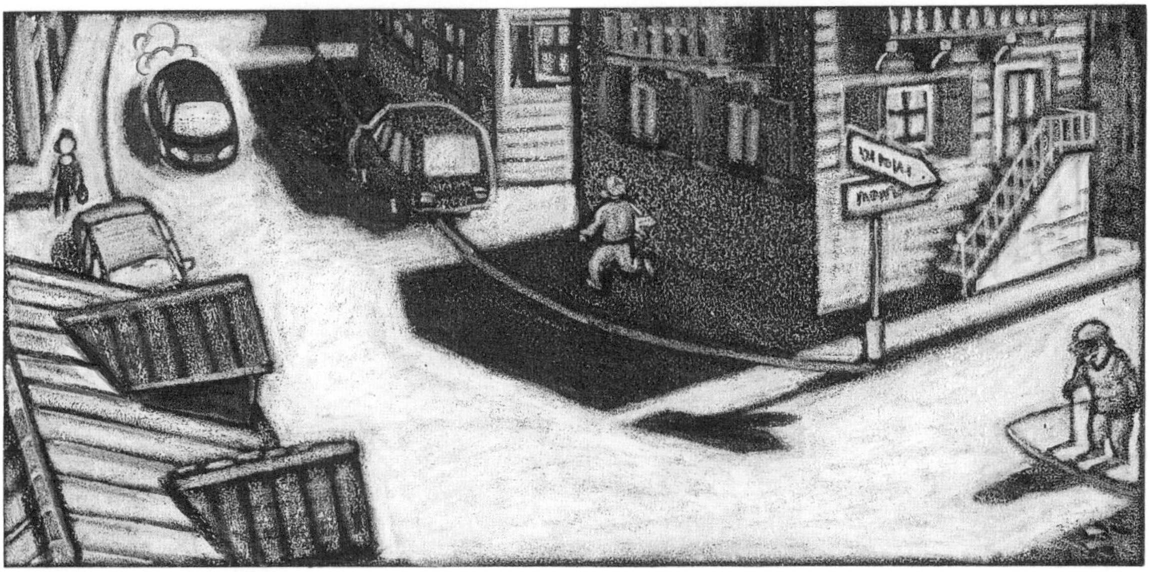

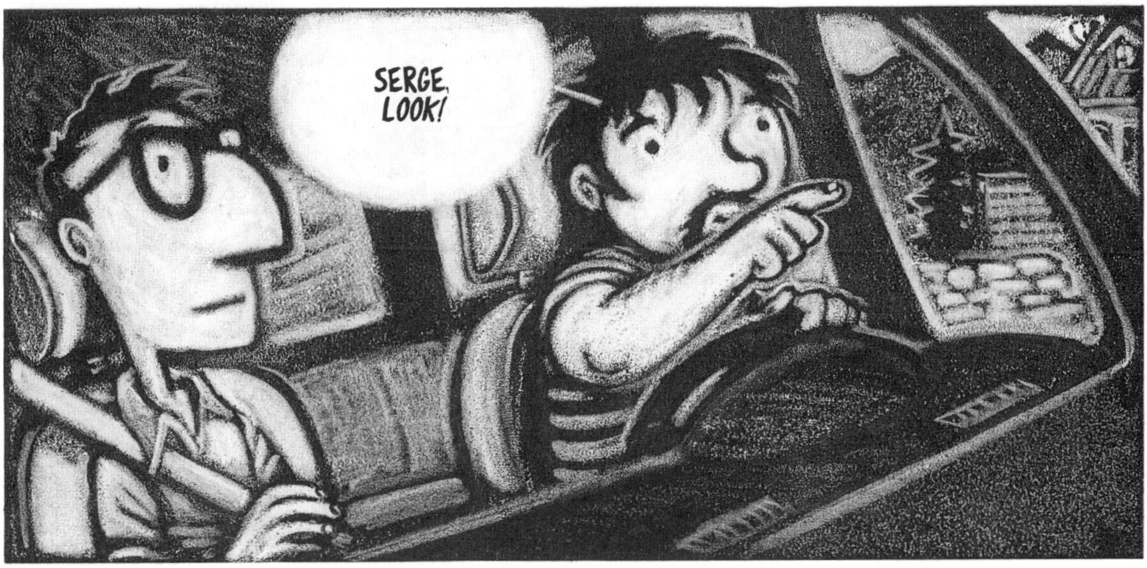
SERGE, LOOK!

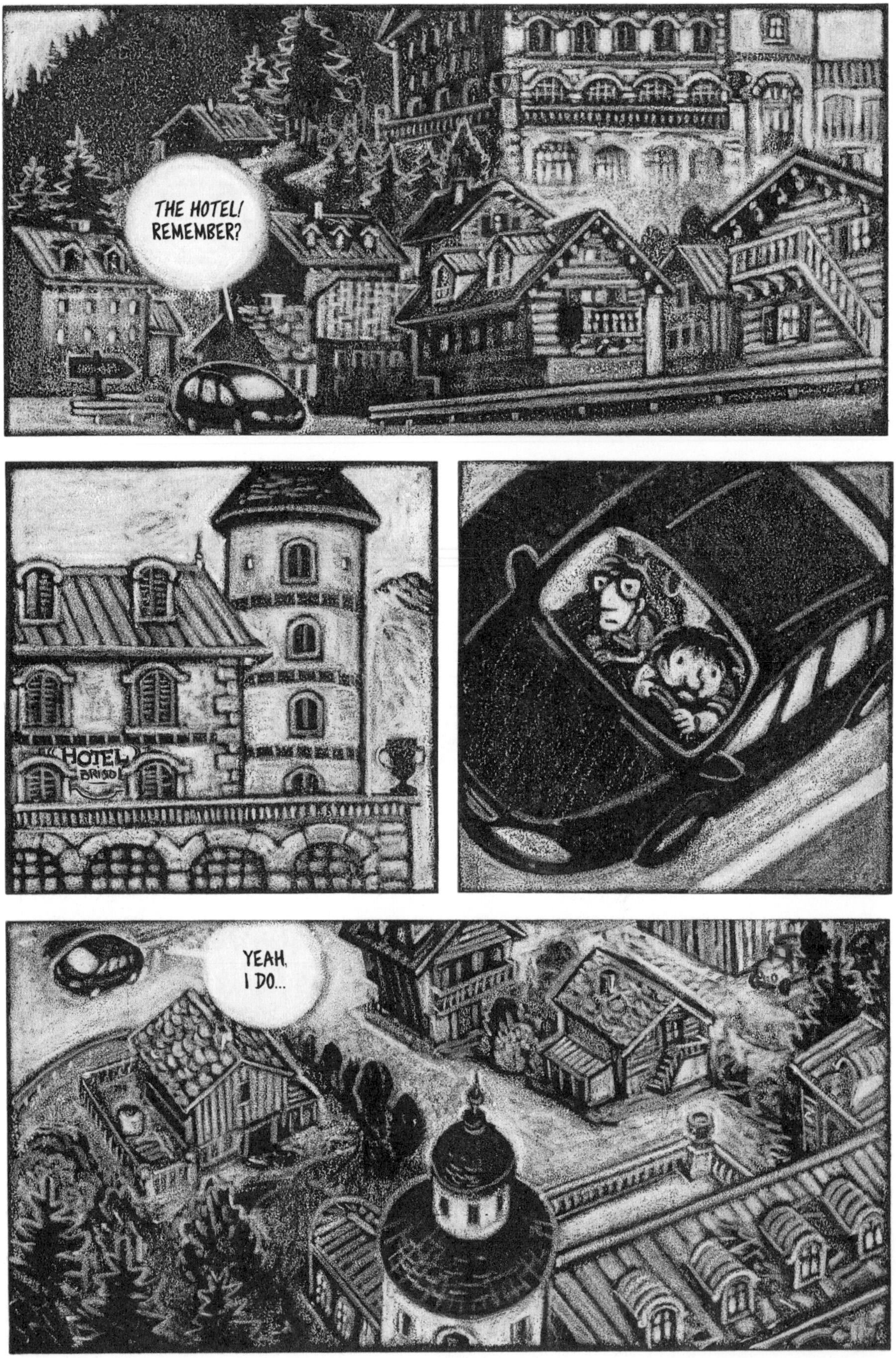
THE HOTEL!
REMEMBER?
HOTEL
BRISOL
YEAH, I DO...

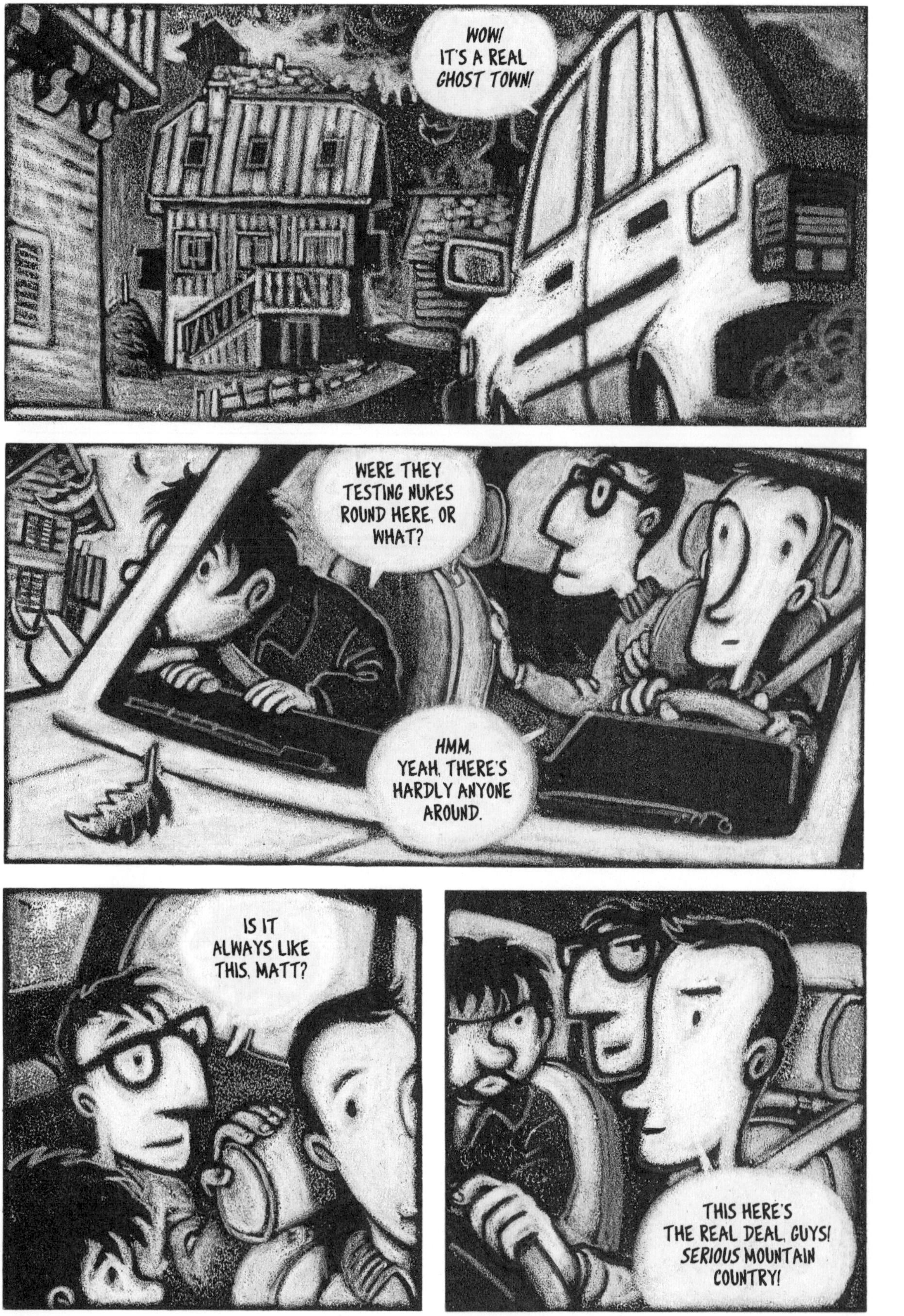
WOW! IT'S A REAL GHOST TOWN!
WERE THEY TESTING NUKES ROUND HERE, OR WHAT?
HMM, YEAH, THERE'S HARDLY ANYONE AROUND.
IS IT ALWAYS LIKE THIS, MATT?
THIS HERE'S THE REAL DEAL, GUYS! *SERIOUS* MOUNTAIN COUNTRY!

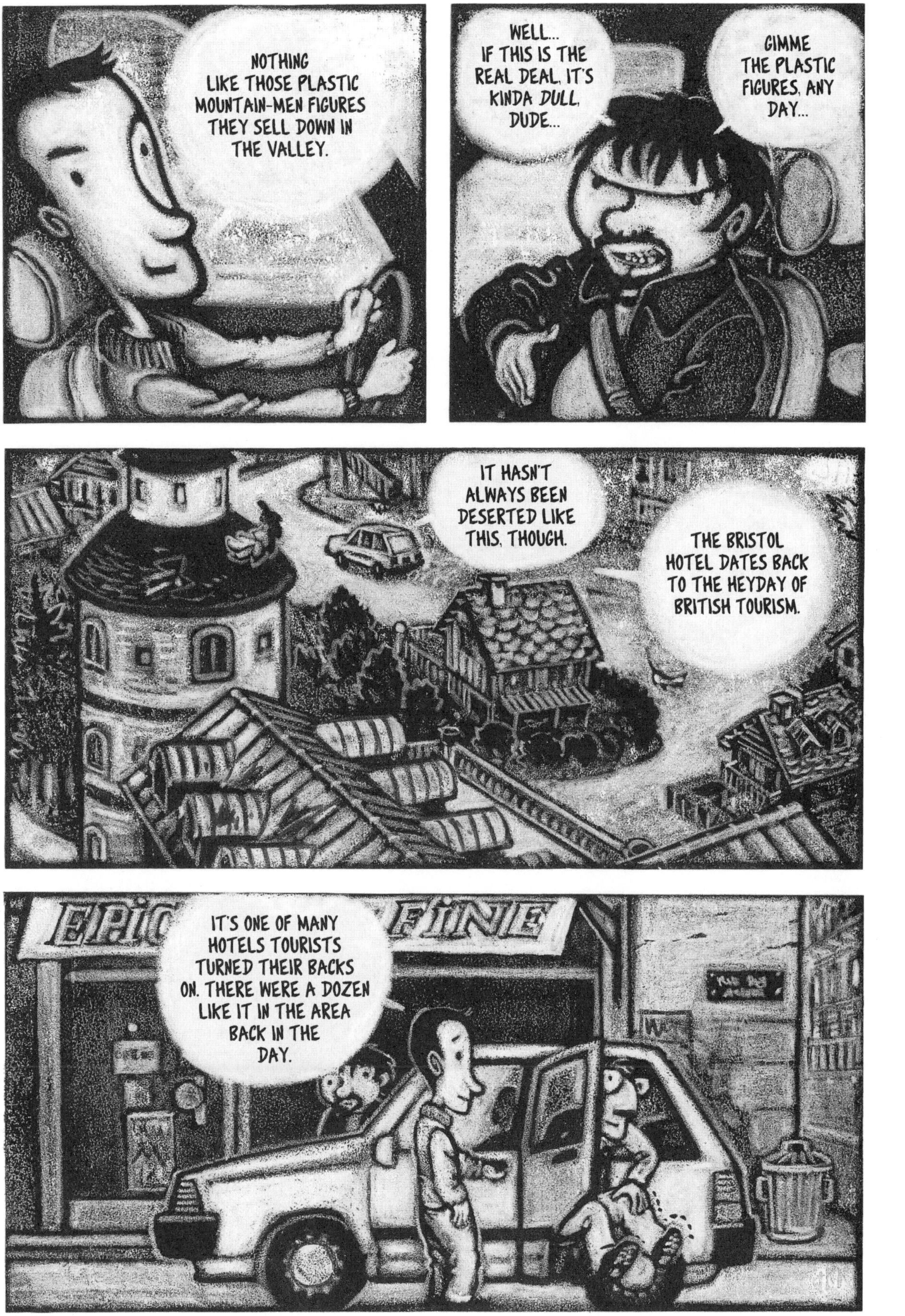
NOTHING LIKE THOSE PLASTIC MOUNTAIN-MEN FIGURES THEY SELL DOWN IN THE VALLEY.
WELL... IF THIS IS THE REAL DEAL, IT'S KINDA *DULL*, DUDE...
GIMME THE PLASTIC FIGURES, ANY DAY...
IT HASN'T ALWAYS BEEN DESERTED LIKE THIS, THOUGH.
THE BRISTOL HOTEL DATES BACK TO THE HEYDAY OF BRITISH TOURISM.
IT'S ONE OF MANY HOTELS TOURISTS TURNED THEIR BACKS ON. THERE WERE A DOZEN LIKE IT IN THE AREA BACK IN THE DAY.

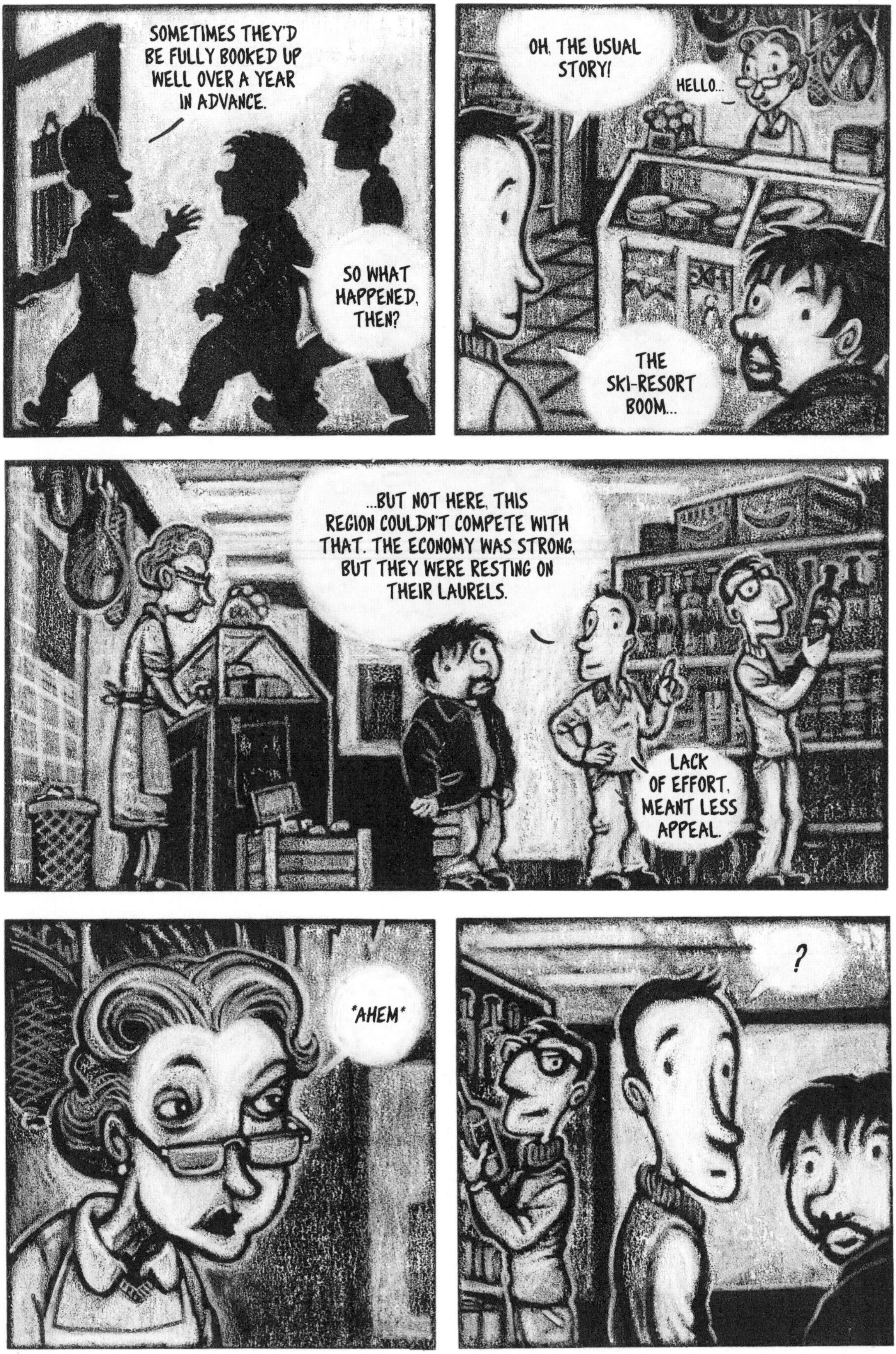
SOMETIMES THEY'D BE FULLY BOOKED UP WELL OVER A YEAR IN ADVANCE.
SO WHAT HAPPENED, THEN?
OH, THE USUAL STORY!
HELLO...
THE SKI-RESORT BOOM...
...BUT NOT HERE, THIS REGION COULDN'T COMPETE WITH THAT. THE ECONOMY WAS STRONG, BUT THEY WERE RESTING ON THEIR LAURELS.
LACK OF EFFORT, MEANT LESS APPEAL.
AHEM
?

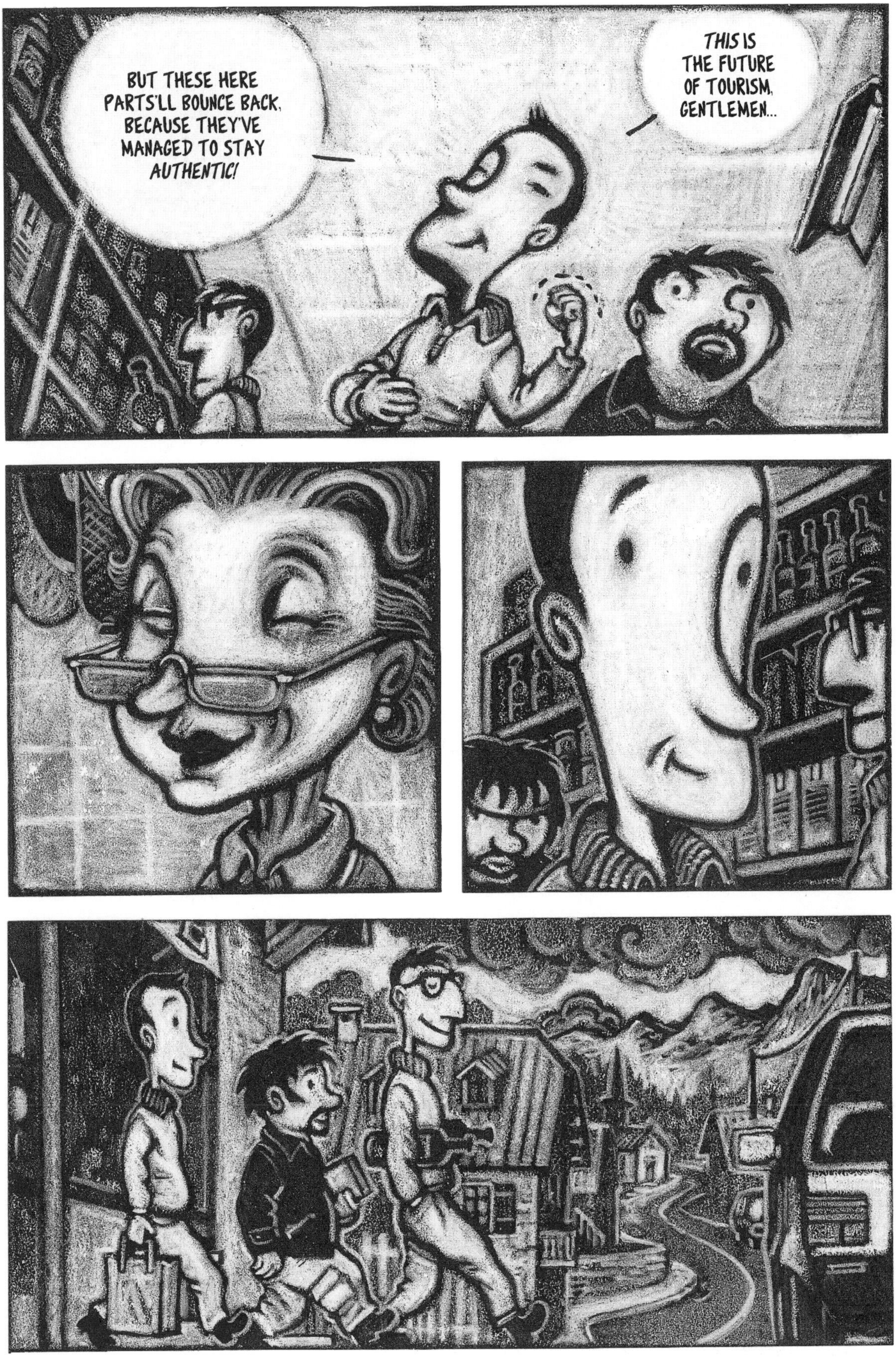
BUT THESE HERE PARTS'LL BOUNCE BACK, BECAUSE THEY'VE MANAGED TO STAY AUTHENTIC!
THIS IS THE FUTURE OF TOURISM, GENTLEMEN...

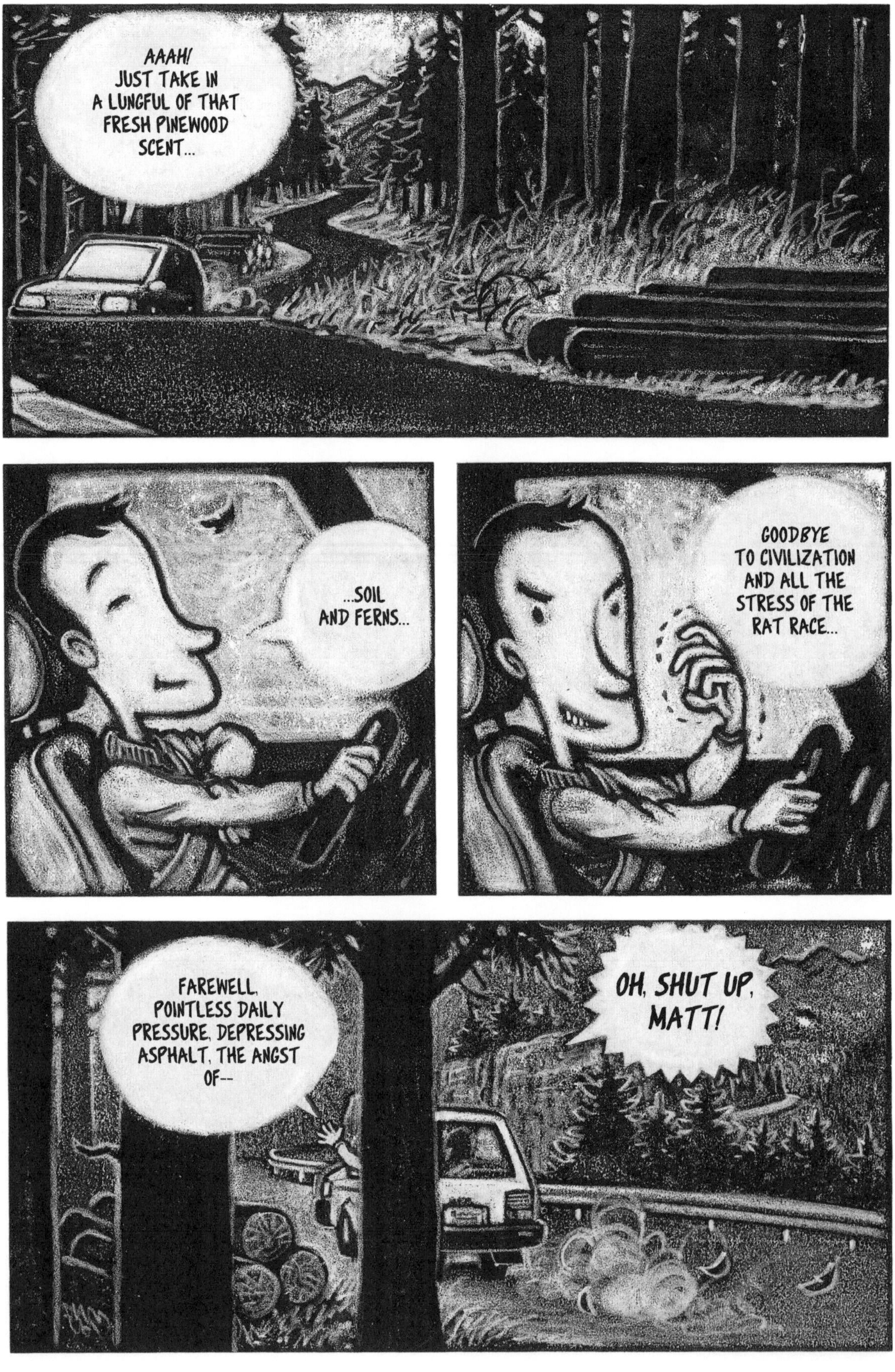
AAAH! JUST TAKE IN A LUNGFUL OF THAT FRESH PINEWOOD SCENT...
...SOIL AND FERNS...
GOODBYE TO CIVILIZATION AND ALL THE STRESS OF THE RAT RACE...
FAREWELL, POINTLESS DAILY PRESSURE, DEPRESSING ASPHALT, THE ANGST OF--
OH, SHUT UP, MATT!

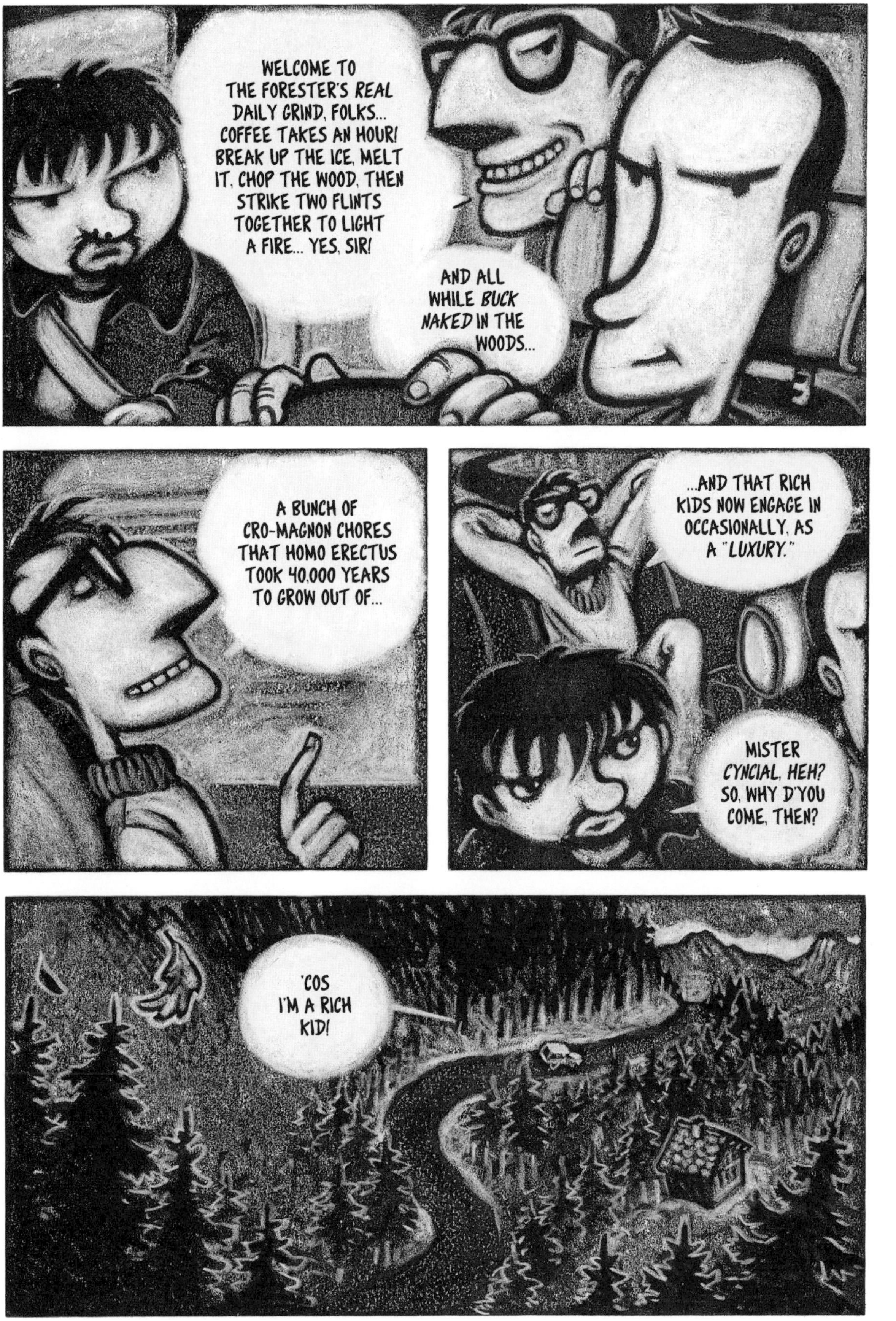
WELCOME TO THE FORESTER'S *REAL* DAILY GRIND, FOLKS... COFFEE TAKES AN HOUR! BREAK UP THE ICE, MELT IT, CHOP THE WOOD, THEN STRIKE TWO FLINTS TOGETHER TO LIGHT A FIRE... YES, SIR!
AND ALL WHILE *BUCK NAKED* IN THE WOODS...
A BUNCH OF CRO-MAGNON CHORES THAT HOMO ERECTUS TOOK 40,000 YEARS TO GROW OUT OF...
...AND THAT RICH KIDS NOW ENGAGE IN OCCASIONALLY, AS A "*LUXURY*."
MISTER *CYNCIAL*, HEH? SO, WHY D'YOU COME, THEN?
'COS I'M A RICH KID!

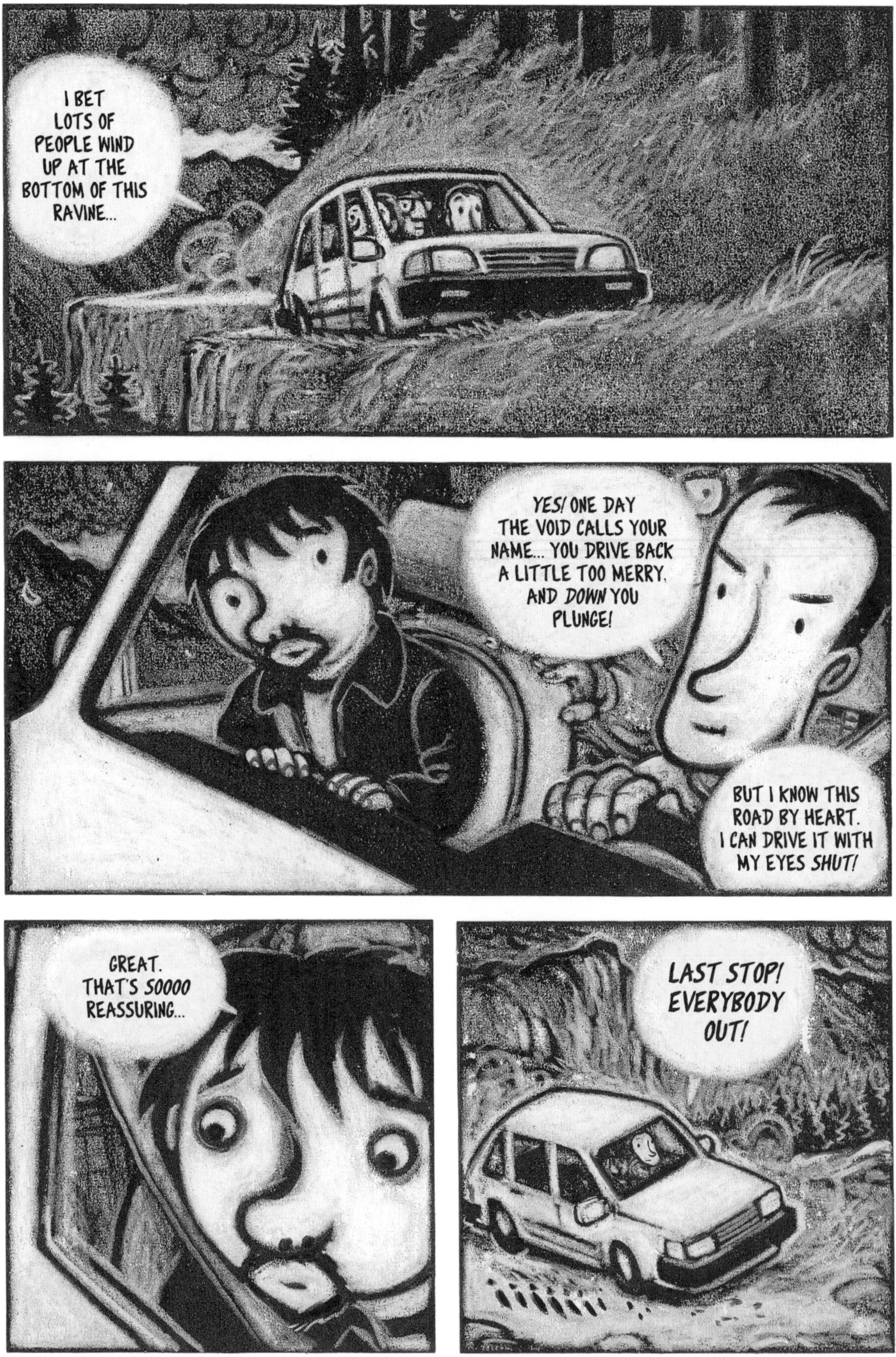
I BET LOTS OF PEOPLE WIND UP AT THE BOTTOM OF THIS RAVINE...
YES! ONE DAY THE VOID CALLS YOUR NAME... YOU DRIVE BACK A LITTLE TOO MERRY, AND *DOWN* YOU PLUNGE!
BUT I KNOW THIS ROAD BY HEART. I CAN DRIVE IT WITH MY EYES *SHUT!*
GREAT. THAT'S *SOOOO* REASSURING...
LAST STOP! EVERYBODY OUT!

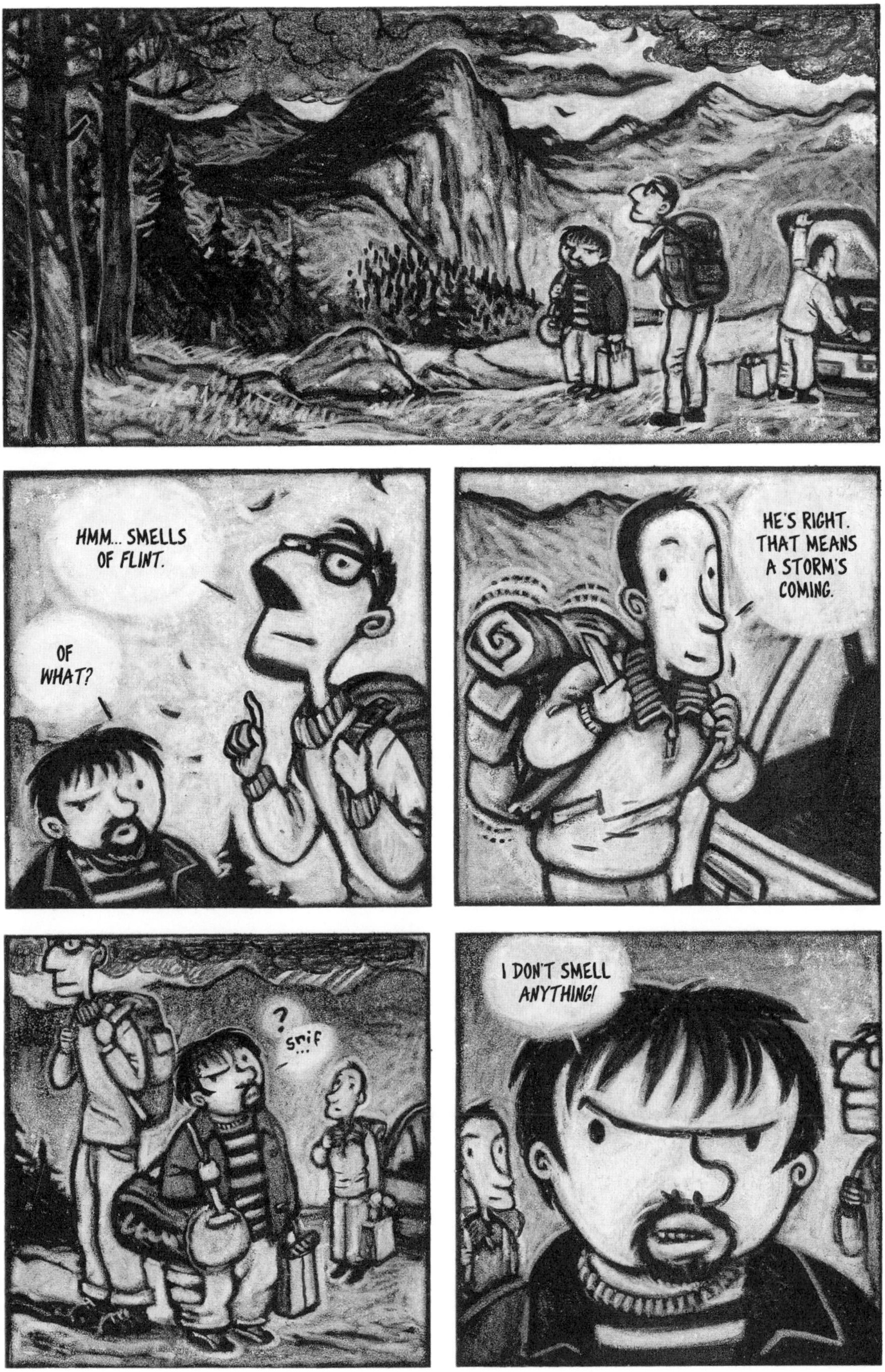
HMM... SMELLS OF FLINT.
OF WHAT?
HE'S RIGHT. THAT MEANS A STORM'S COMING.
?
SNIF...
I DON'T SMELL ANYTHING!

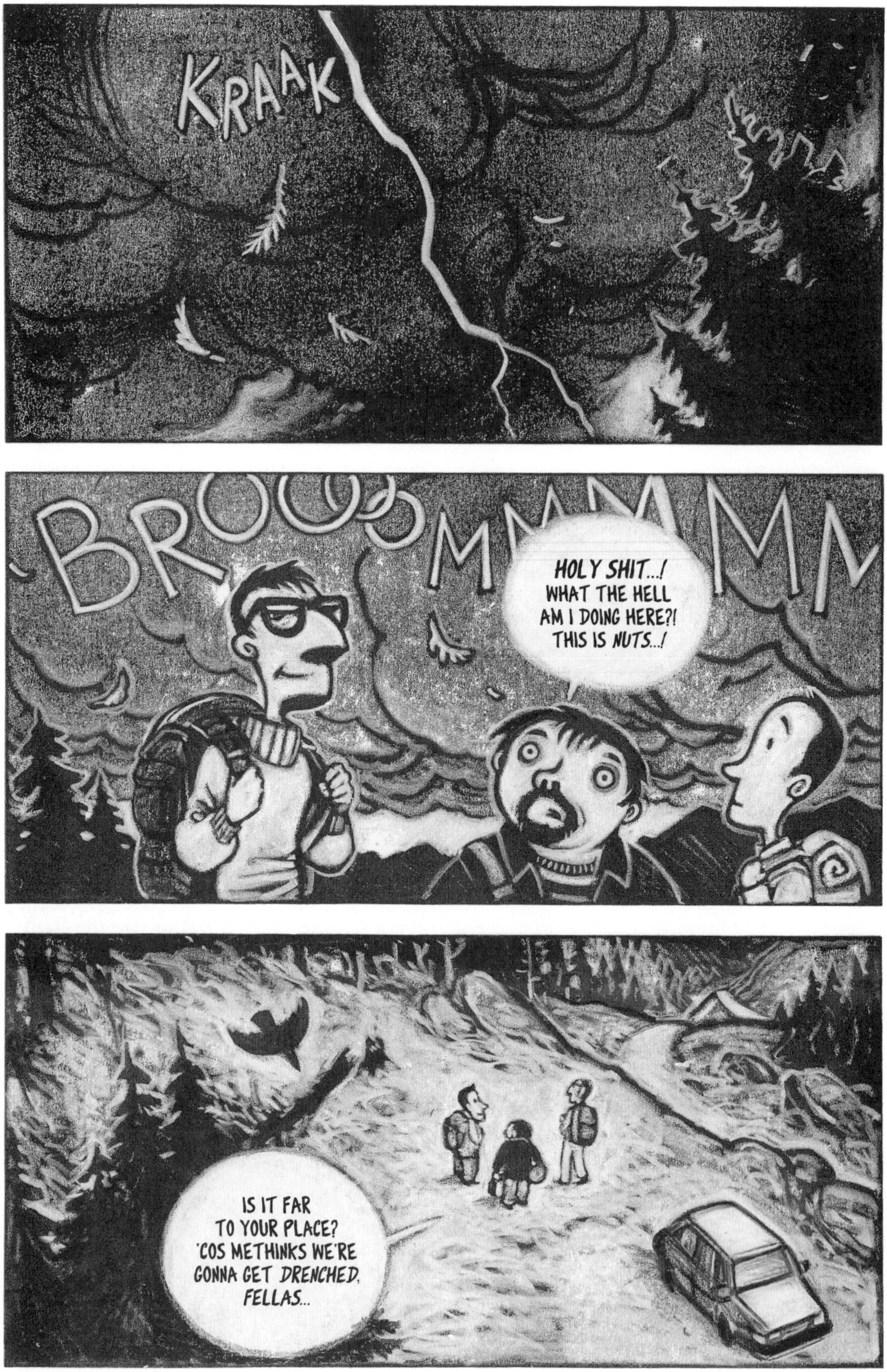
KRAAK
BROOOOMMMMM
HOLY SHIT...! WHAT THE HELL AM I DOING HERE?! THIS IS NUTS...!
IS IT FAR TO YOUR PLACE? 'COS METHINKS WE'RE GONNA GET DRENCHED, FELLAS...

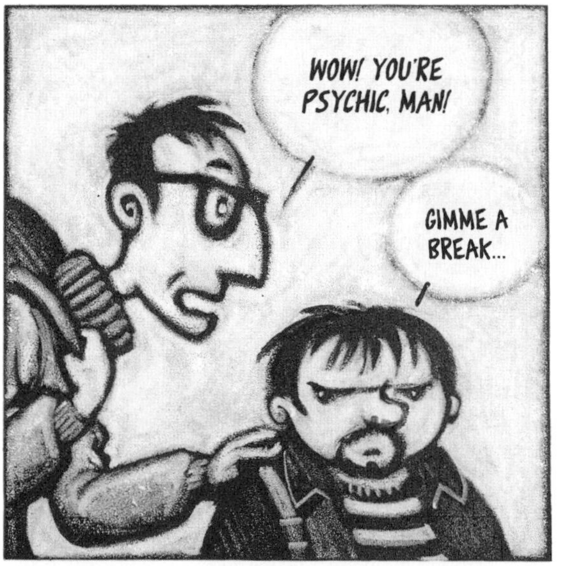
WOW! YOU'RE PSYCHIC, MAN!
GIMME A BREAK...

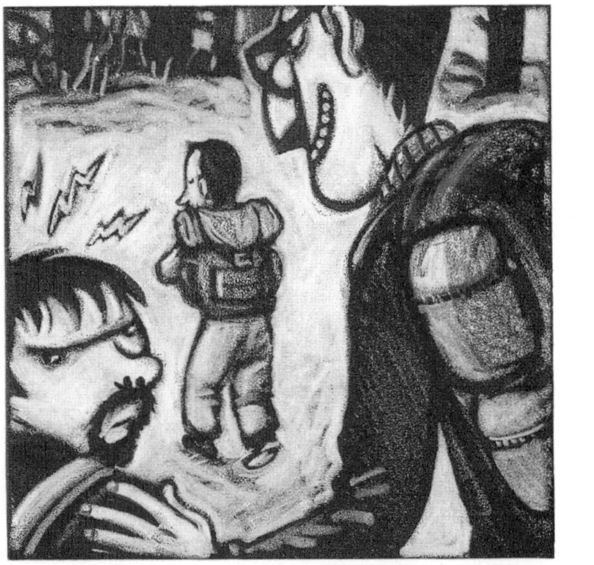

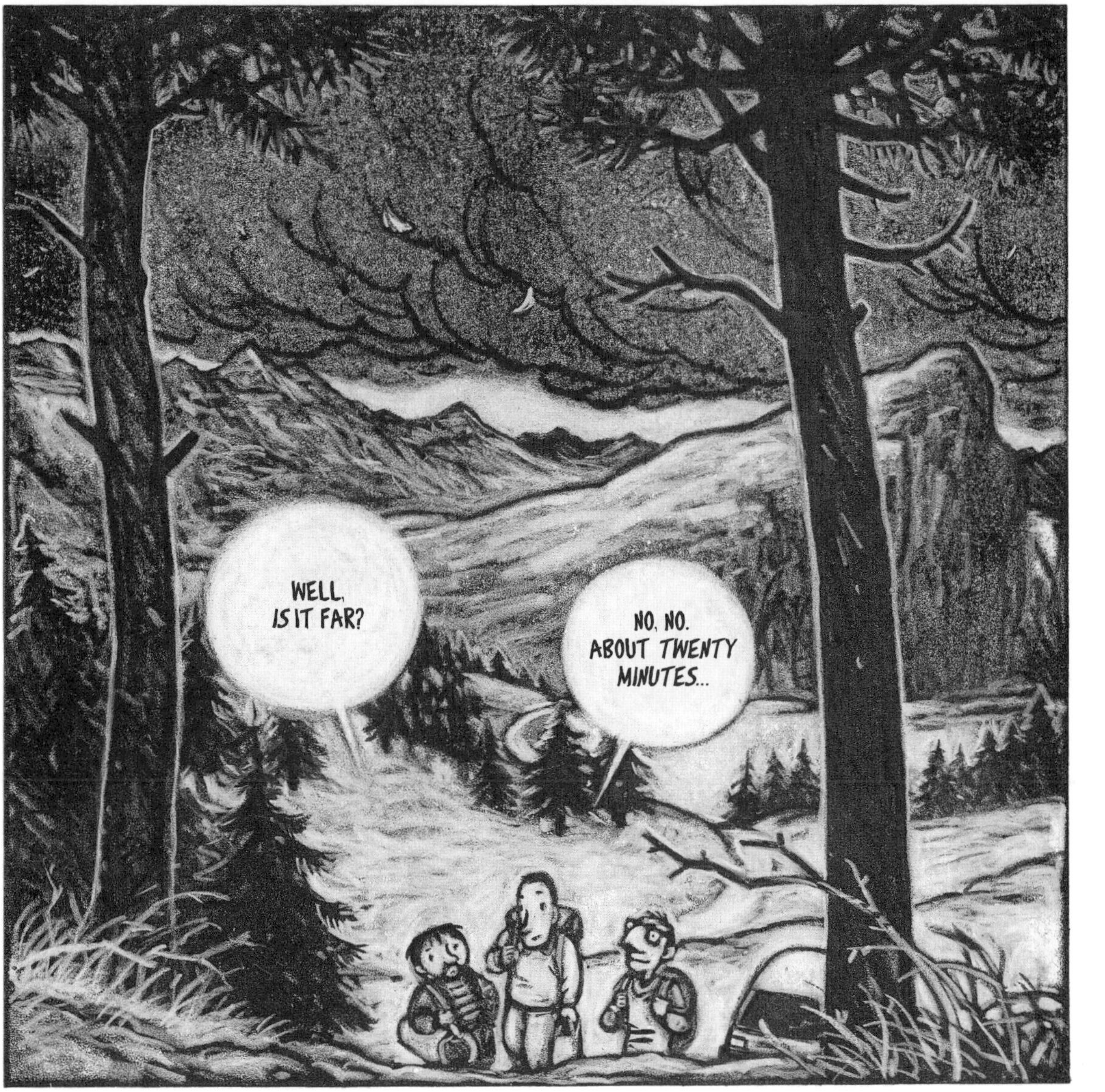
WELL, IS IT FAR?
NO, NO. ABOUT TWENTY MINUTES...

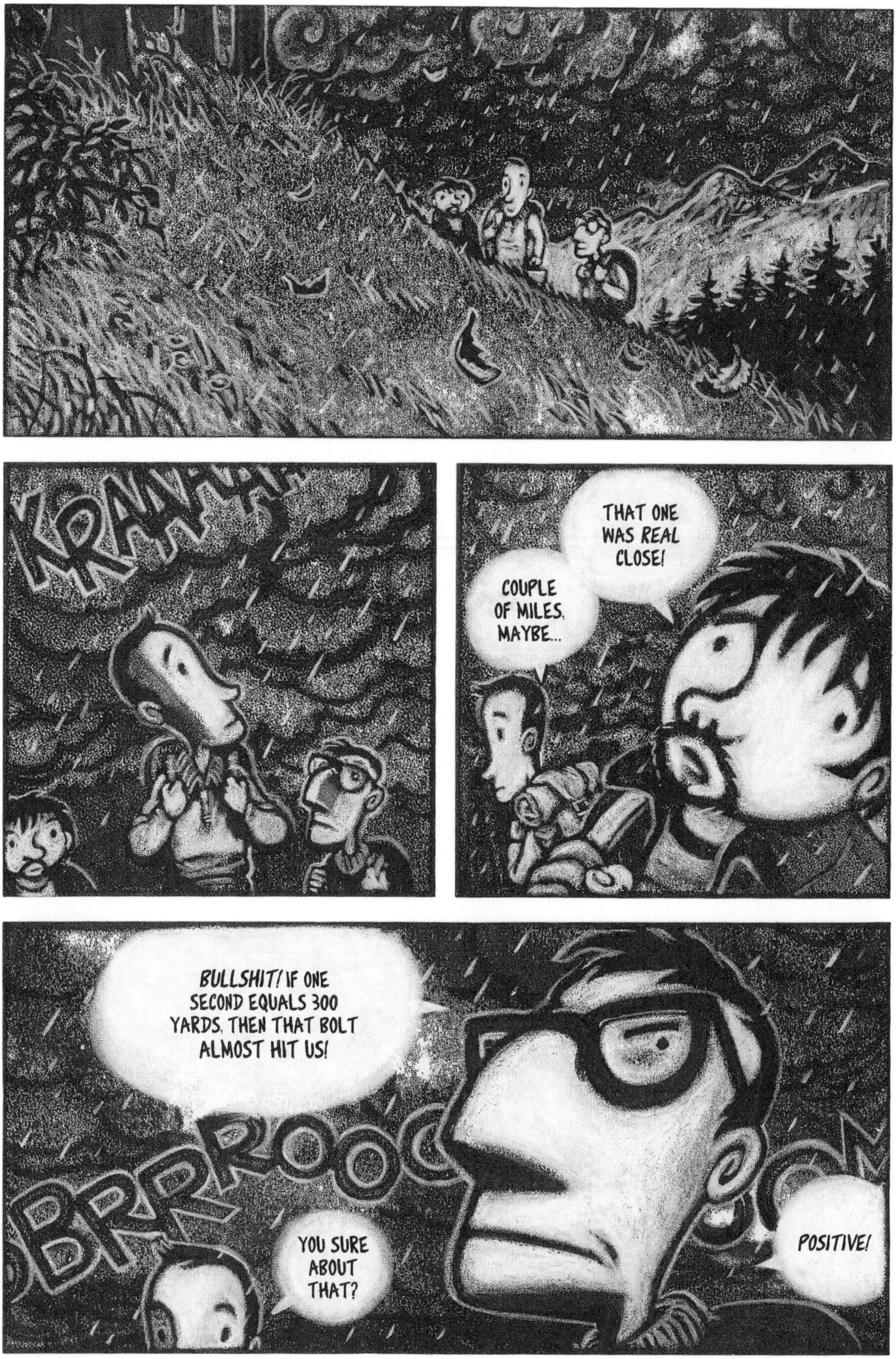
THAT ONE WAS REAL CLOSE!
COUPLE OF MILES, MAYBE...
BULLSHIT! IF ONE SECOND EQUALS 300 YARDS, THEN THAT BOLT ALMOST HIT US!
YOU SURE ABOUT THAT?
POSITIVE!

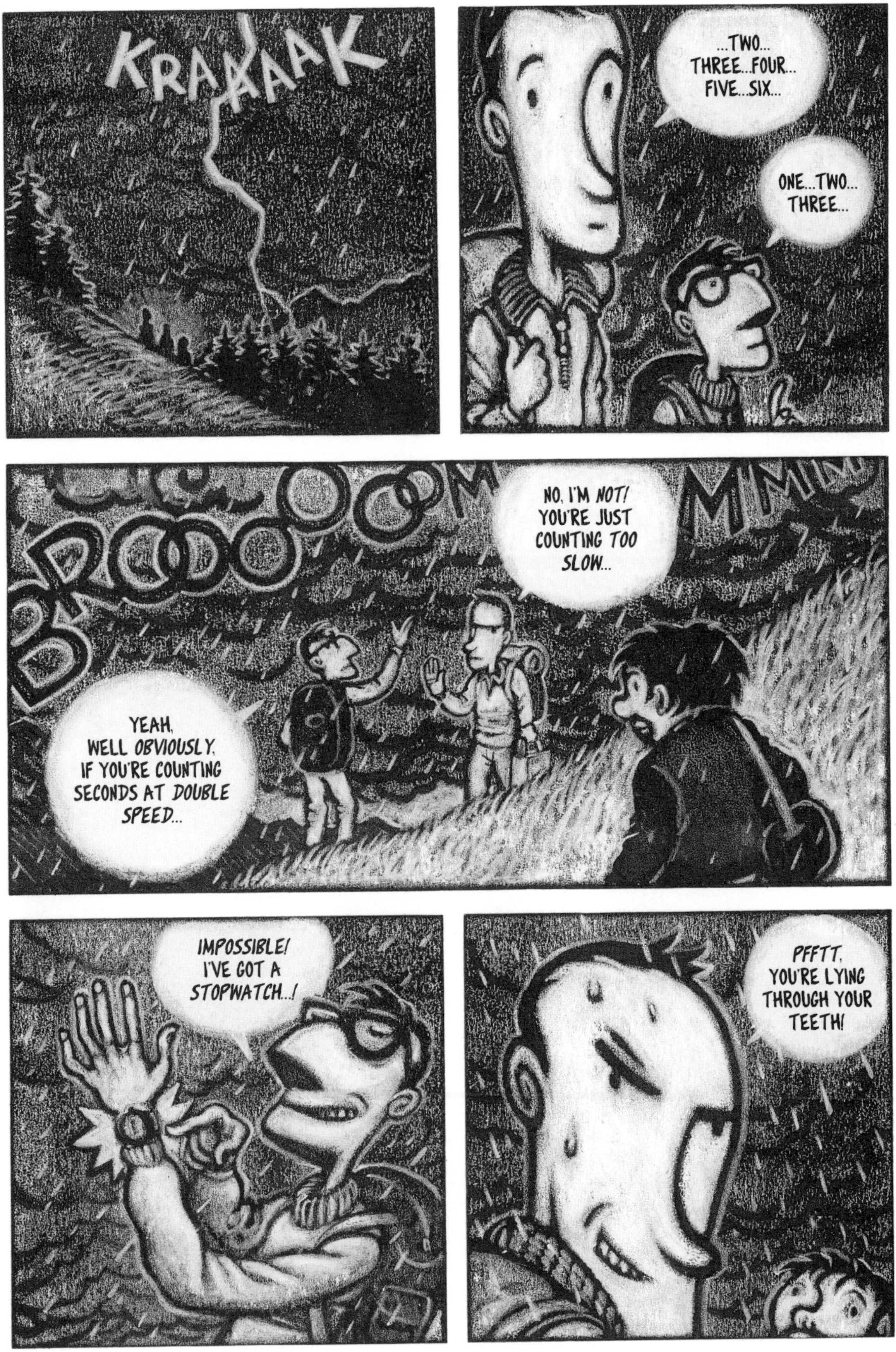
KRAAAAK
...TWO... THREE...FOUR... FIVE...SIX...
ONE...TWO... THREE...
NO, I'M *NOT!* YOU'RE JUST COUNTING *TOO* SLOW...
YEAH, WELL *OBVIOUSLY*, IF YOU'RE COUNTING SECONDS AT *DOUBLE* SPEED...
IMPOSSIBLE! I'VE GOT A STOPWATCH...!
PFFTT, YOU'RE LYING THROUGH YOUR TEETH!

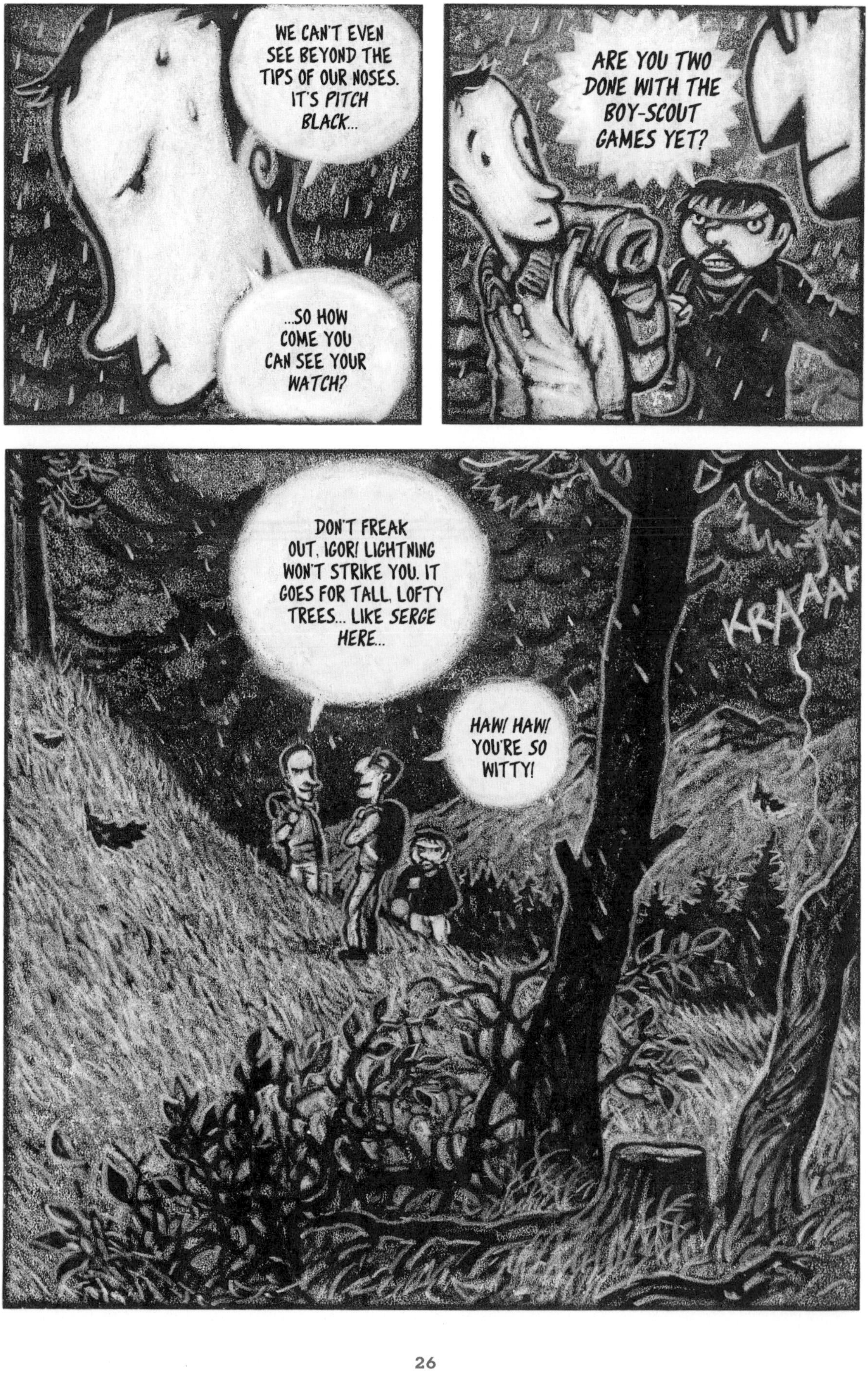
WE CAN'T EVEN SEE BEYOND THE TIPS OF OUR NOSES. IT'S PITCH BLACK...
...SO HOW COME YOU CAN SEE YOUR WATCH?
ARE YOU TWO DONE WITH THE BOY-SCOUT GAMES YET?
DON'T FREAK OUT, IGOR! LIGHTNING WON'T STRIKE YOU. IT GOES FOR TALL, LOFTY TREES... LIKE SERGE HERE...
HAW! HAW! YOU'RE SO WITTY!
KRAAAK

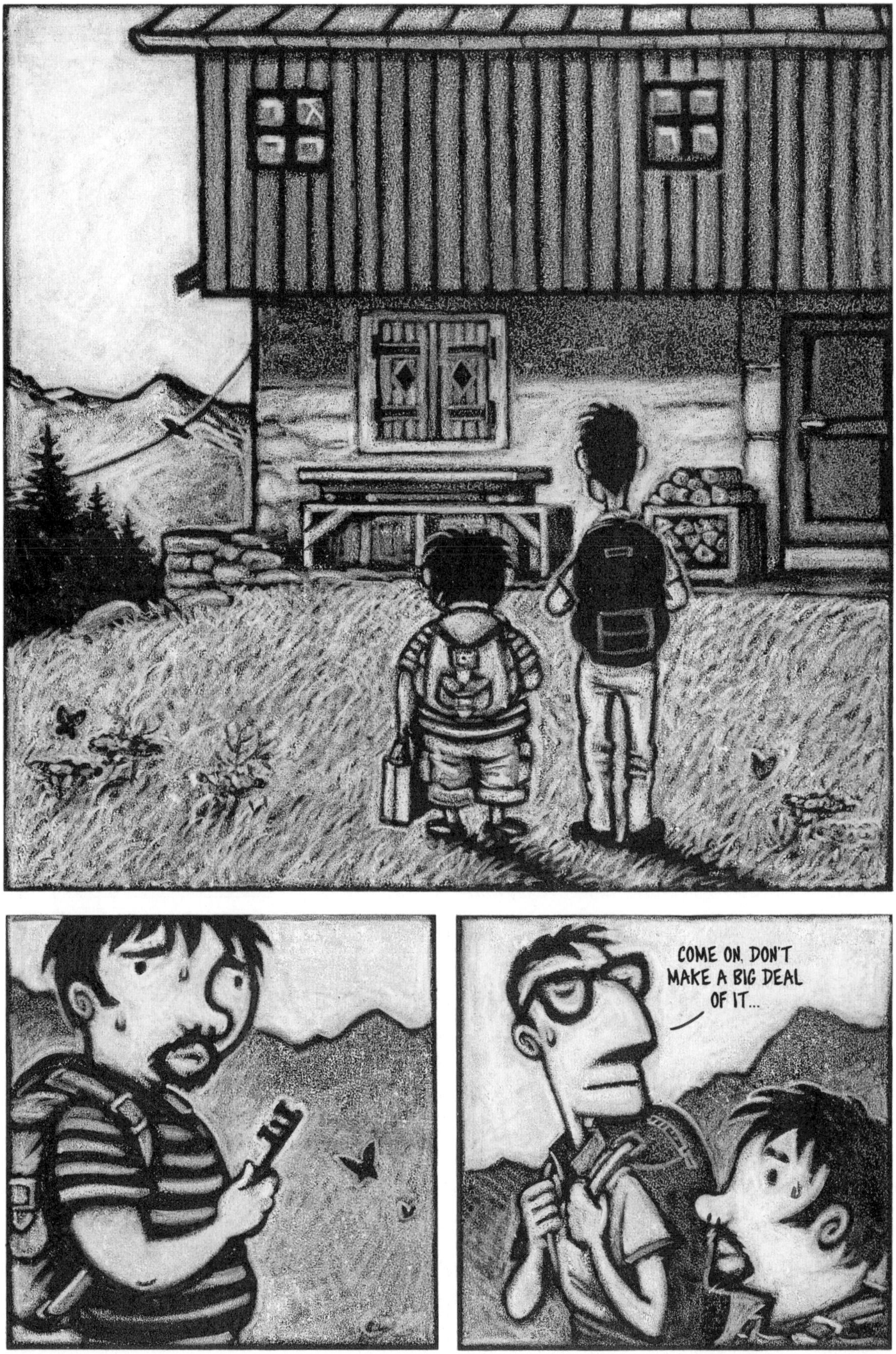
COME ON, DON'T MAKE A BIG DEAL OF IT...

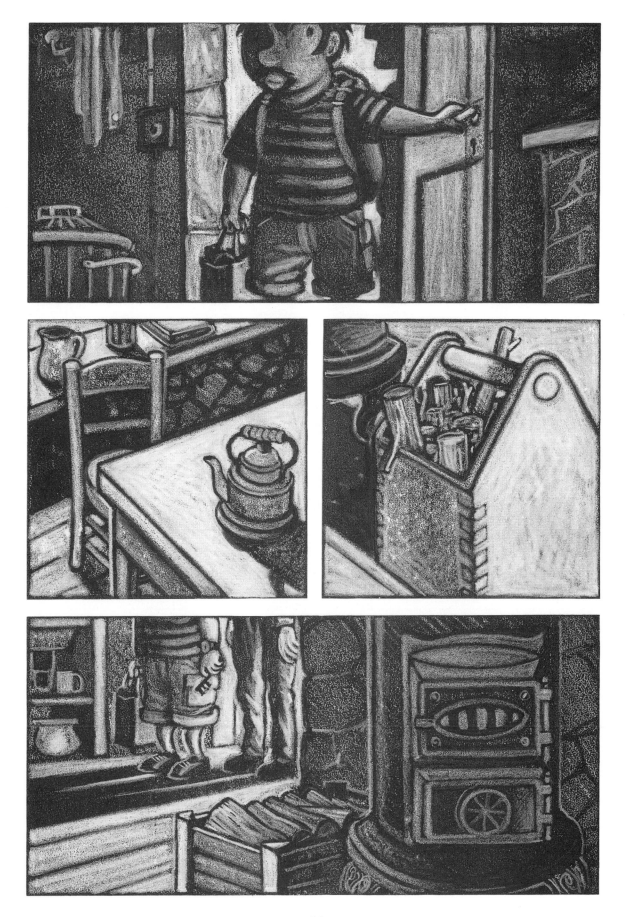

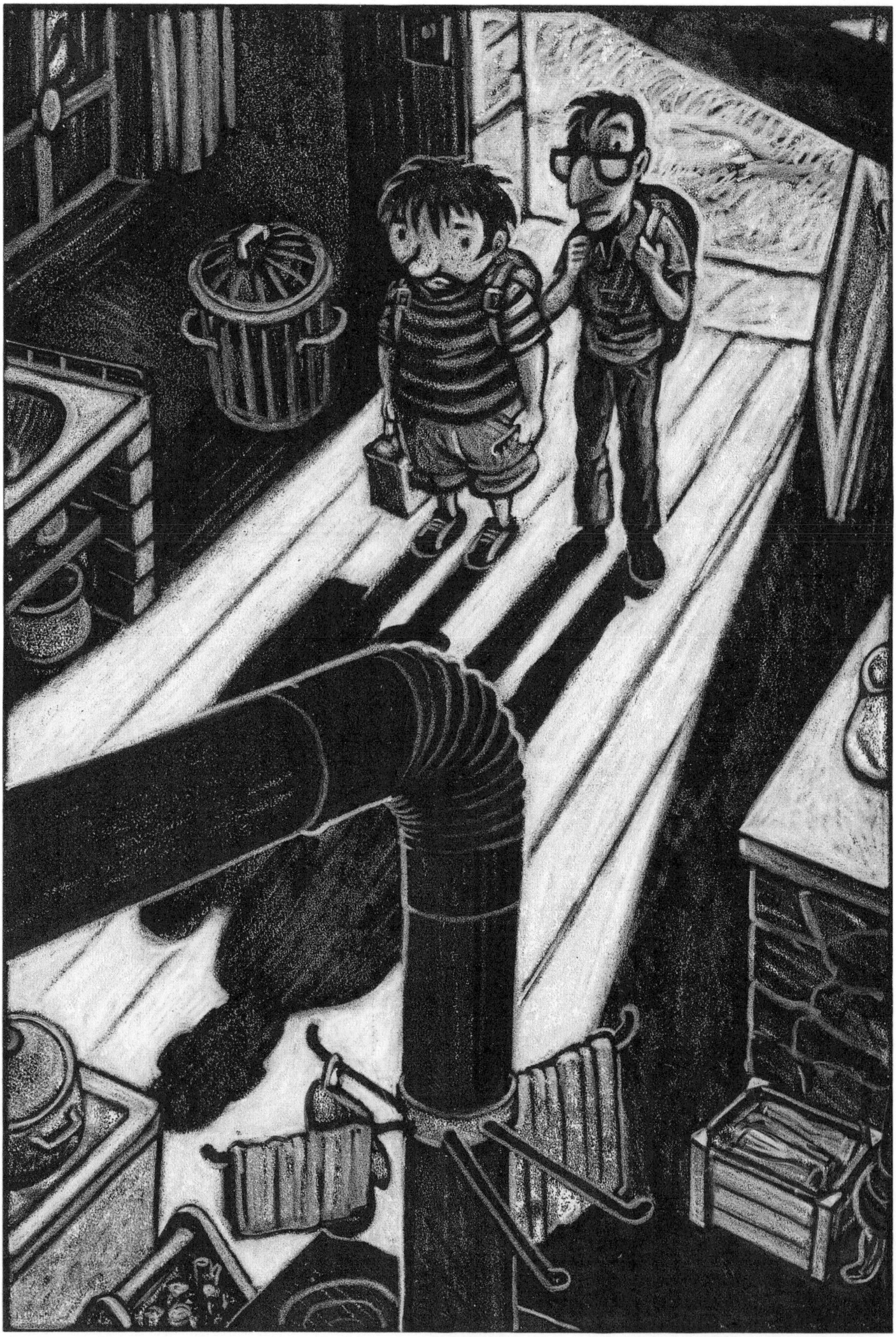

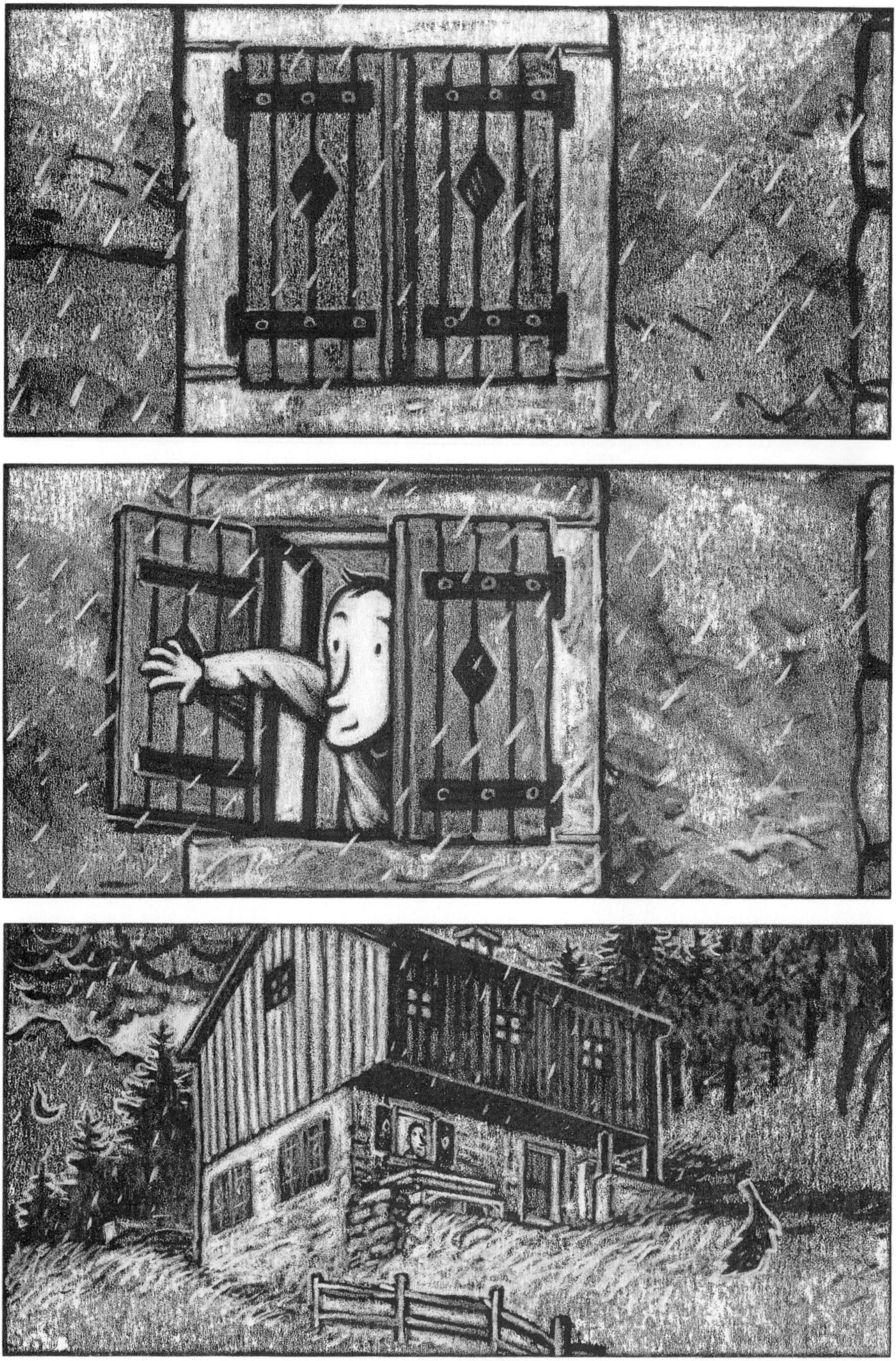

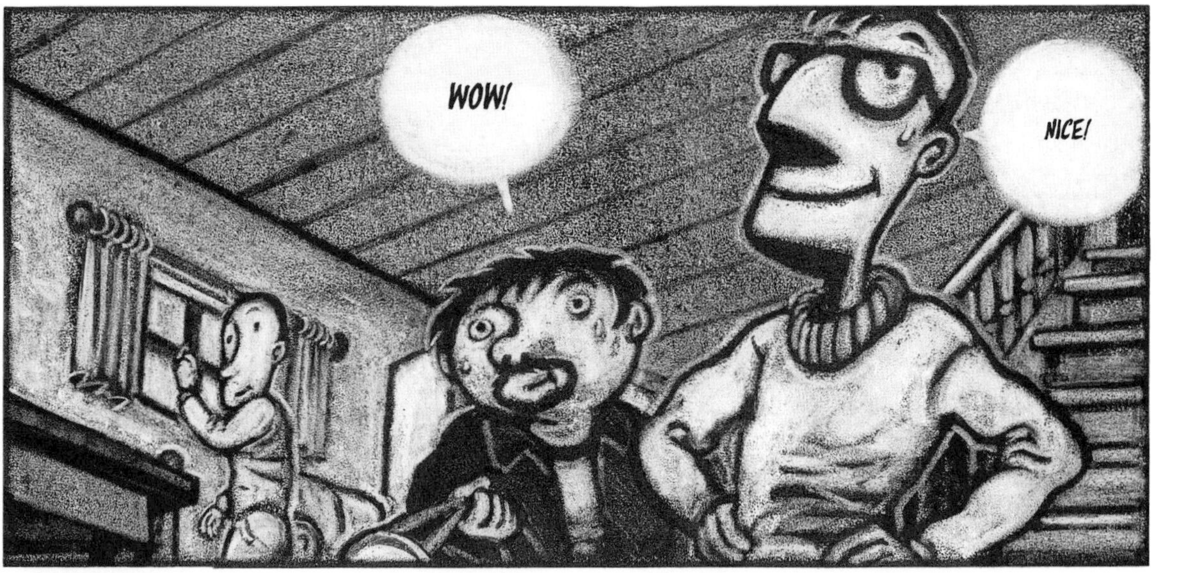
WOW!
NICE!

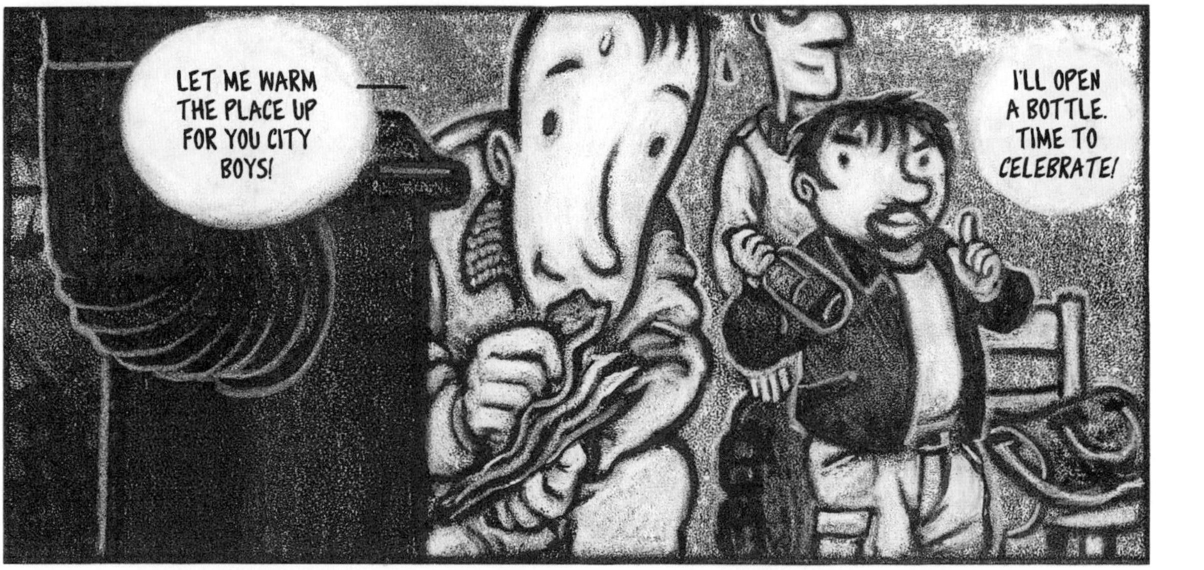
LET ME WARM THE PLACE UP FOR YOU CITY BOYS!
I'LL OPEN A BOTTLE. TIME TO CELEBRATE!

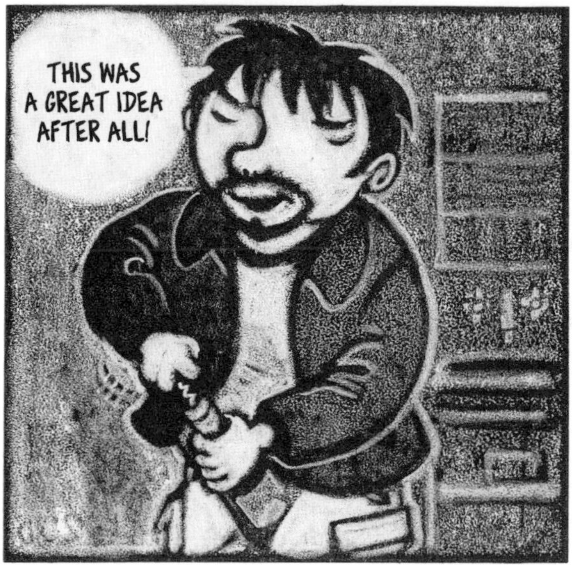
THIS WAS A GREAT IDEA AFTER ALL!

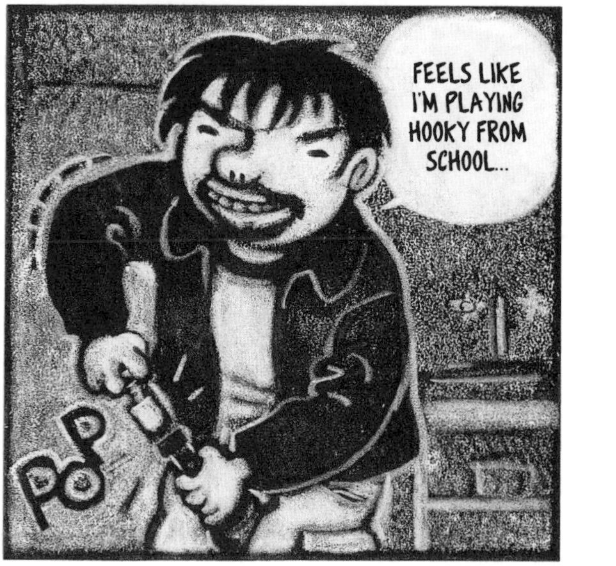
FEELS LIKE I'M PLAYING HOOKY FROM SCHOOL...
POP

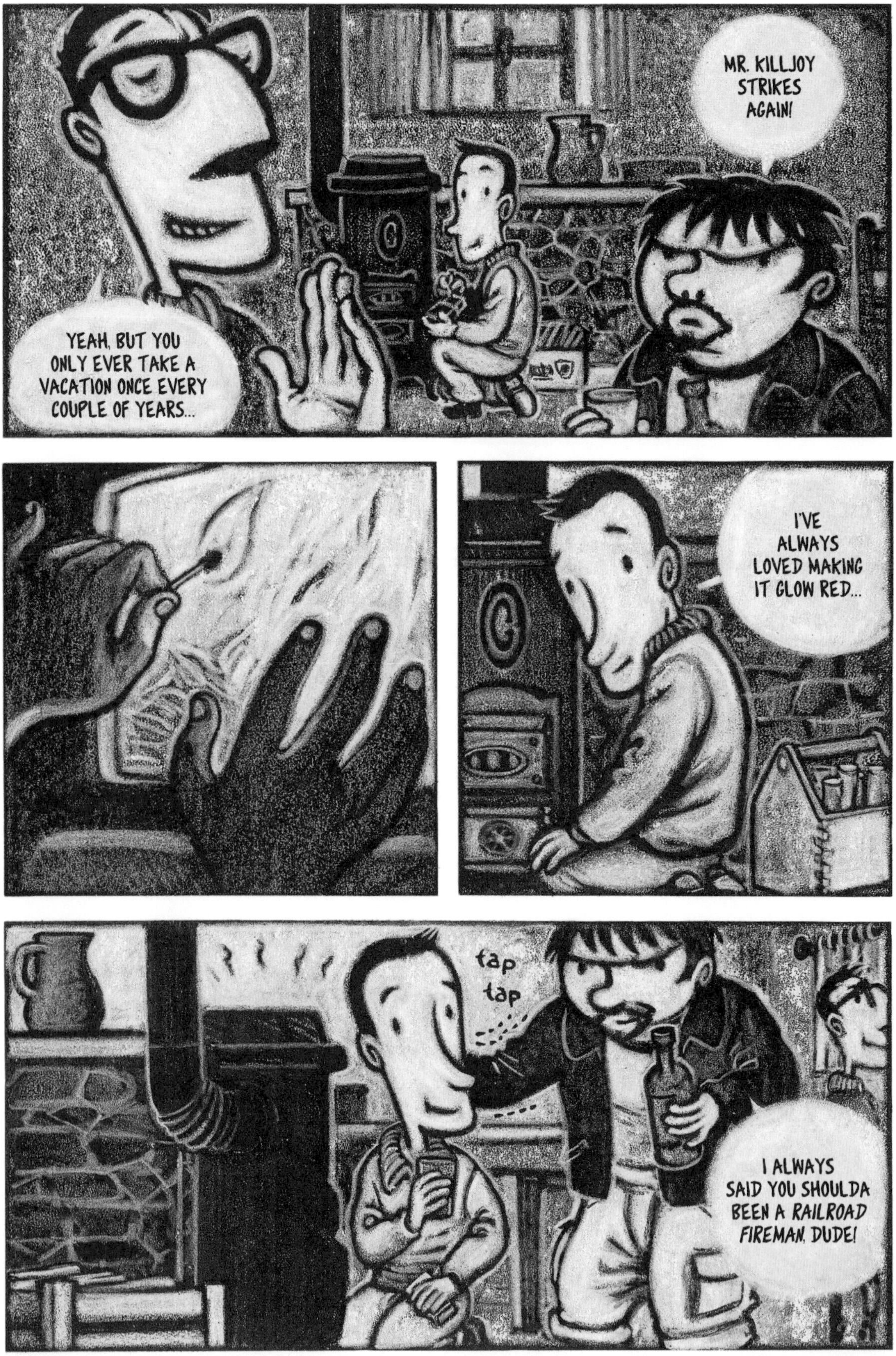
MR. KILLJOY STRIKES AGAIN!
YEAH, BUT YOU ONLY EVER TAKE A VACATION ONCE EVERY COUPLE OF YEARS...
I'VE ALWAYS LOVED MAKING IT GLOW RED...
tap tap
I ALWAYS SAID YOU SHOULDA BEEN A *RAILROAD FIREMAN*, DUDE!

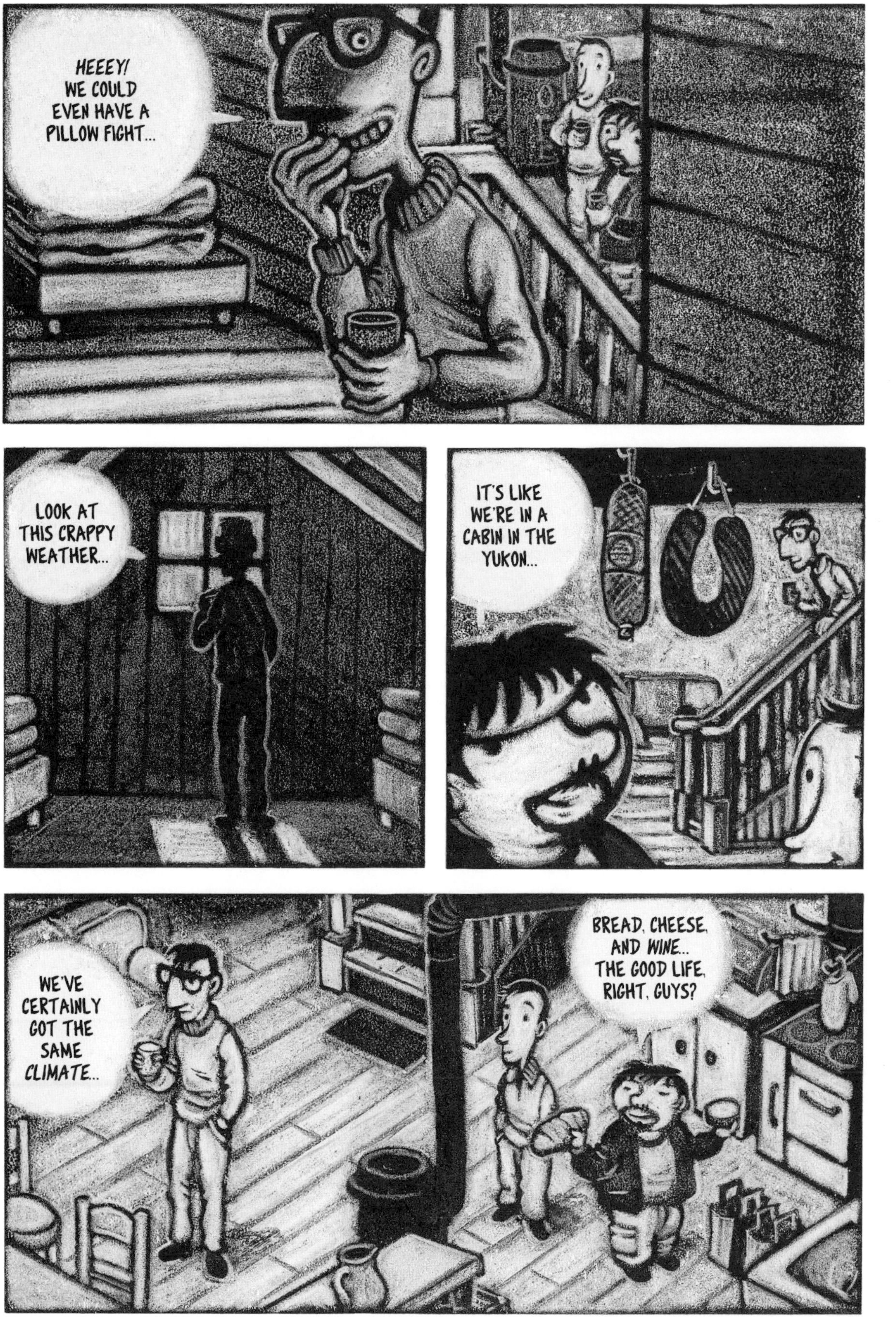
HEEEY! WE COULD EVEN HAVE A PILLOW FIGHT...
LOOK AT THIS CRAPPY WEATHER...
IT'S LIKE WE'RE IN A CABIN IN THE YUKON...
WE'VE CERTAINLY GOT THE SAME CLIMATE...
BREAD, CHEESE, AND WINE... THE GOOD LIFE, RIGHT, GUYS?

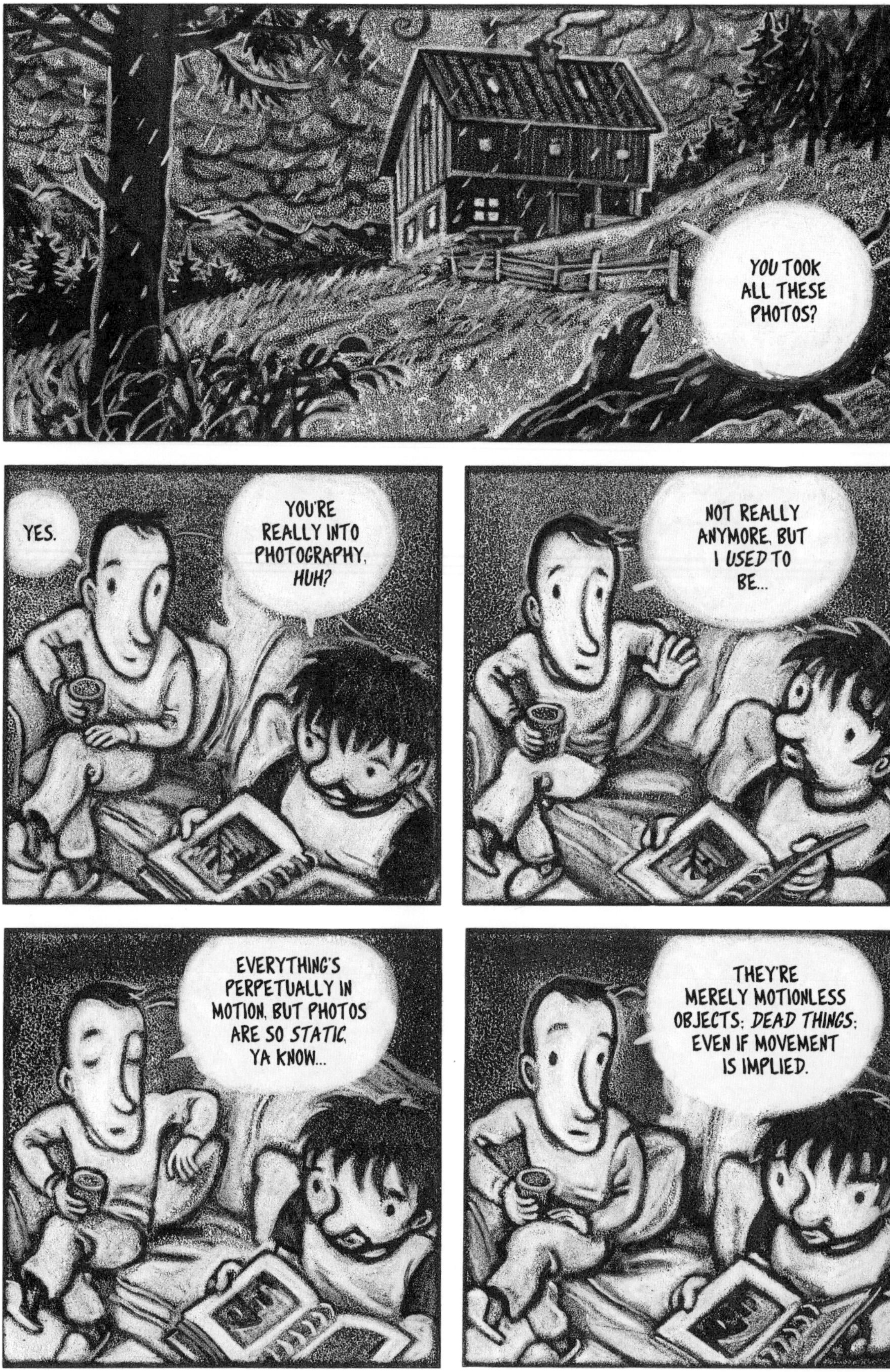
YOU TOOK ALL THESE PHOTOS?
YES.
YOU'RE REALLY INTO PHOTOGRAPHY, HUH?
NOT REALLY ANYMORE, BUT I USED TO BE...
EVERYTHING'S PERPETUALLY IN MOTION, BUT PHOTOS ARE SO STATIC, YA KNOW...
THEY'RE MERELY MOTIONLESS OBJECTS; DEAD THINGS; EVEN IF MOVEMENT IS IMPLIED.

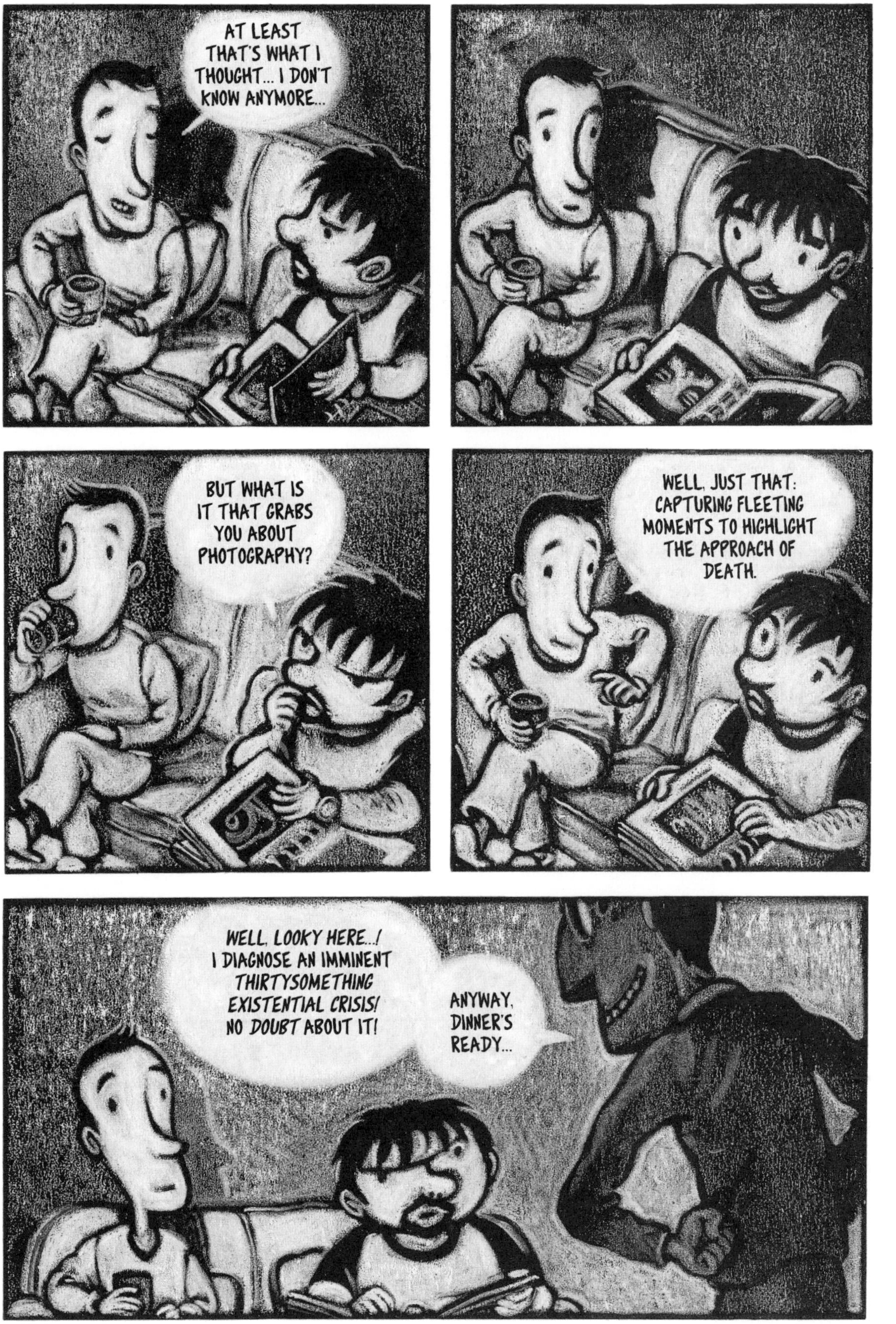
AT LEAST THAT'S WHAT I THOUGHT... I DON'T KNOW ANYMORE...
BUT WHAT IS IT THAT GRABS YOU ABOUT PHOTOGRAPHY?
WELL, JUST THAT: CAPTURING FLEETING MOMENTS TO HIGHLIGHT THE APPROACH OF DEATH.
WELL, LOOKY HERE...! I DIAGNOSE AN IMMINENT THIRTYSOMETHING EXISTENTIAL CRISIS! NO DOUBT ABOUT IT!
ANYWAY, DINNER'S READY...

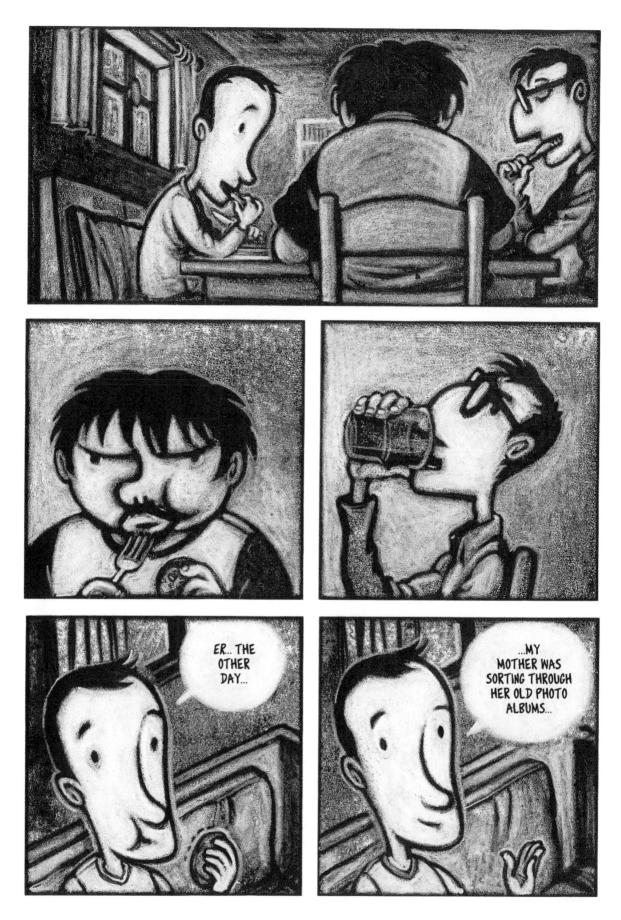

ER... THE OTHER DAY...

...MY MOTHER WAS SORTING THROUGH HER OLD PHOTO ALBUMS...

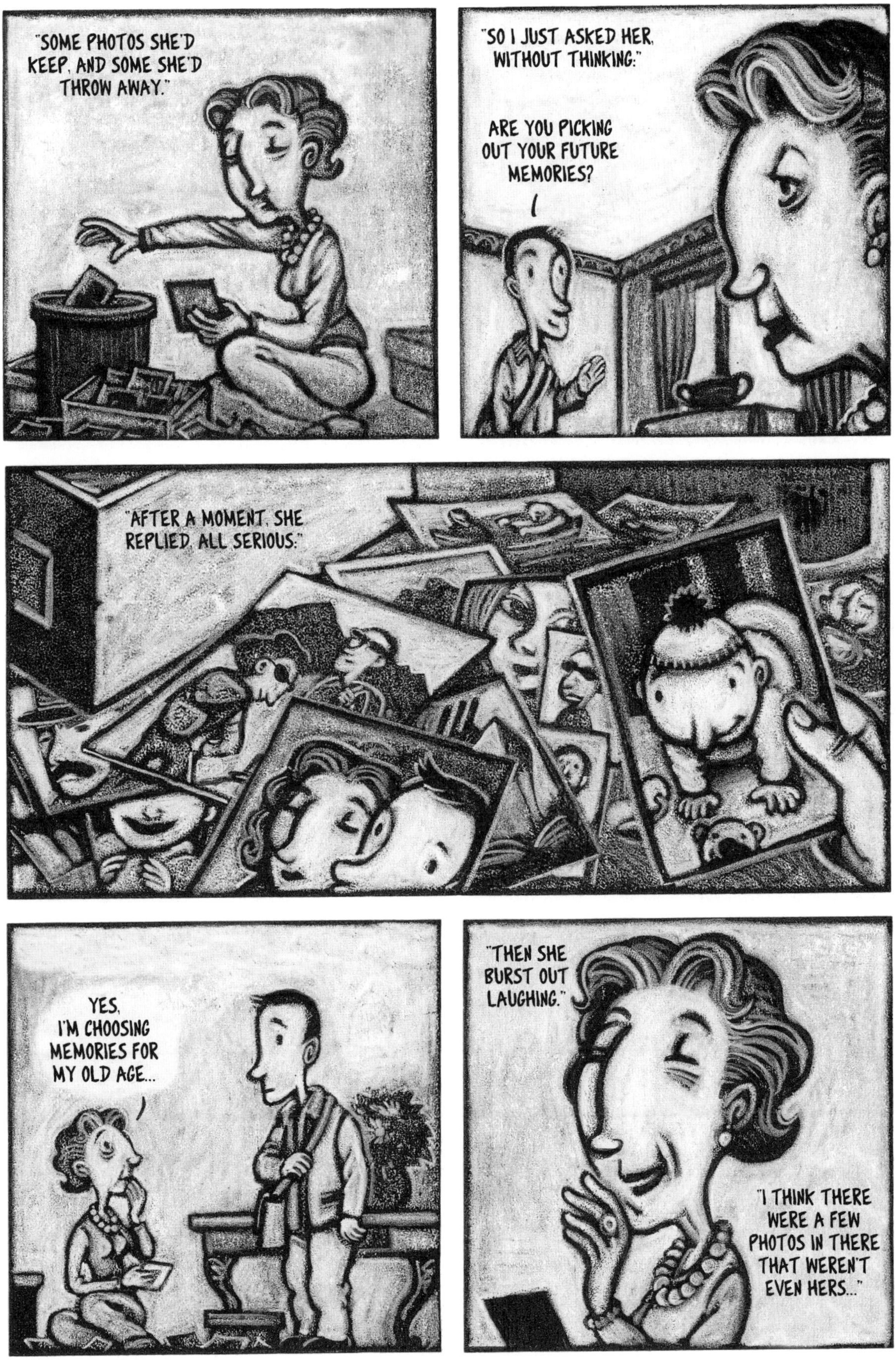
"SOME PHOTOS SHE'D KEEP, AND SOME SHE'D THROW AWAY."
"SO I JUST ASKED HER, WITHOUT THINKING:"
ARE YOU PICKING OUT YOUR FUTURE MEMORIES?
"AFTER A MOMENT, SHE REPLIED, ALL SERIOUS:"
YES, I'M CHOOSING MEMORIES FOR MY OLD AGE...
"THEN SHE BURST OUT LAUGHING."
"I THINK THERE WERE A FEW PHOTOS IN THERE THAT WEREN'T EVEN HERS..."

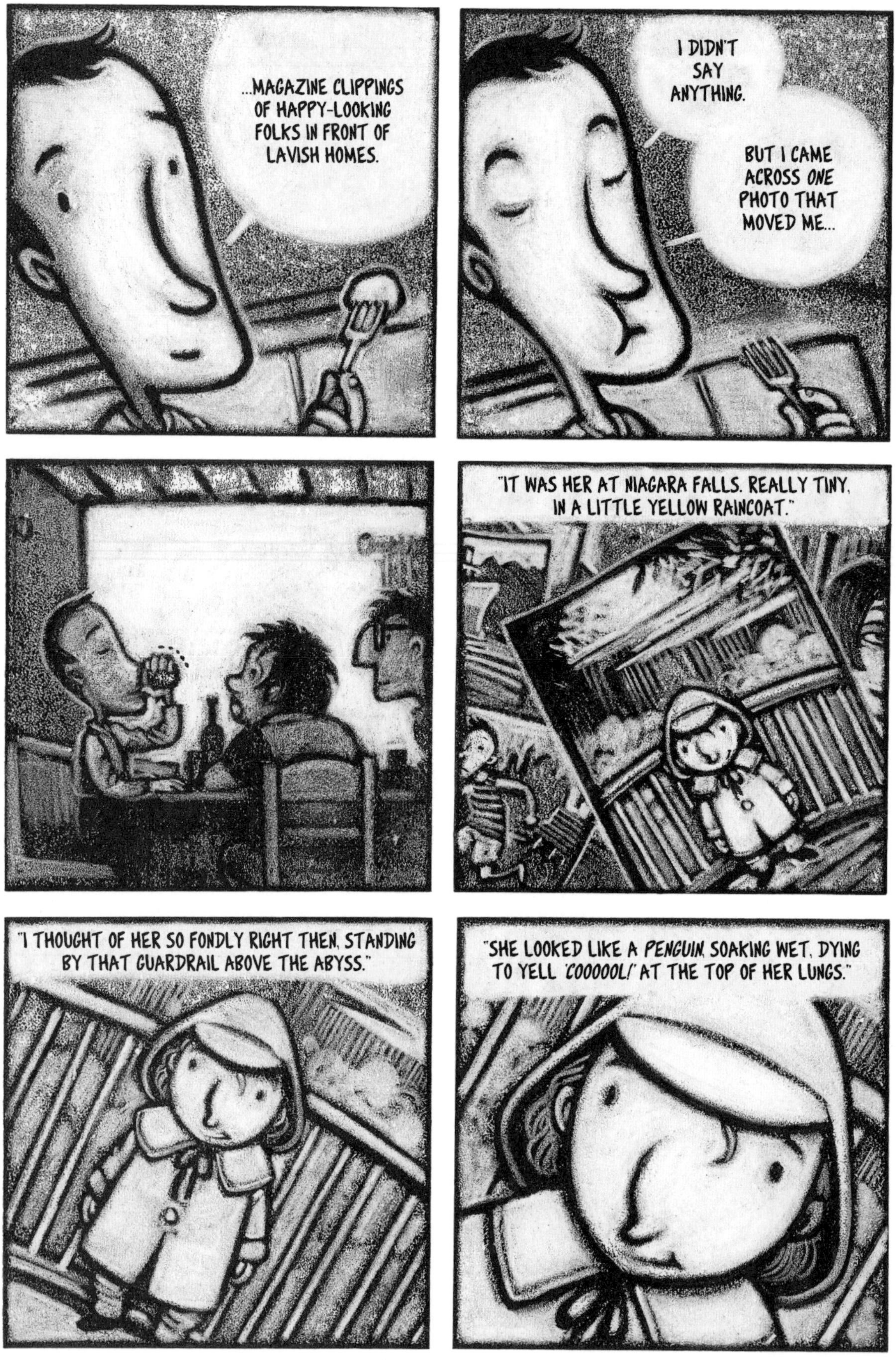
...MAGAZINE CLIPPINGS OF HAPPY-LOOKING FOLKS IN FRONT OF LAVISH HOMES.
I DIDN'T SAY ANYTHING.
BUT I CAME ACROSS ONE PHOTO THAT MOVED ME...
"IT WAS HER AT NIAGARA FALLS. REALLY TINY, IN A LITTLE YELLOW RAINCOAT."
"I THOUGHT OF HER SO FONDLY RIGHT THEN, STANDING BY THAT GUARDRAIL ABOVE THE ABYSS."
"SHE LOOKED LIKE A *PENGUIN*, SOAKING WET, DYING TO YELL *'COOOOOL!'* AT THE TOP OF HER LUNGS."

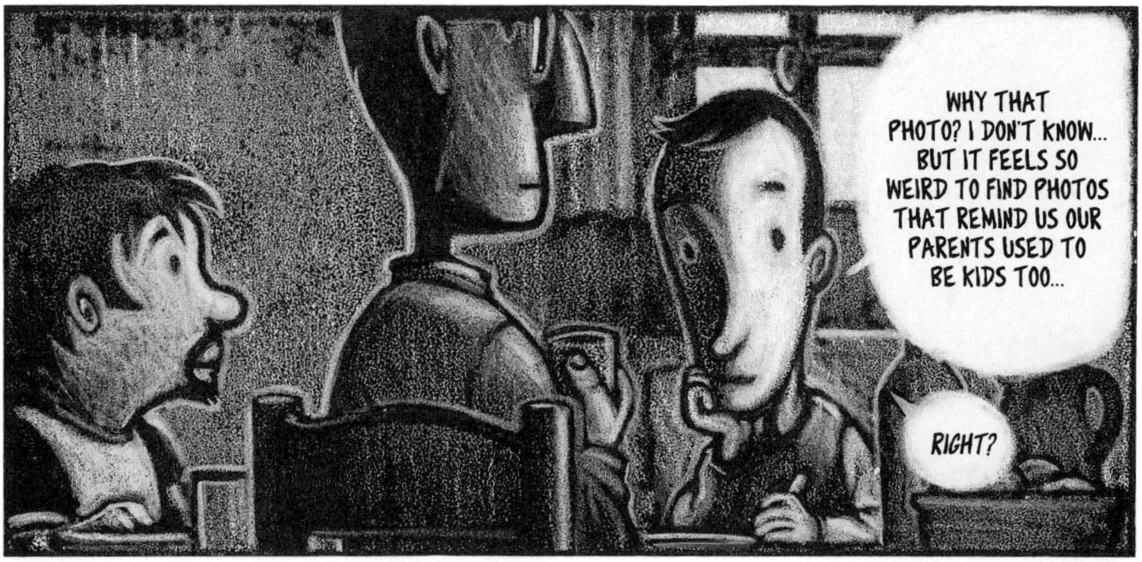
WHY THAT PHOTO? I DON'T KNOW... BUT IT FEELS SO WEIRD TO FIND PHOTOS THAT REMIND US OUR PARENTS USED TO BE KIDS TOO...
RIGHT?

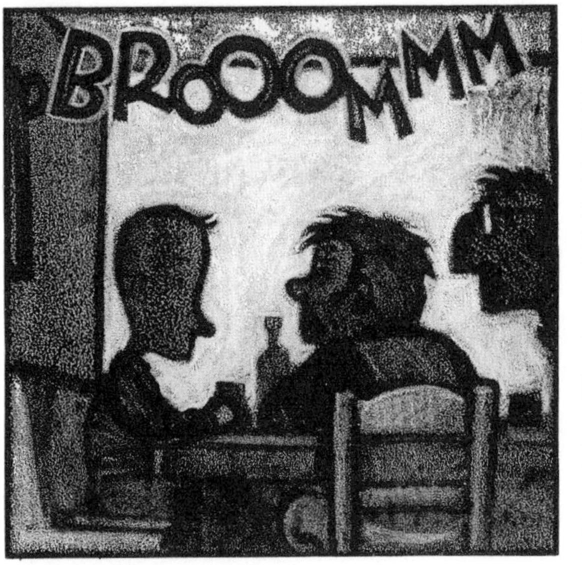
BROOOMMM

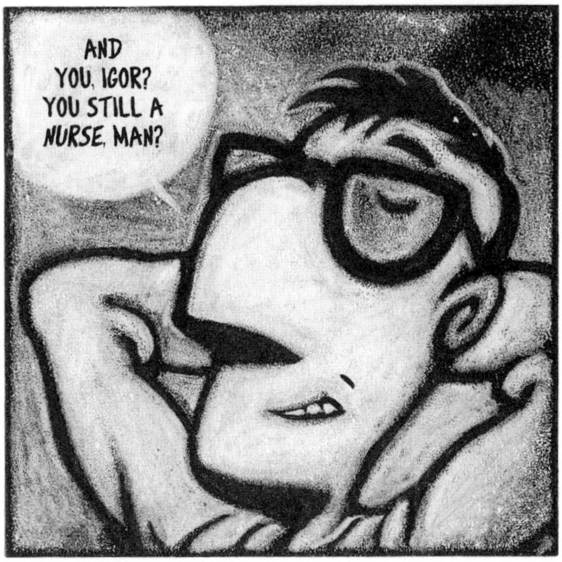
AND YOU, IGOR? YOU STILL A *NURSE*, MAN?

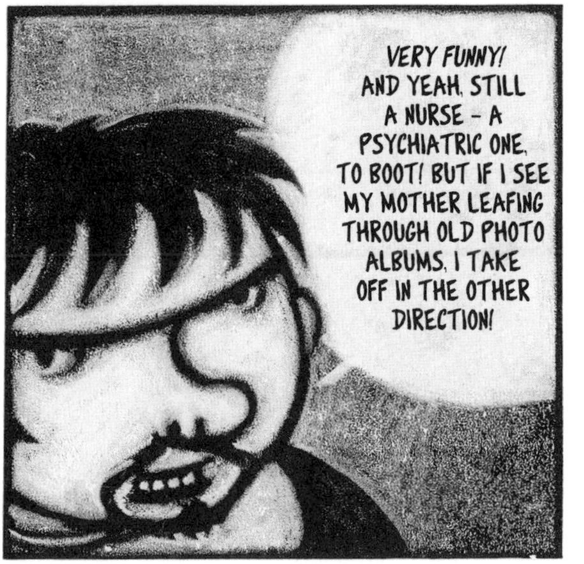
VERY FUNNY! AND YEAH, STILL A NURSE – A PSYCHIATRIC ONE, TO BOOT! BUT IF I SEE MY MOTHER LEAFING THROUGH OLD PHOTO ALBUMS, I TAKE OFF IN THE OTHER DIRECTION!

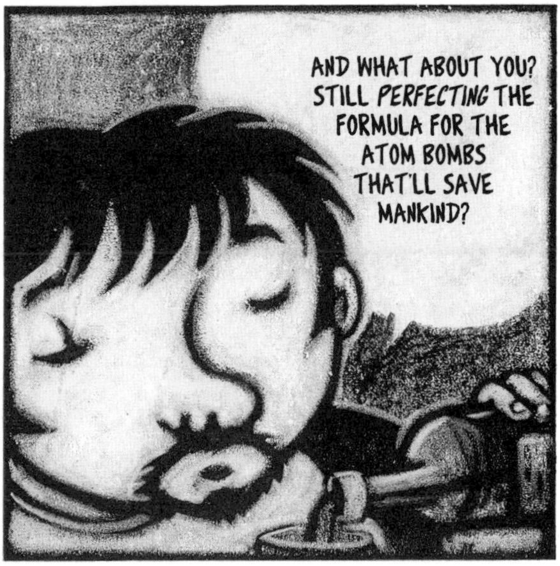
AND WHAT ABOUT YOU? STILL *PERFECTING* THE FORMULA FOR THE ATOM BOMBS THAT'LL SAVE MANKIND?

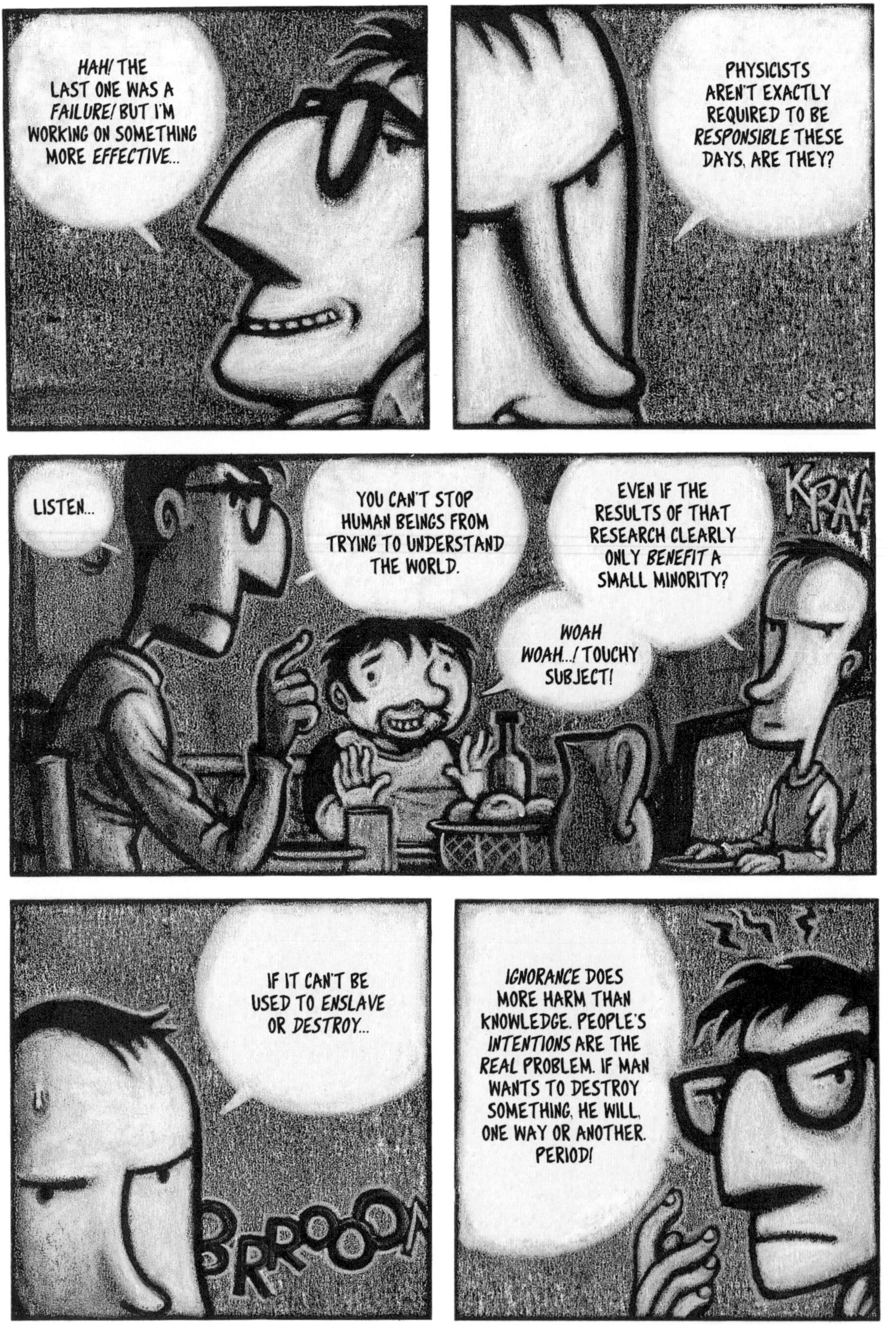
HAH! THE LAST ONE WAS A FAILURE! BUT I'M WORKING ON SOMETHING MORE EFFECTIVE...
PHYSICISTS AREN'T EXACTLY REQUIRED TO BE RESPONSIBLE THESE DAYS, ARE THEY?
LISTEN...
YOU CAN'T STOP HUMAN BEINGS FROM TRYING TO UNDERSTAND THE WORLD.
EVEN IF THE RESULTS OF THAT RESEARCH CLEARLY ONLY BENEFIT A SMALL MINORITY?
WOAH WOAH...! TOUCHY SUBJECT!
IF IT CAN'T BE USED TO ENSLAVE OR DESTROY...
BRROOOM
IGNORANCE DOES MORE HARM THAN KNOWLEDGE. PEOPLE'S INTENTIONS ARE THE REAL PROBLEM. IF MAN WANTS TO DESTROY SOMETHING, HE WILL, ONE WAY OR ANOTHER. PERIOD!

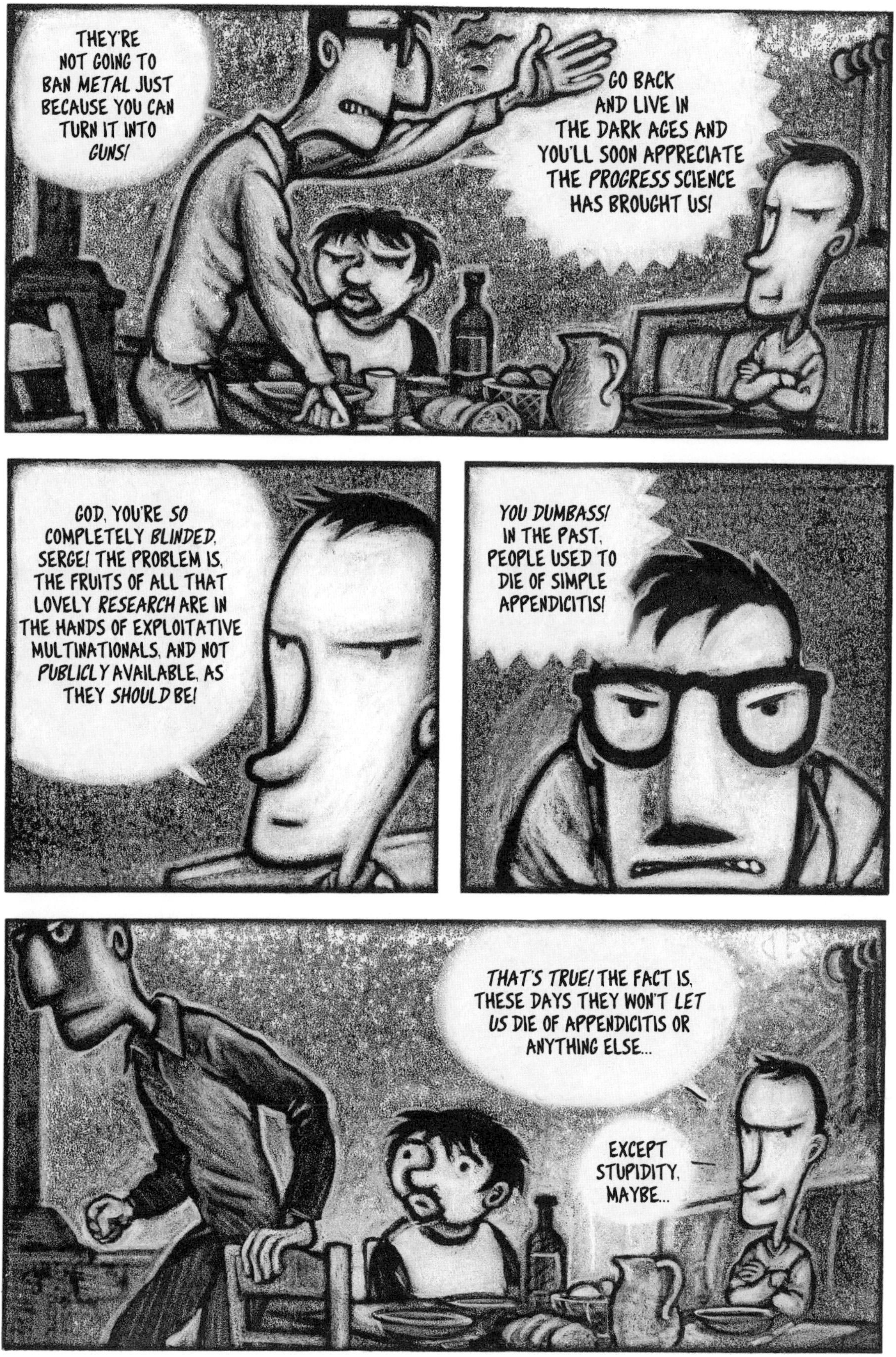
THEY'RE NOT GOING TO BAN *METAL* JUST BECAUSE YOU CAN TURN IT INTO *GUNS!*
GO BACK AND LIVE IN THE DARK AGES AND YOU'LL SOON APPRECIATE THE *PROGRESS* SCIENCE HAS BROUGHT US!
GOD, YOU'RE *SO* COMPLETELY *BLINDED*, SERGE! THE PROBLEM IS, THE FRUITS OF ALL THAT LOVELY *RESEARCH* ARE IN THE HANDS OF EXPLOITATIVE MULTINATIONALS, AND NOT *PUBLICLY* AVAILABLE, AS THEY *SHOULD* BE!
YOU DUMBASS! IN THE PAST, PEOPLE USED TO DIE OF SIMPLE APPENDICITIS!
THAT'S TRUE! THE FACT IS, THESE DAYS THEY WON'T *LET US* DIE OF APPENDICITIS OR ANYTHING ELSE...
EXCEPT STUPIDITY, MAYBE...

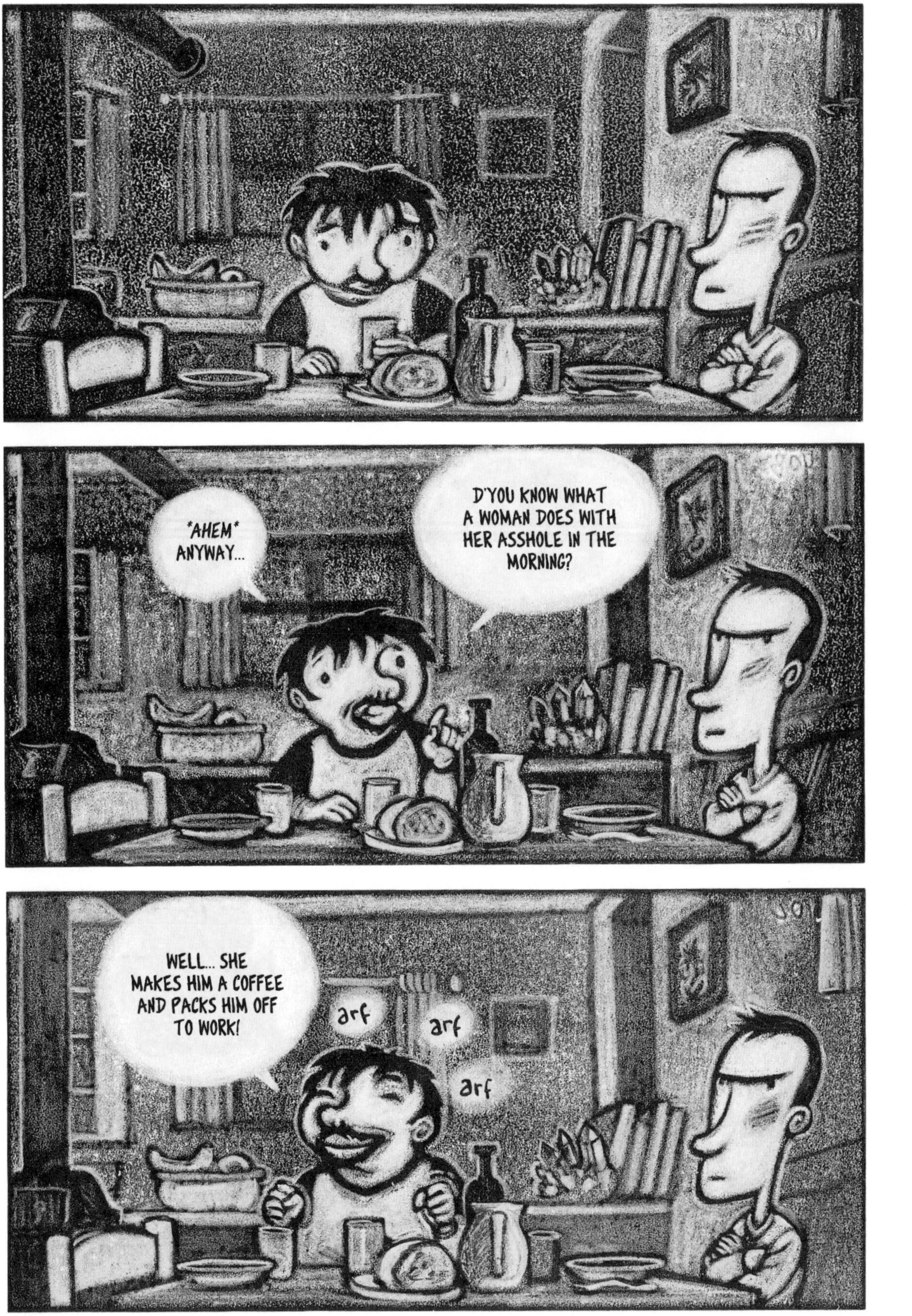
AHEM ANYWAY...
D'YOU KNOW WHAT A WOMAN DOES WITH HER ASSHOLE IN THE MORNING?
WELL... SHE MAKES HIM A COFFEE AND PACKS HIM OFF TO WORK!
arf
arf
arf

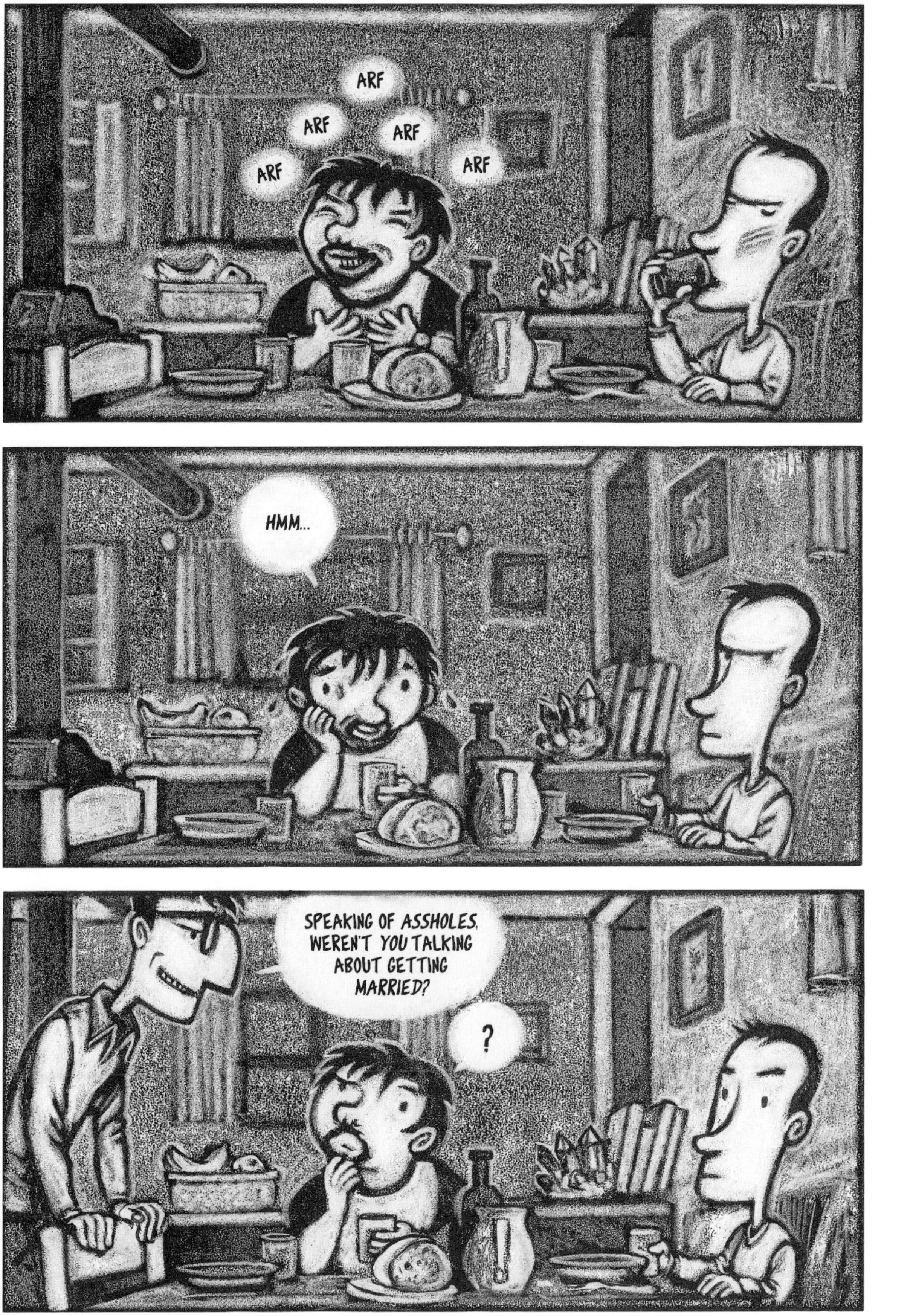
ARF
ARF
ARF
ARF
ARF
HMM...
SPEAKING OF ASSHOLES, WEREN'T YOU TALKING ABOUT GETTING MARRIED?
?

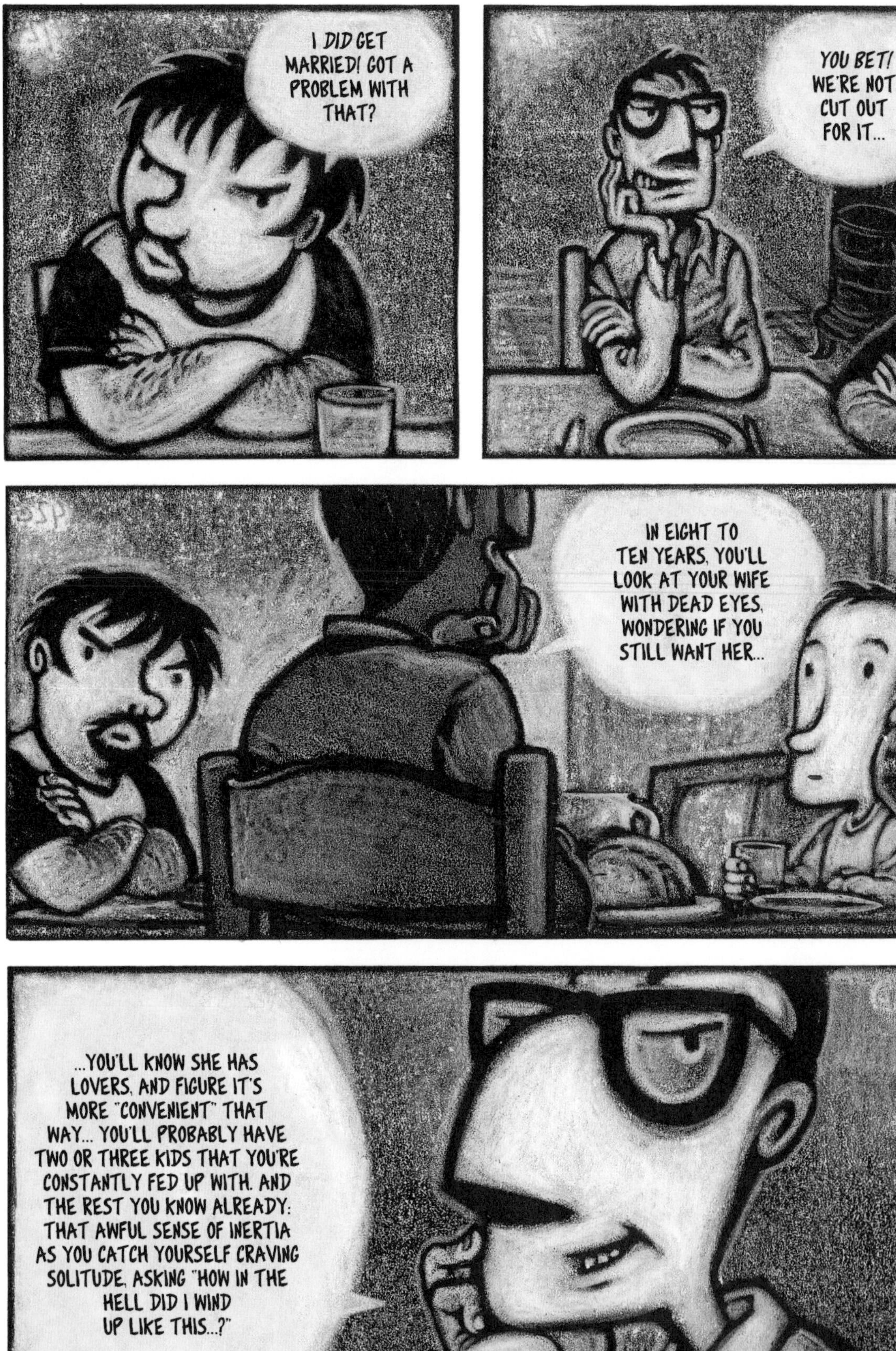
I *DID* GET MARRIED! GOT A PROBLEM WITH THAT?
YOU BET! WE'RE NOT CUT OUT FOR IT...
IN EIGHT TO TEN YEARS, YOU'LL LOOK AT YOUR WIFE WITH DEAD EYES, WONDERING IF YOU STILL WANT HER...
...YOU'LL KNOW SHE HAS LOVERS, AND FIGURE IT'S MORE "CONVENIENT" THAT WAY... YOU'LL PROBABLY HAVE TWO OR THREE KIDS THAT YOU'RE CONSTANTLY FED UP WITH. AND THE REST YOU KNOW ALREADY: THAT AWFUL SENSE OF INERTIA AS YOU CATCH YOURSELF CRAVING SOLITUDE, ASKING "HOW IN THE HELL DID I WIND UP LIKE THIS...?"

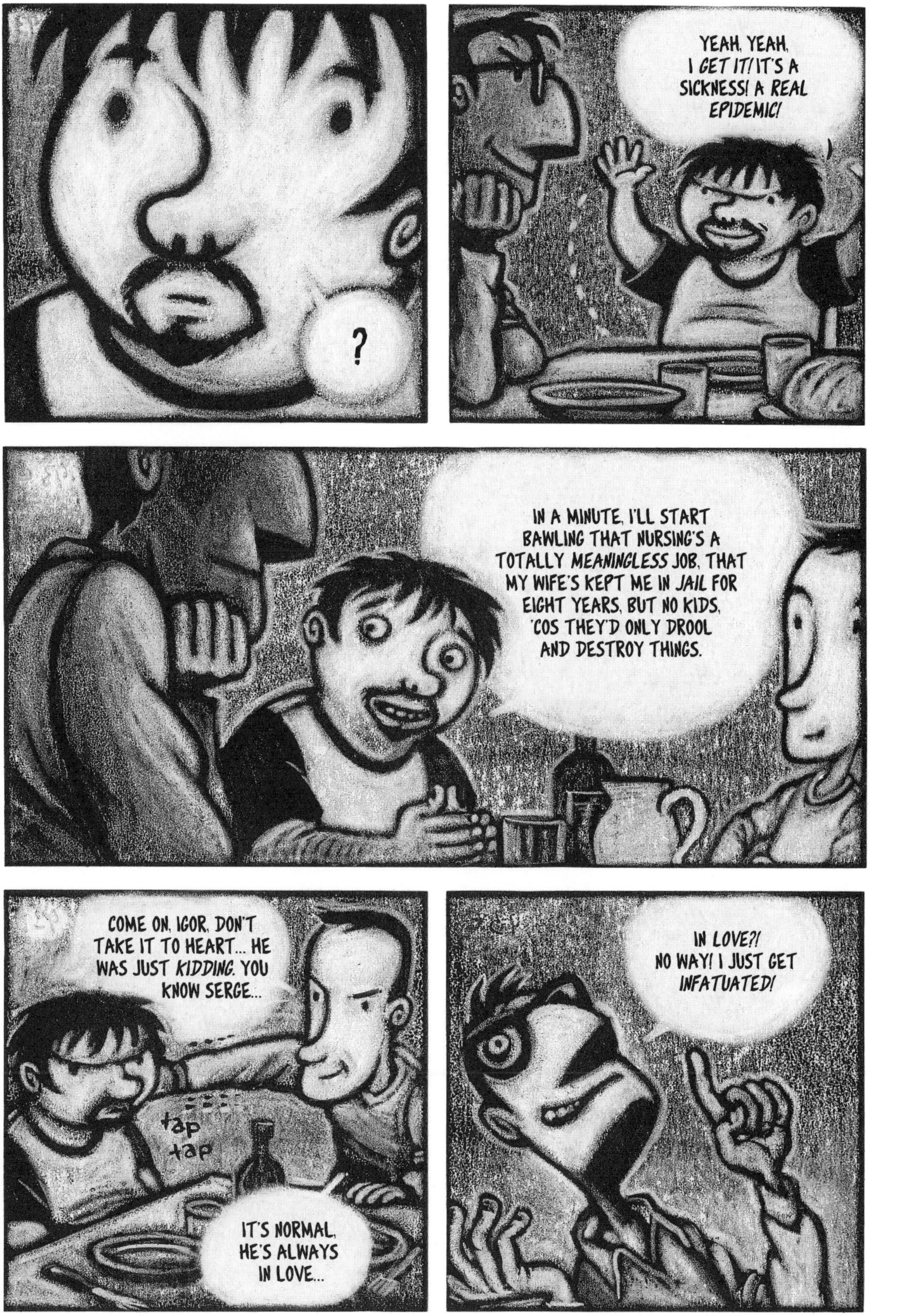
?
YEAH, YEAH, I *GET IT!* IT'S A SICKNESS! A REAL EPIDEMIC!
IN A MINUTE, I'LL START BAWLING THAT NURSING'S A TOTALLY *MEANINGLESS* JOB, THAT MY WIFE'S KEPT ME IN *JAIL* FOR EIGHT YEARS, BUT NO KIDS, 'COS THEY'D ONLY DROOL AND DESTROY THINGS.
COME ON, IGOR, DON'T TAKE IT TO HEART... HE WAS JUST *KIDDING*. YOU KNOW SERGE...
tap tap
IT'S NORMAL, HE'S ALWAYS IN LOVE...
IN LOVE?! NO WAY! I JUST GET *INFATUATED!*

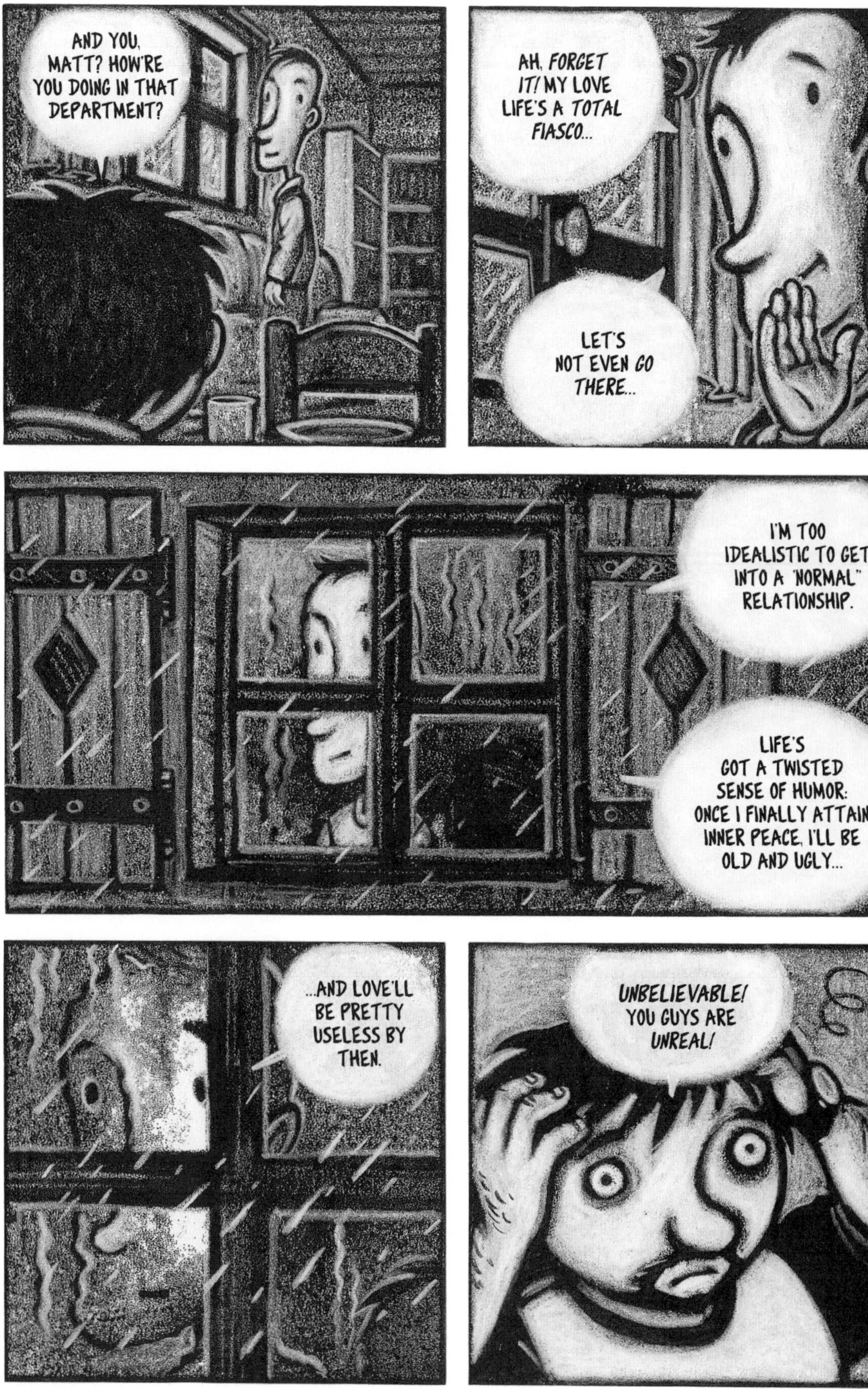
AND YOU, MATT? HOW'RE YOU DOING IN THAT DEPARTMENT?
AH, FORGET IT! MY LOVE LIFE'S A TOTAL FIASCO...
LET'S NOT EVEN GO THERE...
I'M TOO IDEALISTIC TO GET INTO A "NORMAL" RELATIONSHIP.
LIFE'S GOT A TWISTED SENSE OF HUMOR: ONCE I FINALLY ATTAIN INNER PEACE, I'LL BE OLD AND UGLY...
...AND LOVE'LL BE PRETTY USELESS BY THEN.
UNBELIEVABLE! YOU GUYS ARE UNREAL!

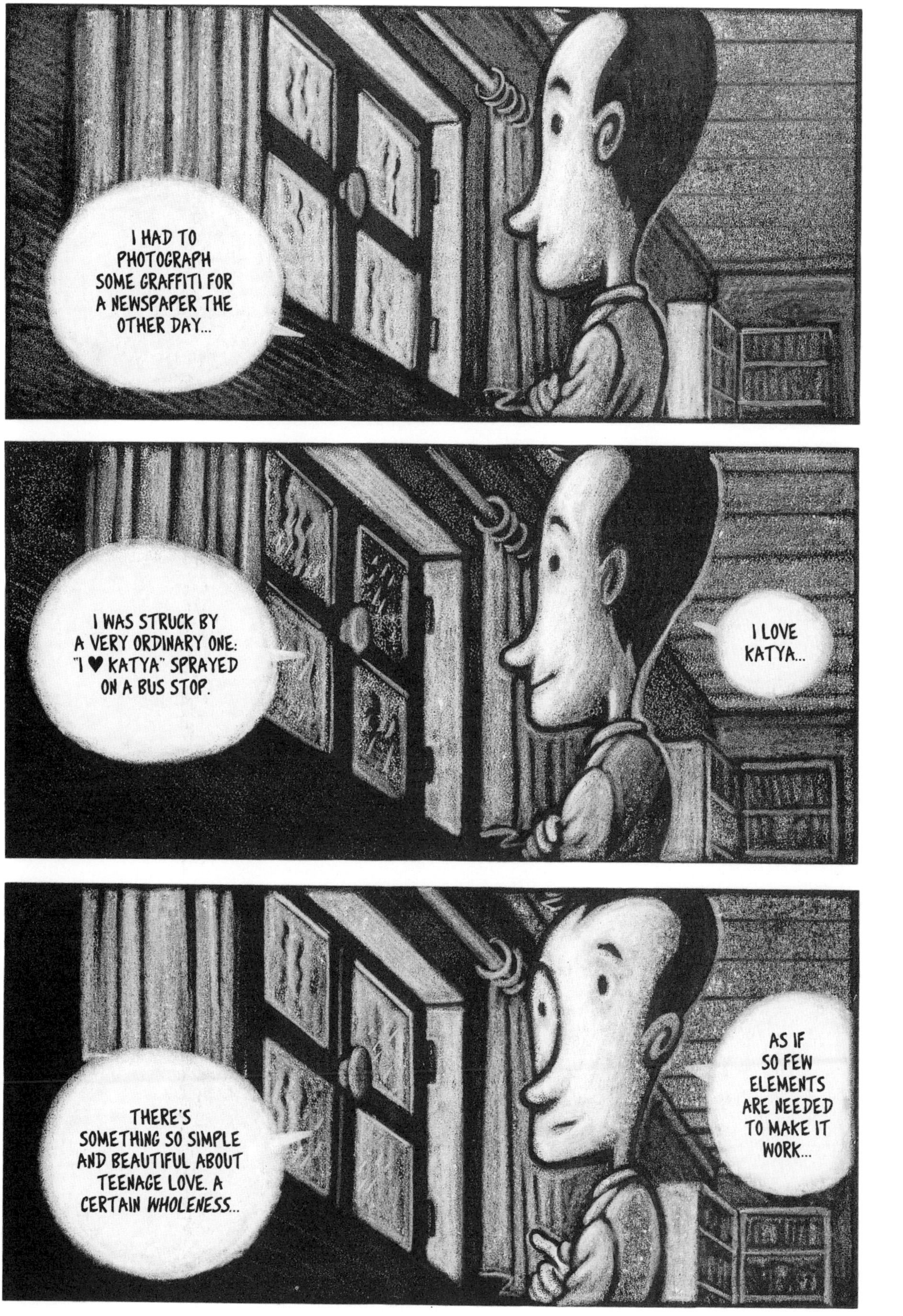
I HAD TO PHOTOGRAPH SOME GRAFFITI FOR A NEWSPAPER THE OTHER DAY...
I WAS STRUCK BY A VERY ORDINARY ONE: "I ♥ KATYA" SPRAYED ON A BUS STOP.
I LOVE KATYA...
THERE'S SOMETHING SO SIMPLE AND BEAUTIFUL ABOUT TEENAGE LOVE. A CERTAIN *WHOLENESS*...
AS IF SO FEW ELEMENTS ARE NEEDED TO MAKE IT WORK...

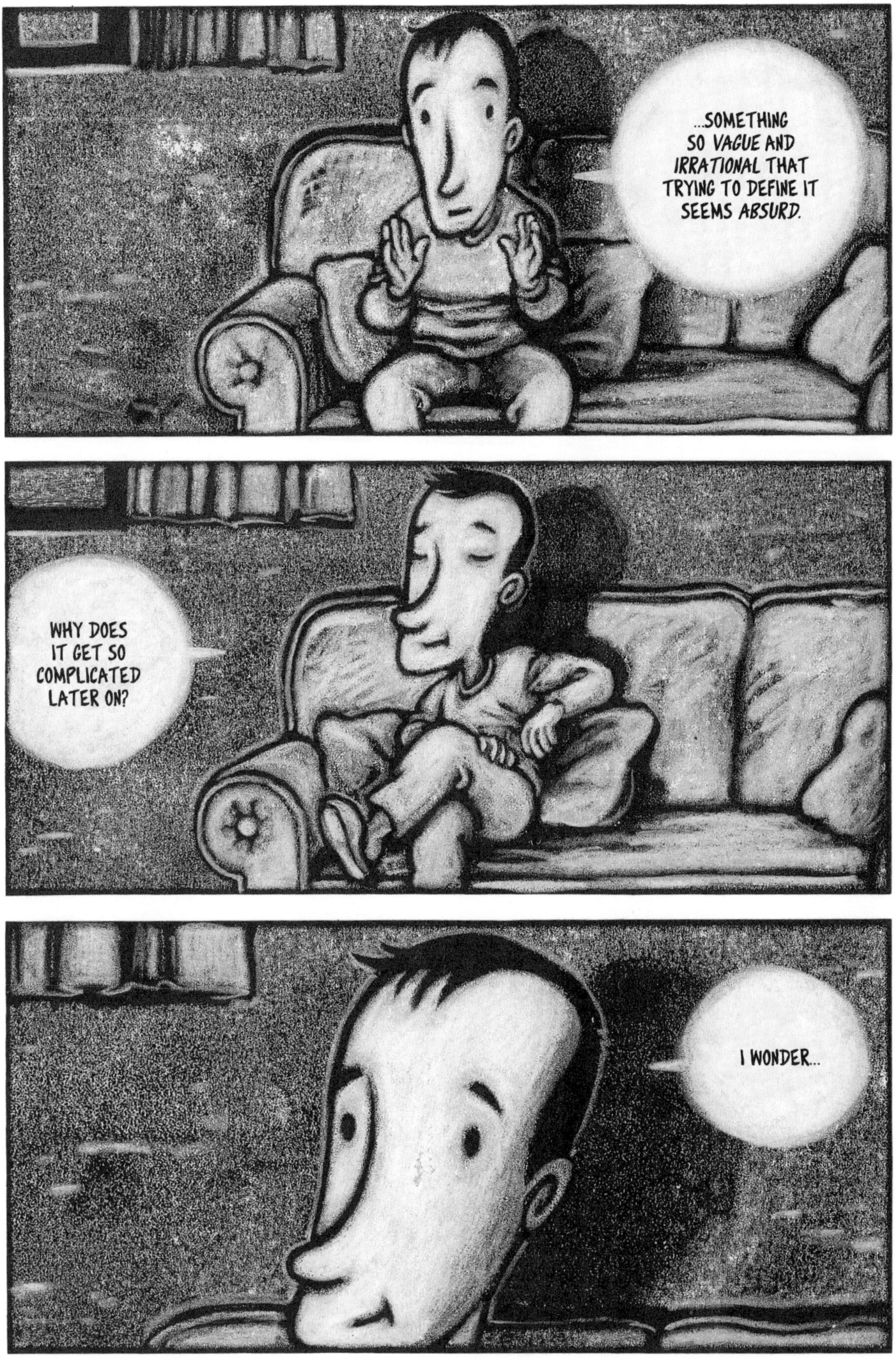
...SOMETHING SO VAGUE AND IRRATIONAL THAT TRYING TO DEFINE IT SEEMS ABSURD.
WHY DOES IT GET SO COMPLICATED LATER ON?
I WONDER...

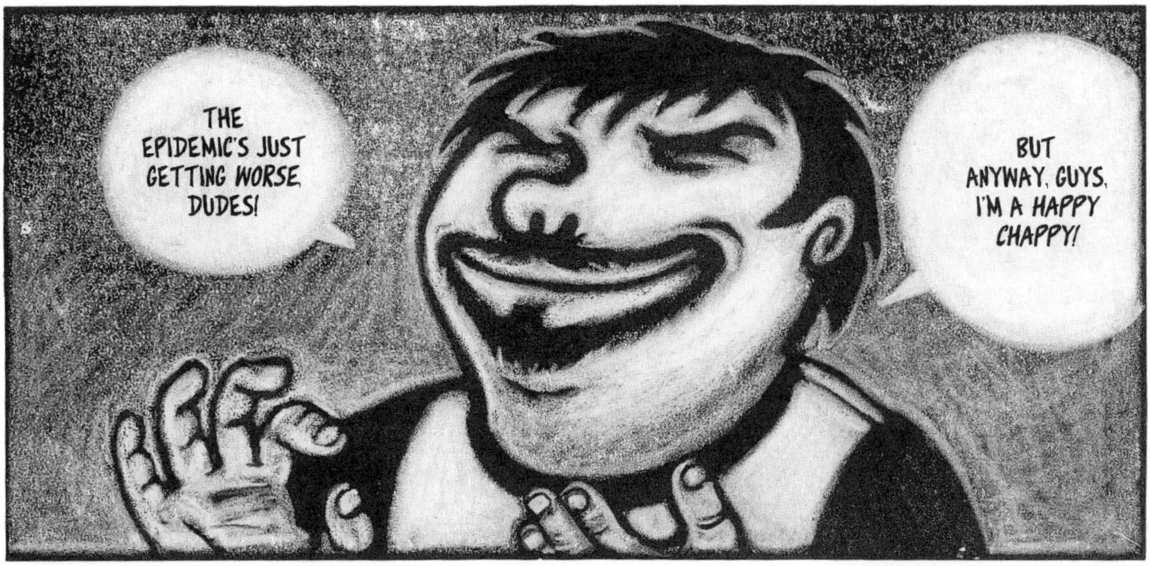
THE EPIDEMIC'S JUST GETTING WORSE, DUDES!
BUT ANYWAY, GUYS, I'M A HAPPY CHAPPY!

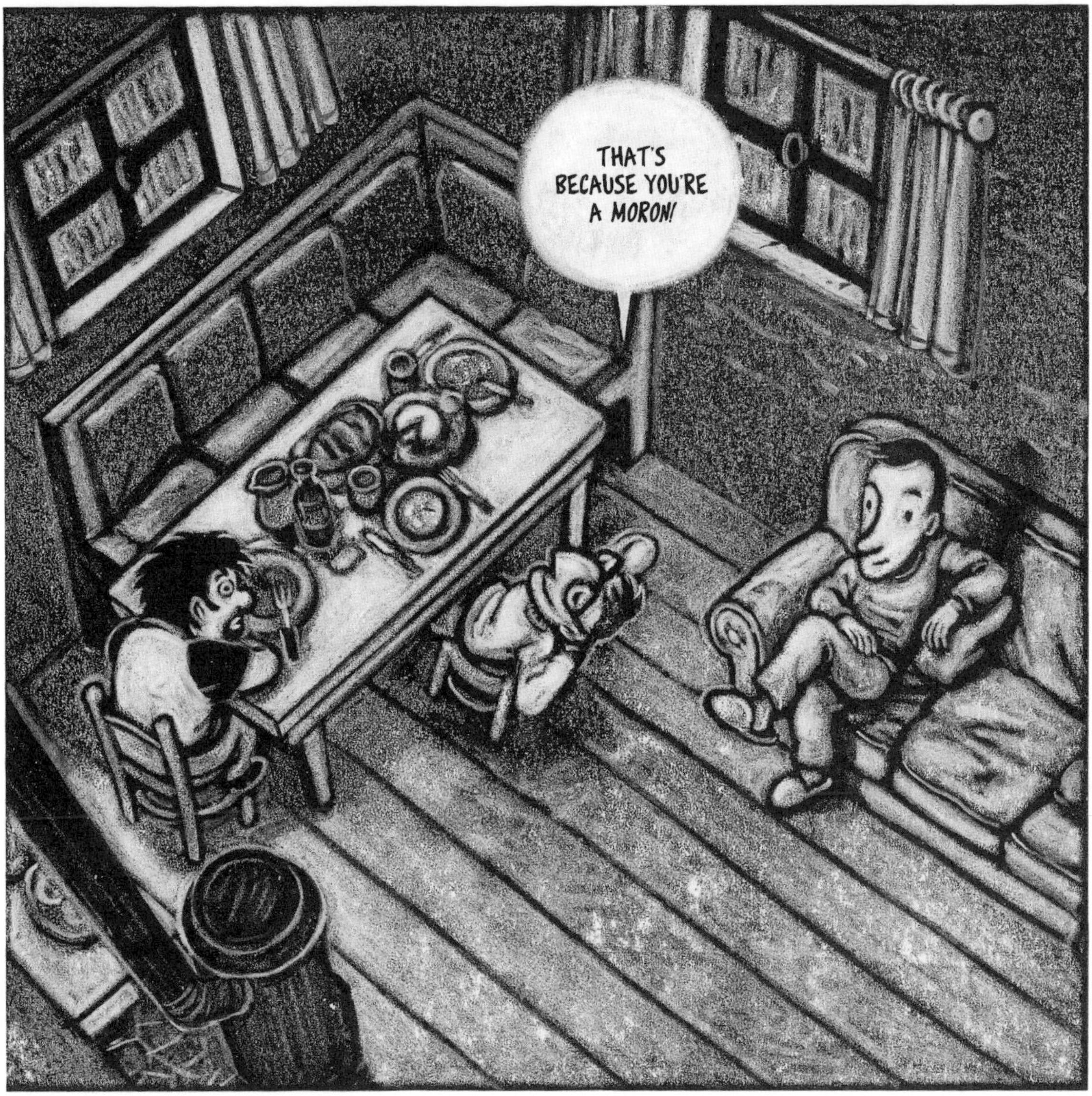
THAT'S BECAUSE YOU'RE A MORON!

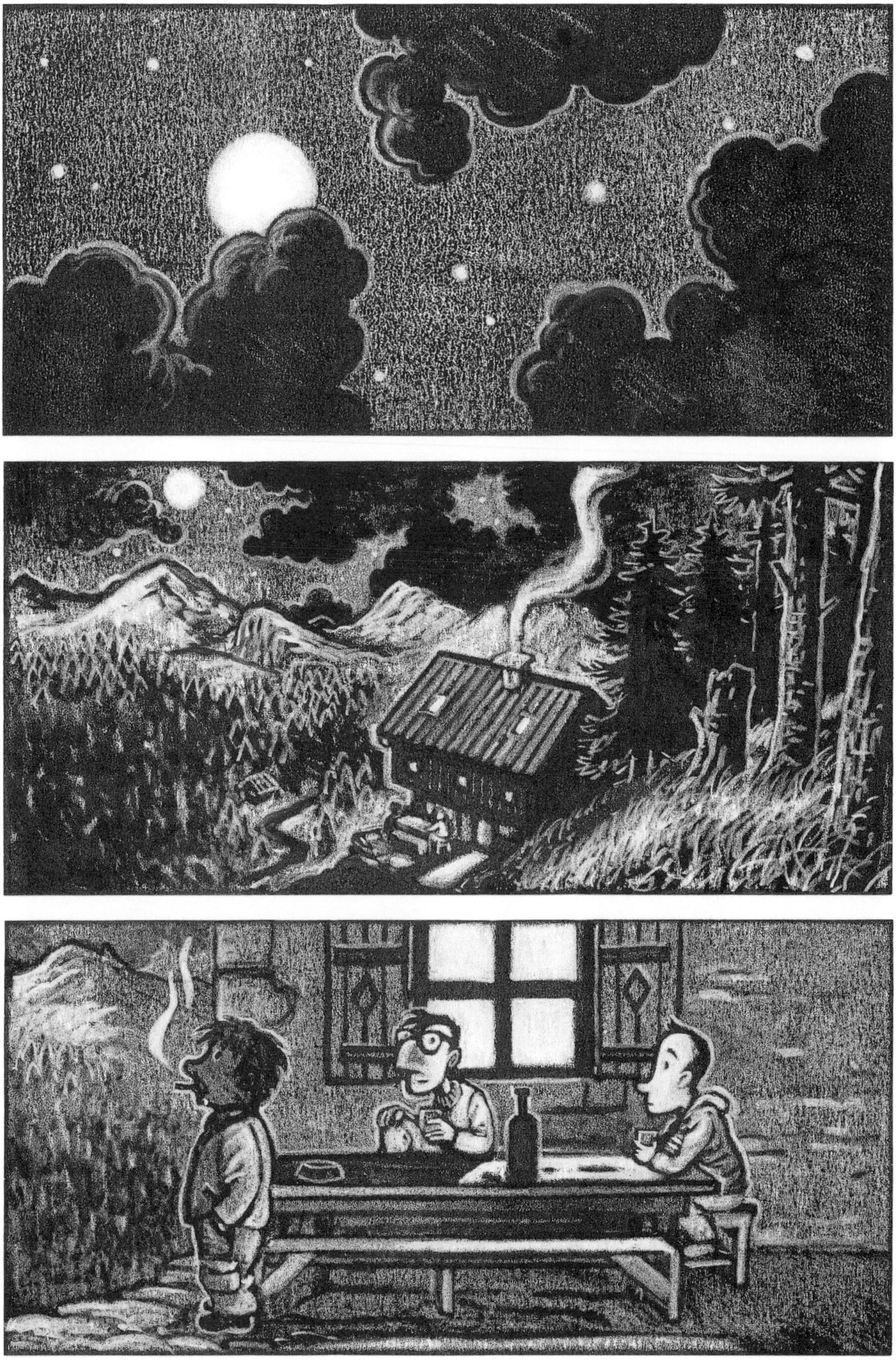

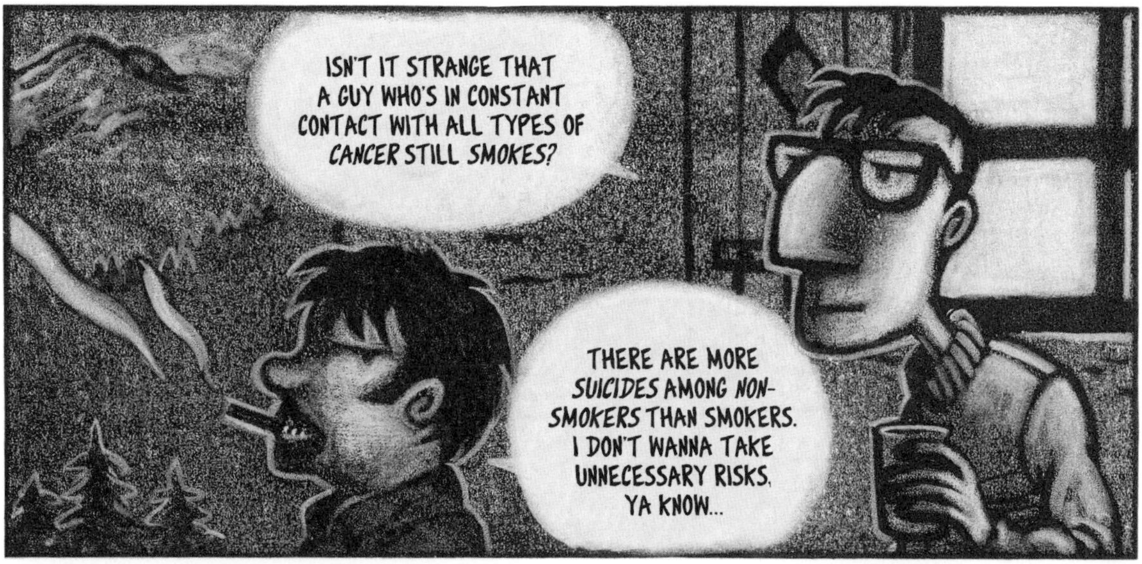
ISN'T IT STRANGE THAT A GUY WHO'S IN CONSTANT CONTACT WITH ALL TYPES OF CANCER STILL SMOKES?
THERE ARE MORE SUICIDES AMONG NON-SMOKERS THAN SMOKERS. I DON'T WANNA TAKE UNNECESSARY RISKS, YA KNOW...

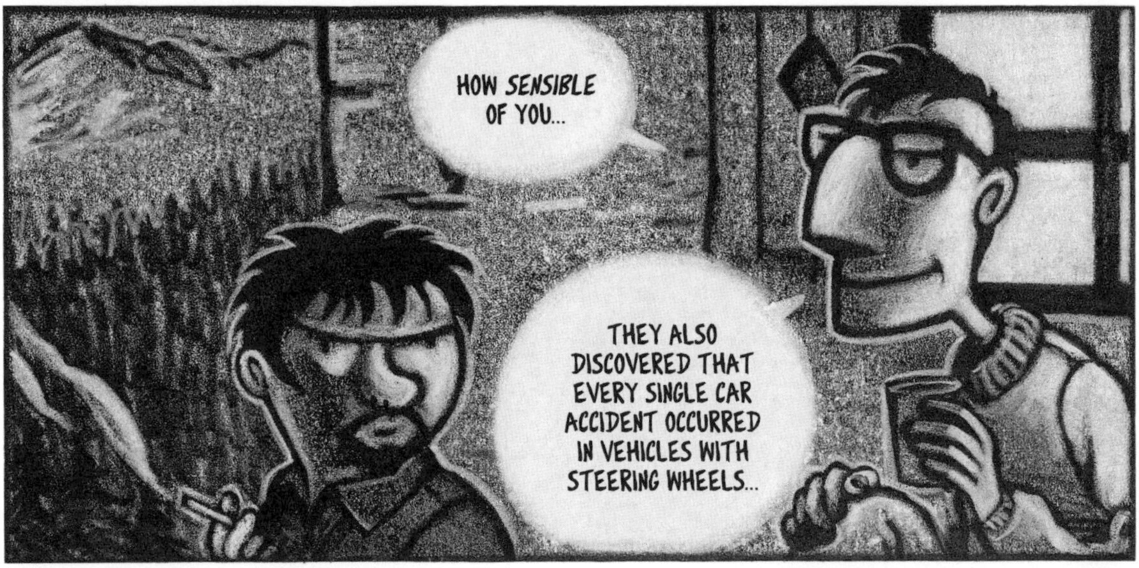
HOW SENSIBLE OF YOU...
THEY ALSO DISCOVERED THAT EVERY SINGLE CAR ACCIDENT OCCURRED IN VEHICLES WITH STEERING WHEELS...

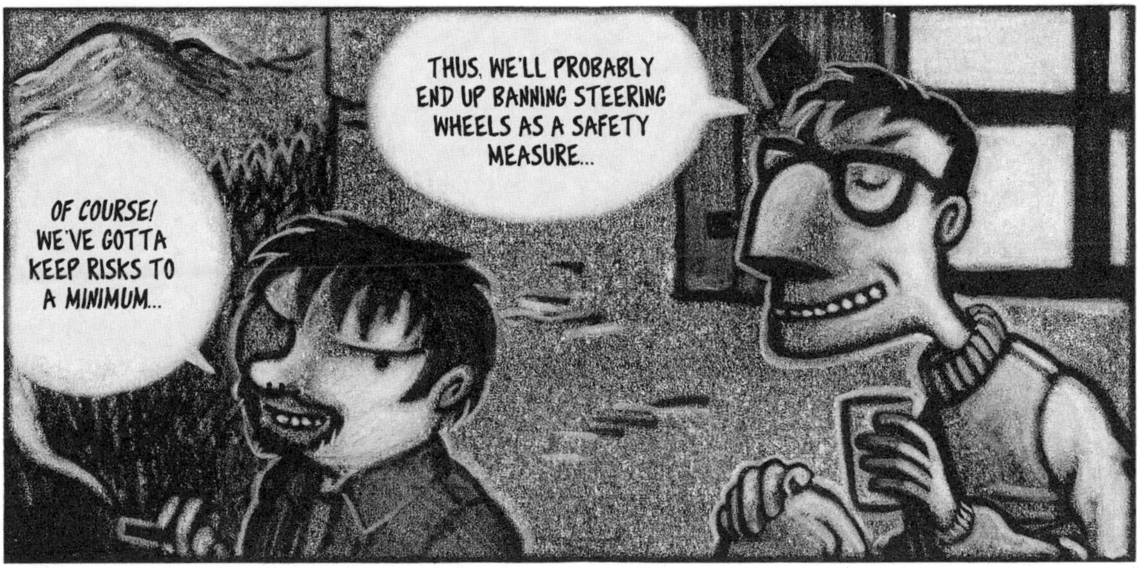
THUS, WE'LL PROBABLY END UP BANNING STEERING WHEELS AS A SAFETY MEASURE...
OF COURSE! WE'VE GOTTA KEEP RISKS TO A MINIMUM...

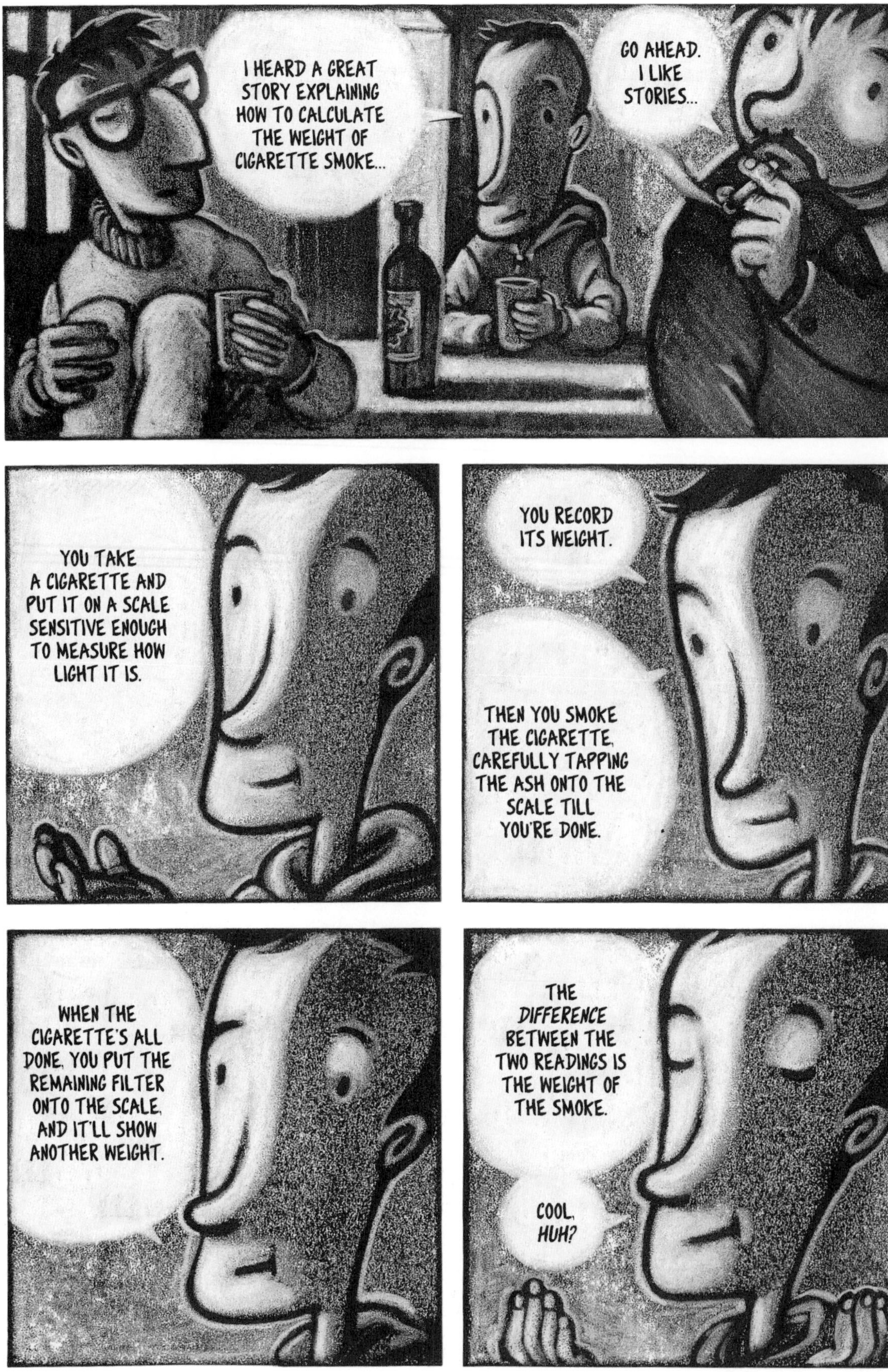
I HEARD A GREAT STORY EXPLAINING HOW TO CALCULATE THE WEIGHT OF CIGARETTE SMOKE...
GO AHEAD. I LIKE STORIES...
YOU TAKE A CIGARETTE AND PUT IT ON A SCALE SENSITIVE ENOUGH TO MEASURE HOW LIGHT IT IS.
YOU RECORD ITS WEIGHT.
THEN YOU SMOKE THE CIGARETTE, CAREFULLY TAPPING THE ASH ONTO THE SCALE TILL YOU'RE DONE.
WHEN THE CIGARETTE'S ALL DONE, YOU PUT THE REMAINING FILTER ONTO THE SCALE, AND IT'LL SHOW ANOTHER WEIGHT.
THE *DIFFERENCE* BETWEEN THE TWO READINGS IS THE WEIGHT OF THE SMOKE.
COOL, HUH?

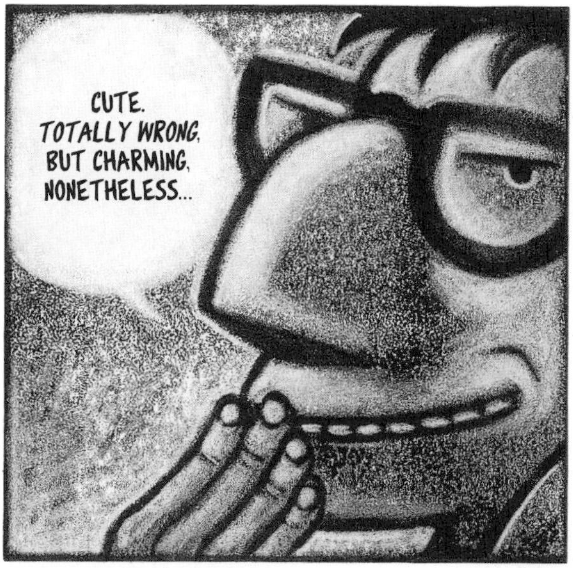
CUTE.
TOTALLY WRONG,
BUT CHARMING,
NONETHELESS...

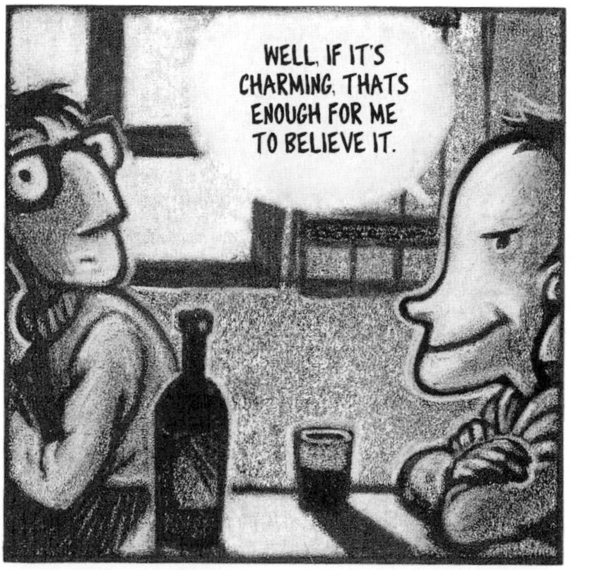
WELL, IF IT'S
CHARMING, THATS
ENOUGH FOR ME
TO BELIEVE IT.

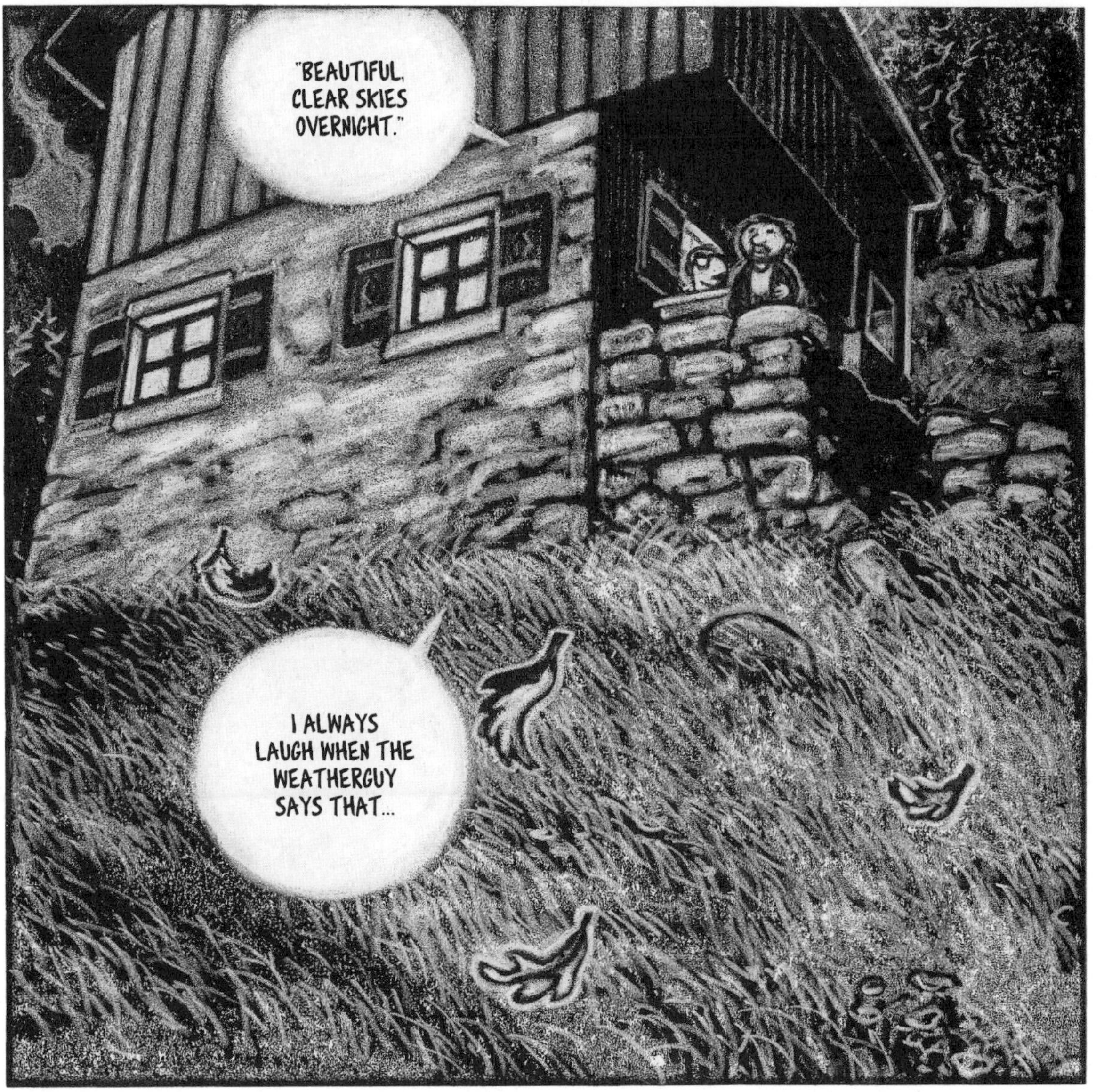
"BEAUTIFUL,
CLEAR SKIES
OVERNIGHT."
I ALWAYS
LAUGH WHEN THE
WEATHERGUY
SAYS THAT...

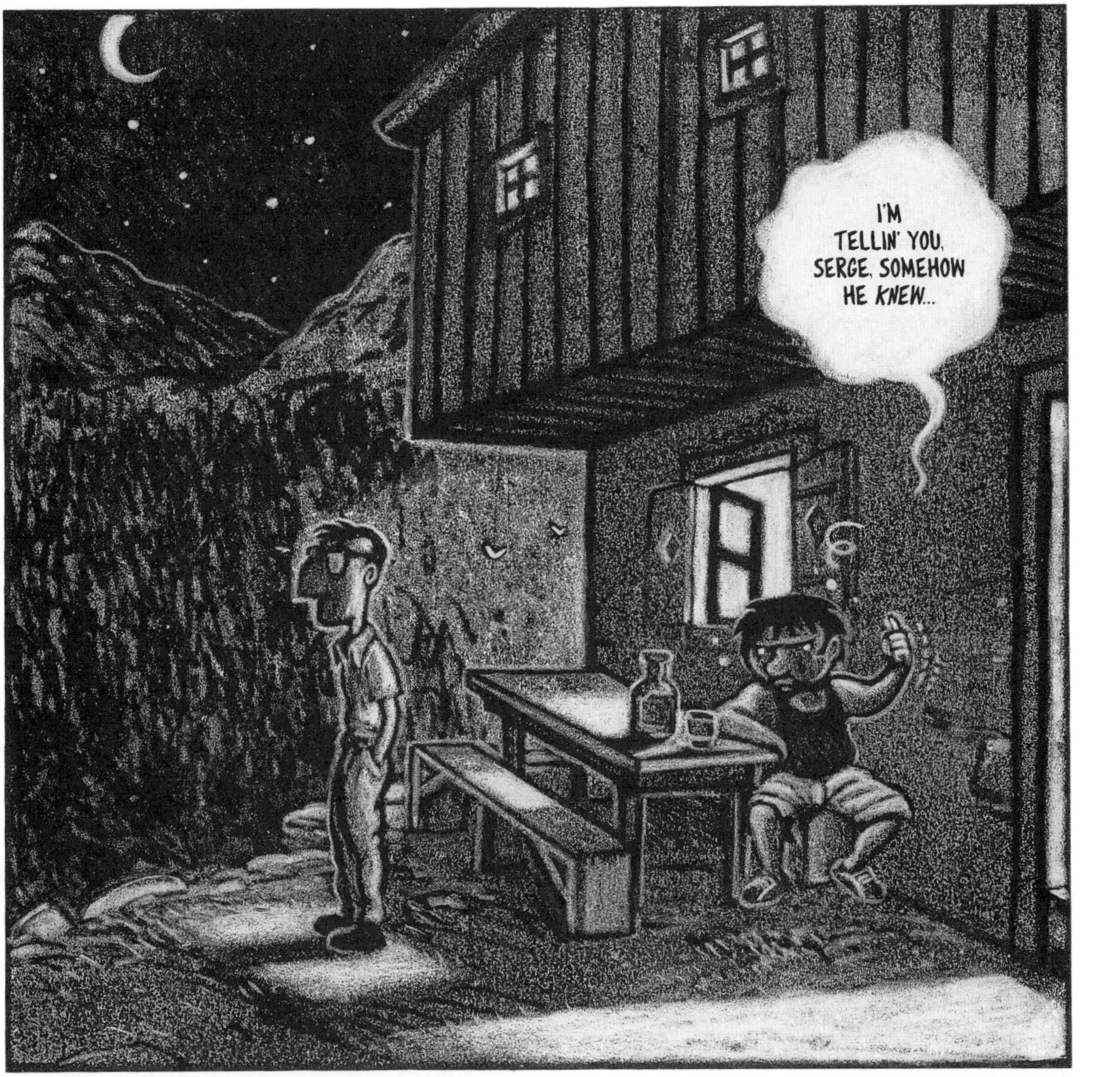
I'M TELLIN' YOU, SERGE, SOMEHOW HE *KNEW*...

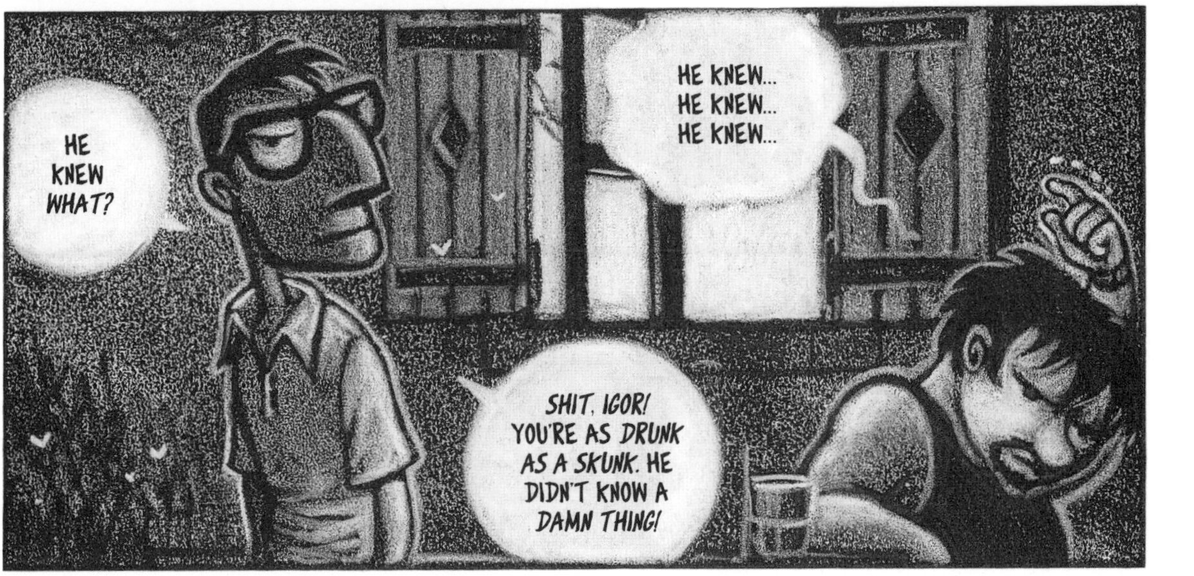
HE KNEW *WHAT?*
HE KNEW... HE KNEW... HE KNEW...
SHIT, IGOR! YOU'RE AS *DRUNK* AS A *SKUNK*. HE DIDN'T KNOW A *DAMN THING!*

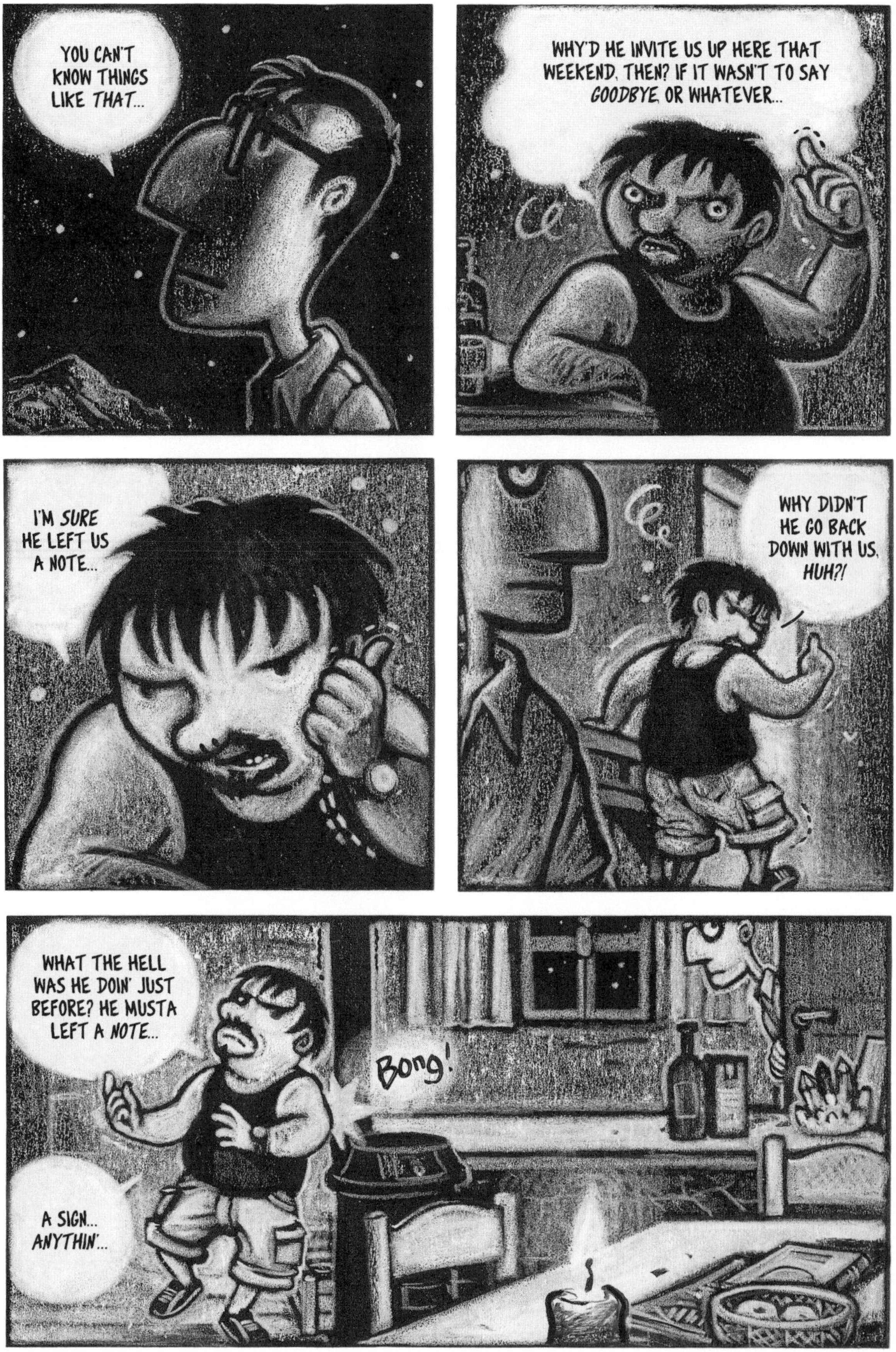
YOU CAN'T KNOW THINGS LIKE *THAT*...
WHY'D HE INVITE US UP HERE THAT WEEKEND, THEN? IF IT WASN'T TO SAY *GOODBYE*, OR WHATEVER...
I'M *SURE* HE LEFT US A NOTE...
WHY DIDN'T HE GO BACK DOWN WITH US, *HUH?!*
WHAT THE HELL WAS HE DOIN' JUST BEFORE? HE MUSTA LEFT A *NOTE*...
Bong!
A SIGN... ANYTHIN'...

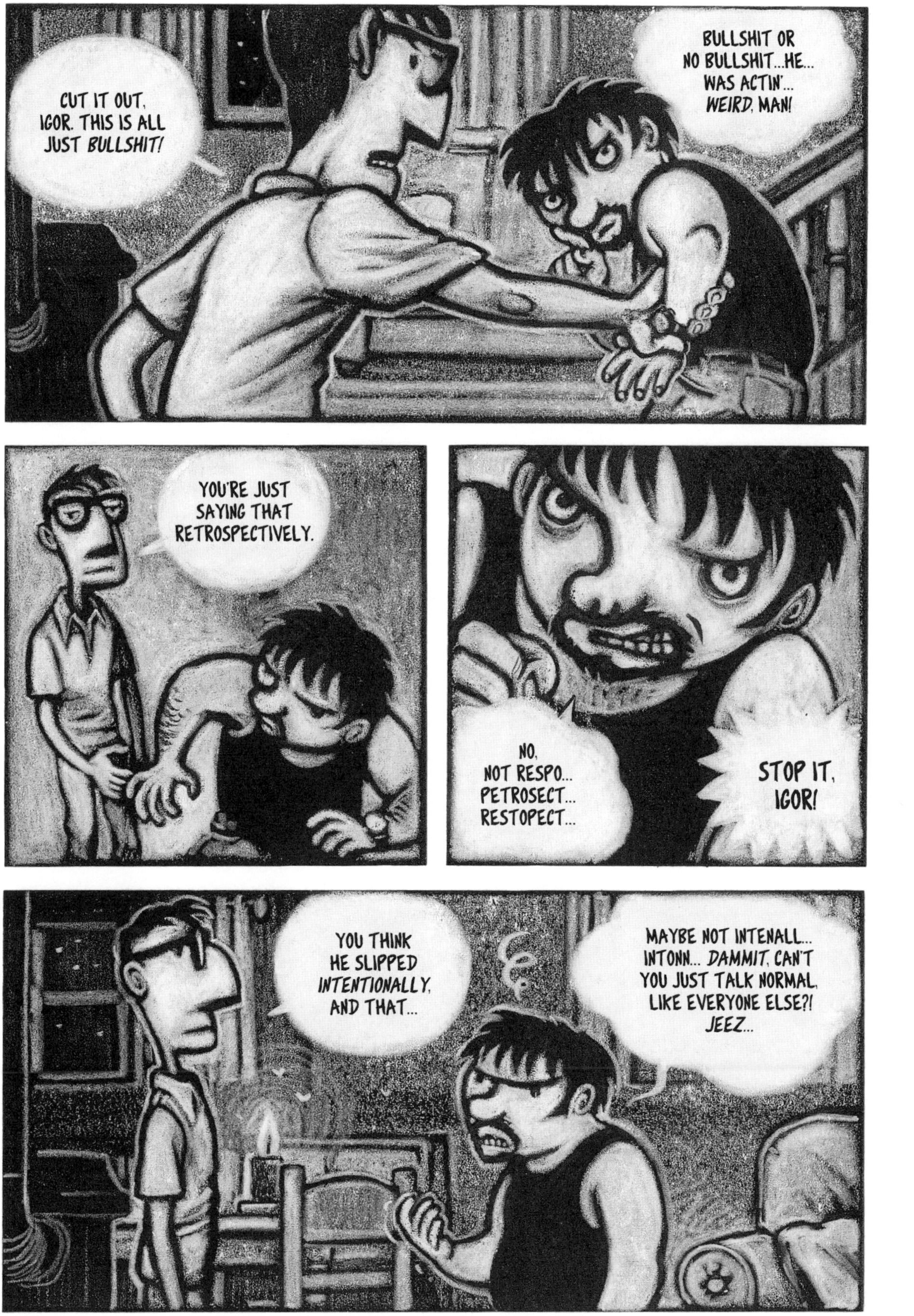
CUT IT OUT, IGOR. THIS IS ALL JUST BULLSHIT!
BULLSHIT OR NO BULLSHIT...HE... WAS ACTIN'... WEIRD, MAN!
YOU'RE JUST SAYING THAT RETROSPECTIVELY.
NO, NOT RESPO... PETROSECT... RESTOPECT...
STOP IT, IGOR!
YOU THINK HE SLIPPED INTENTIONALLY, AND THAT...
MAYBE NOT INTENALL... INTONN... DAMMIT, CAN'T YOU JUST TALK NORMAL, LIKE EVERYONE ELSE?! JEEZ...

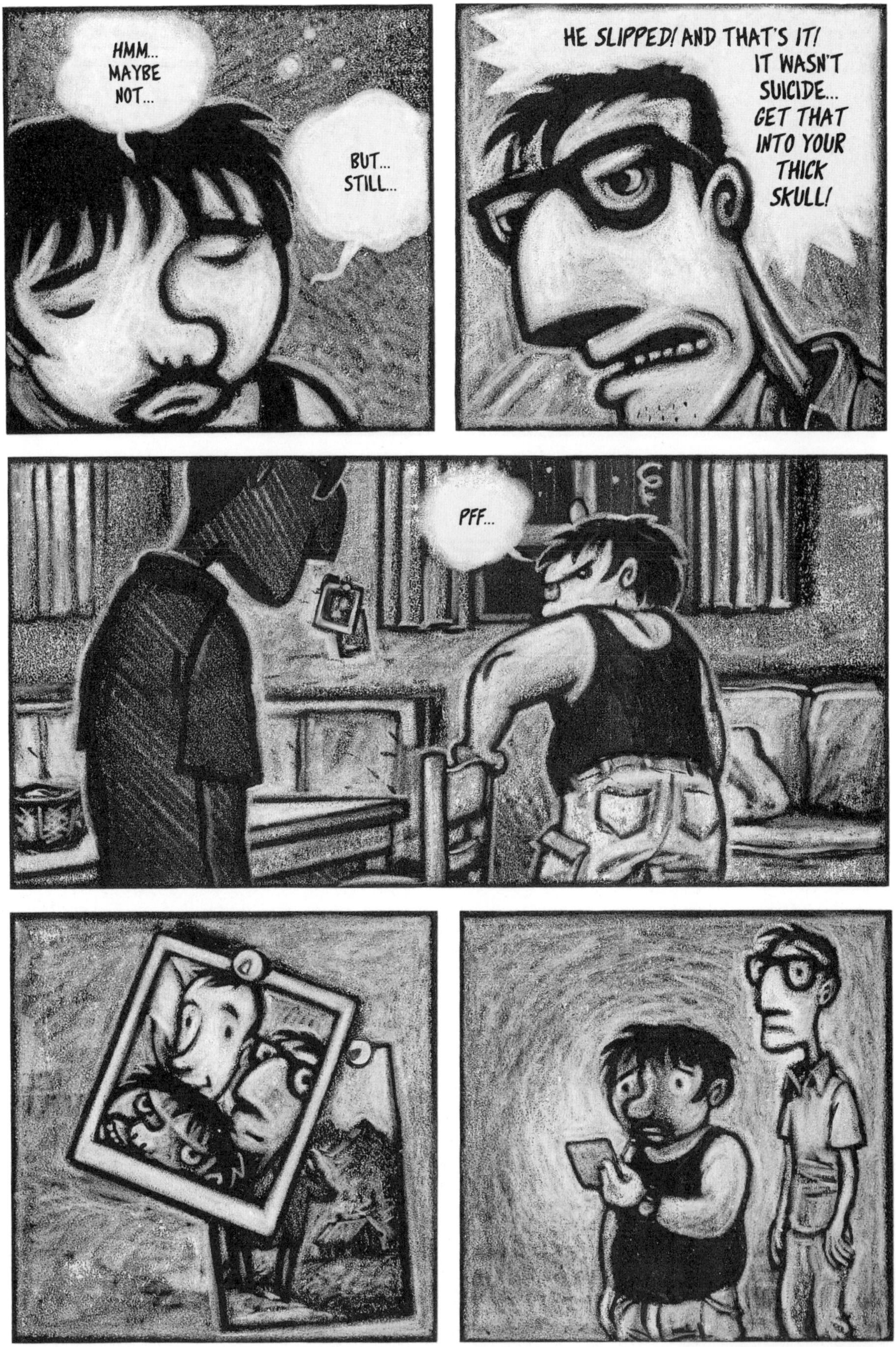
HMM... MAYBE NOT...
BUT... STILL...
HE SLIPPED! AND THAT'S IT! IT WASN'T SUICIDE... GET THAT INTO YOUR THICK SKULL!
PFF...

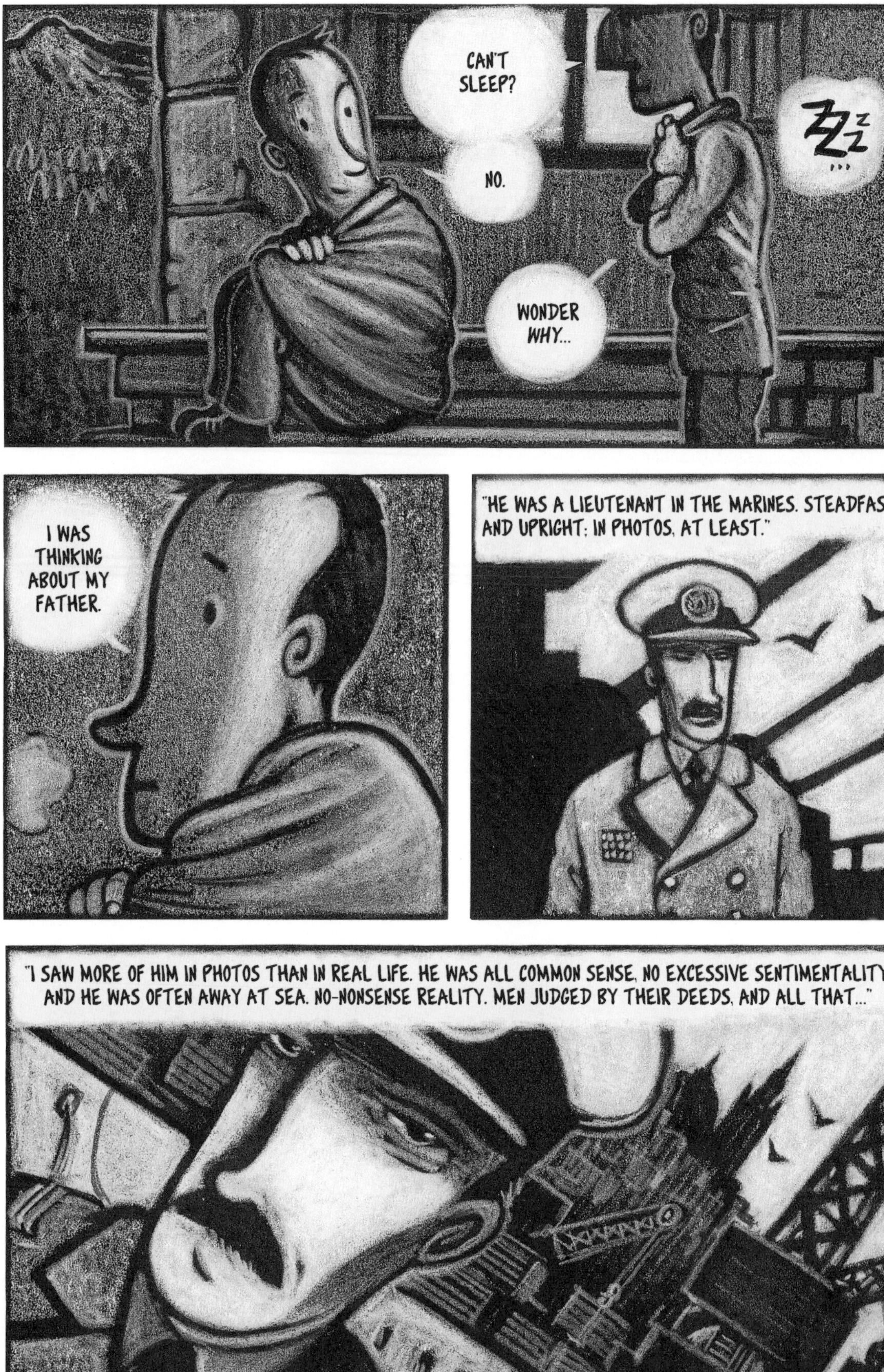
CAN'T SLEEP?
NO.
WONDER WHY...
ZZZ
I WAS THINKING ABOUT MY FATHER.
"HE WAS A LIEUTENANT IN THE MARINES. STEADFAST AND UPRIGHT: IN PHOTOS, AT LEAST."
"I SAW MORE OF HIM IN PHOTOS THAN IN REAL LIFE. HE WAS ALL COMMON SENSE, NO EXCESSIVE SENTIMENTALITY, AND HE WAS OFTEN AWAY AT SEA. NO-NONSENSE REALITY. MEN JUDGED BY THEIR DEEDS, AND ALL THAT..."

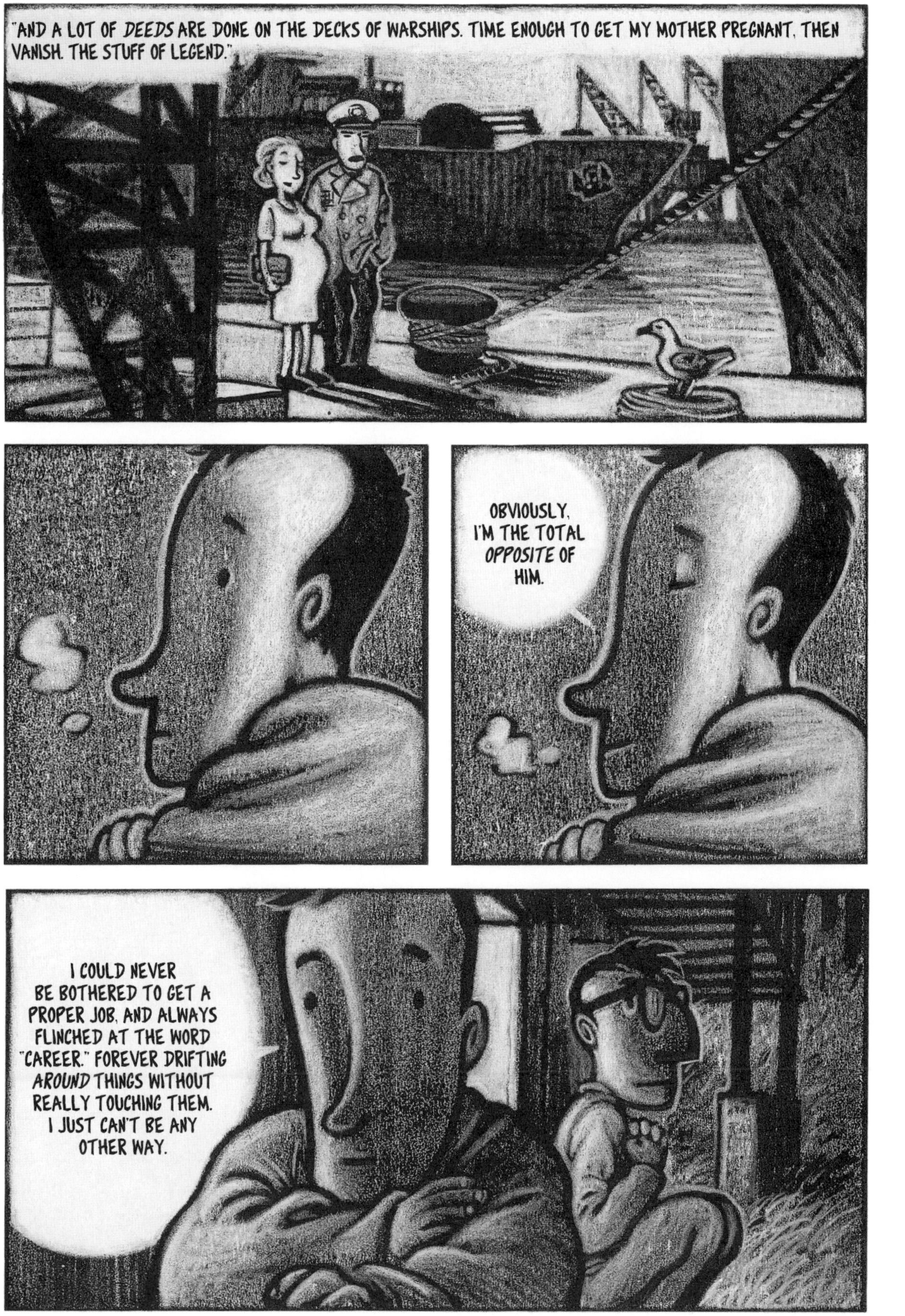
"AND A LOT OF *DEEDS* ARE DONE ON THE DECKS OF WARSHIPS. TIME ENOUGH TO GET MY MOTHER PREGNANT, THEN VANISH. THE STUFF OF LEGEND."
OBVIOUSLY, I'M THE TOTAL *OPPOSITE* OF HIM.
I COULD NEVER BE BOTHERED TO GET A PROPER JOB, AND ALWAYS FLINCHED AT THE WORD "CAREER." FOREVER DRIFTING *AROUND* THINGS WITHOUT REALLY TOUCHING THEM. I JUST CAN'T BE ANY OTHER WAY.

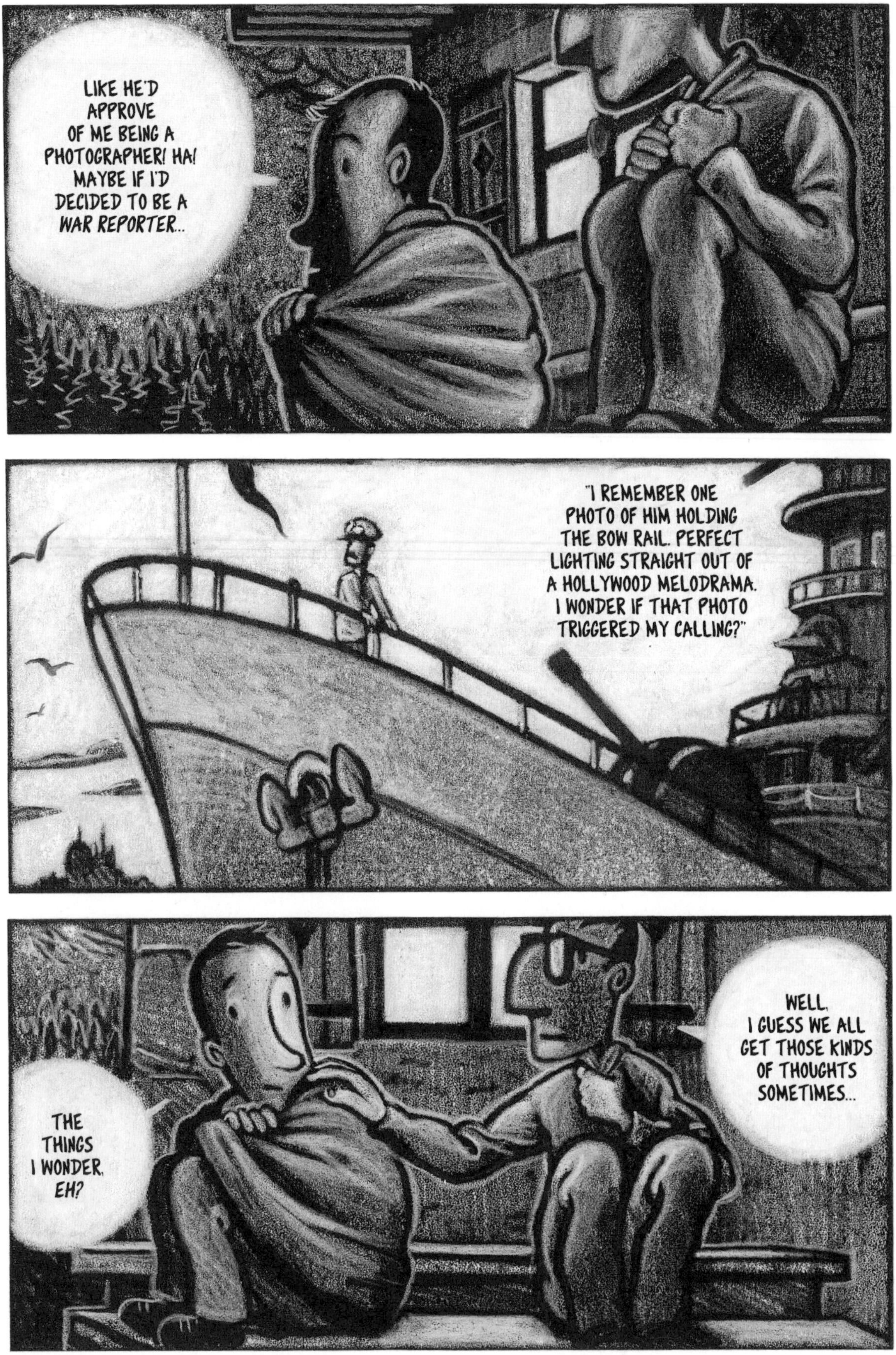
LIKE HE'D APPROVE OF ME BEING A PHOTOGRAPHER! HA! MAYBE IF I'D DECIDED TO BE A WAR REPORTER...
"I REMEMBER ONE PHOTO OF HIM HOLDING THE BOW RAIL. PERFECT LIGHTING STRAIGHT OUT OF A HOLLYWOOD MELODRAMA. I WONDER IF THAT PHOTO TRIGGERED MY CALLING?"
THE THINGS I WONDER, EH?
WELL, I GUESS WE ALL GET THOSE KINDS OF THOUGHTS SOMETIMES...

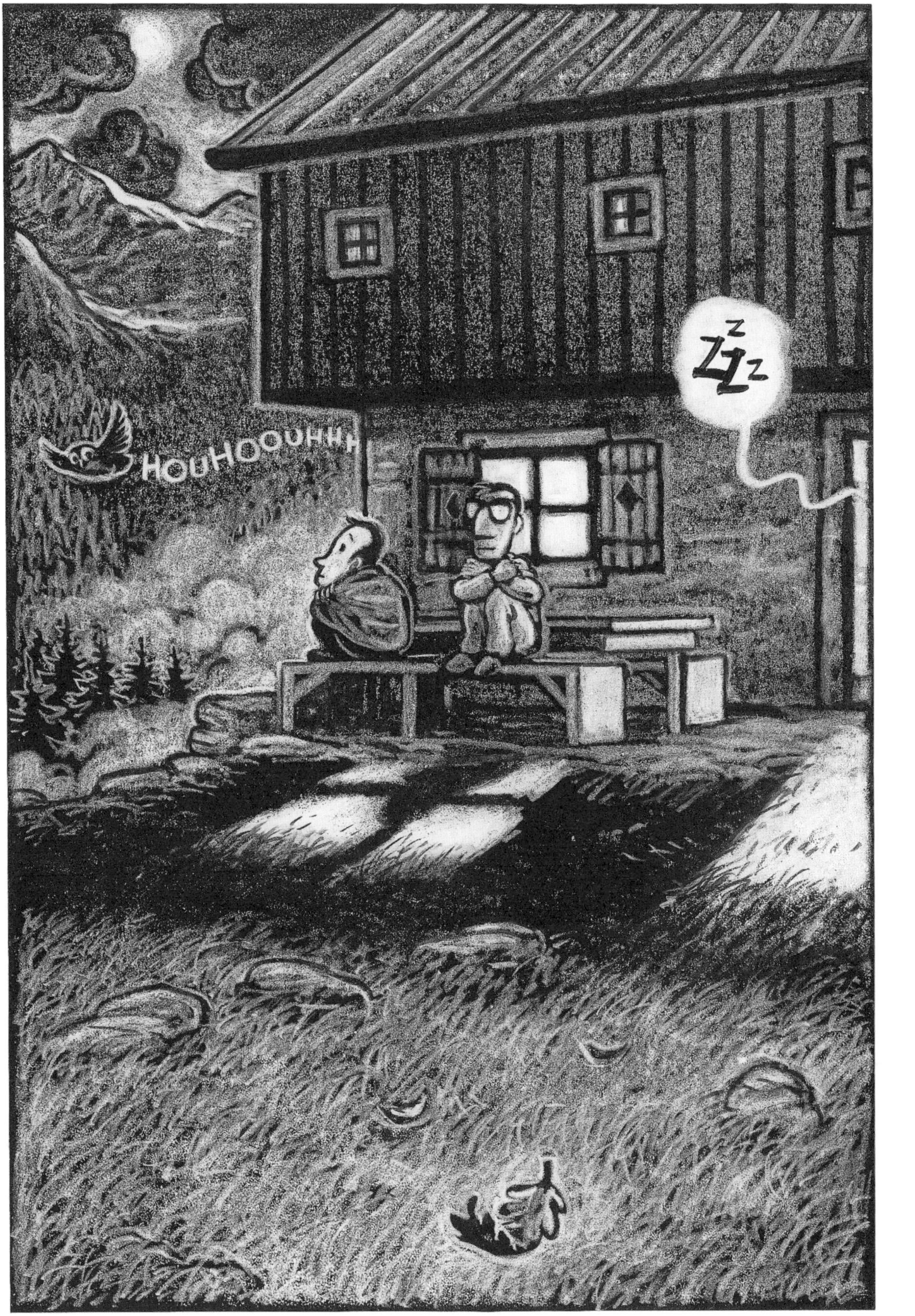
HOUHOOUHHH
ZZZ

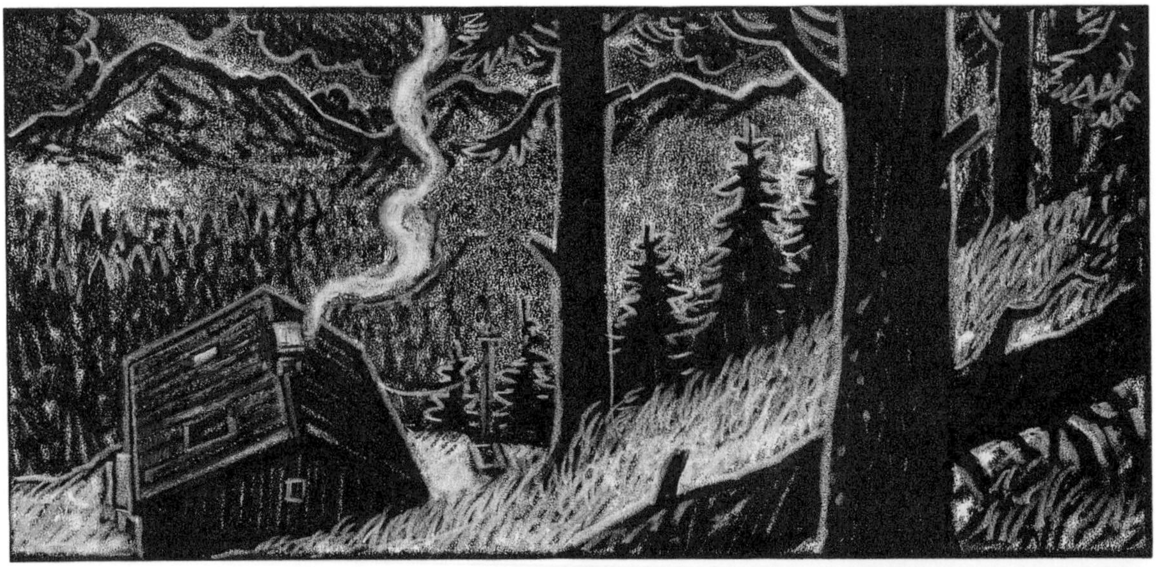

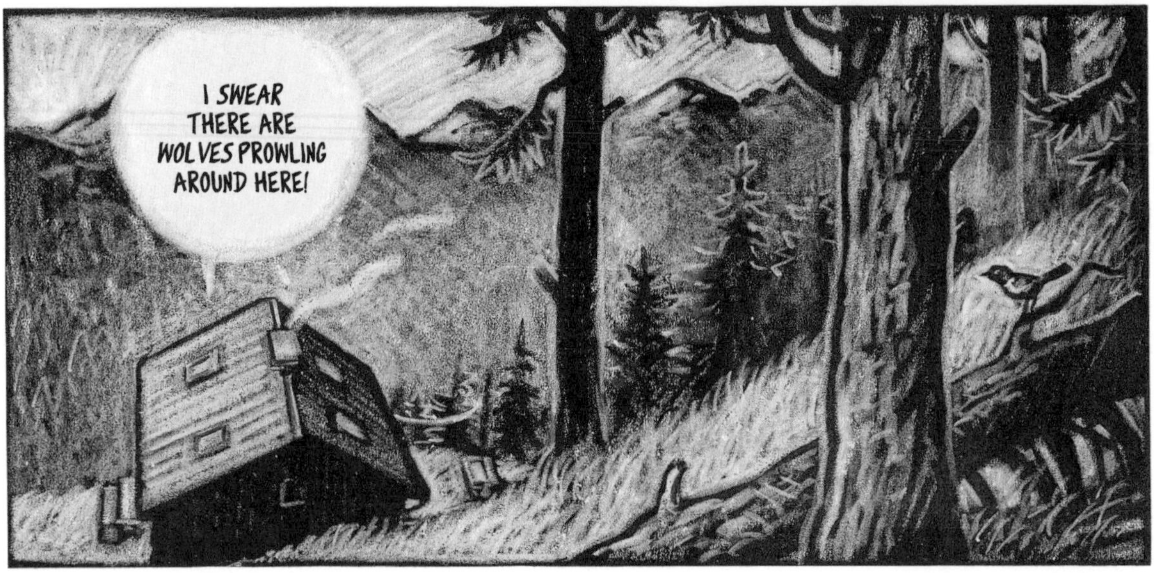
I SWEAR THERE ARE WOLVES PROWLING AROUND HERE!

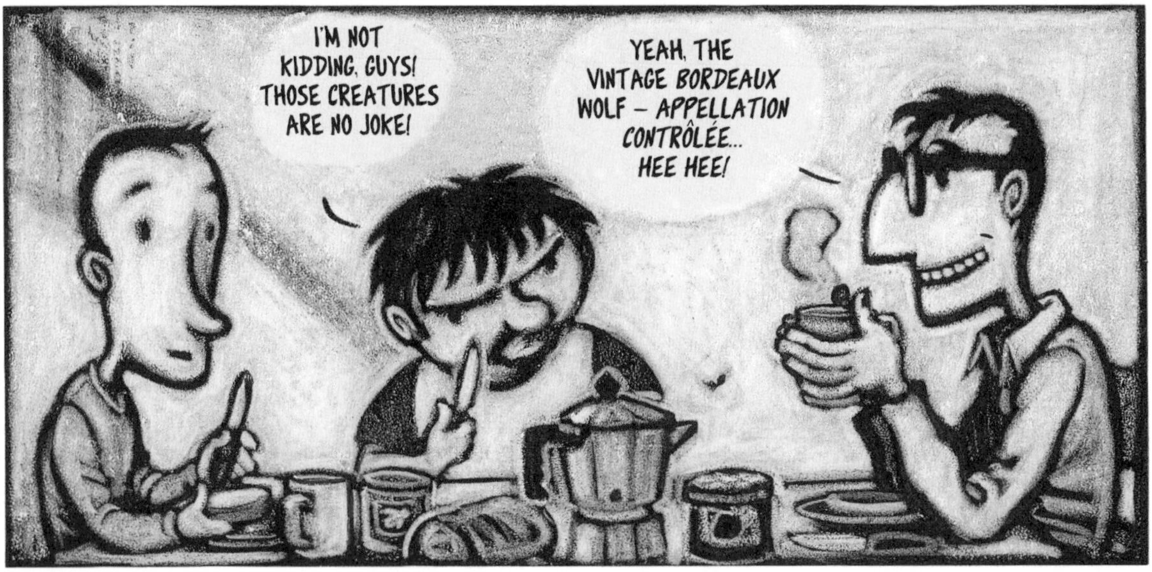
I'M NOT KIDDING, GUYS! THOSE CREATURES ARE NO JOKE!
YEAH, THE VINTAGE BORDEAUX WOLF – APPELLATION CONTRÔLÉE... HEE HEE!

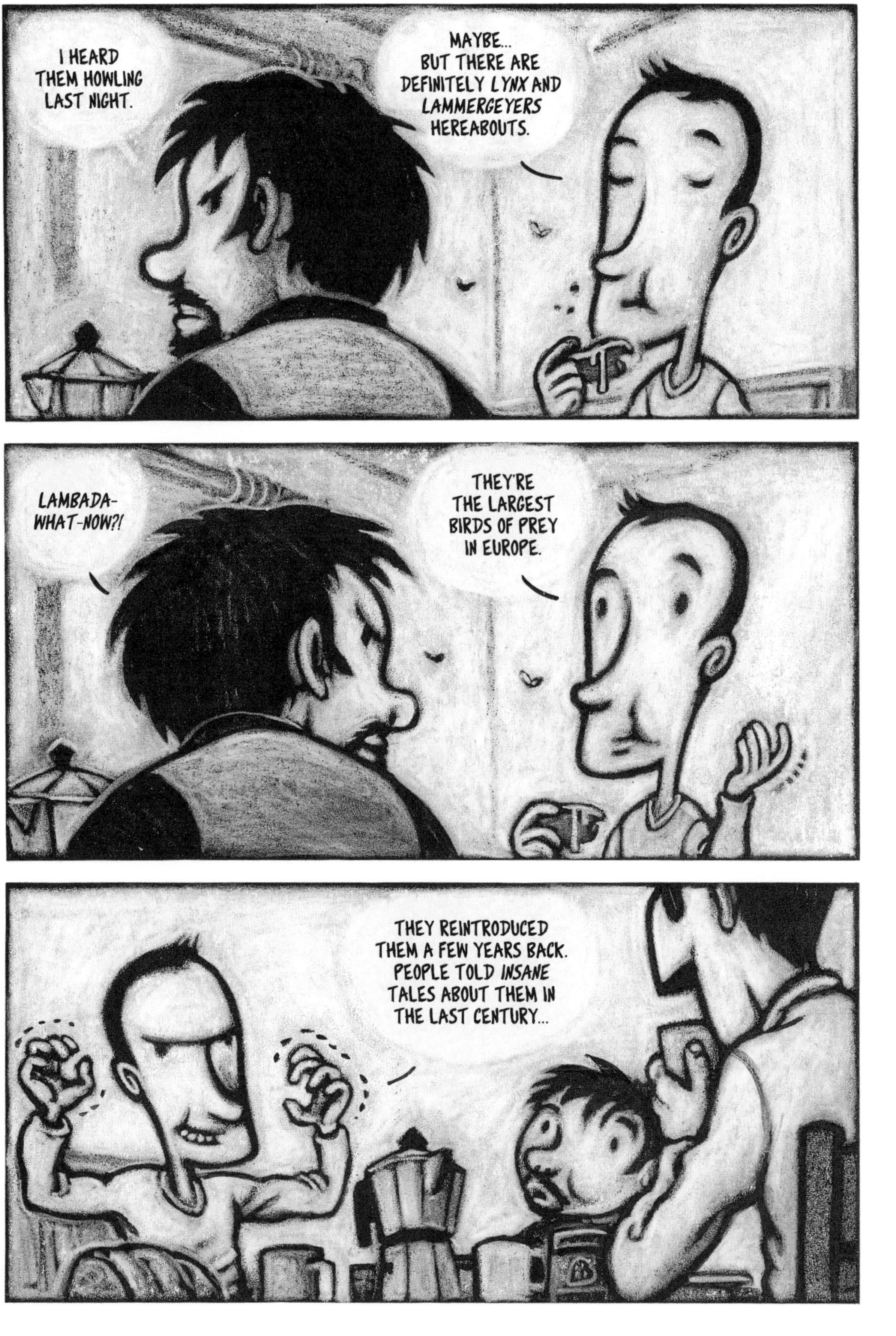
I HEARD THEM HOWLING LAST NIGHT.
MAYBE... BUT THERE ARE DEFINITELY *LYNX* AND *LAMMERGEYERS* HEREABOUTS.
LAMBADA-WHAT-NOW?!
THEY'RE THE LARGEST BIRDS OF PREY IN EUROPE.
THEY REINTRODUCED THEM A FEW YEARS BACK. PEOPLE TOLD *INSANE* TALES ABOUT THEM IN THE LAST CENTURY...

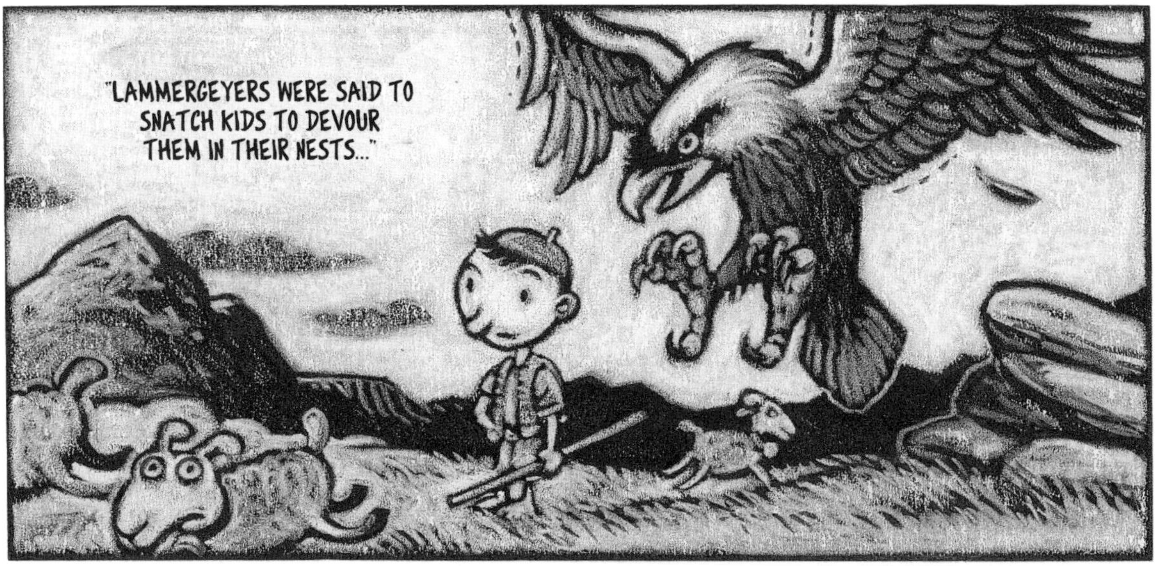
"LAMMERGEYERS WERE SAID TO SNATCH KIDS TO DEVOUR THEM IN THEIR NESTS..."

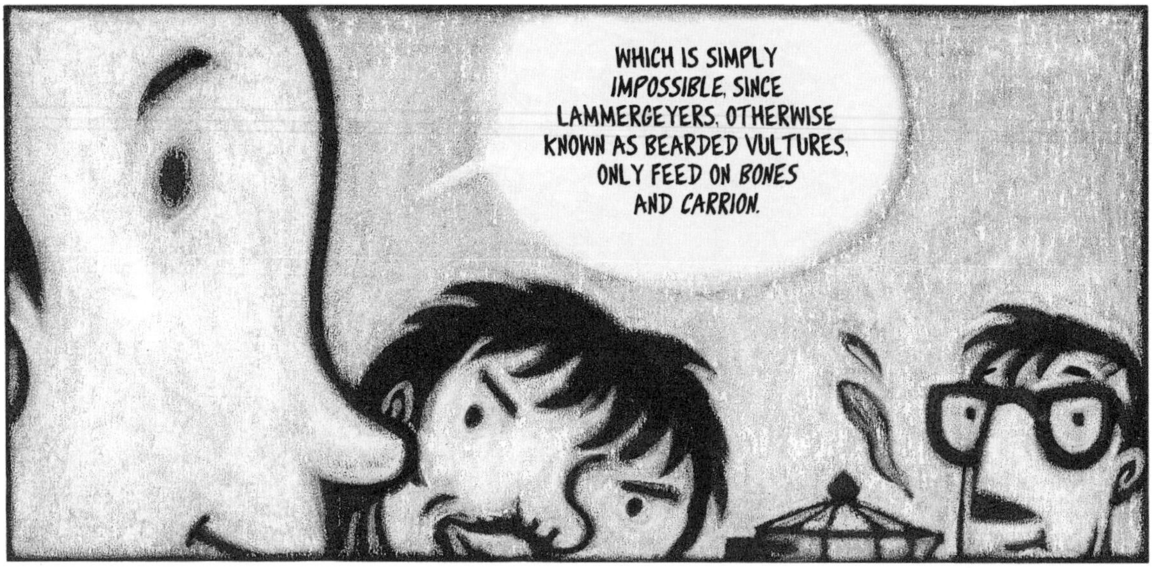
WHICH IS SIMPLY *IMPOSSIBLE*, SINCE LAMMERGEYERS, OTHERWISE KNOWN AS BEARDED VULTURES, ONLY FEED ON *BONES* AND *CARRION*.

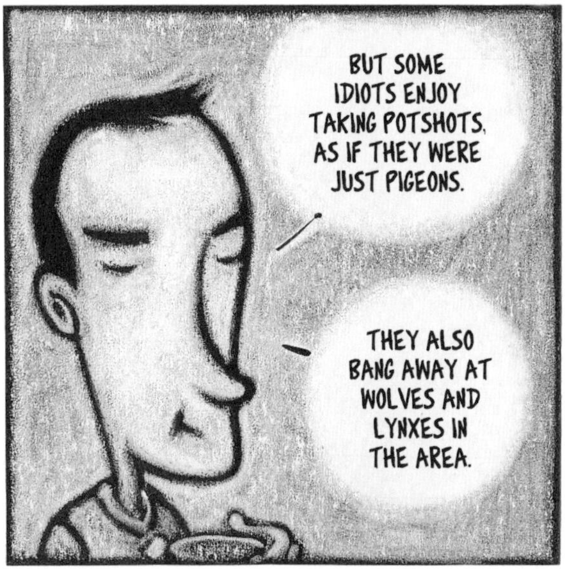
BUT SOME IDIOTS ENJOY TAKING POTSHOTS, AS IF THEY WERE JUST PIGEONS.
THEY ALSO BANG AWAY AT WOLVES AND LYNXES IN THE AREA.

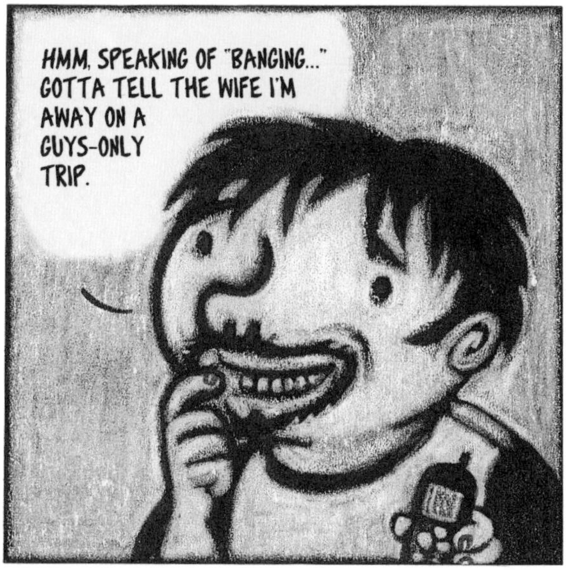
HMM, SPEAKING OF "BANGING..." GOTTA TELL THE WIFE I'M AWAY ON A GUYS-ONLY TRIP.

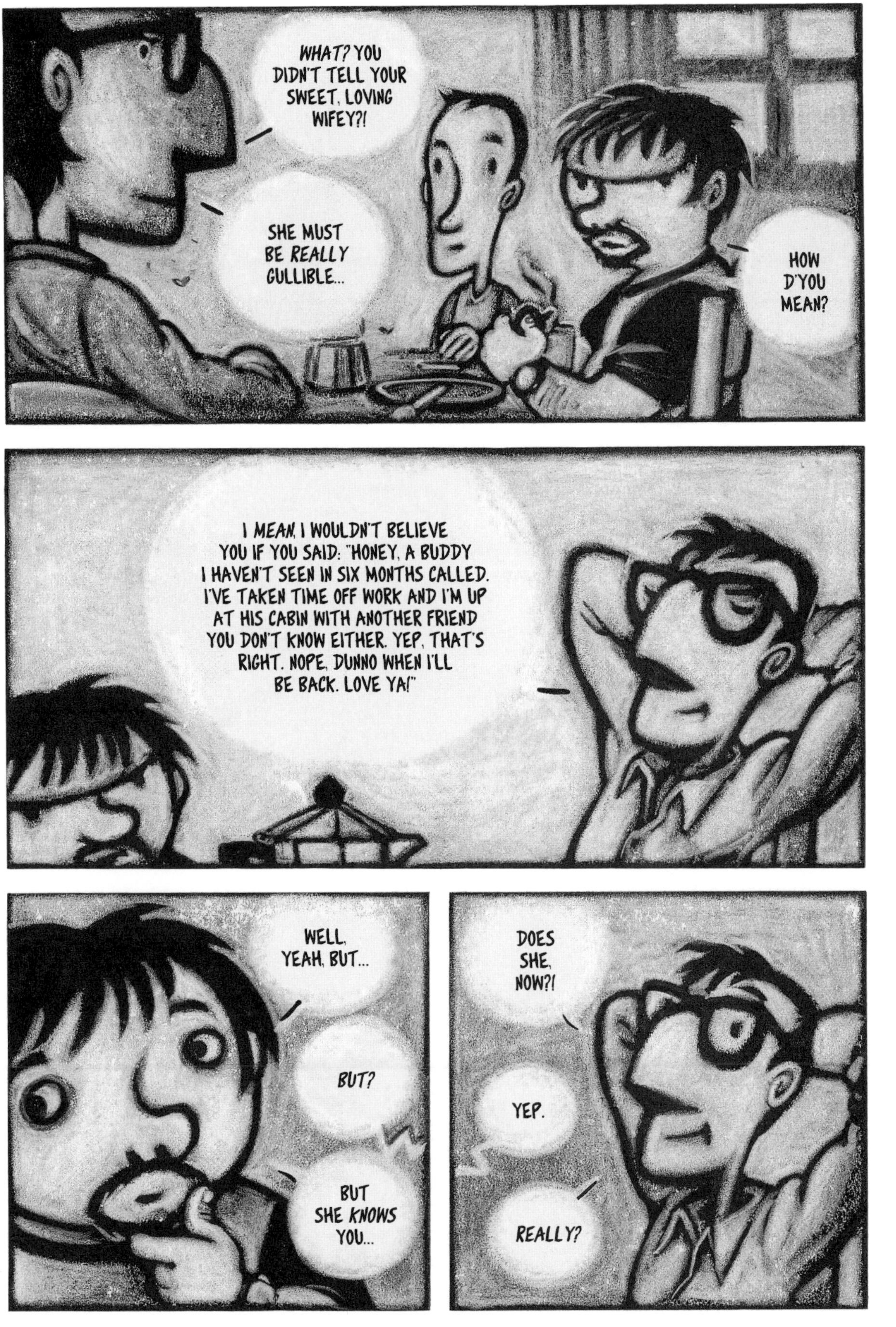

WHAT? YOU DIDN'T TELL YOUR SWEET, LOVING WIFEY?!
SHE MUST BE REALLY GULLIBLE...
HOW D'YOU MEAN?
I MEAN, I WOULDN'T BELIEVE YOU IF YOU SAID: "HONEY, A BUDDY I HAVEN'T SEEN IN SIX MONTHS CALLED. I'VE TAKEN TIME OFF WORK AND I'M UP AT HIS CABIN WITH ANOTHER FRIEND YOU DON'T KNOW EITHER. YEP, THAT'S RIGHT. NOPE, DUNNO WHEN I'LL BE BACK. LOVE YA!"
WELL, YEAH, BUT...
BUT?
BUT SHE KNOWS YOU...
DOES SHE, NOW?!
YEP.
REALLY?

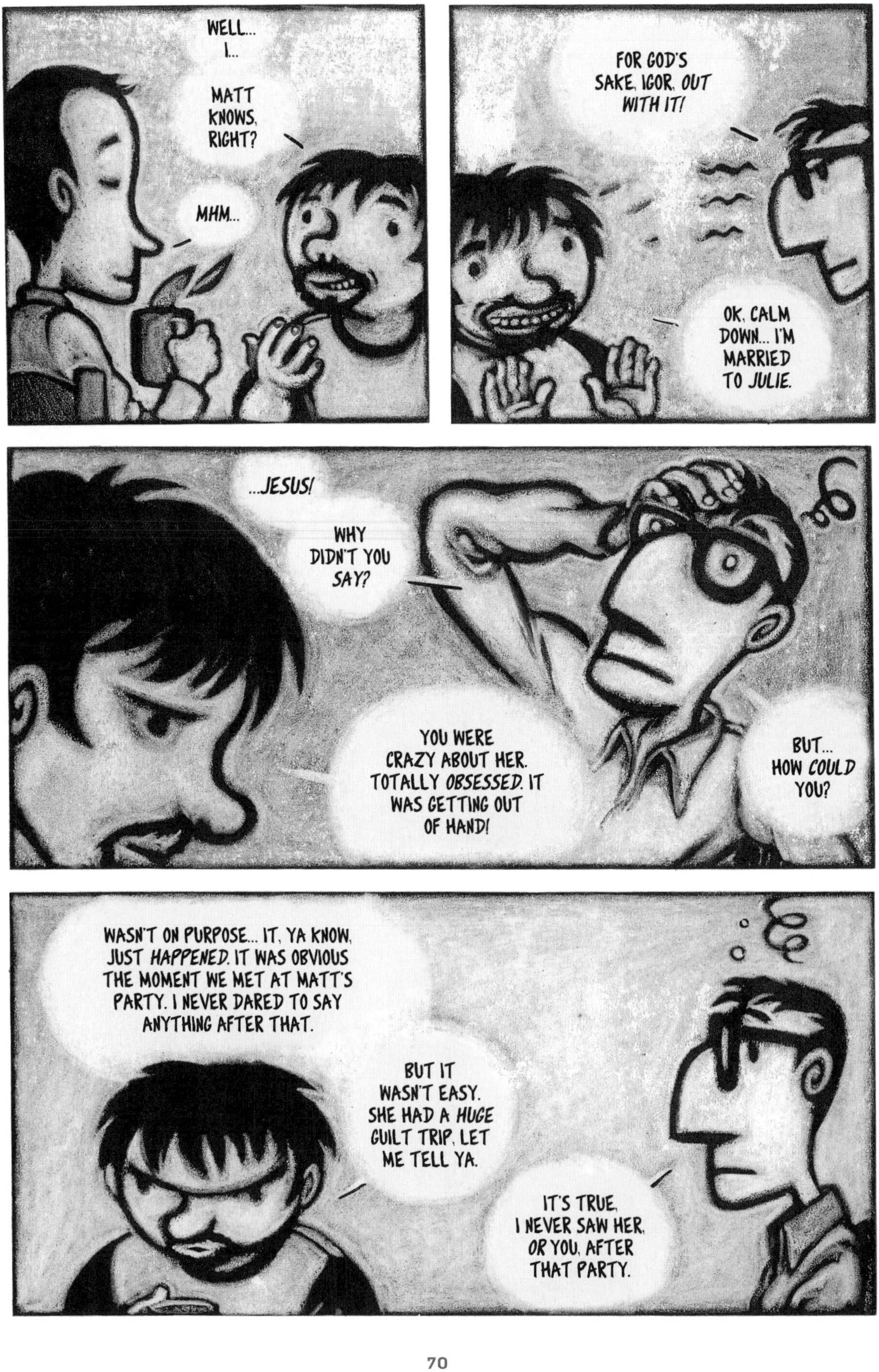
WELL... I...
MATT KNOWS, RIGHT?
MHM...
FOR GOD'S SAKE, IGOR, OUT WITH IT!
OK, CALM DOWN... I'M MARRIED TO JULIE.
...JESUS!
WHY DIDN'T YOU SAY?
YOU WERE CRAZY ABOUT HER. TOTALLY OBSESSED. IT WAS GETTING OUT OF HAND!
BUT... HOW COULD YOU?
WASN'T ON PURPOSE... IT, YA KNOW, JUST HAPPENED. IT WAS OBVIOUS THE MOMENT WE MET AT MATT'S PARTY. I NEVER DARED TO SAY ANYTHING AFTER THAT.
BUT IT WASN'T EASY. SHE HAD A HUGE GUILT TRIP, LET ME TELL YA.
IT'S TRUE, I NEVER SAW HER, OR YOU, AFTER THAT PARTY.

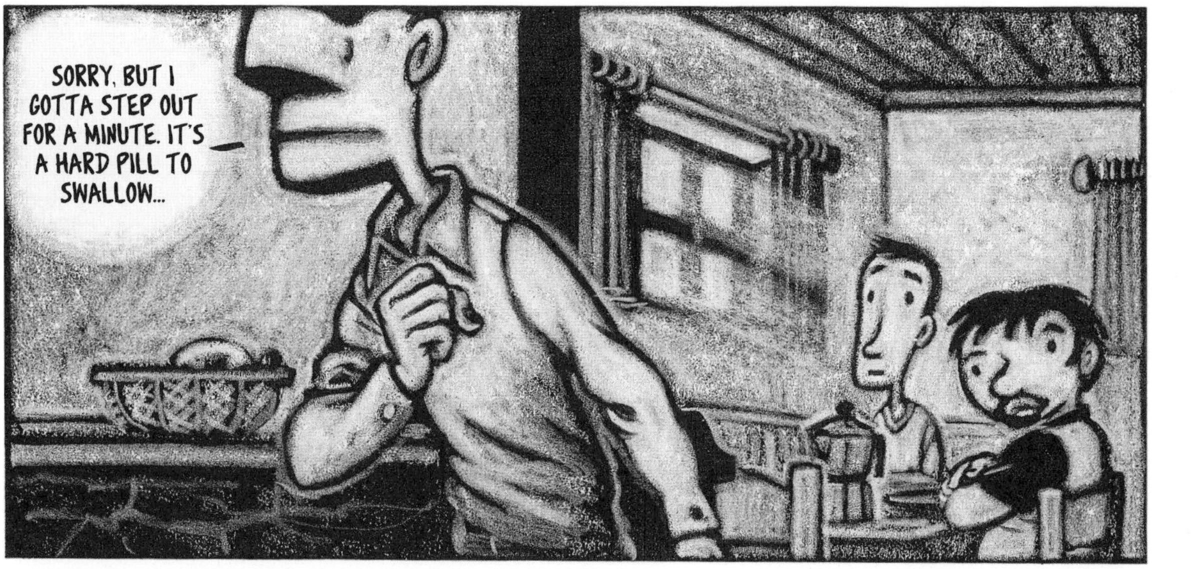
SORRY, BUT I GOTTA STEP OUT FOR A MINUTE. IT'S A HARD PILL TO SWALLOW...

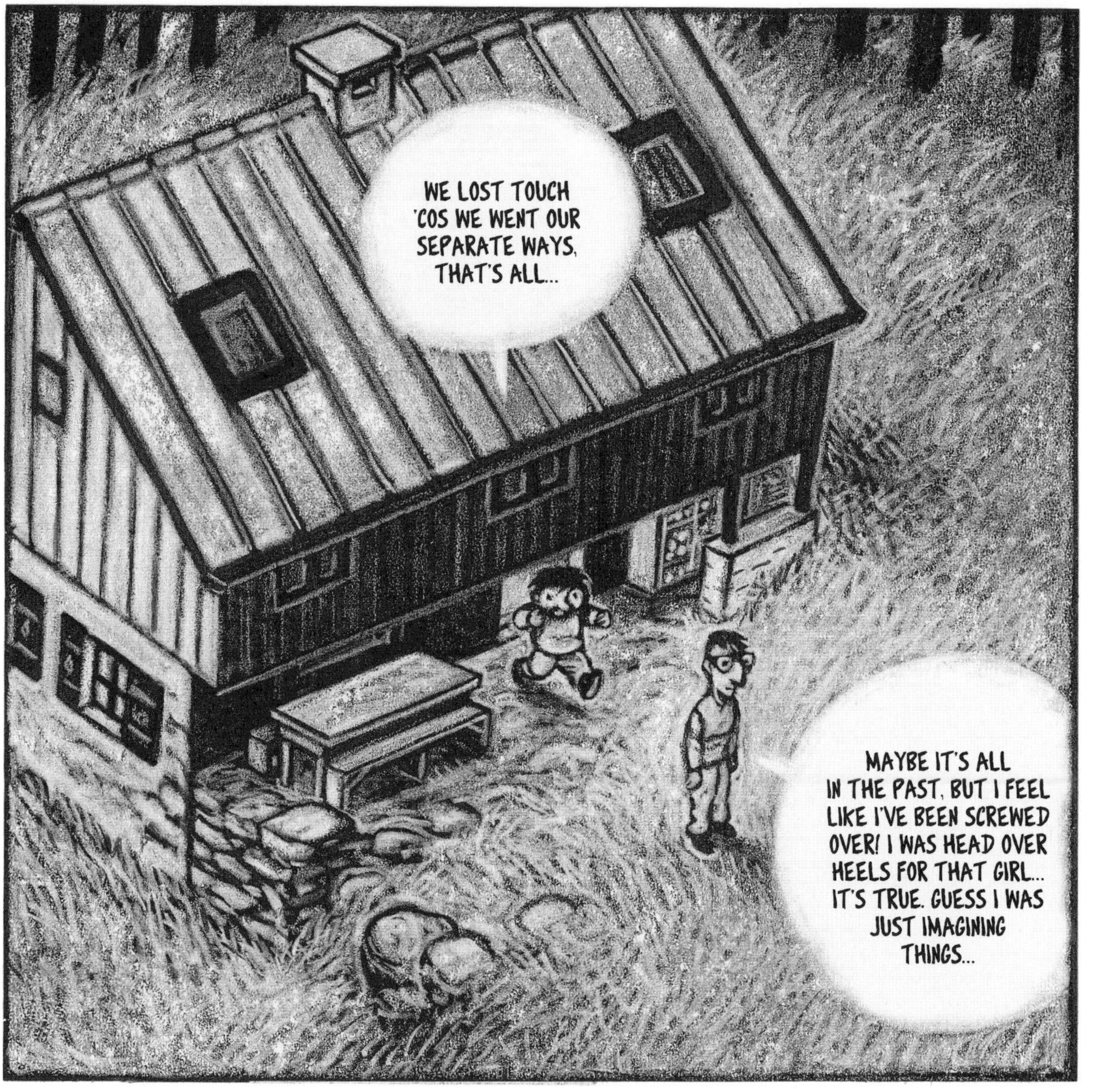
WE LOST TOUCH 'COS WE WENT OUR SEPARATE WAYS, THAT'S ALL...
MAYBE IT'S ALL IN THE PAST, BUT I FEEL LIKE I'VE BEEN SCREWED OVER! I WAS HEAD OVER HEELS FOR THAT GIRL... IT'S TRUE. GUESS I WAS JUST IMAGINING THINGS...

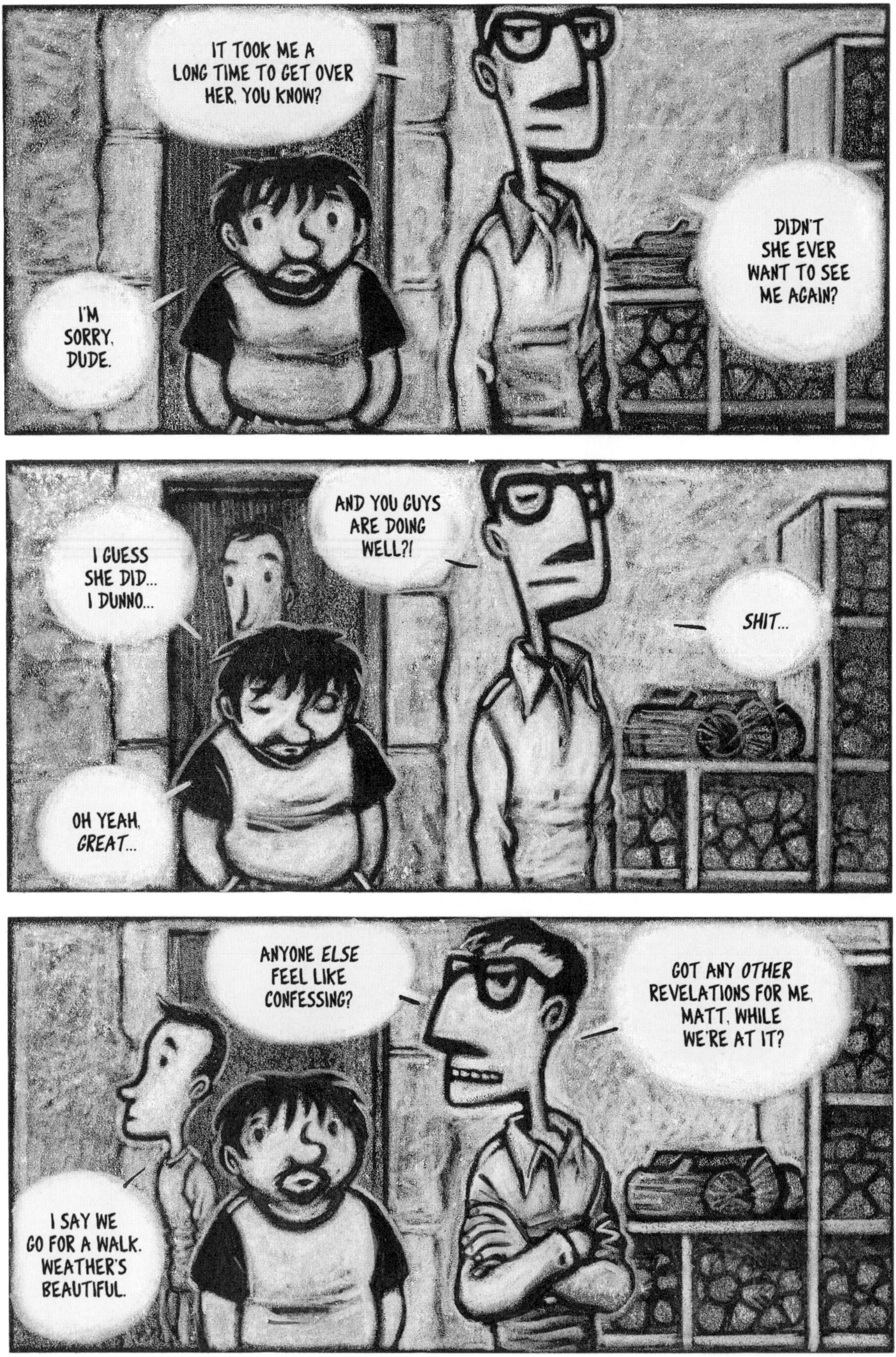
IT TOOK ME A LONG TIME TO GET OVER HER, YOU KNOW?
I'M SORRY, DUDE.
DIDN'T SHE EVER WANT TO SEE ME AGAIN?
I GUESS SHE DID... I DUNNO...
AND YOU GUYS ARE DOING WELL?!
OH YEAH, GREAT...
SHIT...
ANYONE ELSE FEEL LIKE CONFESSING?
GOT ANY OTHER REVELATIONS FOR ME, MATT, WHILE WE'RE AT IT?
I SAY WE GO FOR A WALK. WEATHER'S BEAUTIFUL.

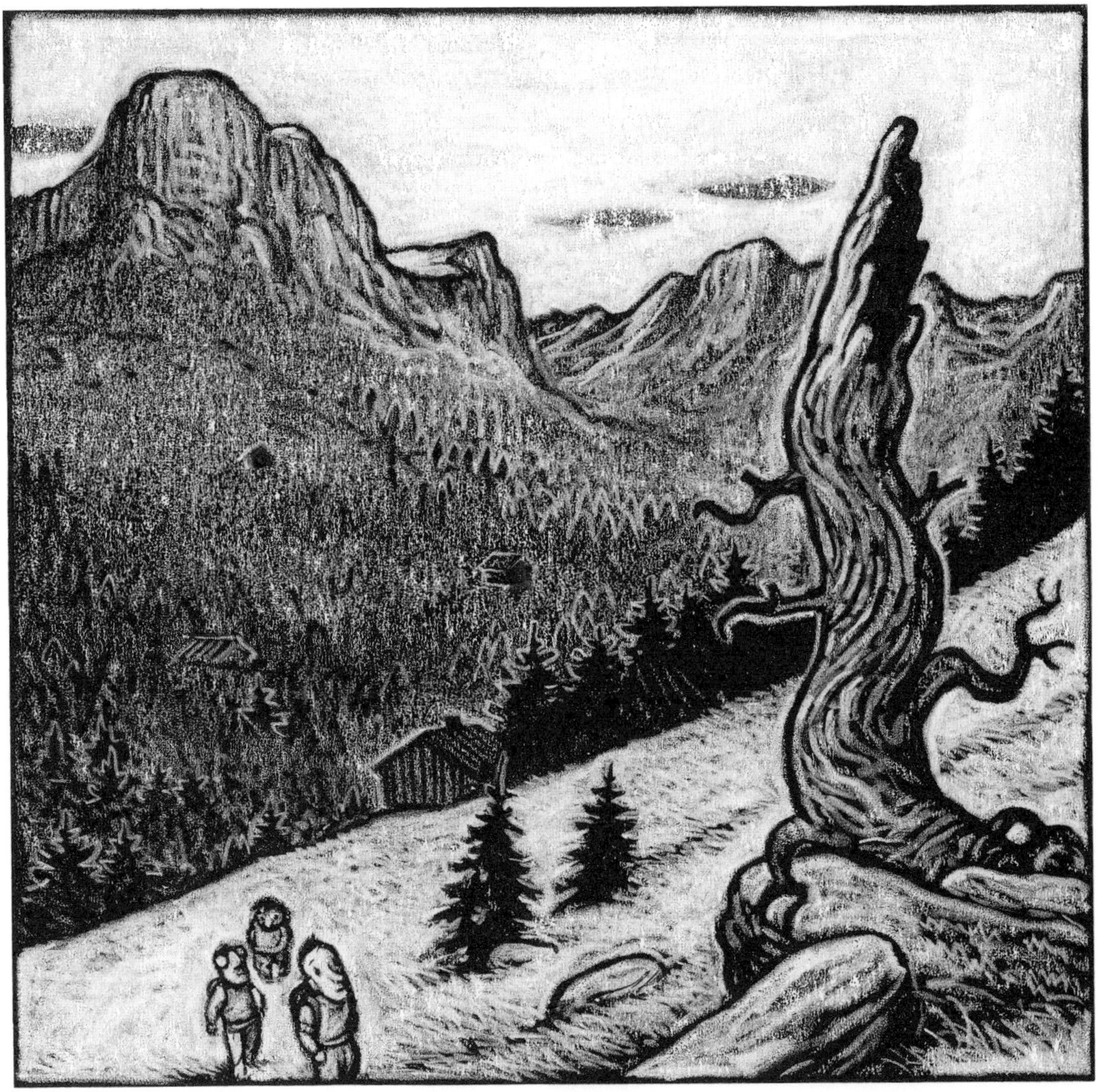

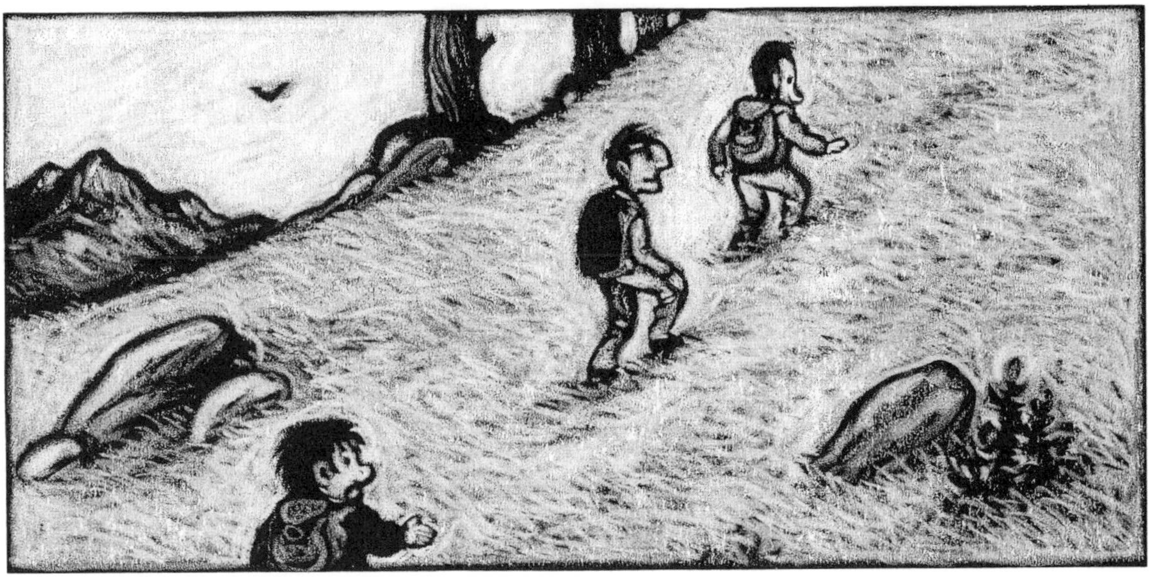

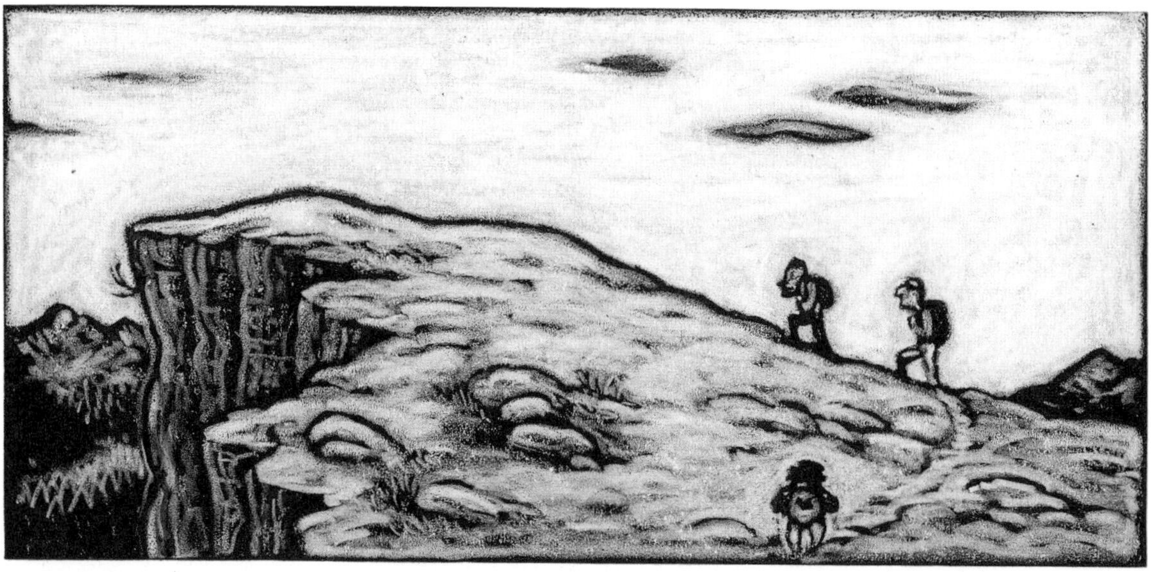

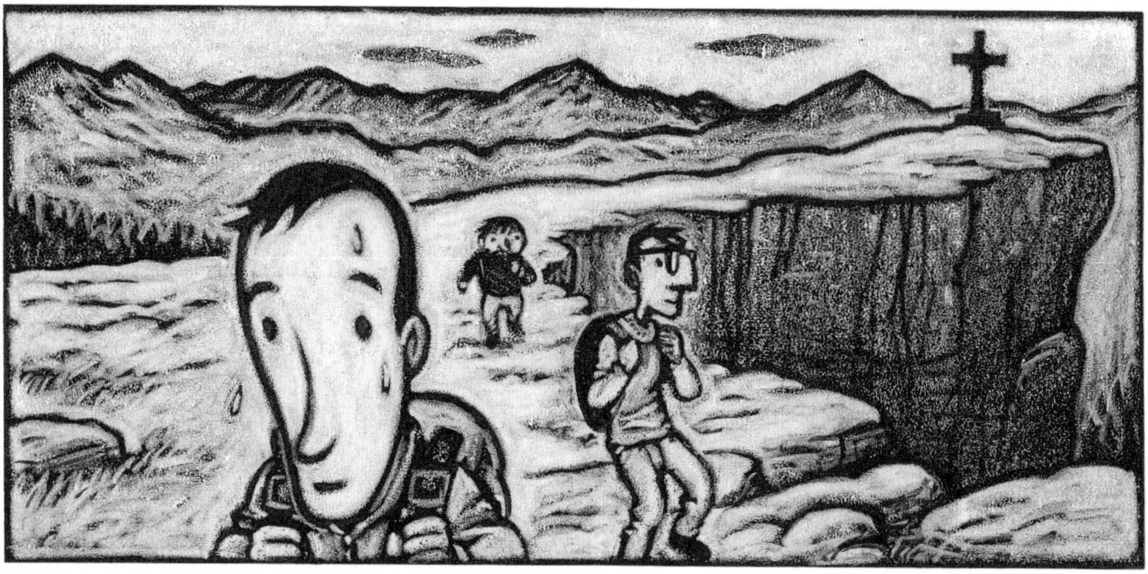

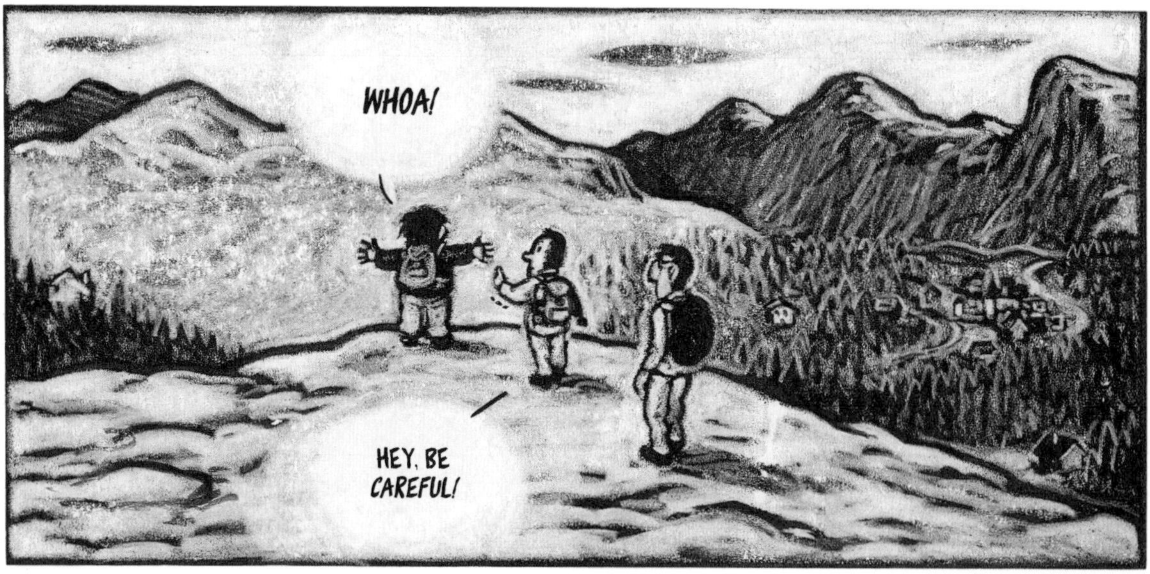
WHOA!
HEY, BE CAREFUL!

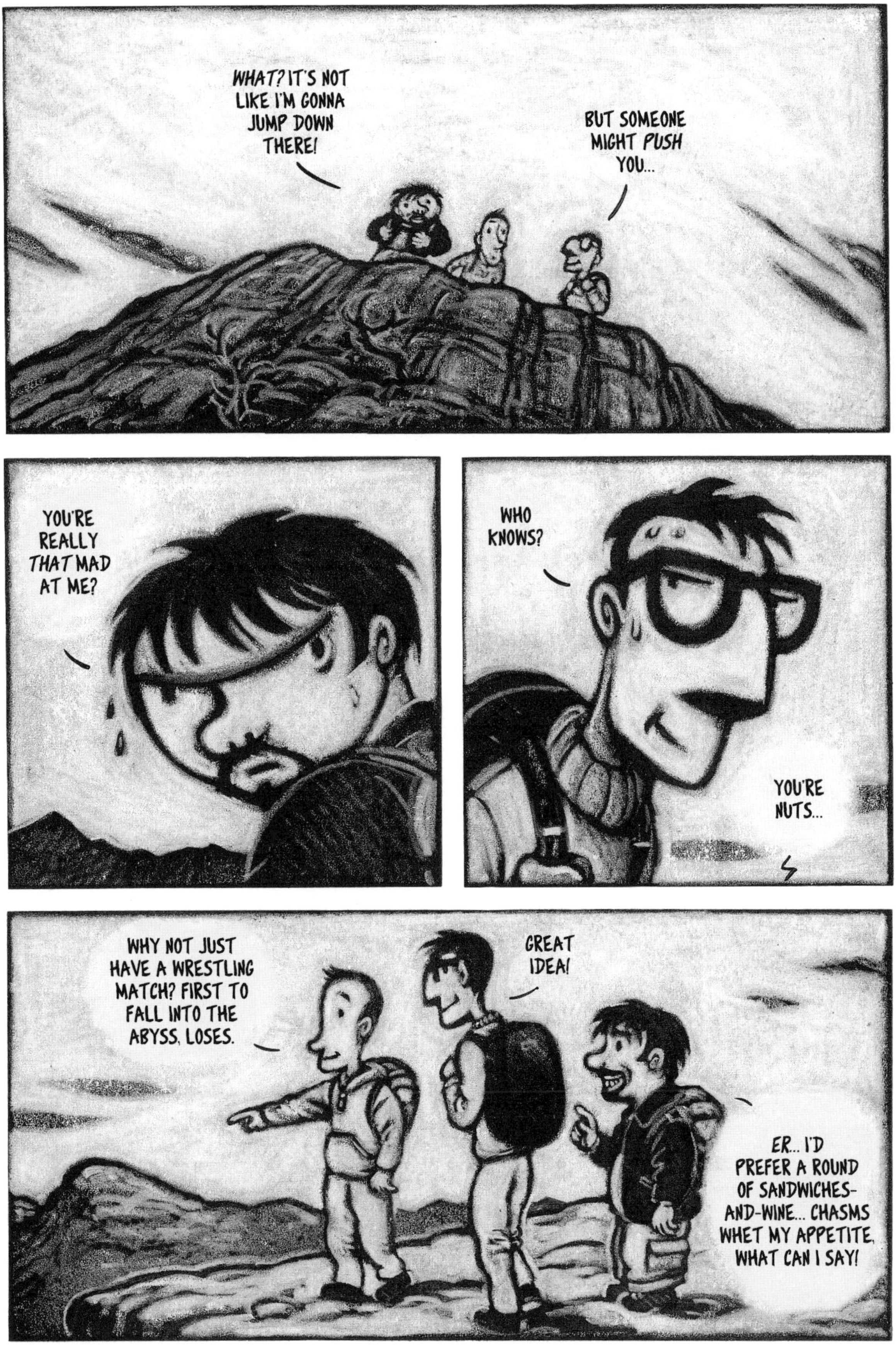
WHAT? IT'S NOT LIKE I'M GONNA JUMP DOWN THERE!
BUT SOMEONE MIGHT PUSH YOU...
YOU'RE REALLY THAT MAD AT ME?
WHO KNOWS?
YOU'RE NUTS...
WHY NOT JUST HAVE A WRESTLING MATCH? FIRST TO FALL INTO THE ABYSS, LOSES.
GREAT IDEA!
ER... I'D PREFER A ROUND OF SANDWICHES-AND-WINE... CHASMS WHET MY APPETITE, WHAT CAN I SAY!

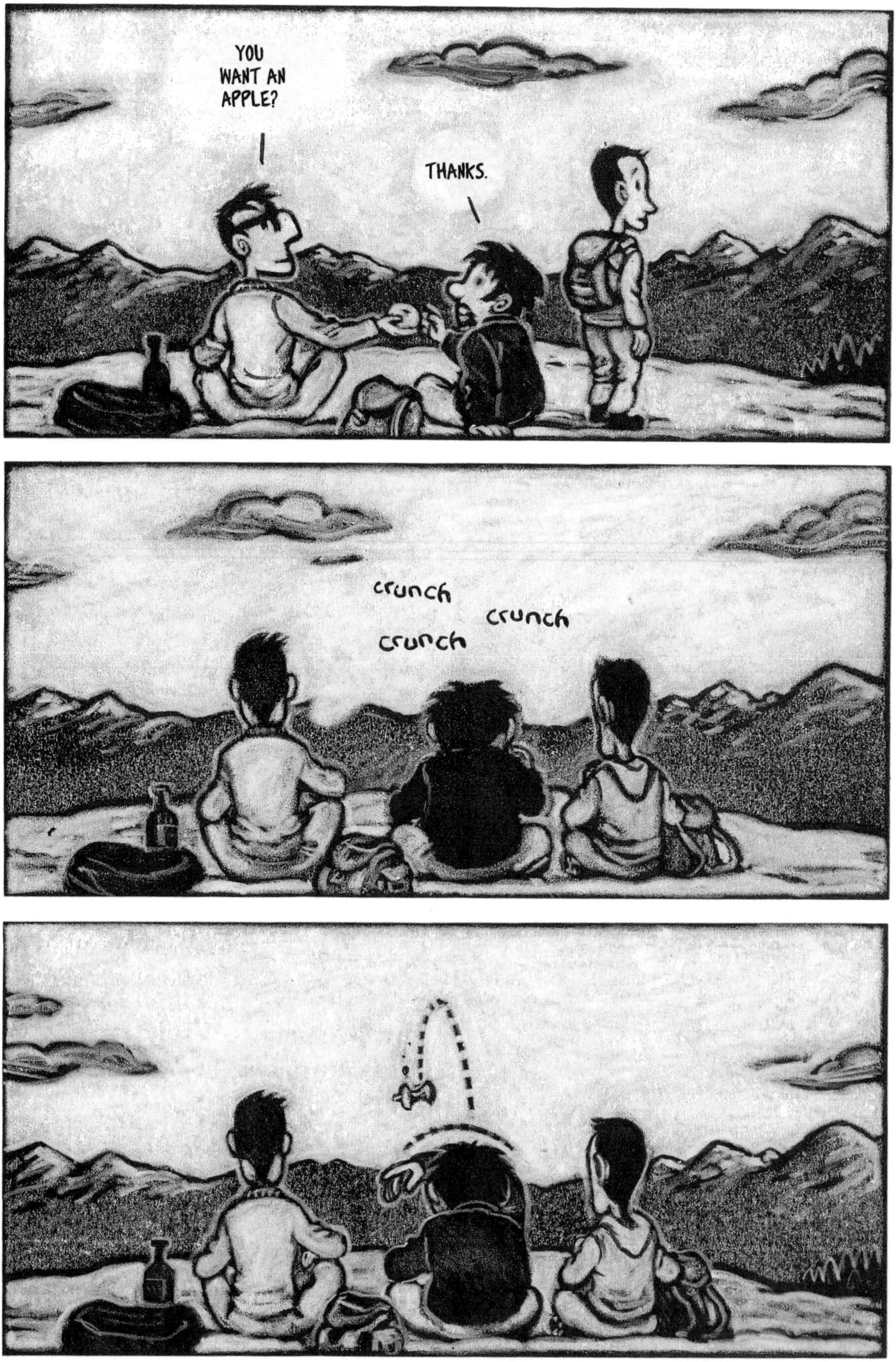
YOU WANT AN APPLE?
THANKS.
crunch
crunch
crunch

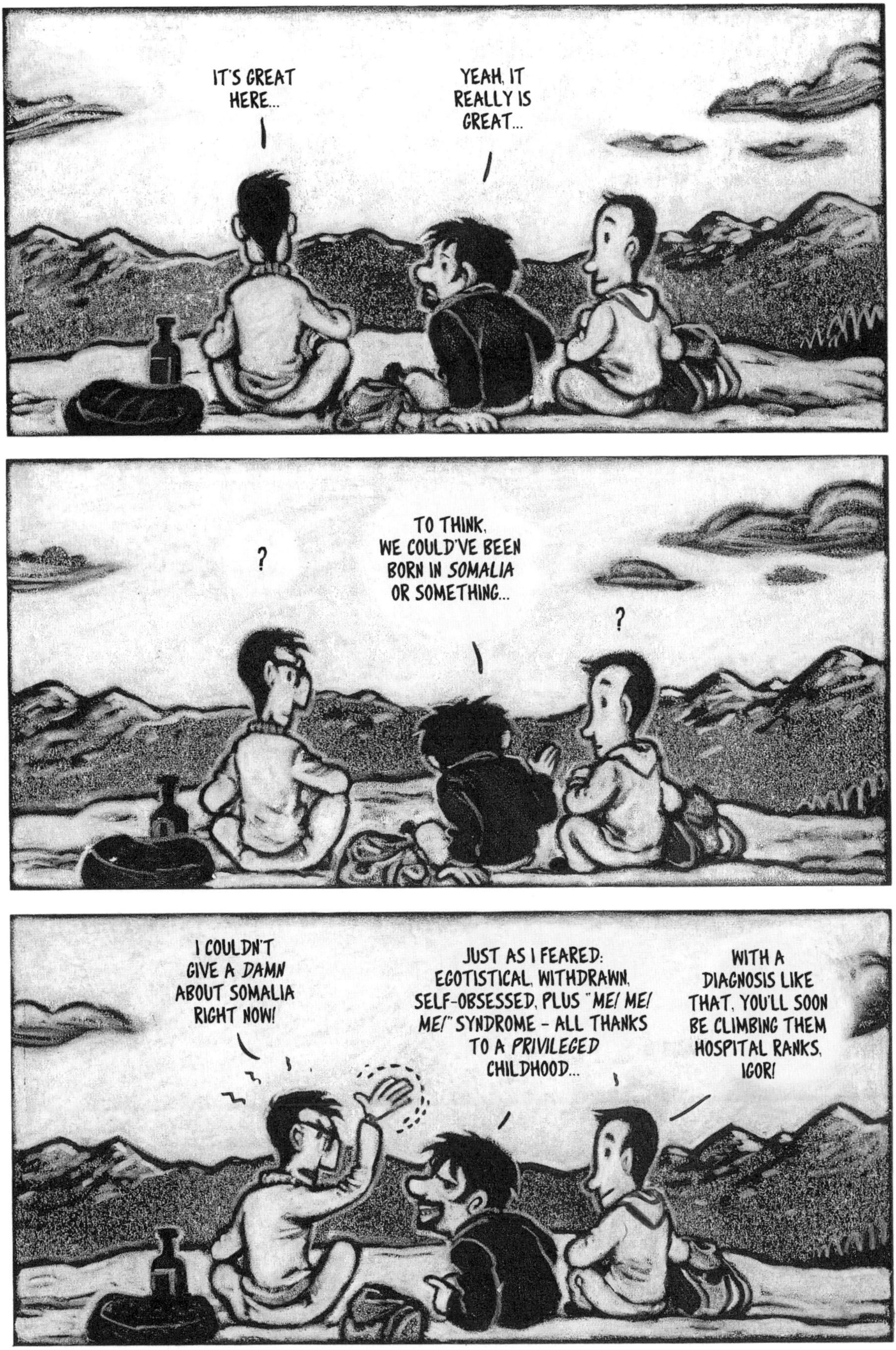

IT'S GREAT HERE...
YEAH, IT REALLY IS GREAT...
?
TO THINK, WE COULD'VE BEEN BORN IN *SOMALIA* OR SOMETHING...
?
I COULDN'T GIVE A *DAMN* ABOUT SOMALIA RIGHT NOW!
JUST AS I FEARED: EGOTISTICAL, WITHDRAWN, SELF-OBSESSED, PLUS "ME! ME! ME!" SYNDROME – ALL THANKS TO A *PRIVILEGED* CHILDHOOD...
WITH A DIAGNOSIS LIKE THAT, YOU'LL SOON BE CLIMBING THEM HOSPITAL RANKS, IGOR!

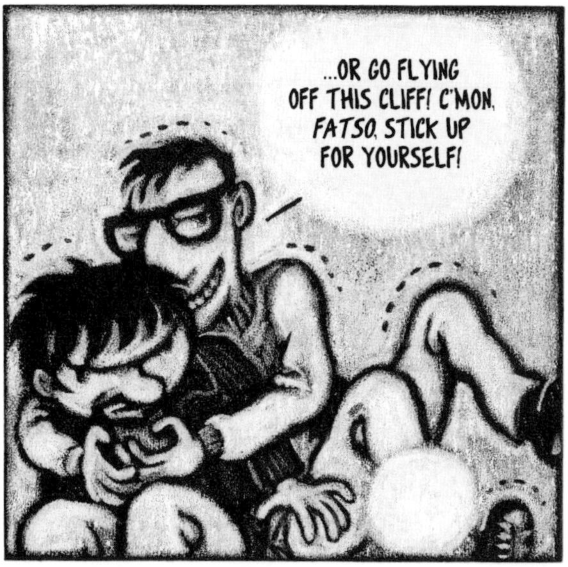
...OR GO FLYING OFF THIS CLIFF! C'MON, FATSO, STICK UP FOR YOURSELF!
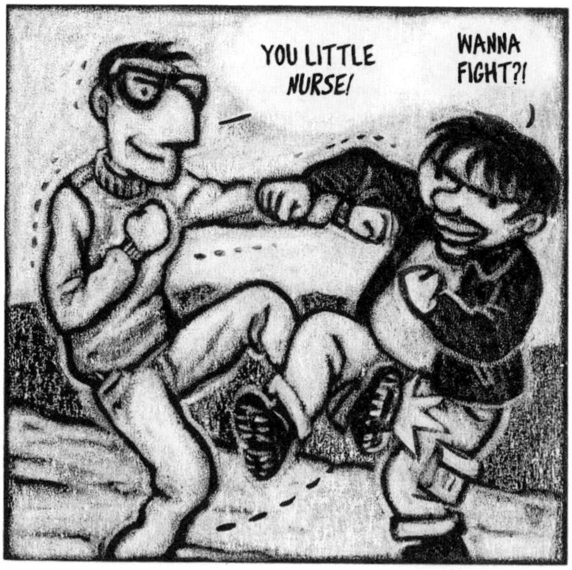
YOU LITTLE NURSE!
WANNA FIGHT?!
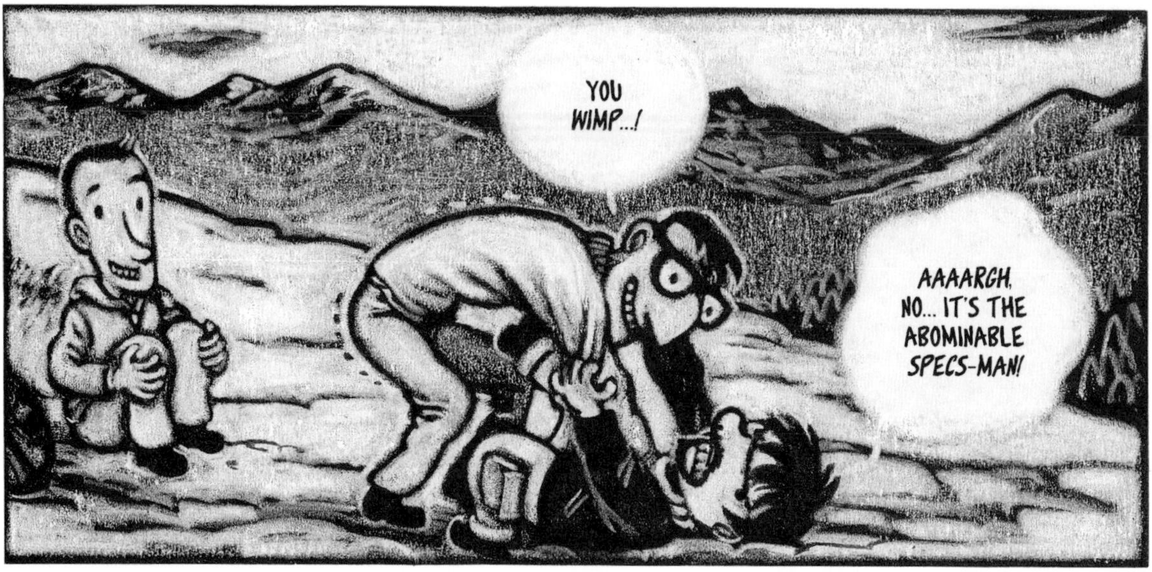
YOU WIMP...!
AAAARGH, NO... IT'S THE ABOMINABLE SPECS-MAN!
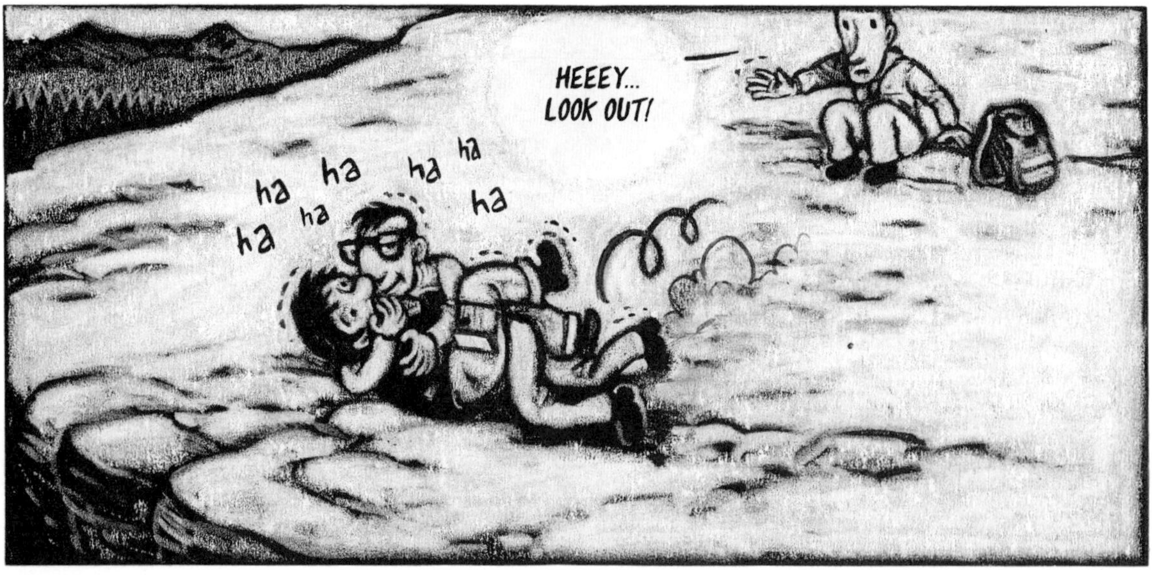
HEEEY... LOOK OUT!
ha ha ha ha ha ha ha ha

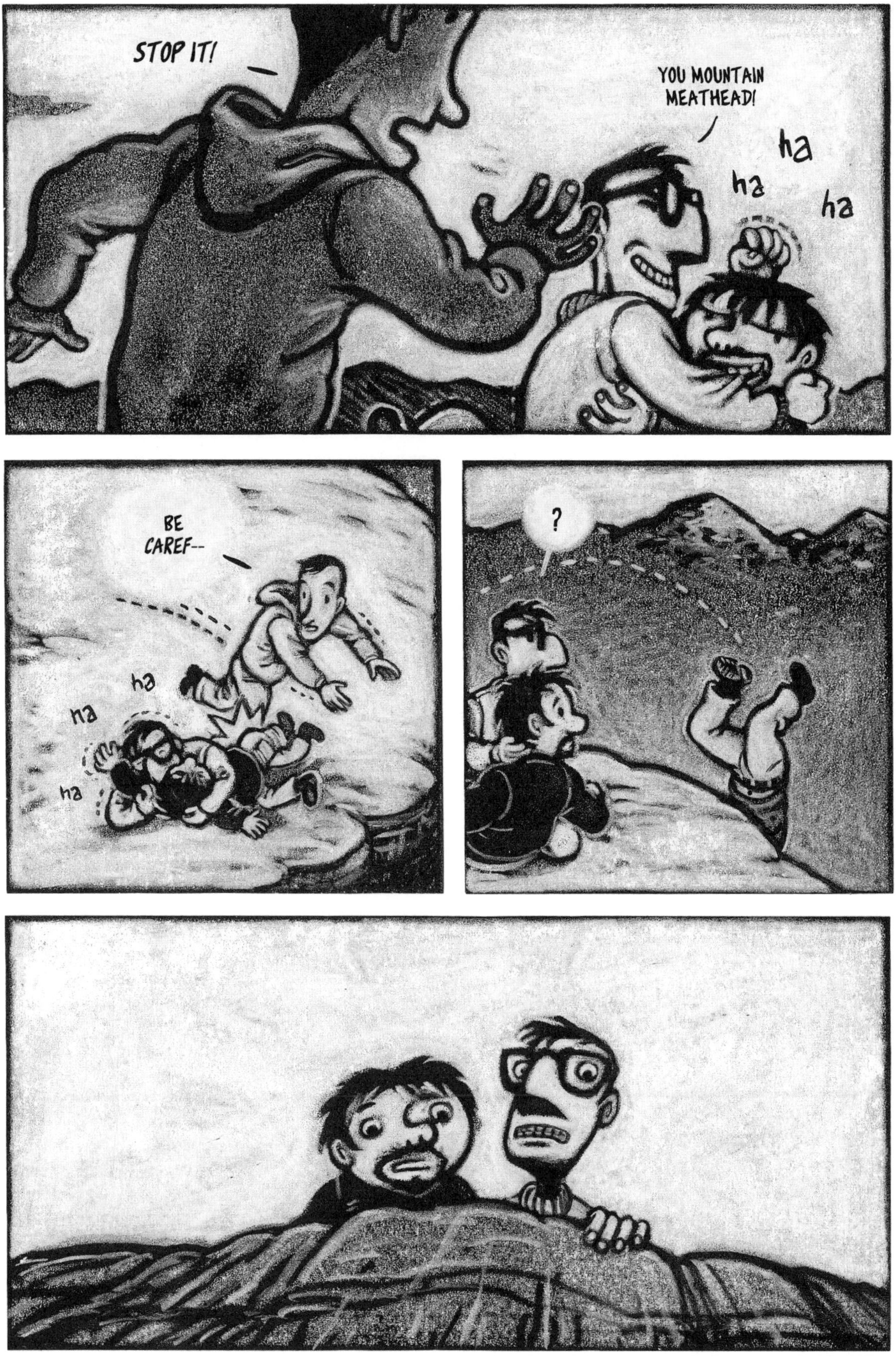
STOP IT!
YOU MOUNTAIN MEATHEAD!
ha
ha
ha
BE CAREF--
ha
ha
ha
?

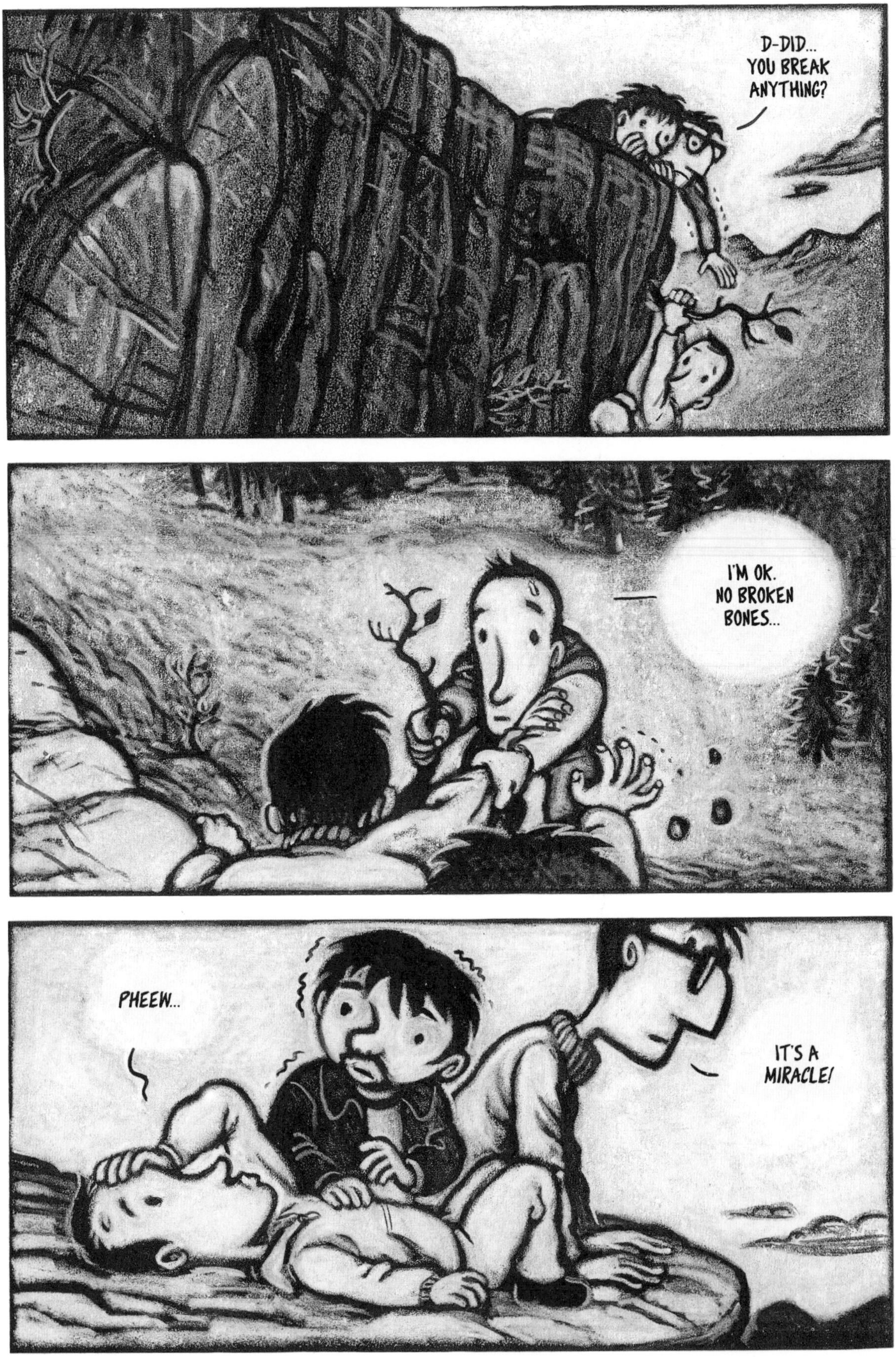
D-DID... YOU BREAK ANYTHING?
I'M OK. NO BROKEN BONES...
PHEEW...
IT'S A MIRACLE!

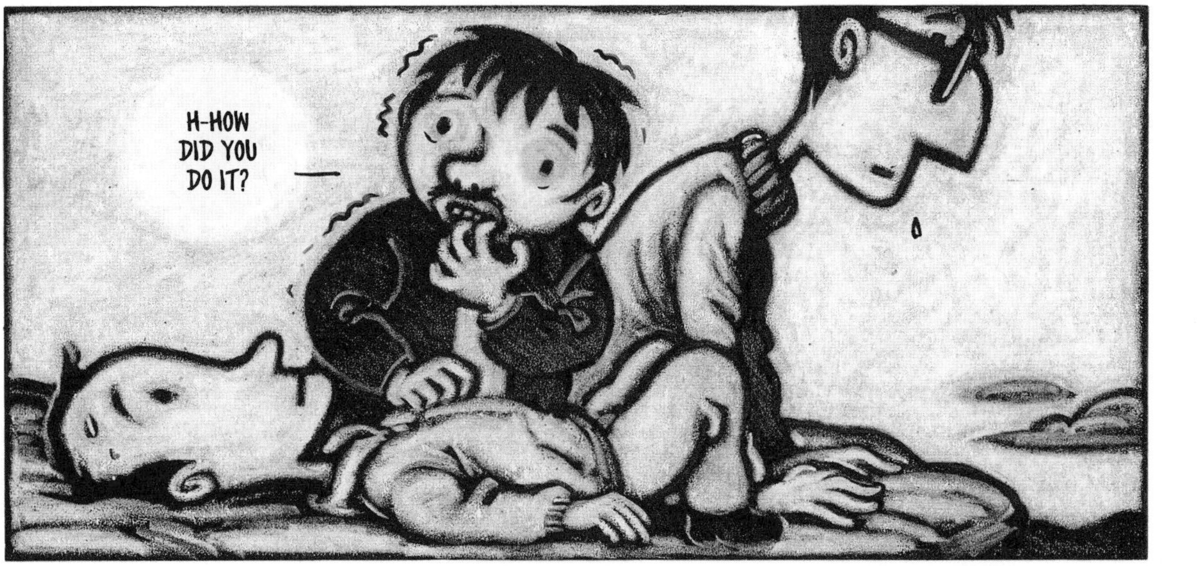
H-HOW DID YOU DO IT?

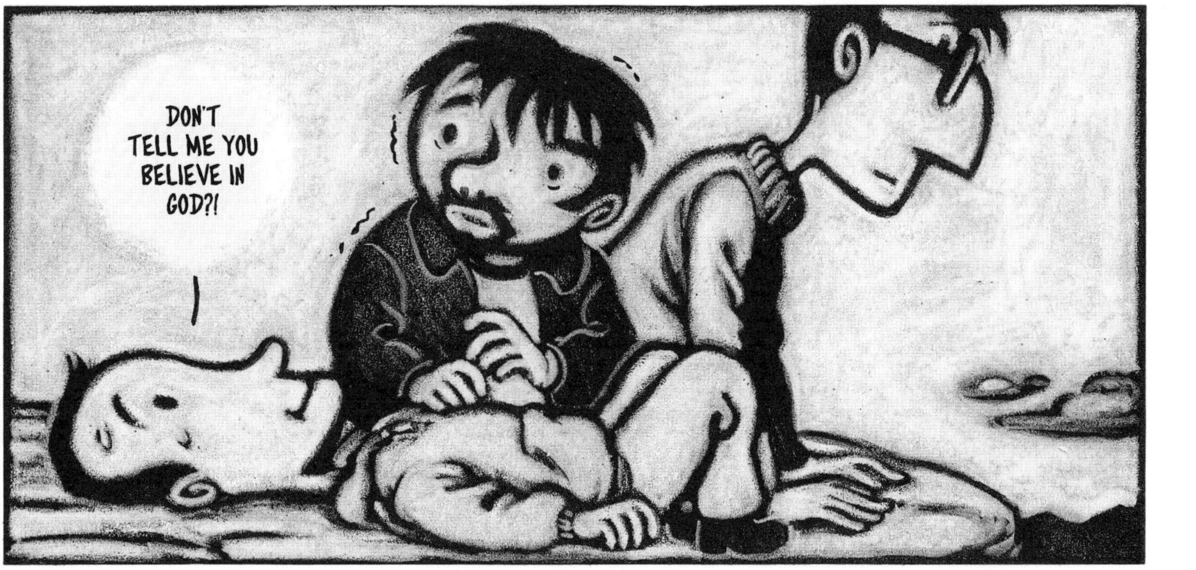
DON'T TELL ME YOU BELIEVE IN GOD?!

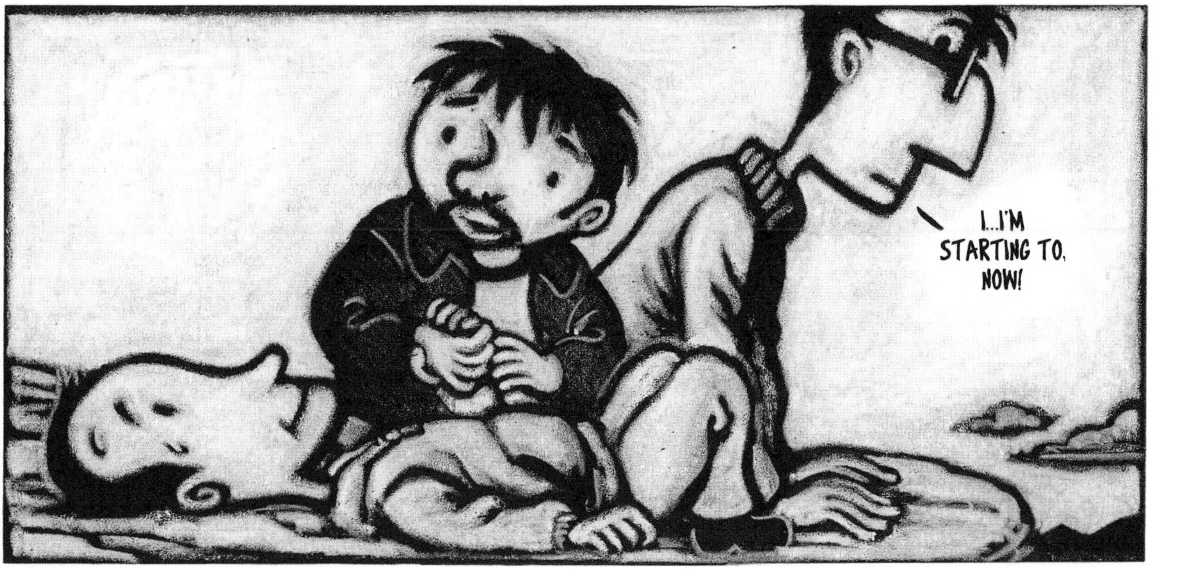
I...I'M STARTING TO, NOW!

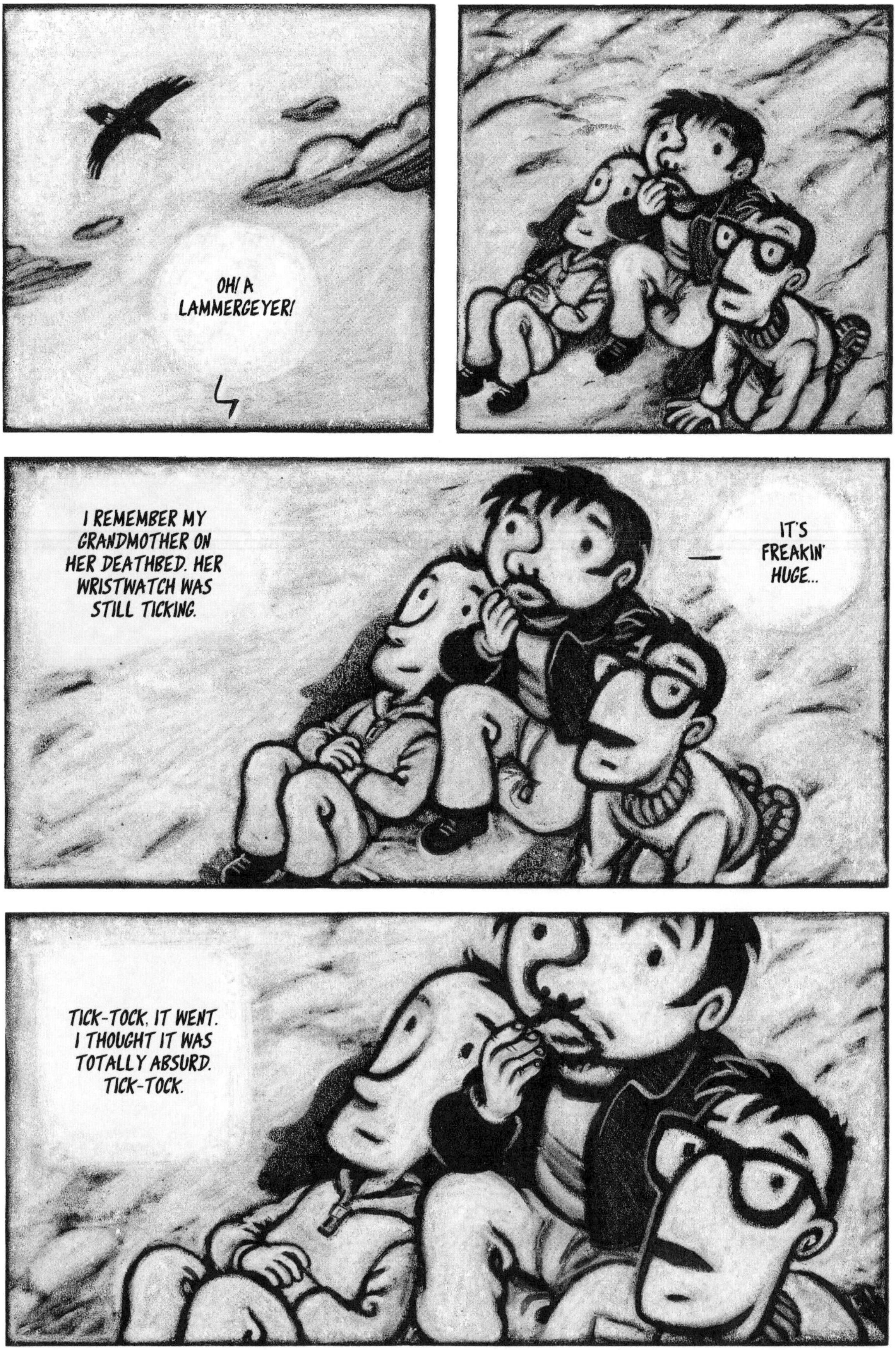
OH! A LAMMERGEYER!
I REMEMBER MY GRANDMOTHER ON HER DEATHBED. HER WRISTWATCH WAS STILL TICKING.
IT'S FREAKIN' HUGE...
TICK-TOCK, IT WENT. I THOUGHT IT WAS TOTALLY ABSURD. TICK-TOCK.

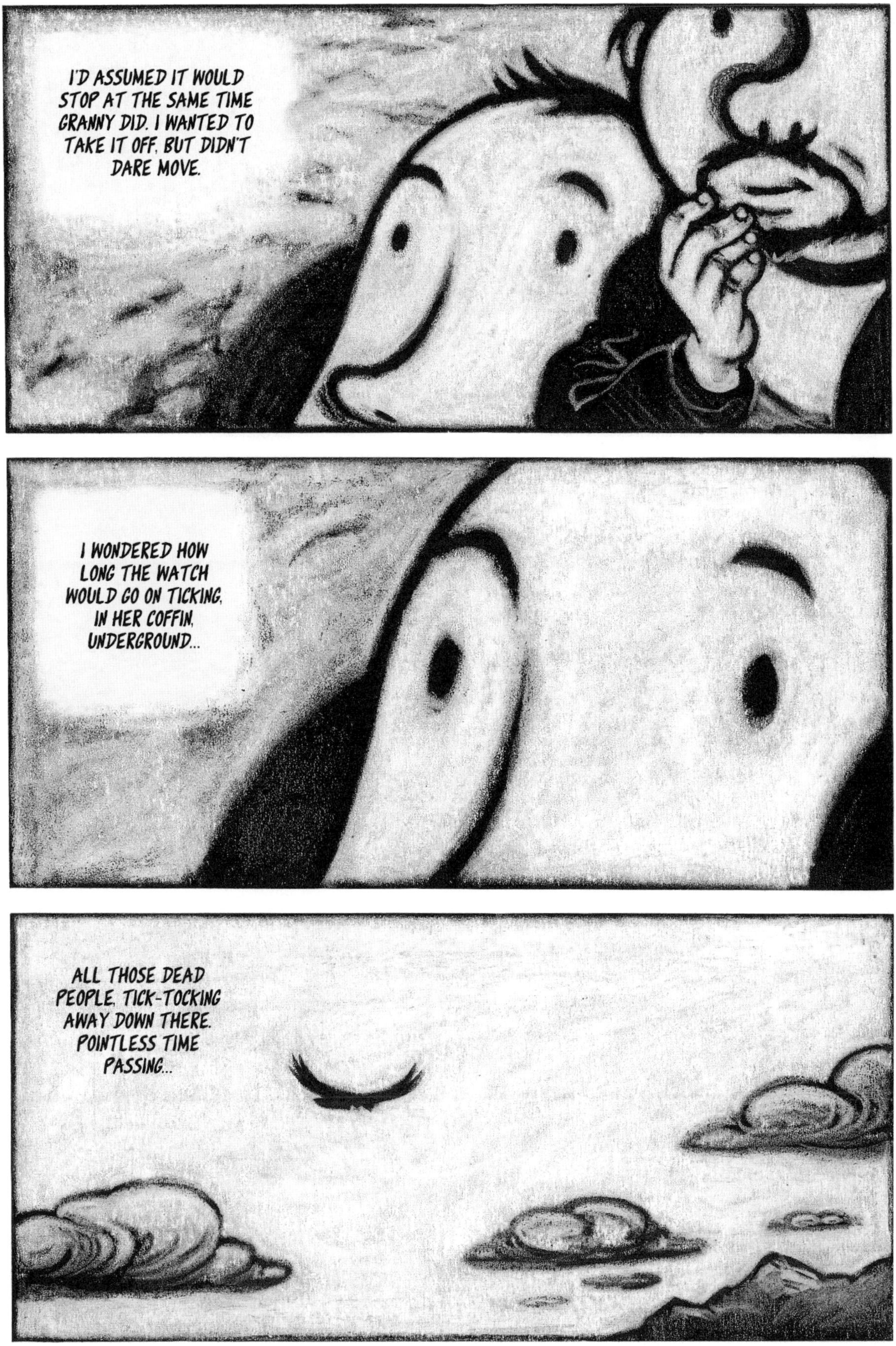
I'D ASSUMED IT WOULD STOP AT THE SAME TIME GRANNY DID. I WANTED TO TAKE IT OFF, BUT DIDN'T DARE MOVE.
I WONDERED HOW LONG THE WATCH WOULD GO ON TICKING, IN HER COFFIN, UNDERGROUND...
ALL THOSE DEAD PEOPLE, TICK-TOCKING AWAY DOWN THERE. POINTLESS TIME PASSING...

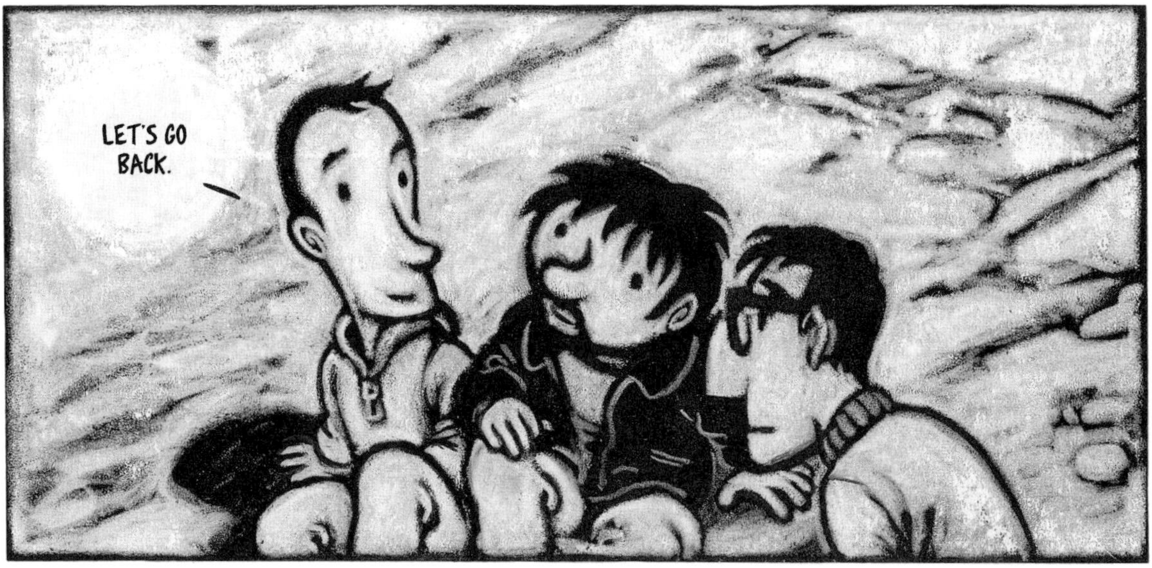
LET'S GO BACK.

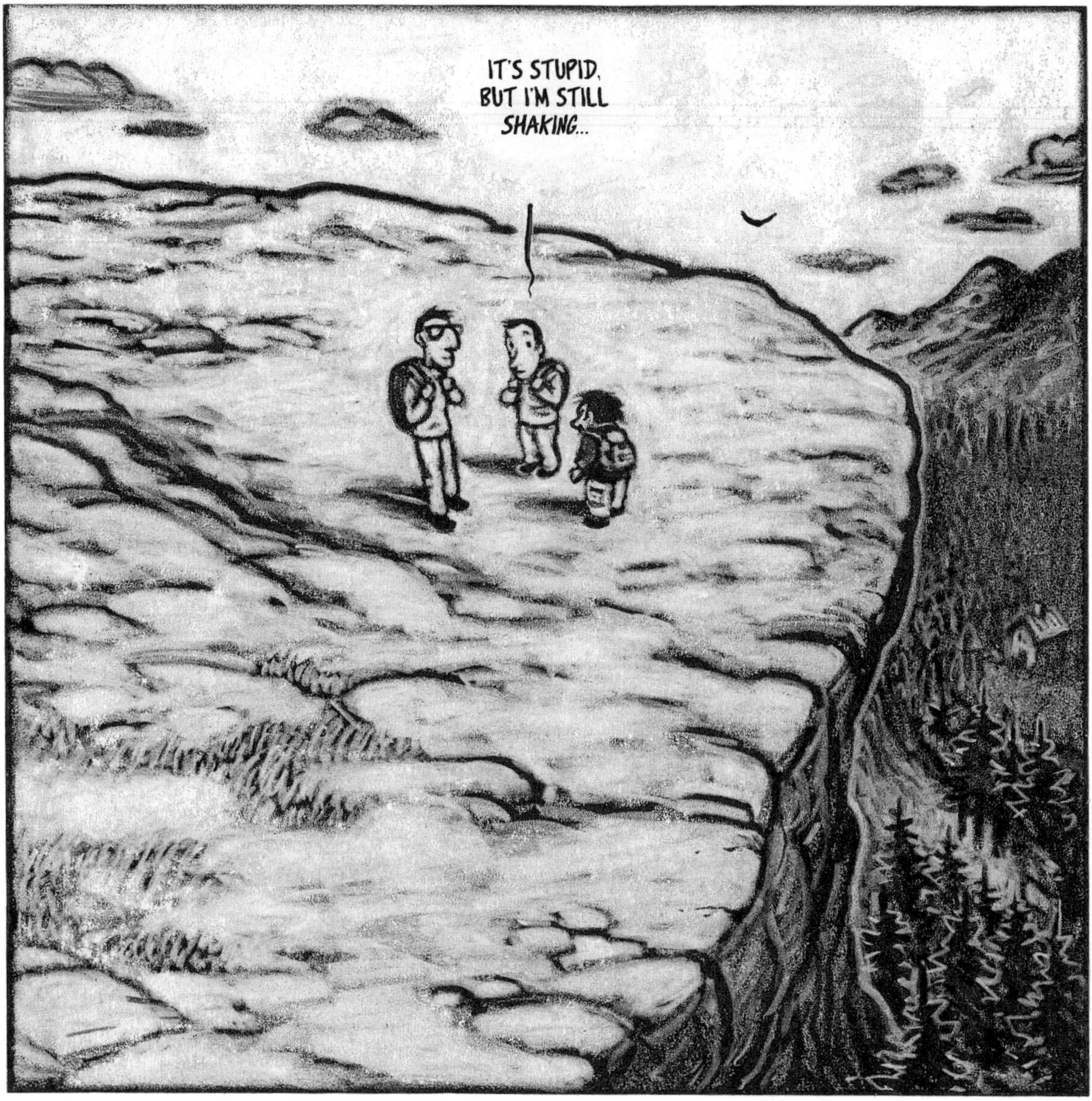
IT'S STUPID, BUT I'M STILL *SHAKING*...

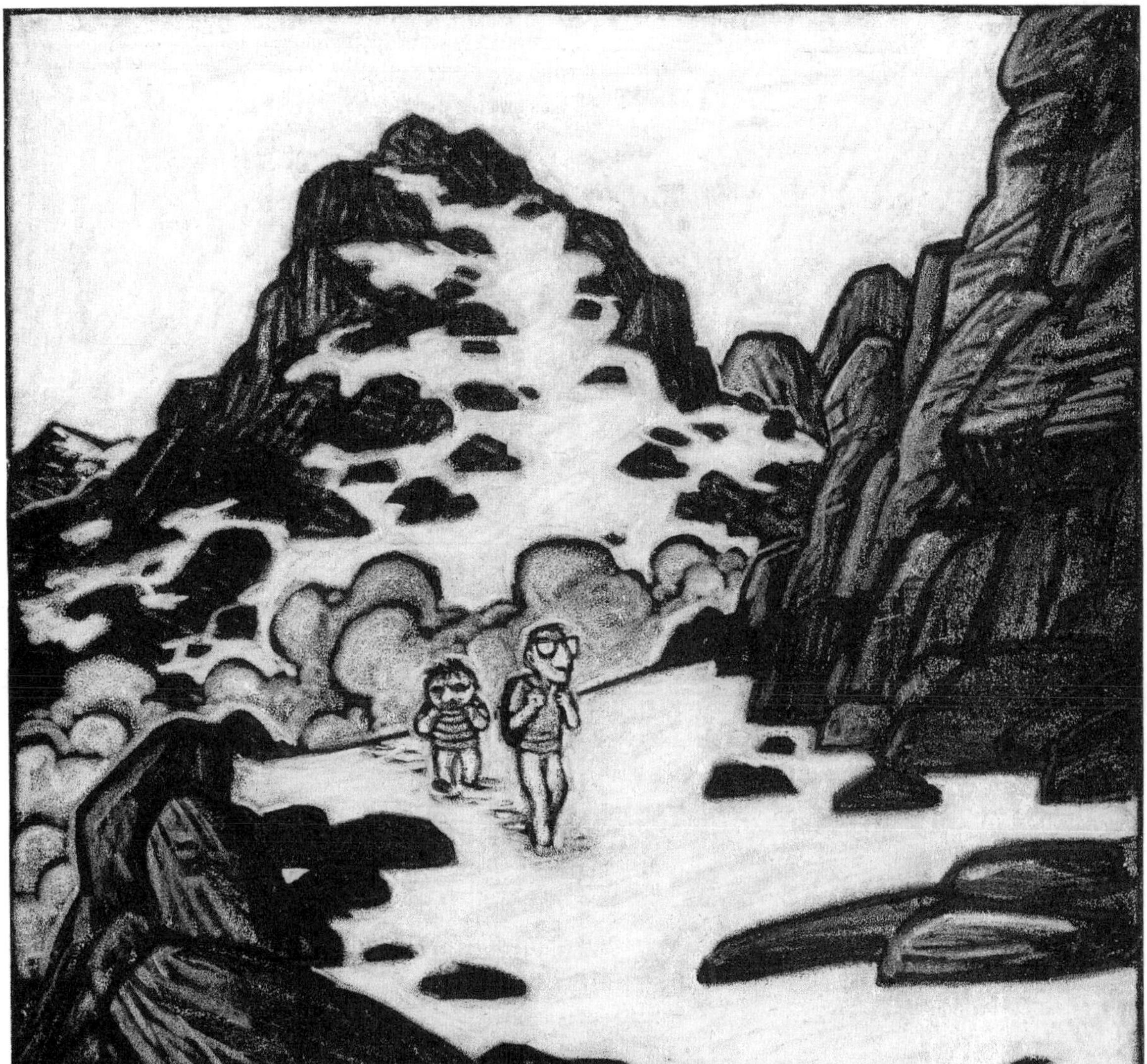

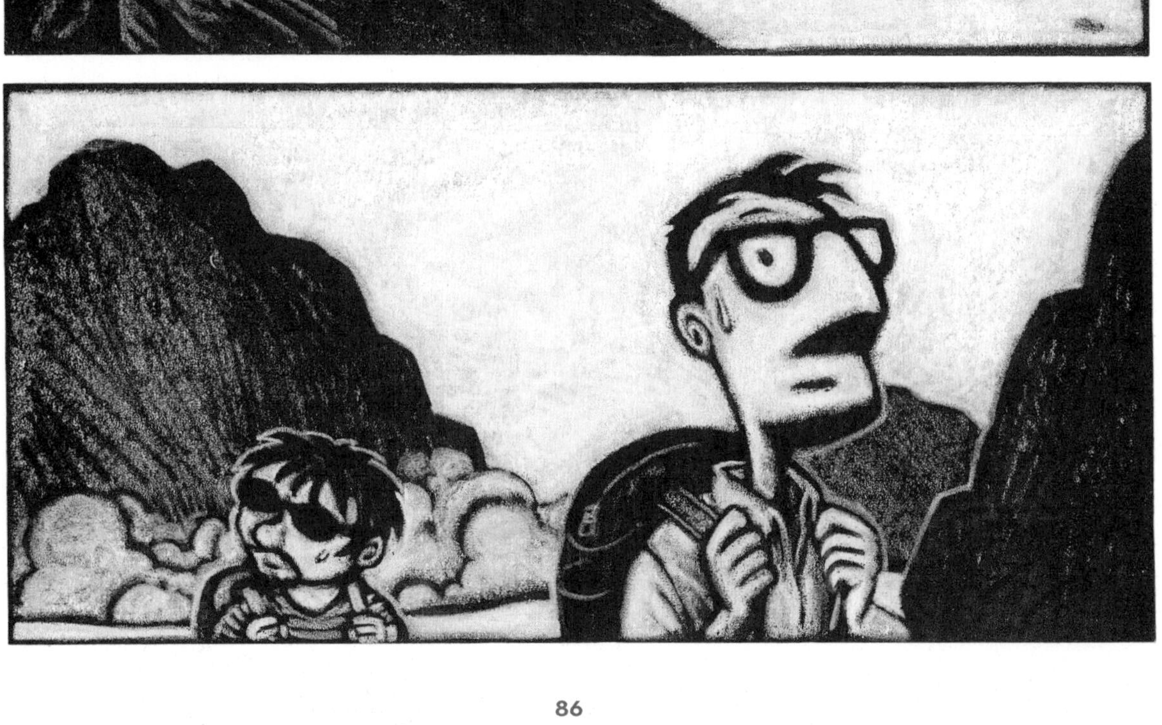

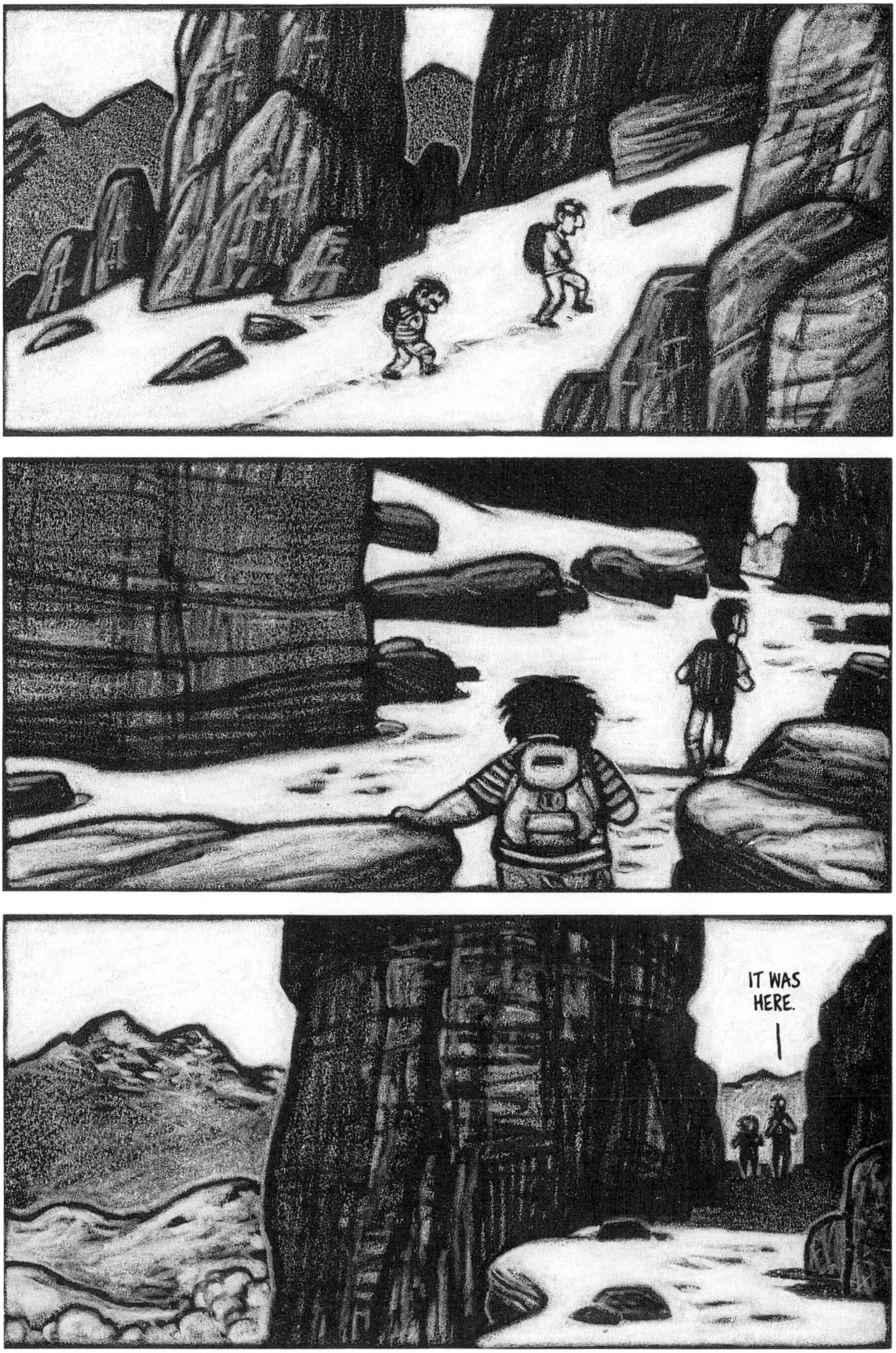
IT WAS
HERE.

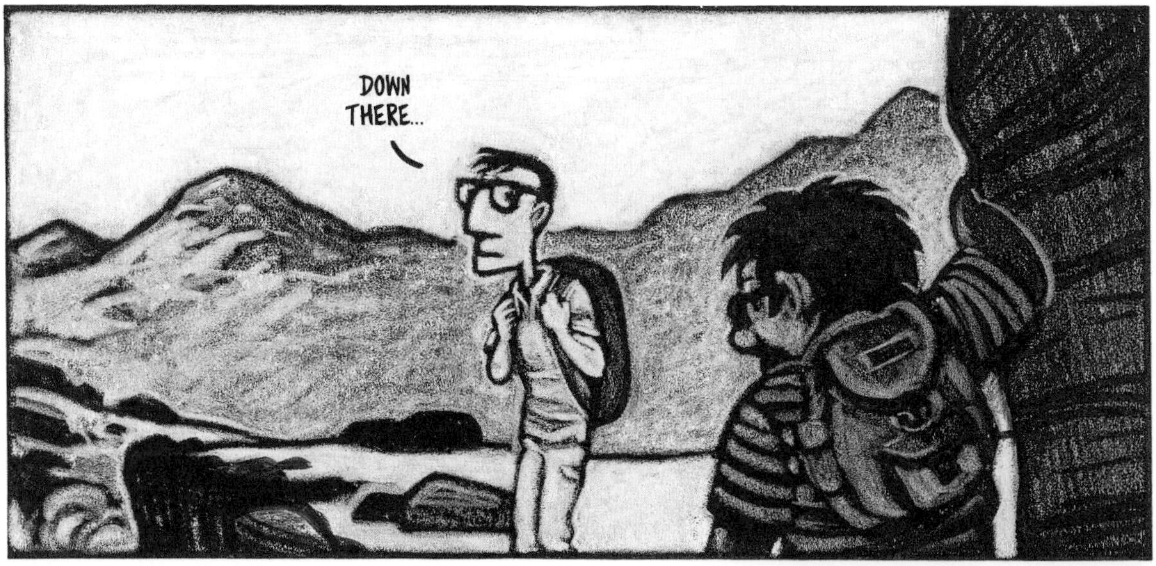
DOWN THERE...

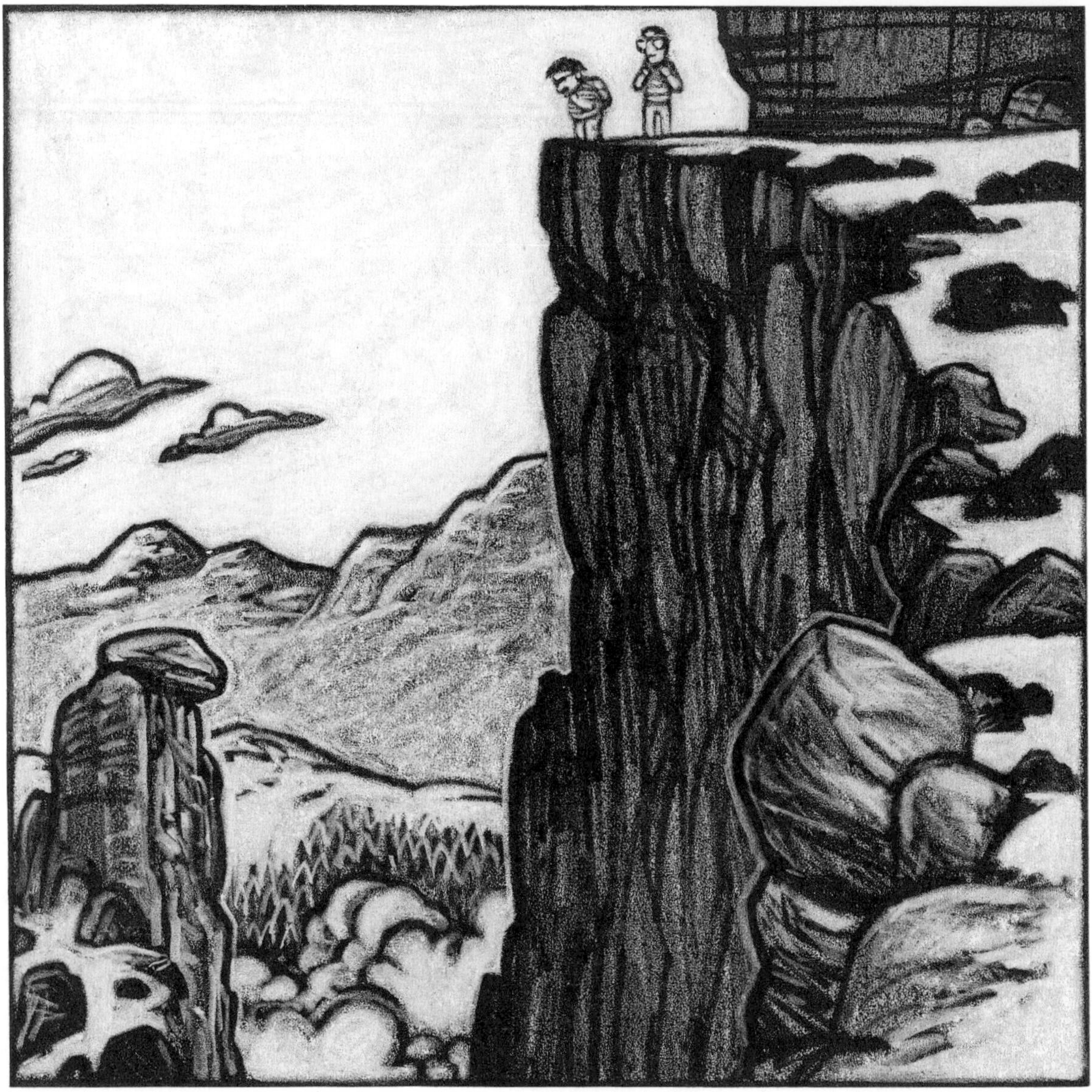

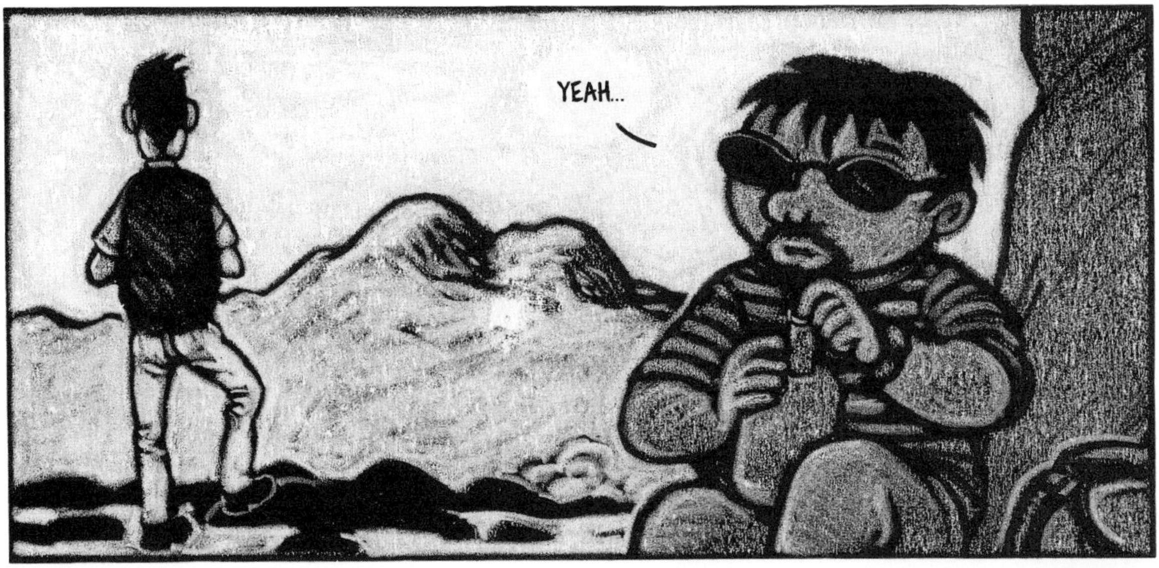
YEAH...

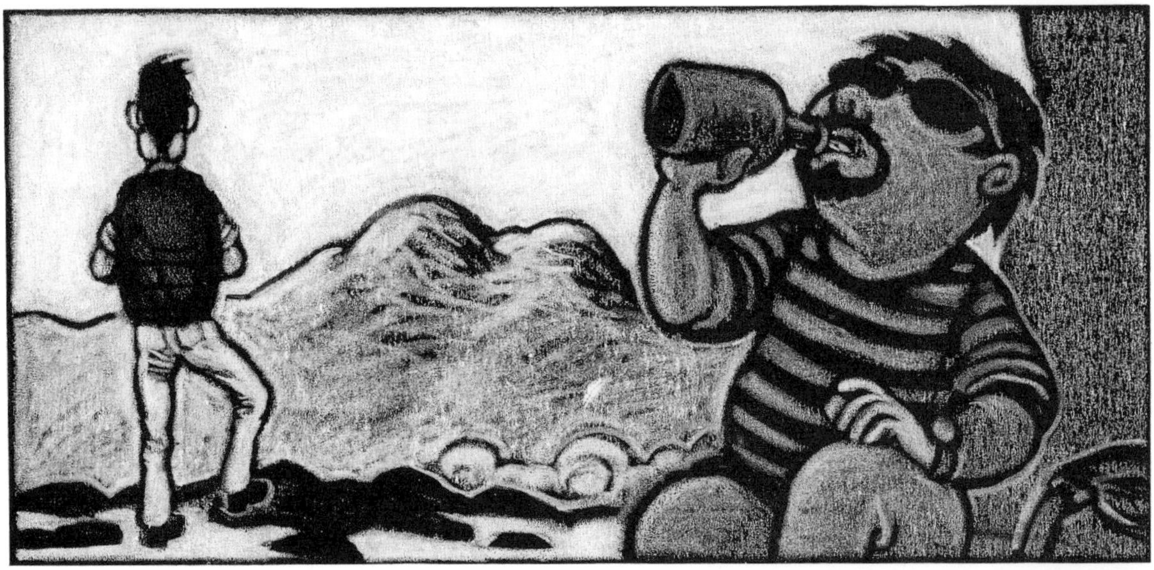

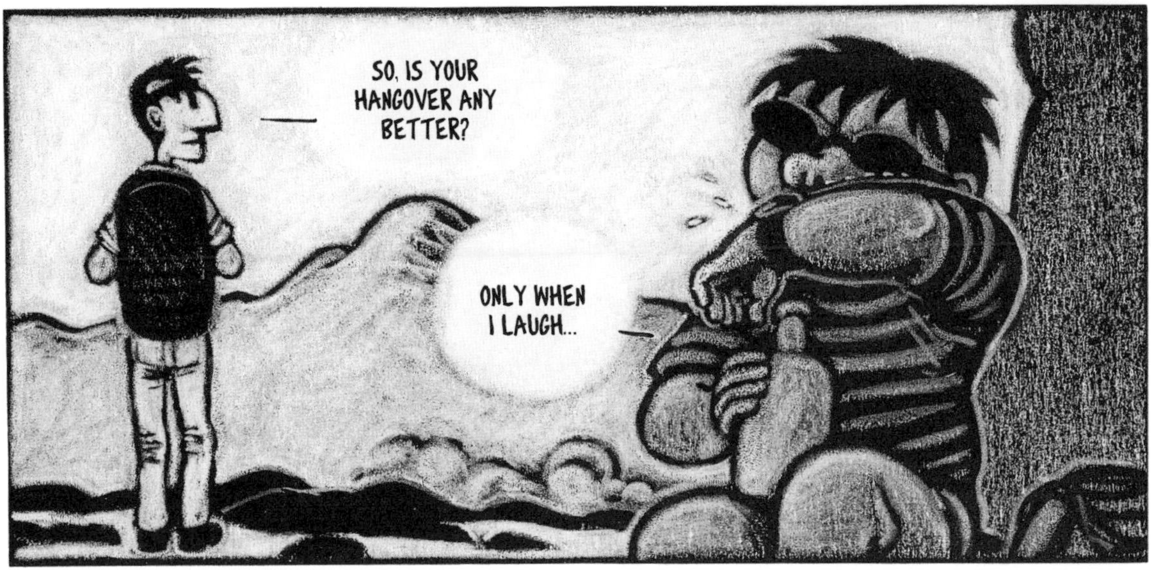
SO, IS YOUR HANGOVER ANY BETTER?
ONLY WHEN I LAUGH...

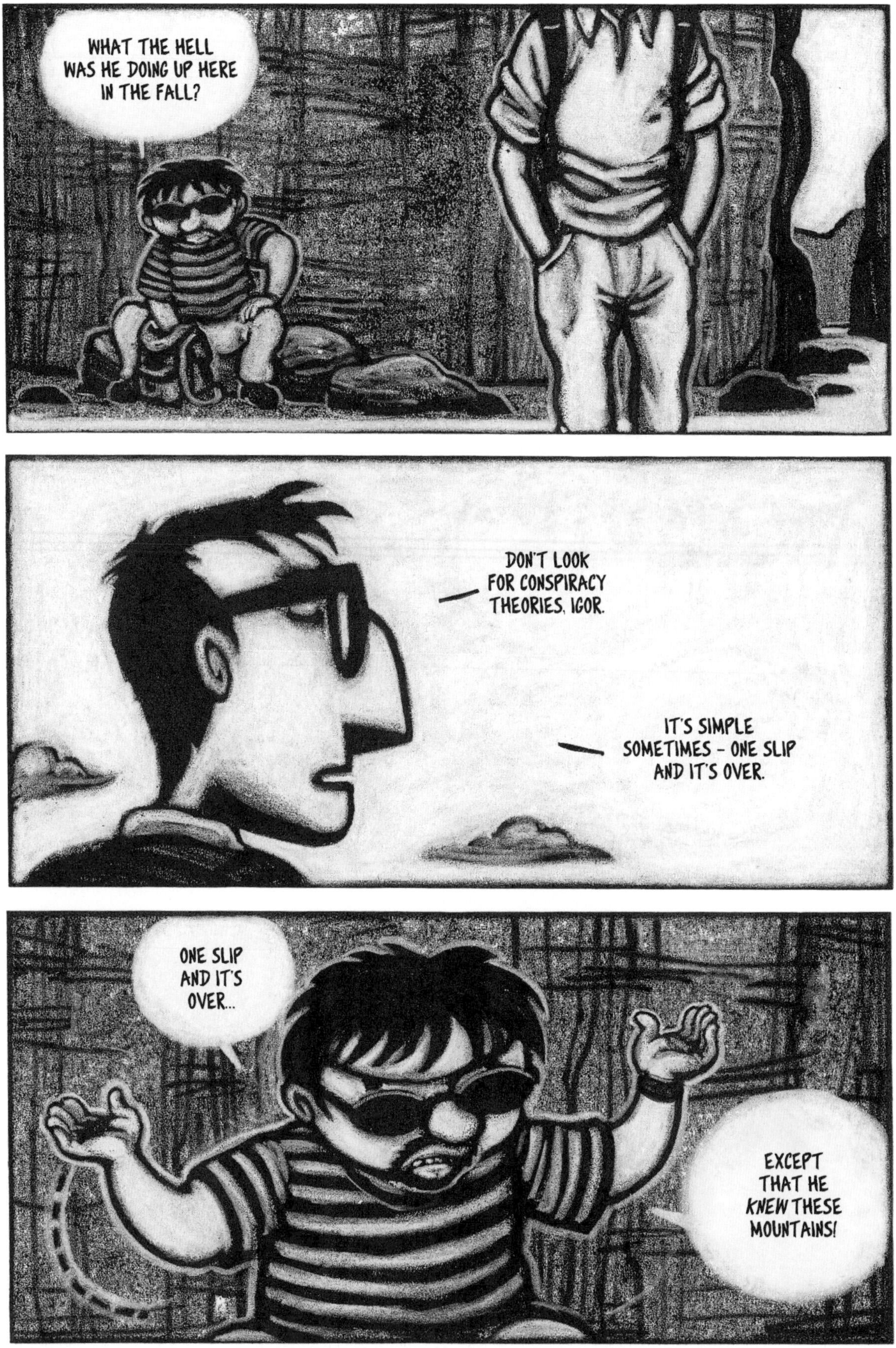
WHAT THE HELL WAS HE DOING UP HERE IN THE FALL?
DON'T LOOK FOR CONSPIRACY THEORIES, IGOR.
IT'S SIMPLE SOMETIMES – ONE SLIP AND IT'S OVER.
ONE SLIP AND IT'S OVER...
EXCEPT THAT HE *KNEW* THESE MOUNTAINS!

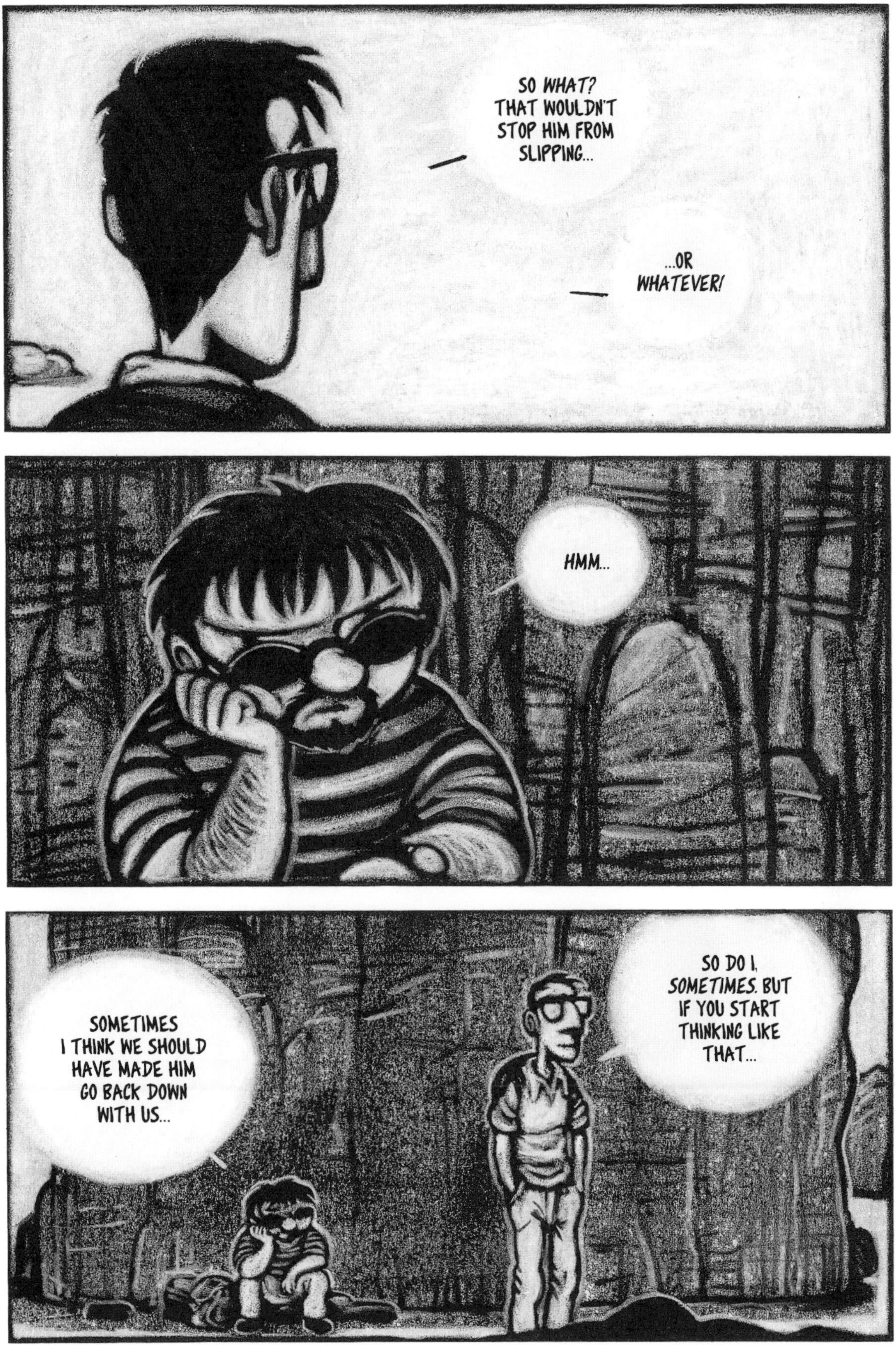
SO WHAT? THAT WOULDN'T STOP HIM FROM SLIPPING...
...OR WHATEVER!
HMM...
SOMETIMES I THINK WE SHOULD HAVE MADE HIM GO BACK DOWN WITH US...
SO DO I, SOMETIMES. BUT IF YOU START THINKING LIKE THAT...

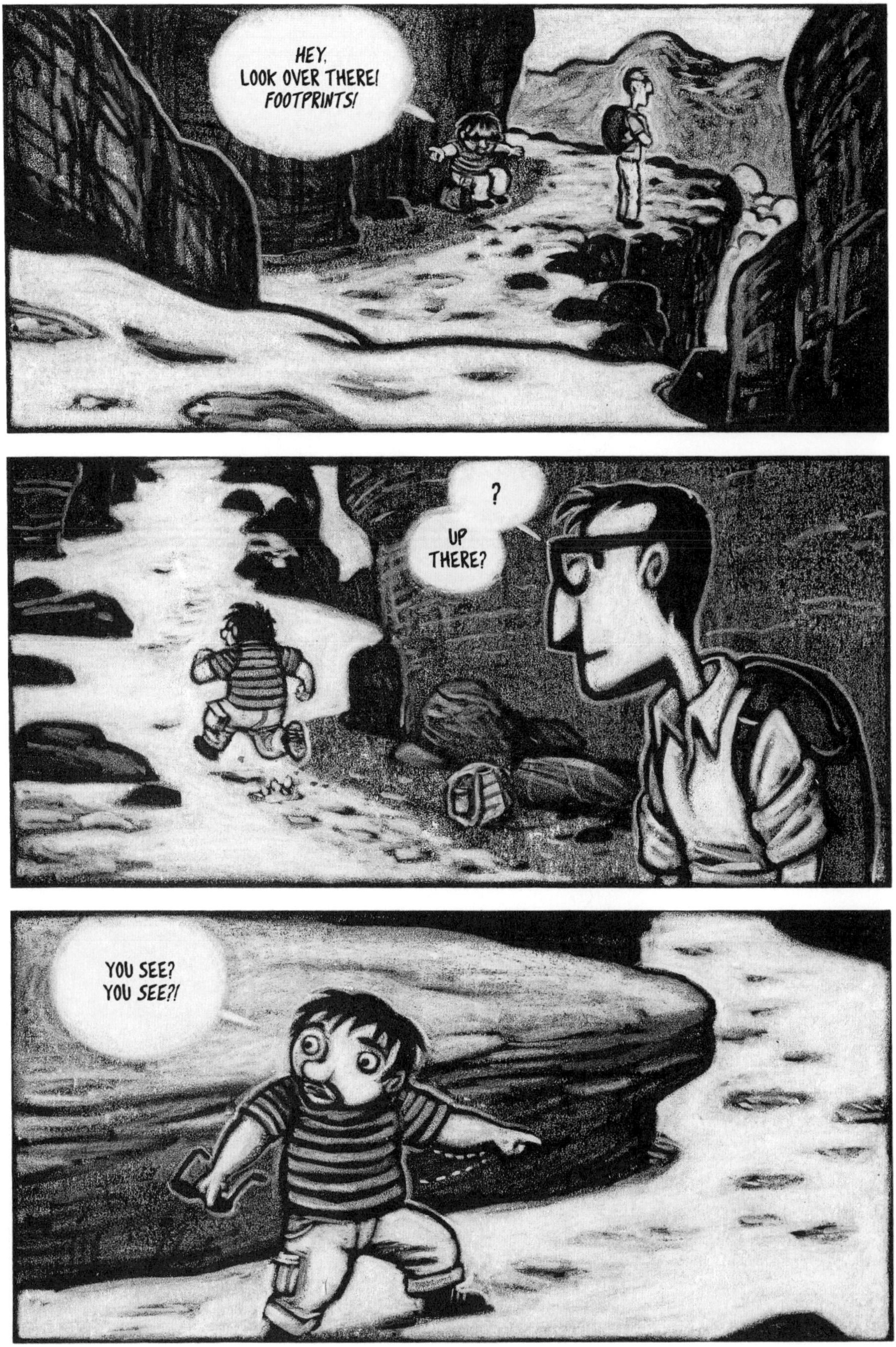
HEY, LOOK OVER THERE! FOOTPRINTS!
?
UP THERE?
YOU SEE? YOU SEE?!

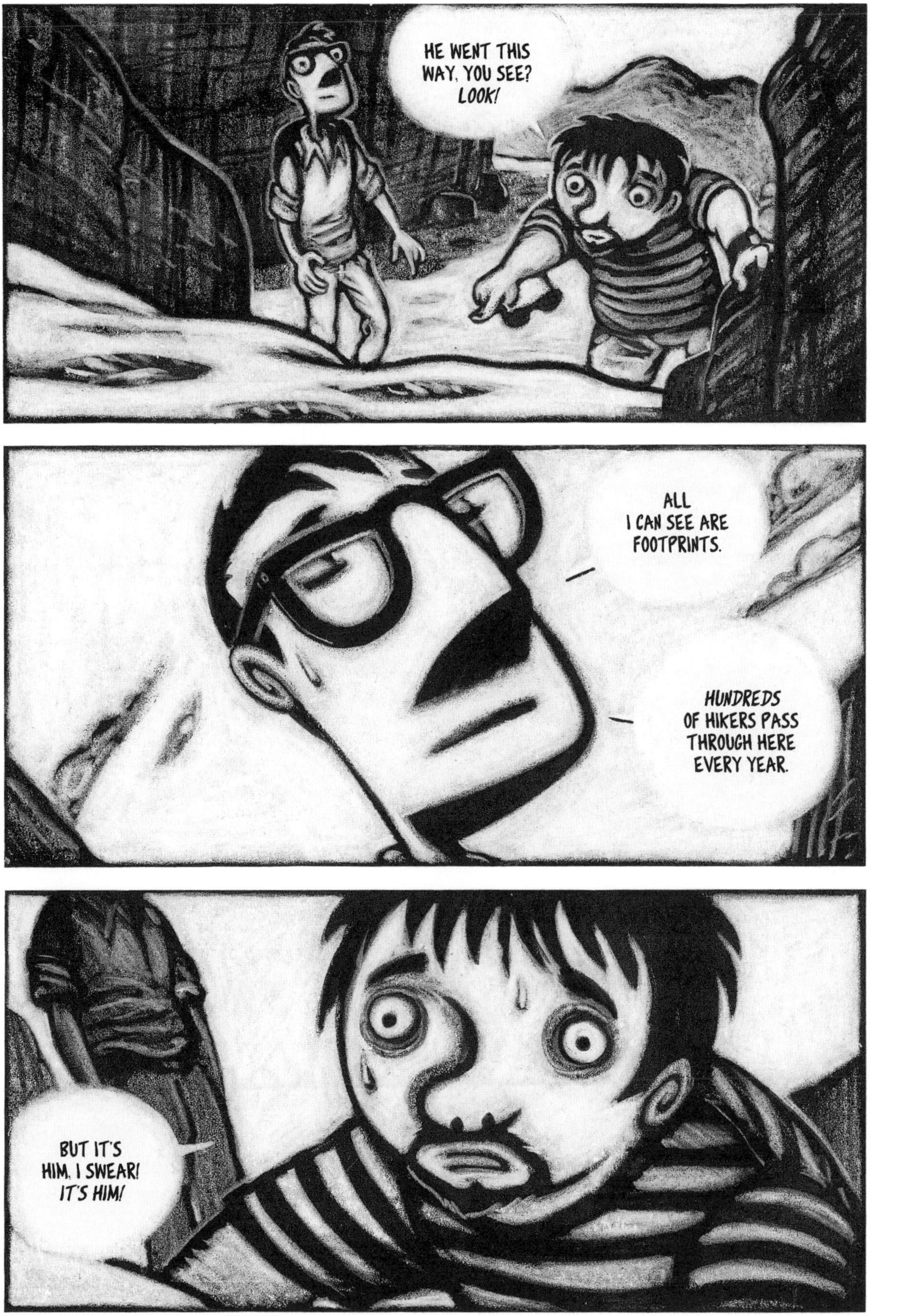
HE WENT THIS WAY, YOU SEE? LOOK!
ALL I CAN SEE ARE FOOTPRINTS.
HUNDREDS OF HIKERS PASS THROUGH HERE EVERY YEAR.
BUT IT'S HIM, I SWEAR! IT'S HIM!

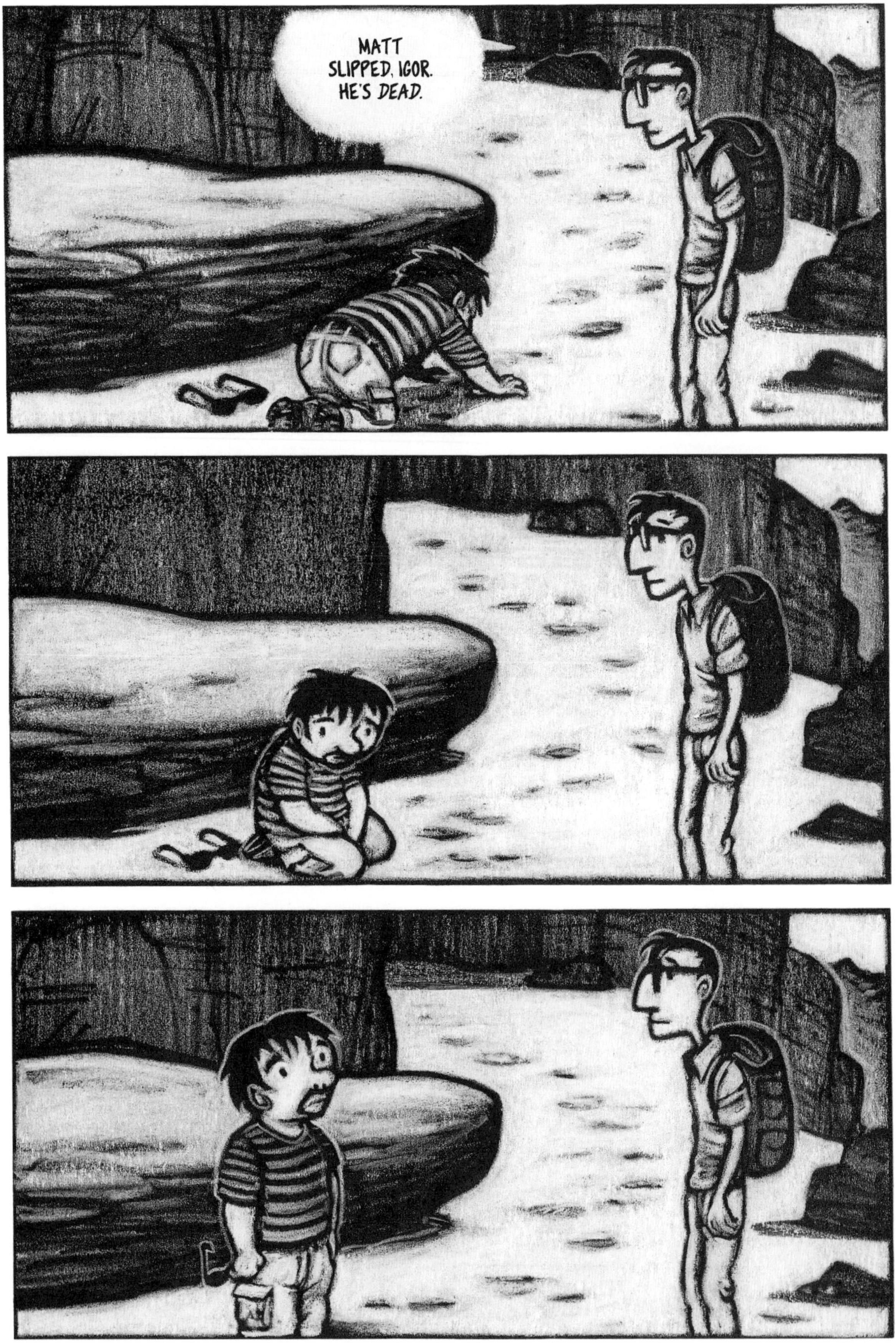
MATT SLIPPED, IGOR. HE'S *DEAD*.

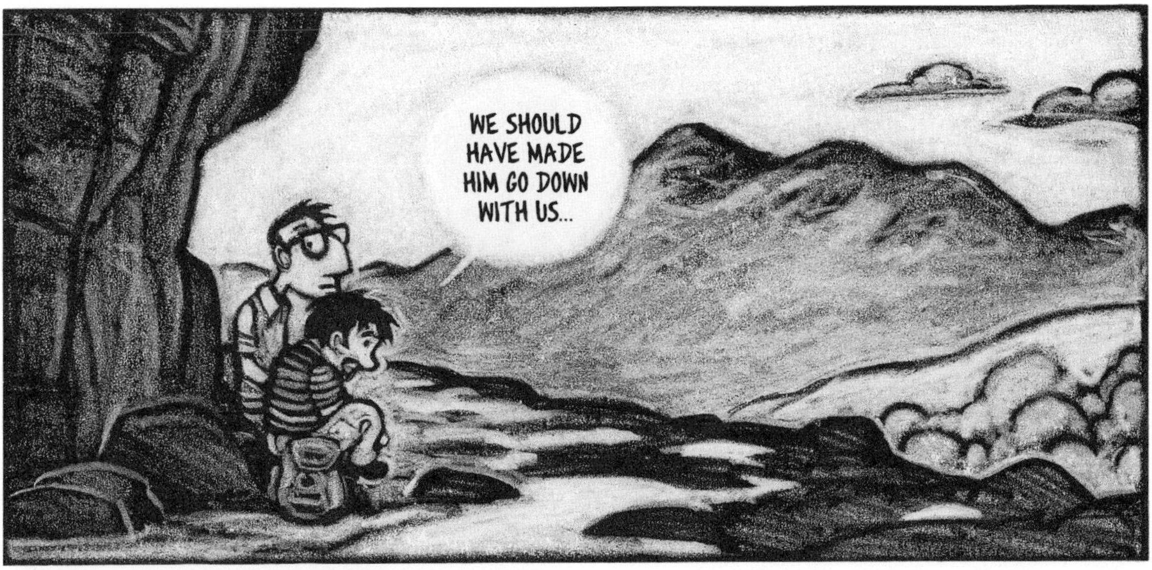
WE SHOULD HAVE MADE HIM GO DOWN WITH US...

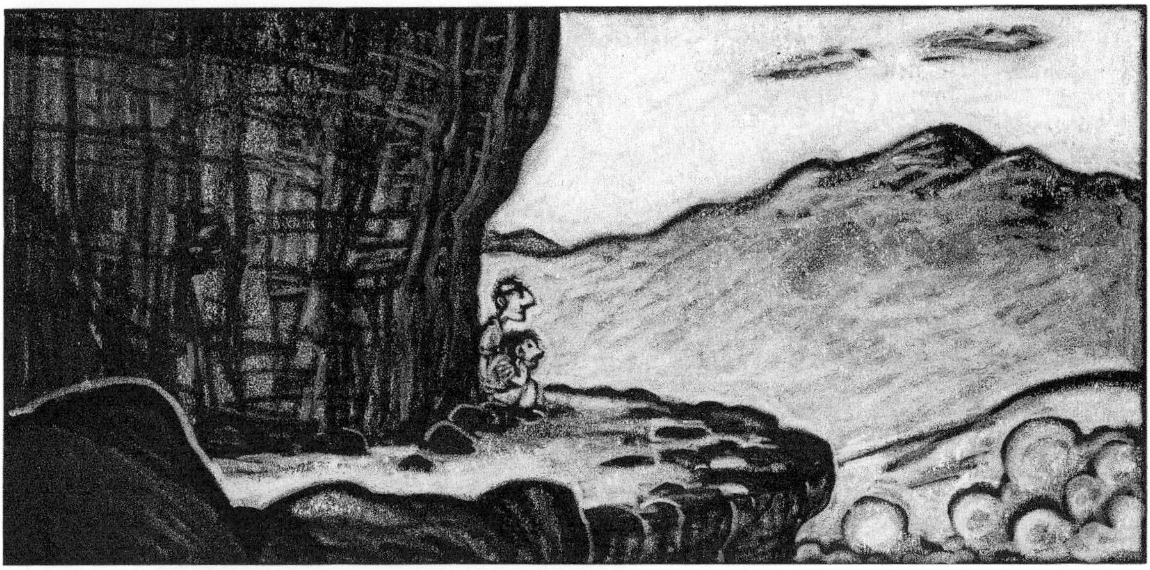

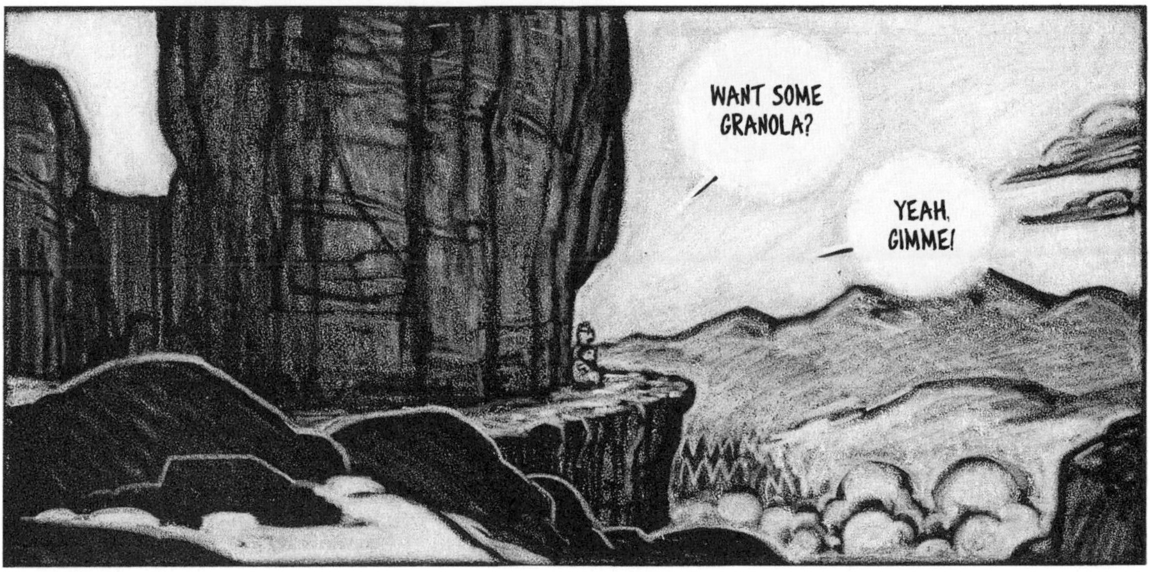
WANT SOME GRANOLA?
YEAH, GIMME!

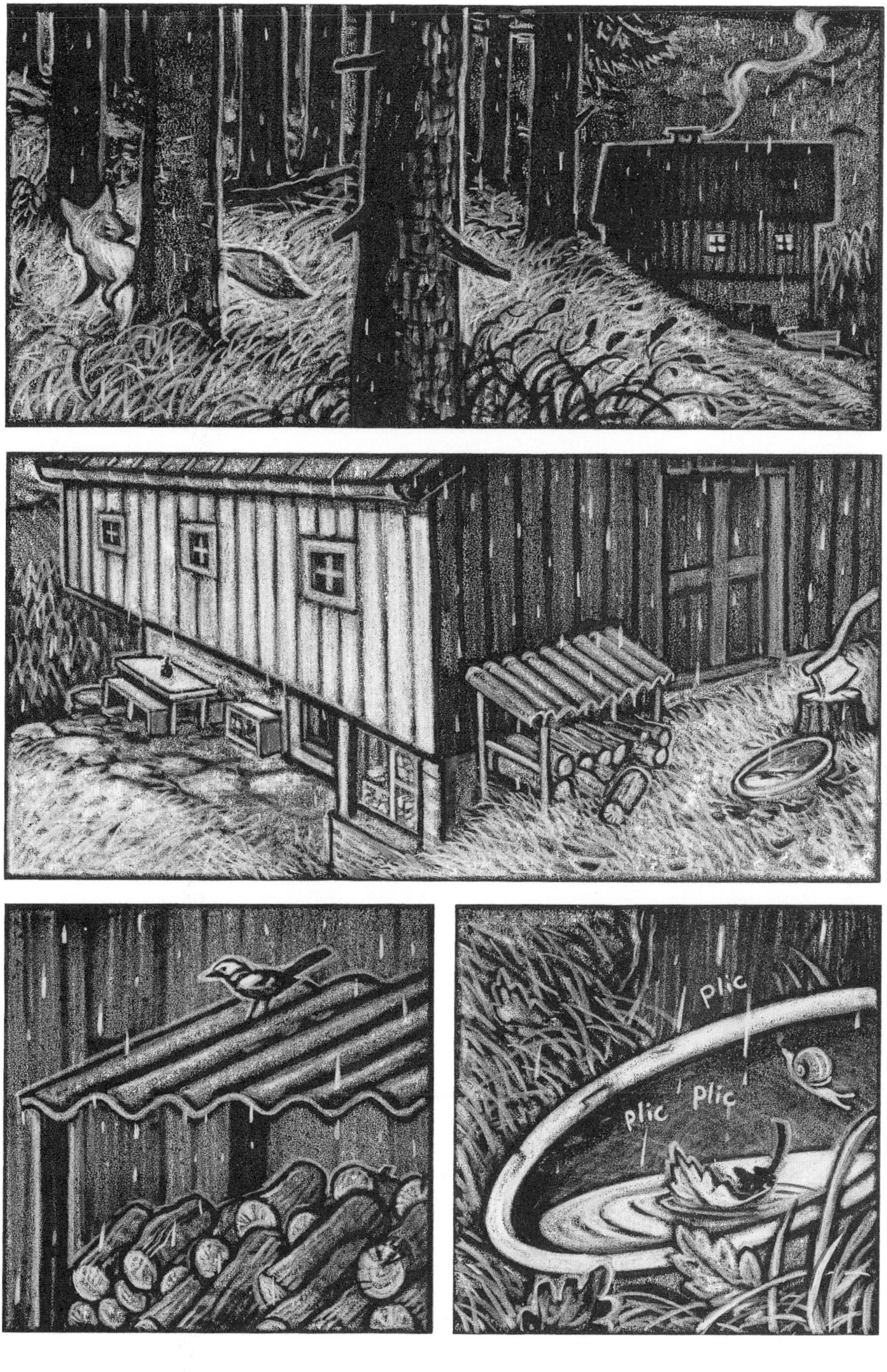
plic
plic plic

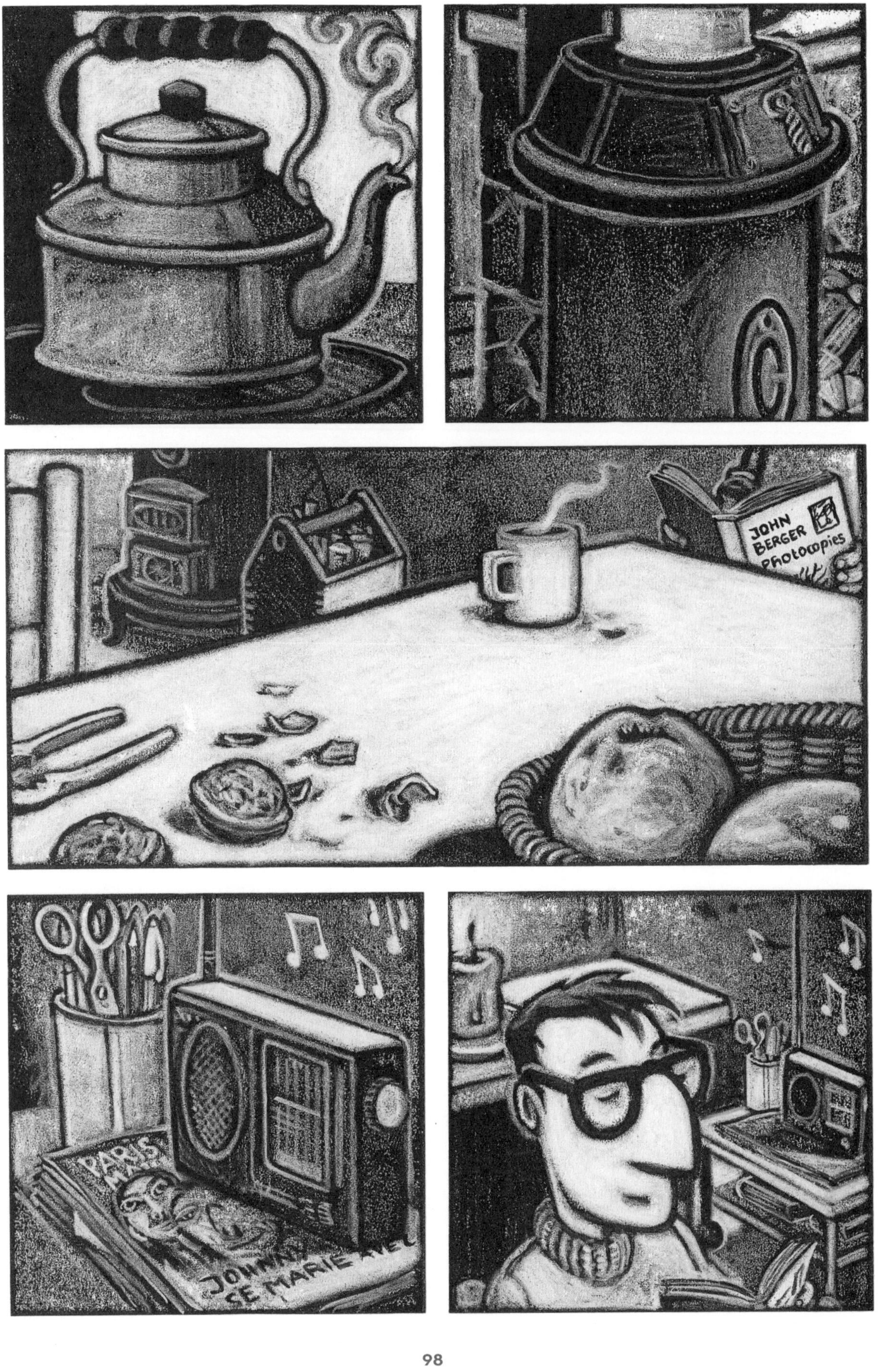
JOHN BERGER
Photocopies
PARIS
SE MARIE

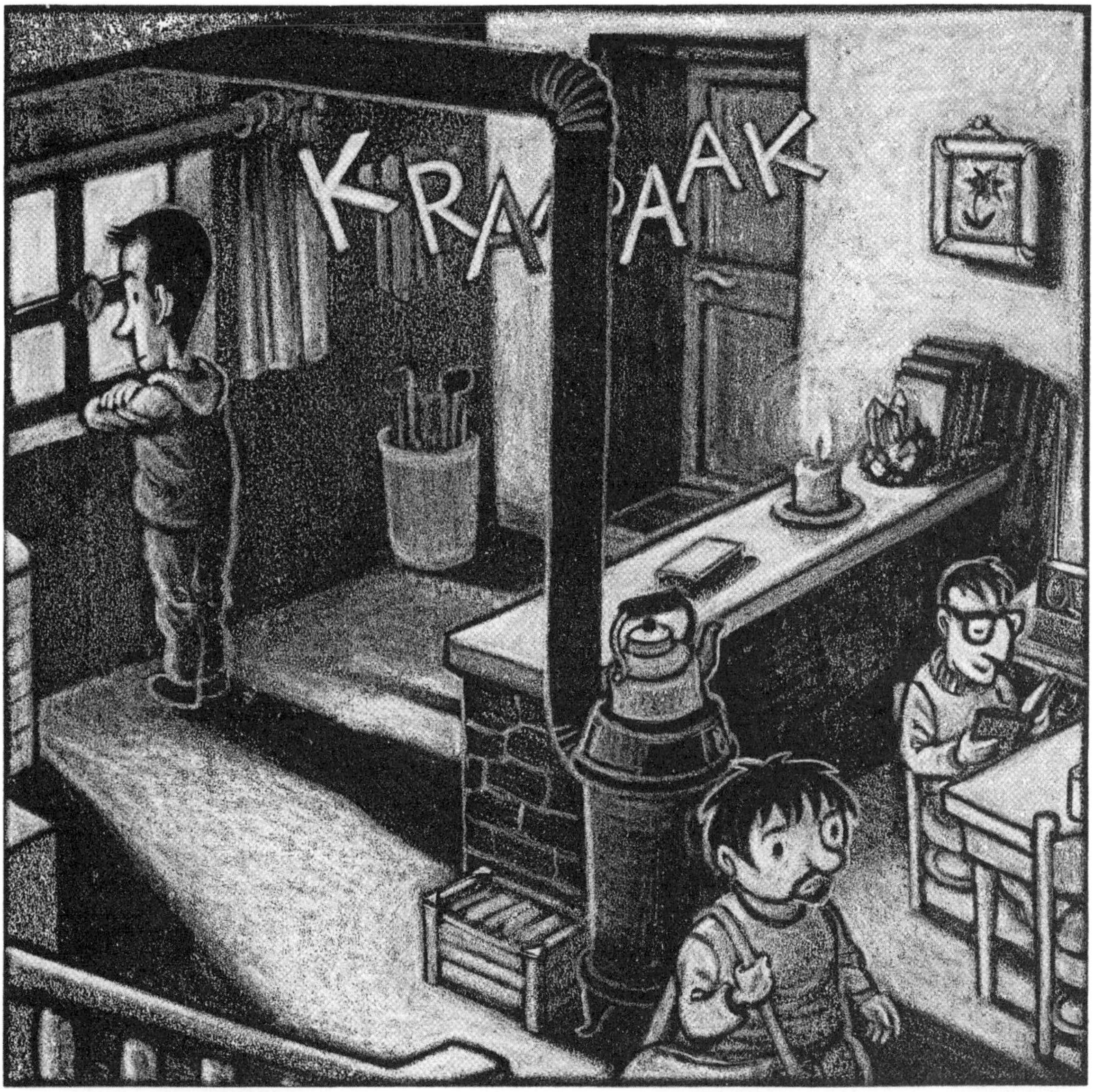
KRAAK

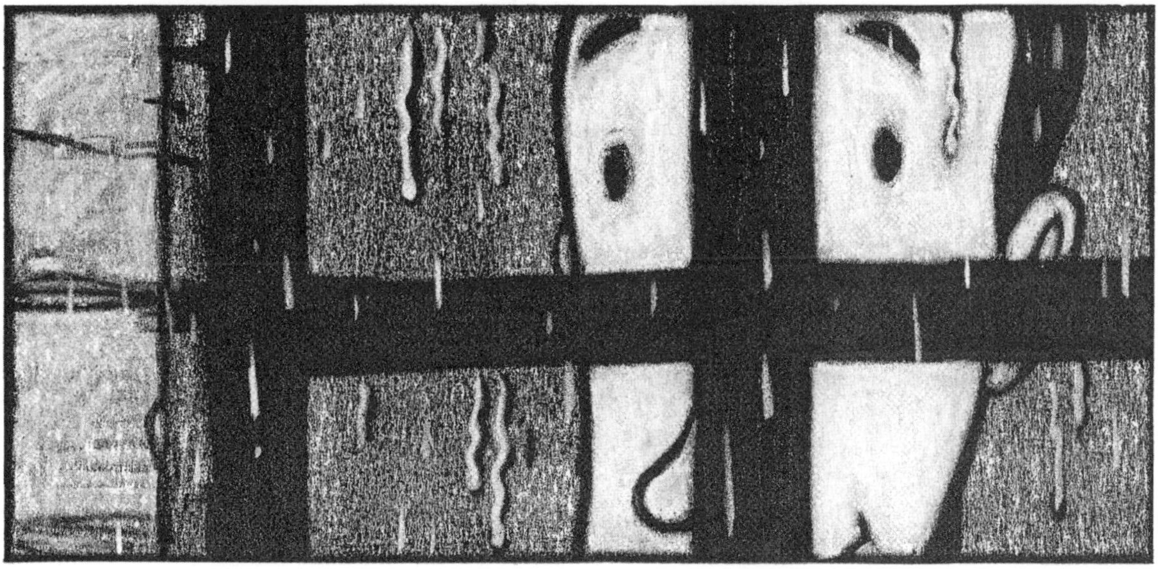

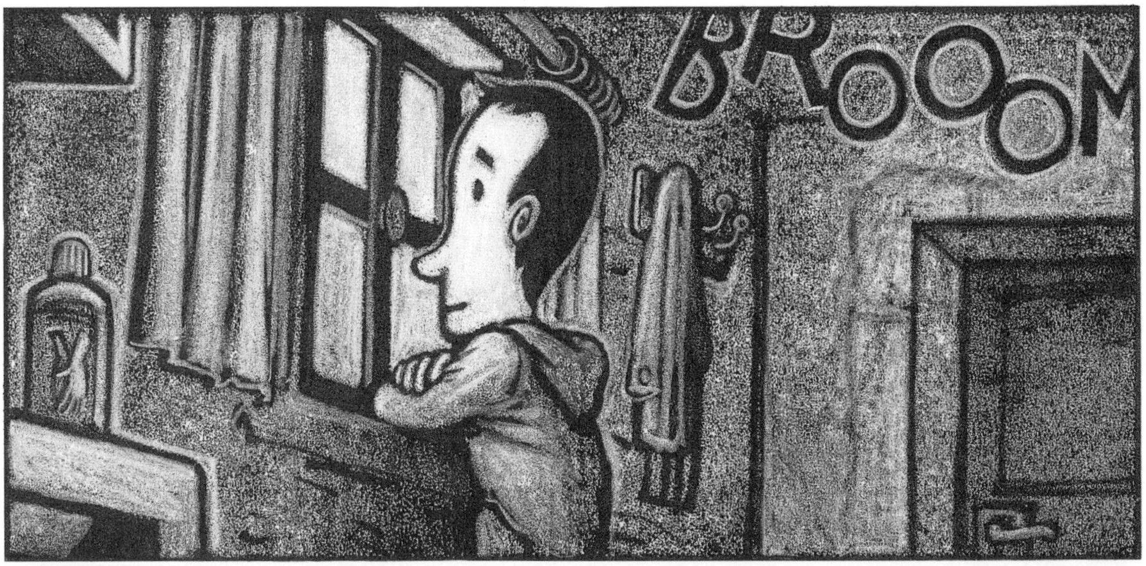
BROOOM

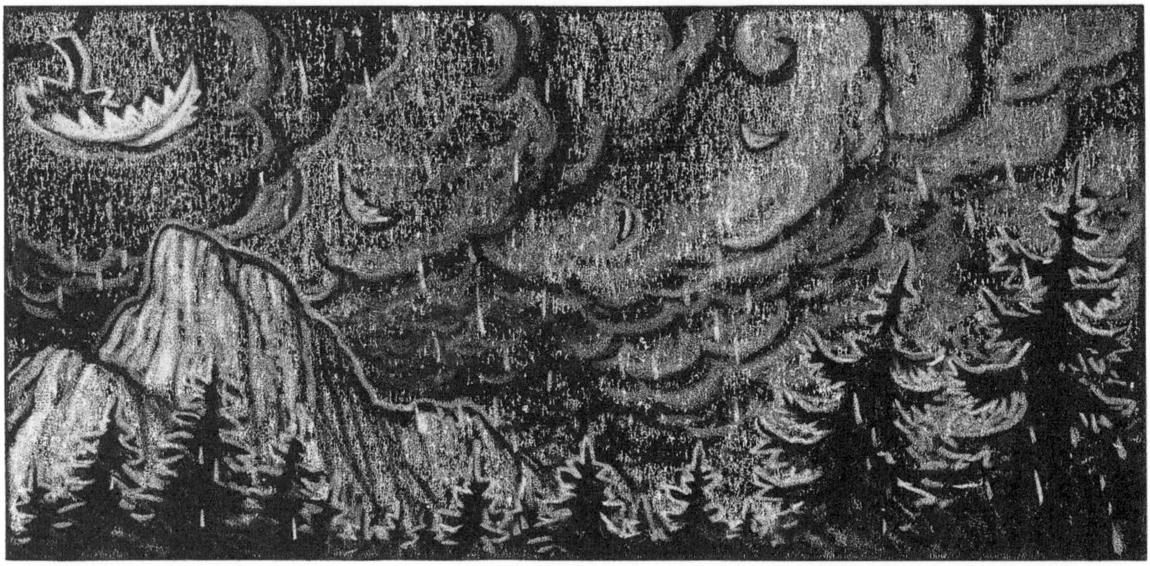

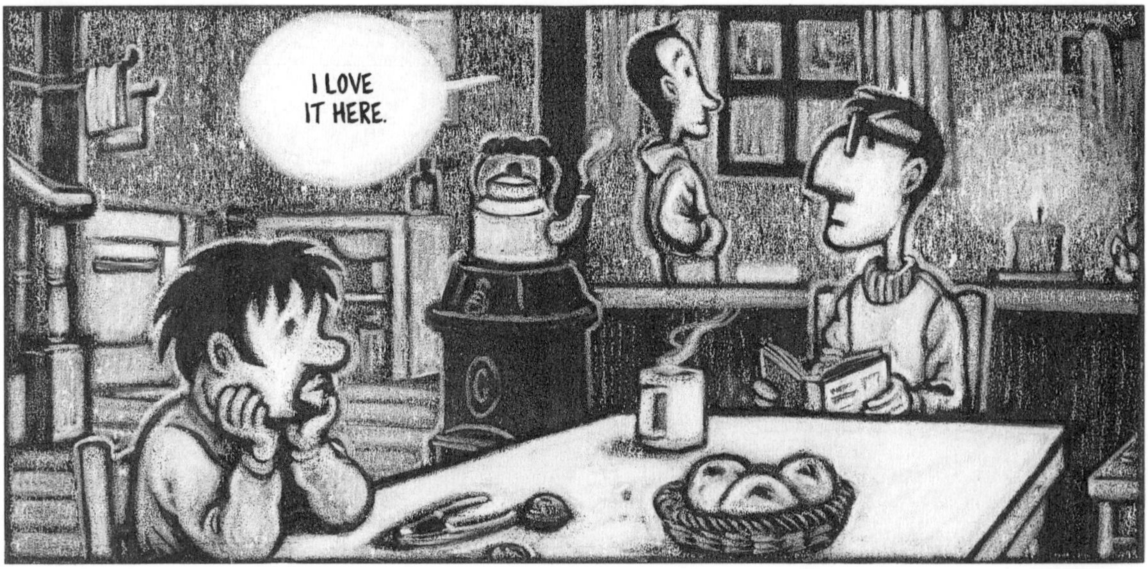
I LOVE
IT HERE.

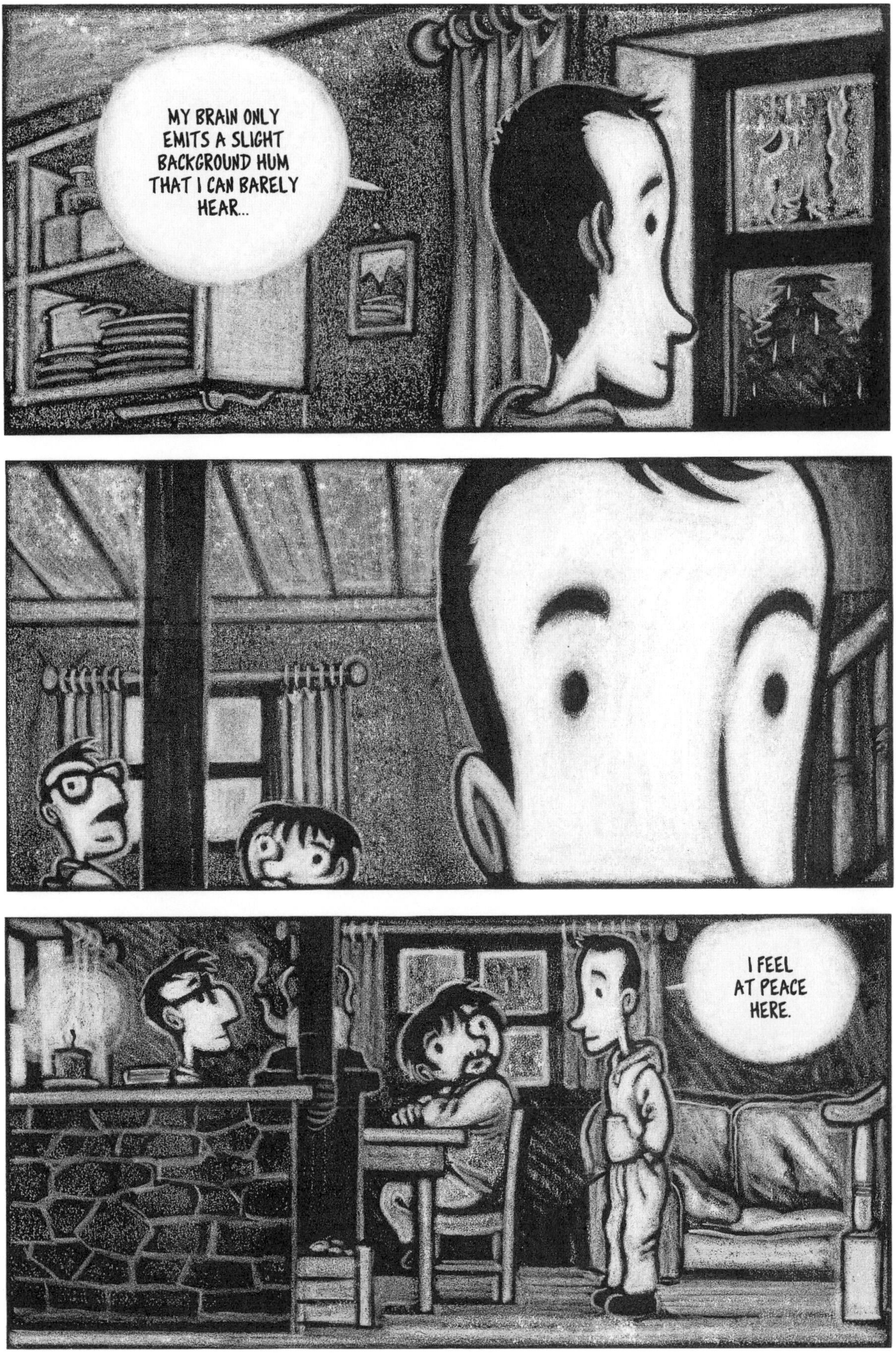
MY BRAIN ONLY EMITS A SLIGHT BACKGROUND HUM THAT I CAN BARELY HEAR...
I FEEL AT PEACE HERE.

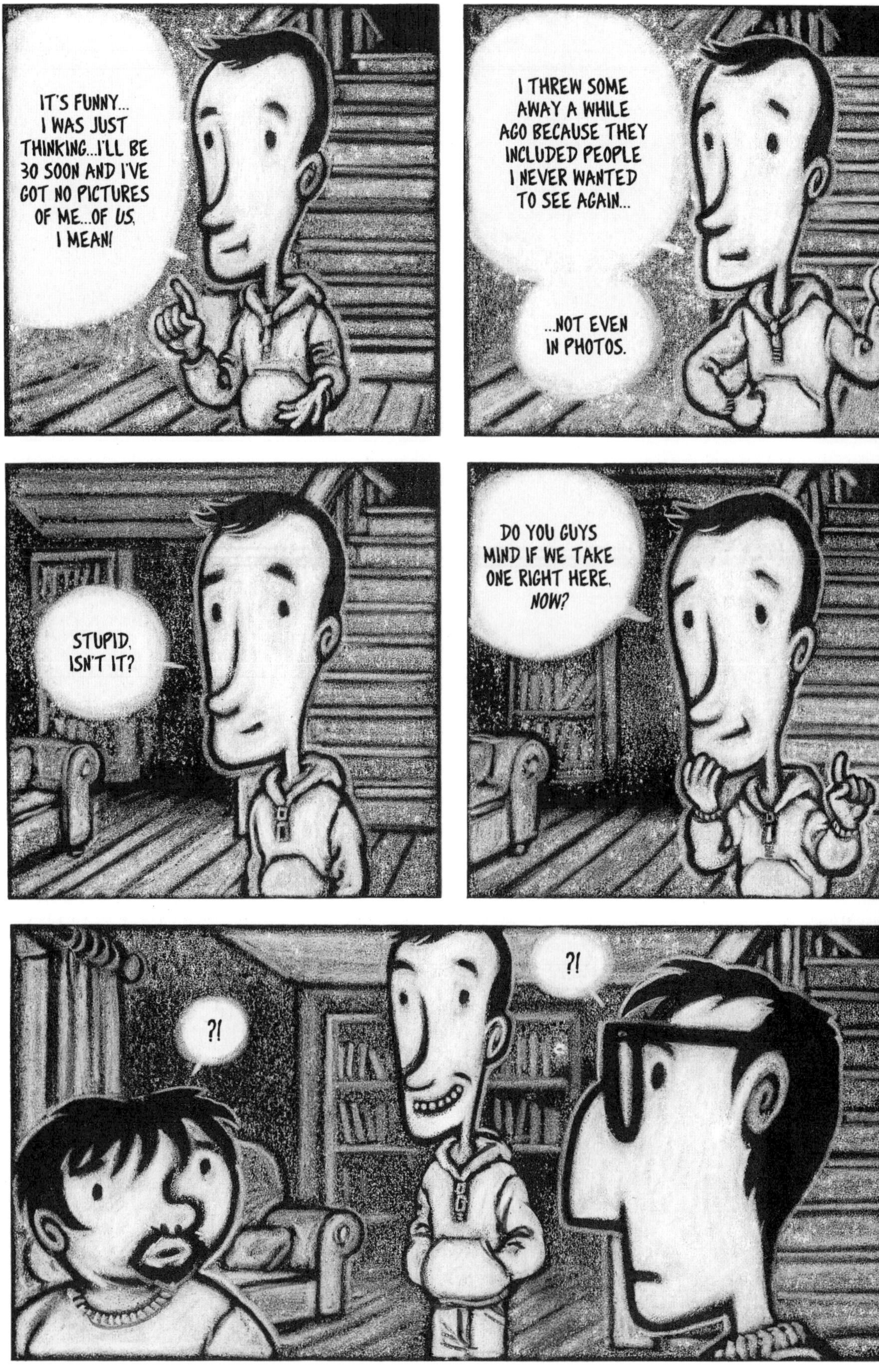
IT'S FUNNY... I WAS JUST THINKING...I'LL BE 30 SOON AND I'VE GOT NO PICTURES OF ME...OF US, I MEAN!
I THREW SOME AWAY A WHILE AGO BECAUSE THEY INCLUDED PEOPLE I NEVER WANTED TO SEE AGAIN...
...NOT EVEN IN PHOTOS.
STUPID, ISN'T IT?
DO YOU GUYS MIND IF WE TAKE ONE RIGHT HERE, NOW?
?!
?!

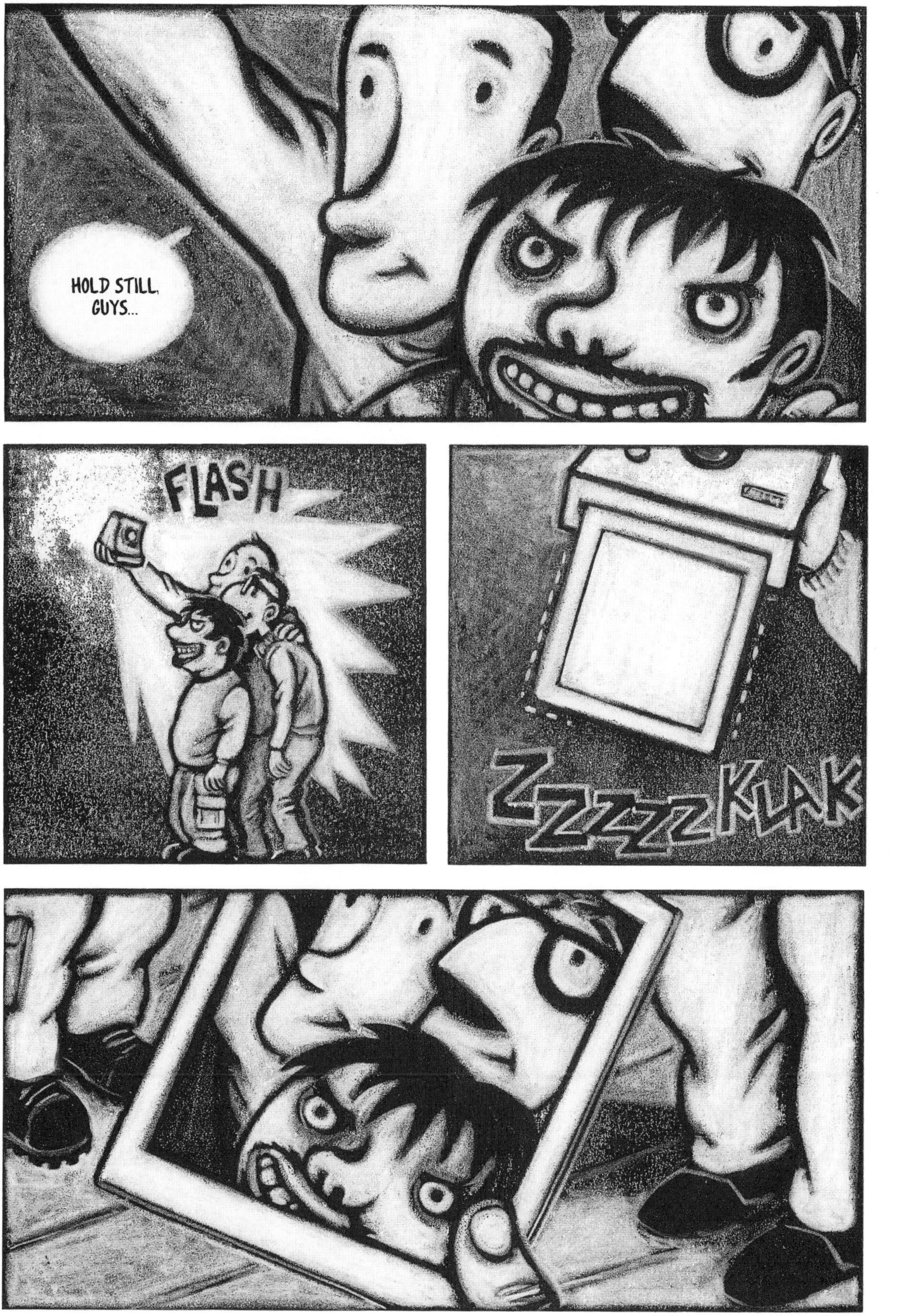
HOLD STILL, GUYS...
FLASH
ZZZZZKLAK

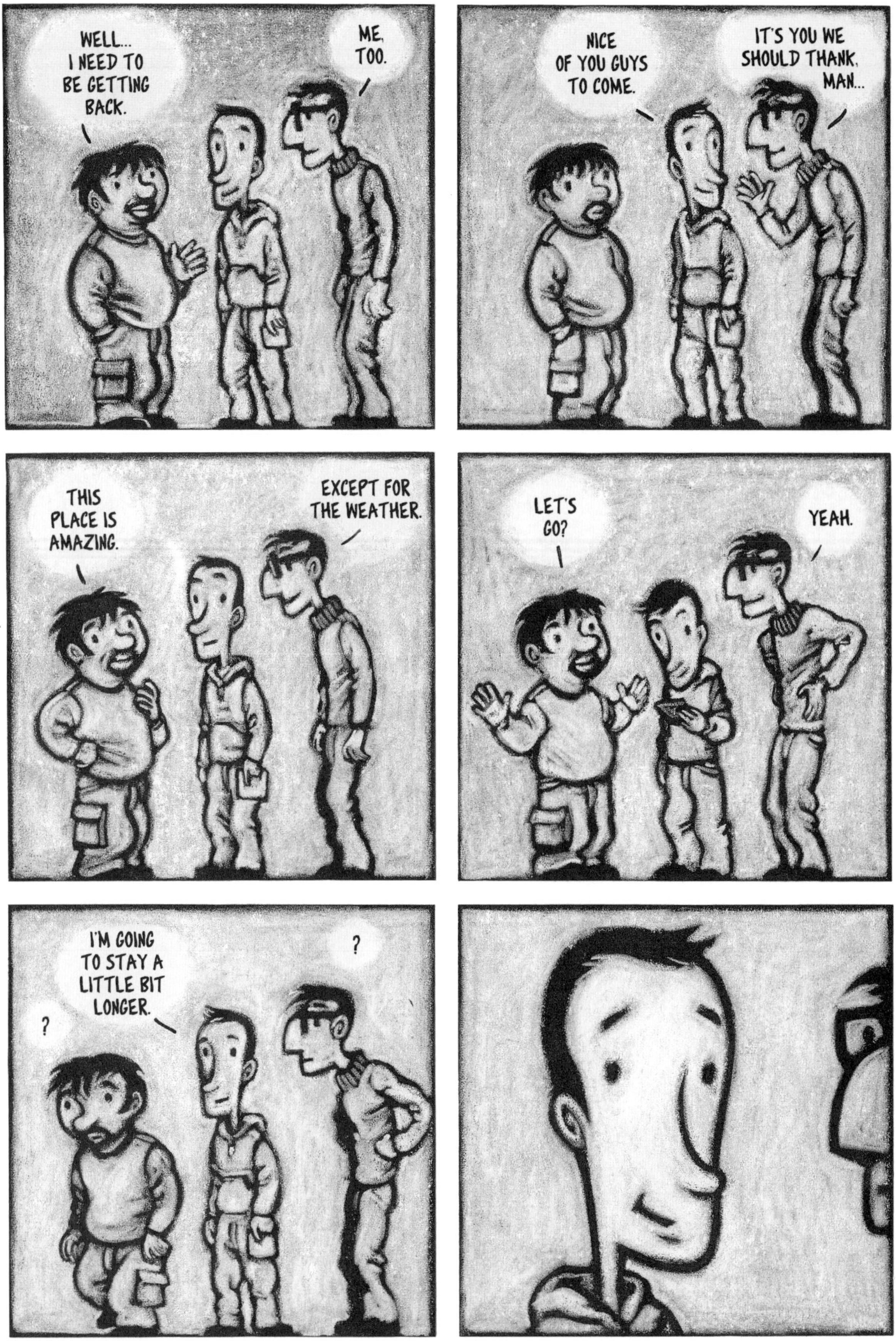
WELL... I NEED TO BE GETTING BACK.
ME, TOO.
NICE OF YOU GUYS TO COME.
IT'S YOU WE SHOULD THANK, MAN...
THIS PLACE IS AMAZING.
EXCEPT FOR THE WEATHER.
LET'S GO?
YEAH.
I'M GOING TO STAY A LITTLE BIT LONGER.
?
?

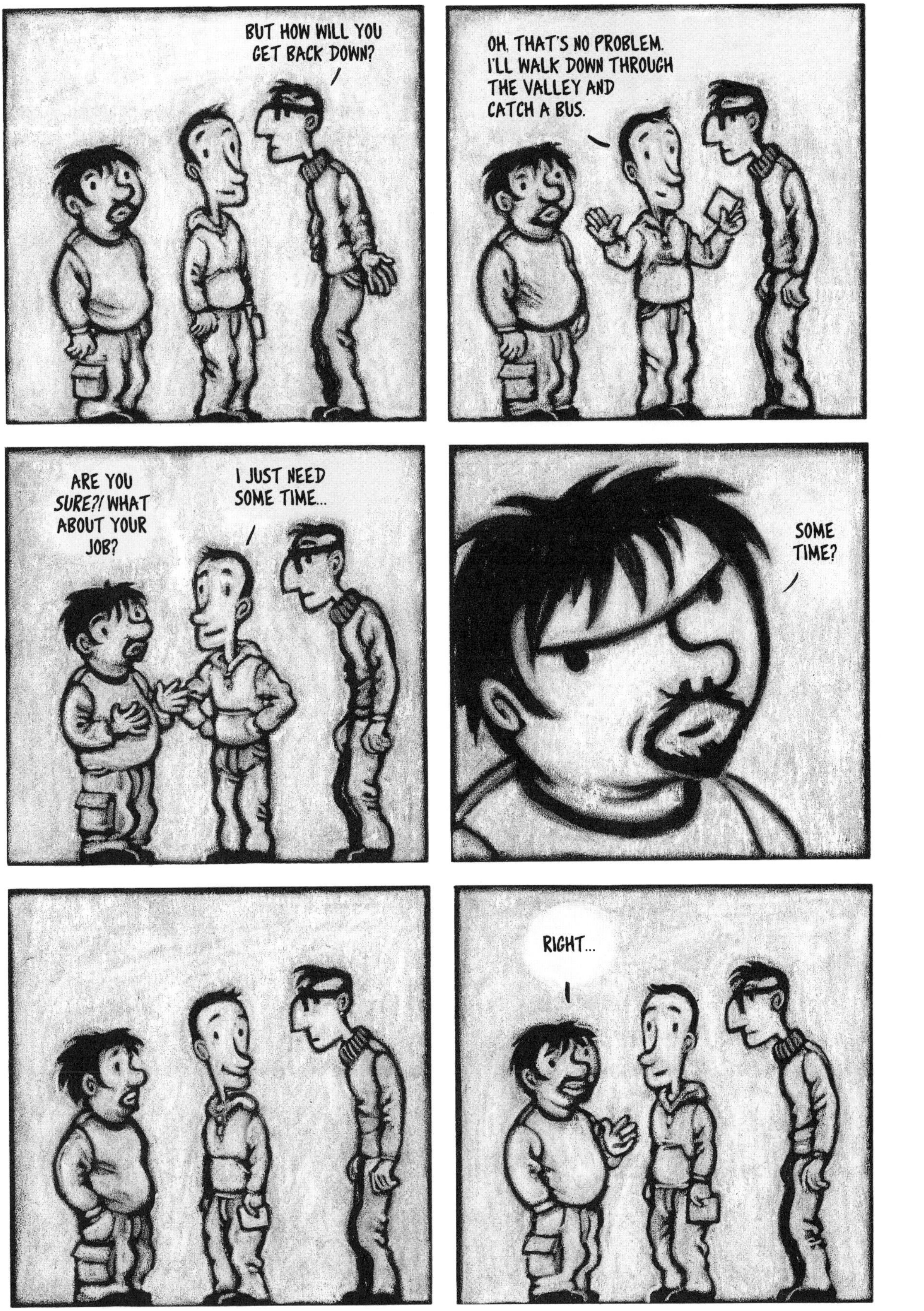
BUT HOW WILL YOU GET BACK DOWN?
OH, THAT'S NO PROBLEM. I'LL WALK DOWN THROUGH THE VALLEY AND CATCH A BUS.
ARE YOU *SURE?!* WHAT ABOUT YOUR JOB?
I JUST NEED SOME TIME...
SOME TIME?
RIGHT...

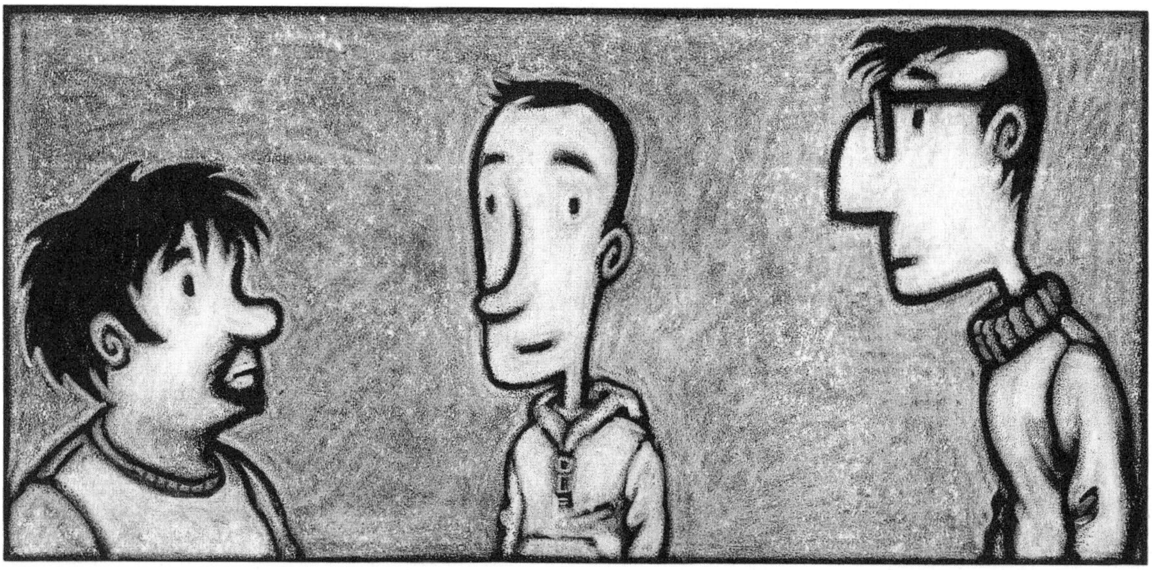

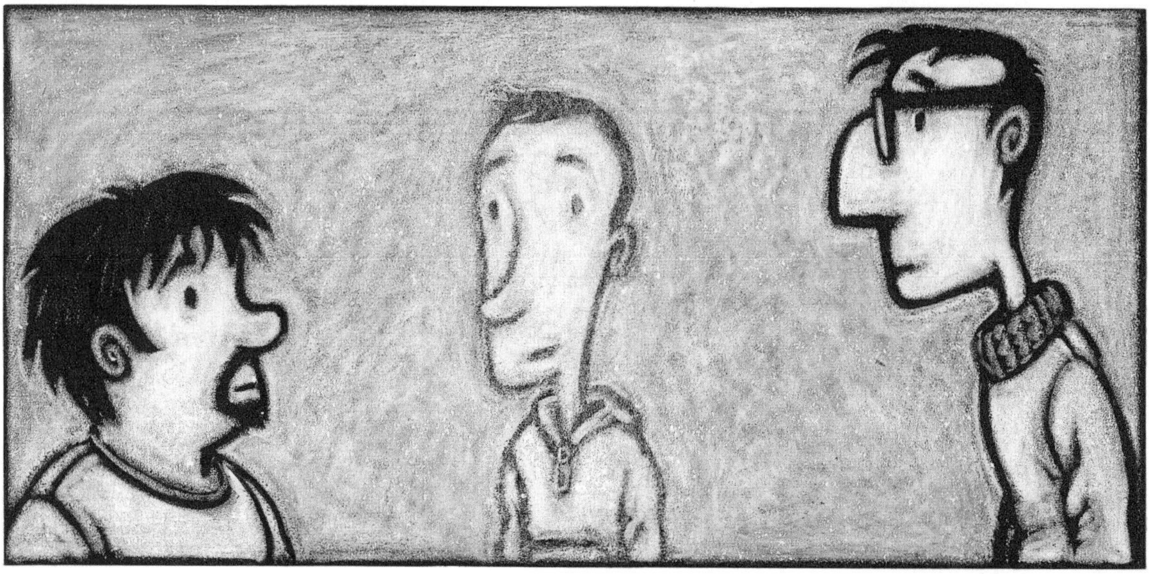

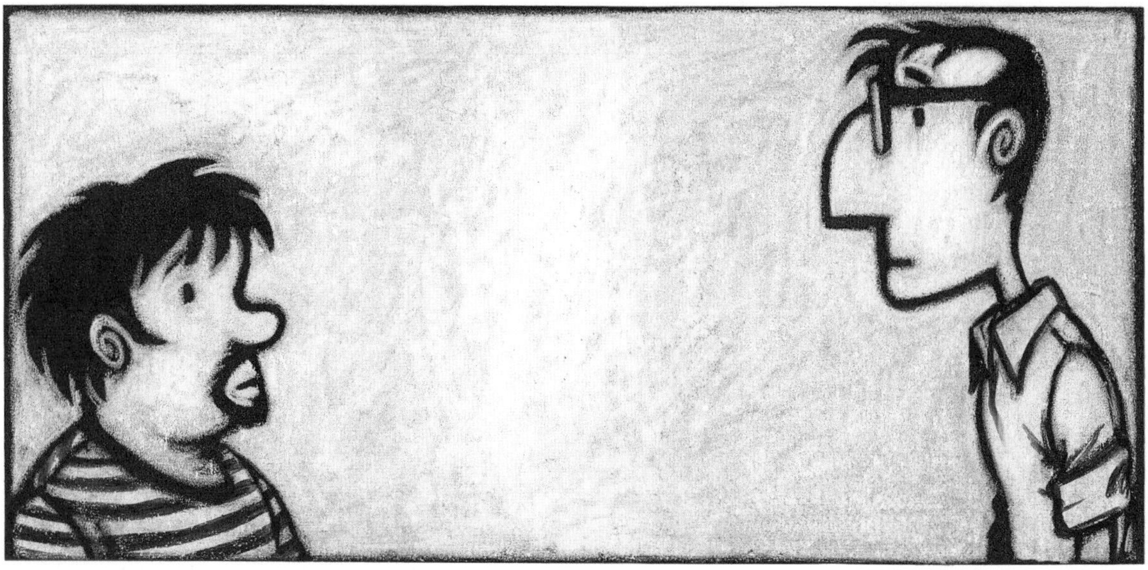

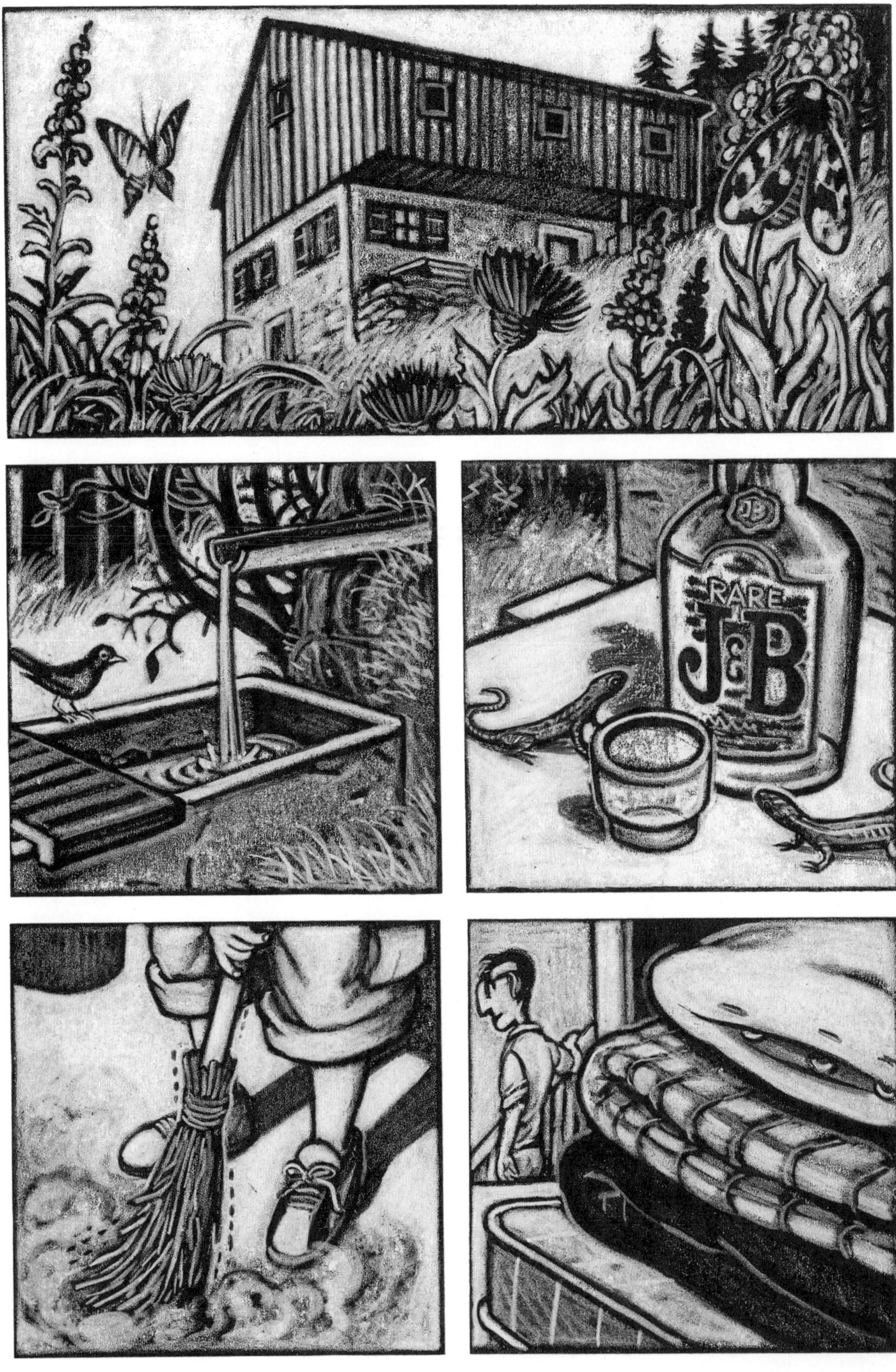
RARE
J&B

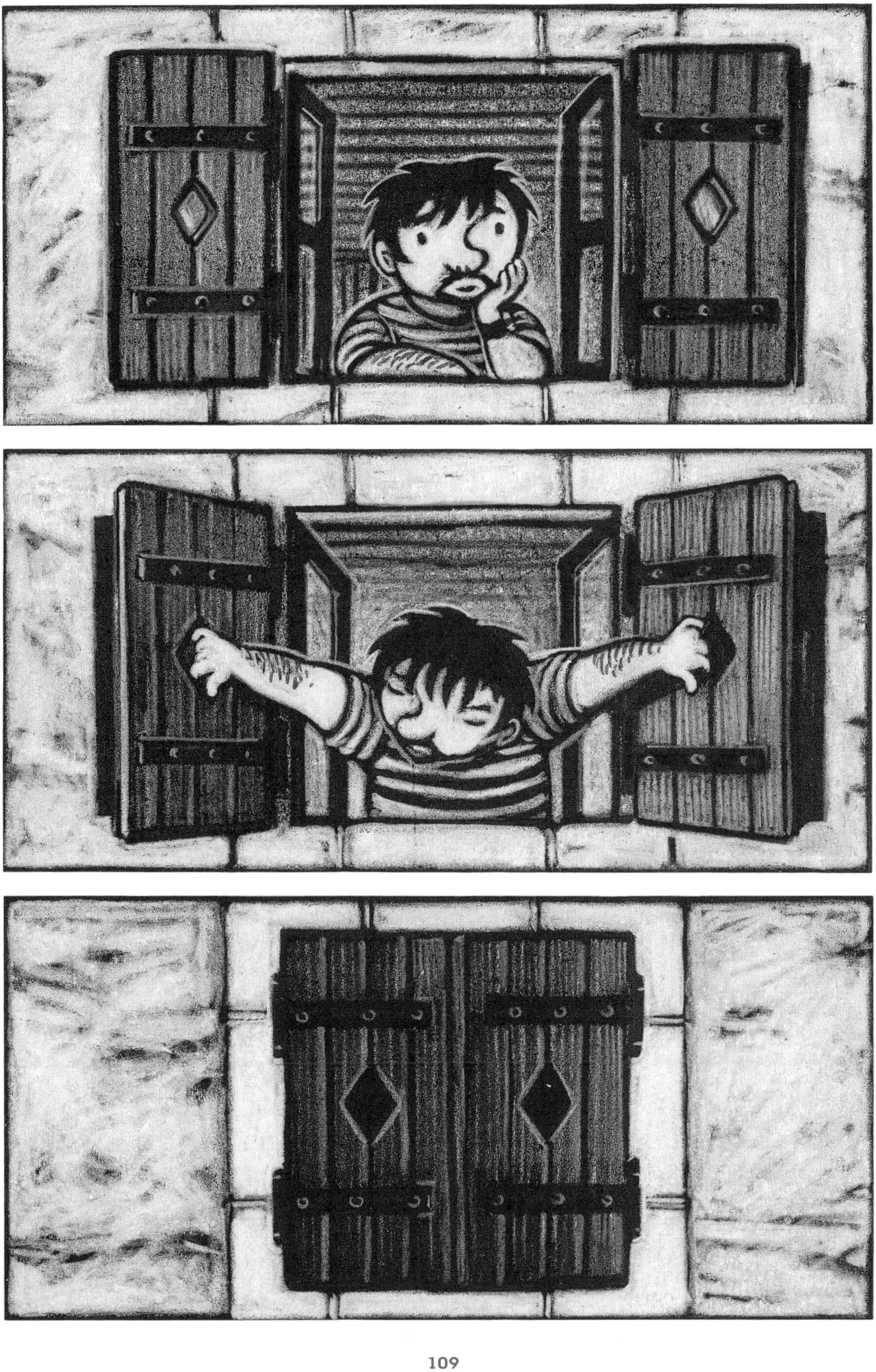

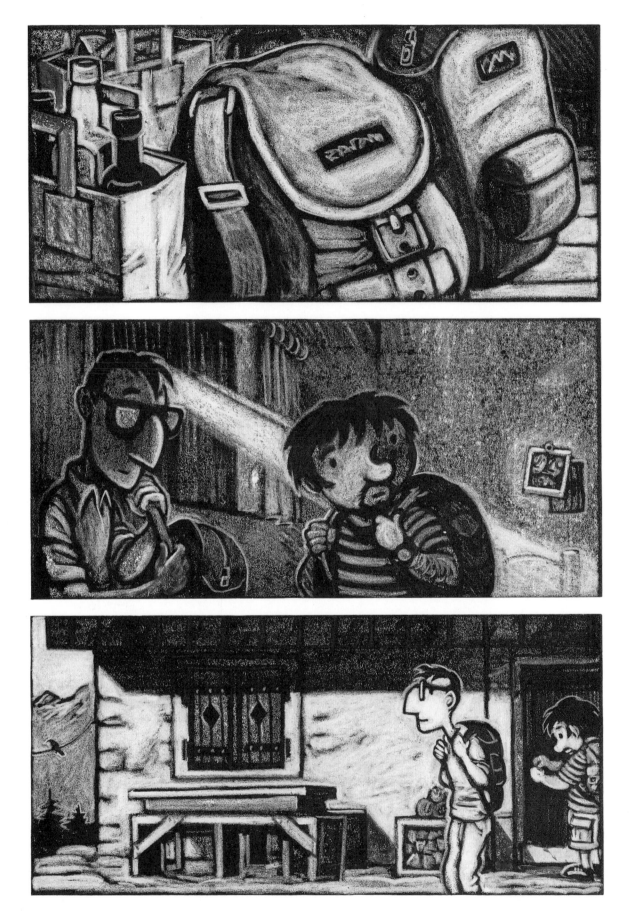

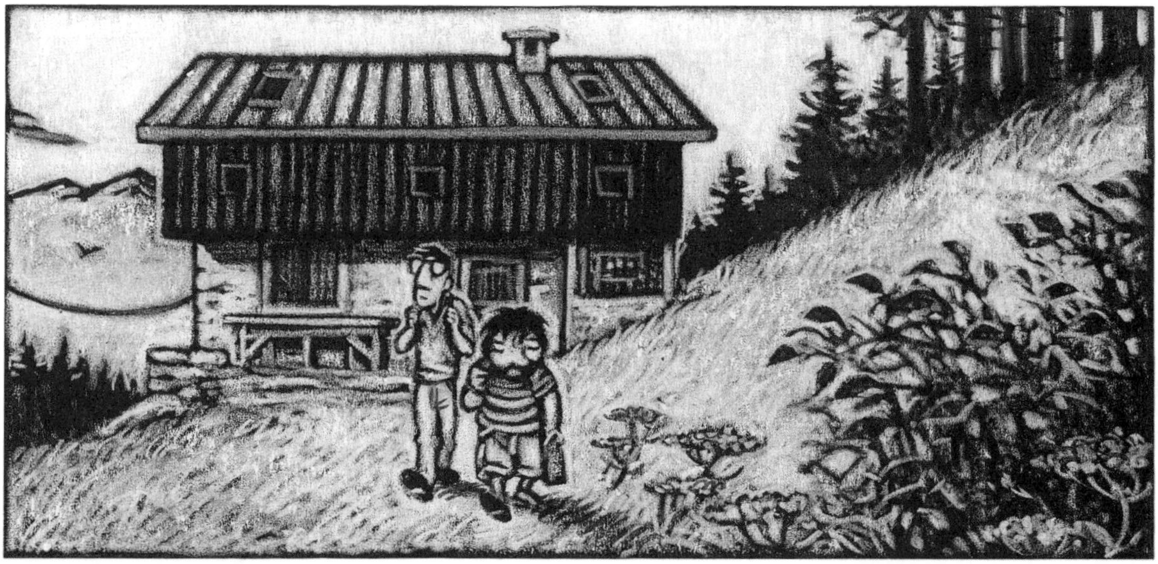

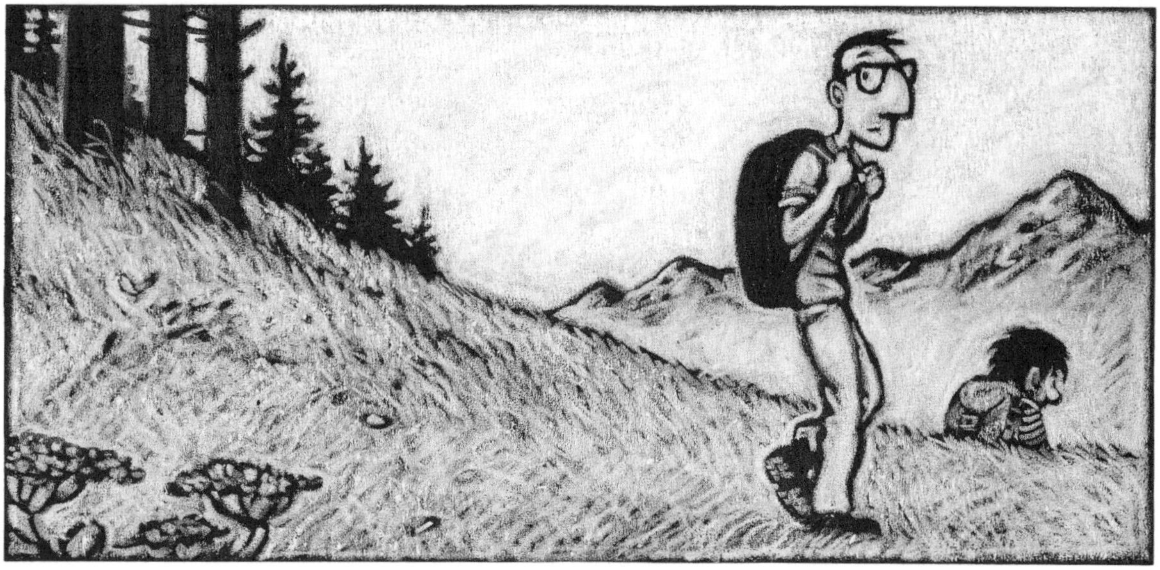

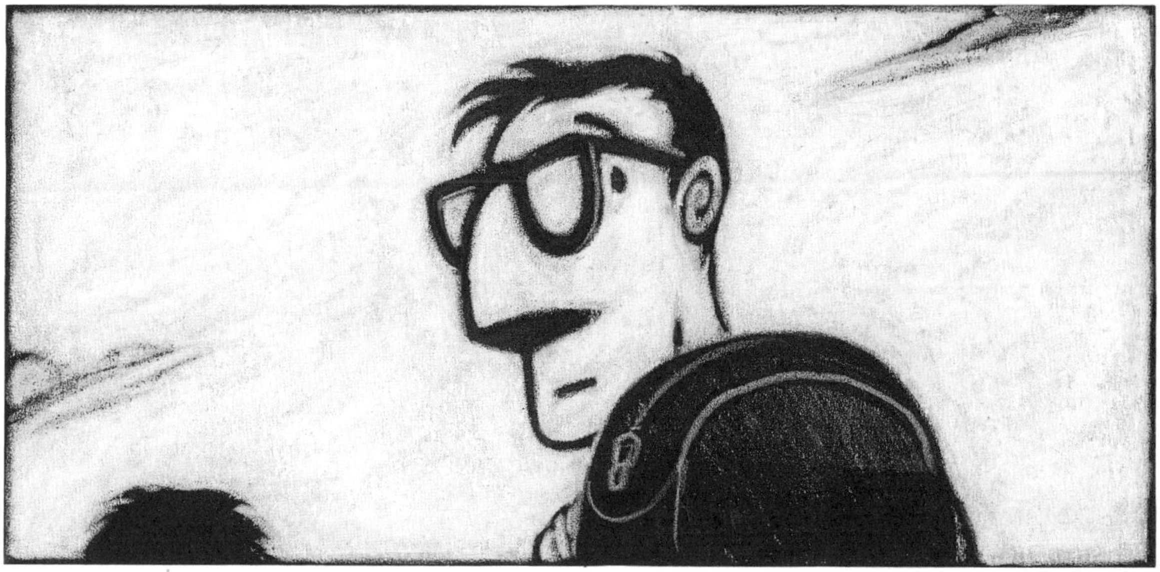

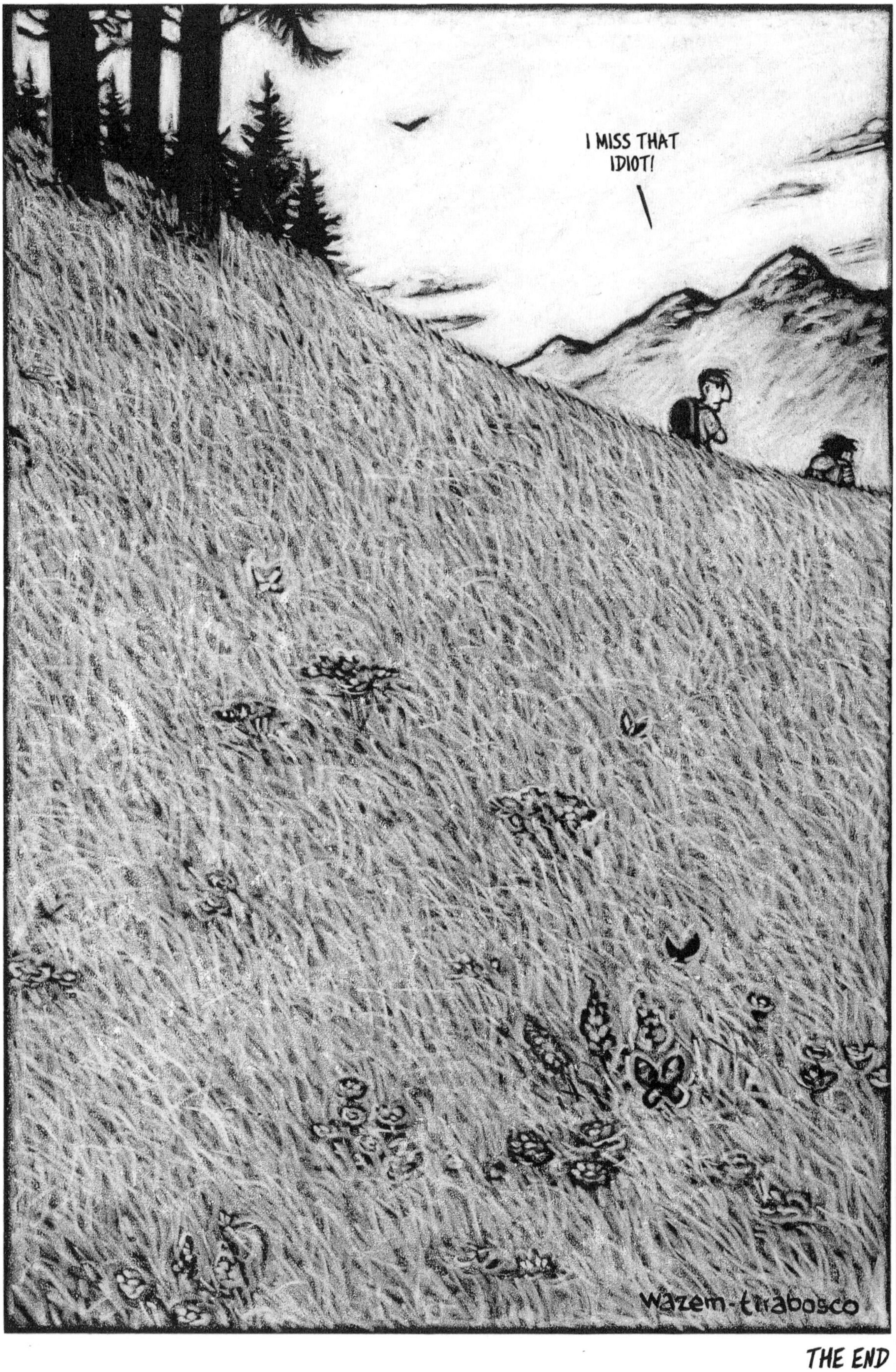
I MISS THAT IDIOT!
wazem-tirabosco

THE END